WINTER
RISING

For Stuart,

thankyou !

Alex x

BOOKS BY ALEX CALLISTER

Winter Dark
Winter Rising

WINTER RISING

ALEX CALLISTER

bookouture

Published by Bookouture in 2020

An imprint of Storyfire Ltd.
Carmelite House
50 Victoria Embankment
London EC4Y 0DZ

www.bookouture.com

ISBN: 978-1-83888-222-8
eBook ISBN: 978-1-83888-221-1

For Winter's friends
Ben and Harriet

PROLOGUE

2 weeks to go...

The girl sat up and opened her eyes.

She could see nothing and it was disorientating. Which way was up and which way down? One minute she had been in a bar on a blind date and the next minute, she was here.

Her senses strained into the dark. Night air warm on her face, traffic far away, a feeling of space above. A wide, open sky. She was sitting on hard ground. A hint of a breeze rustling Long grass and leaves on trees. A smell of old roses.

Why was it so dark?

Her hands flew to her eyes, scrabbling at the lids. Lashes fluttered under her fingers. There should be some light. Even in the middle of the night, London never got completely dark. She had heard you could see the sodium from space.

Nothing.

Her heart thudded as the panic hit.

She lunged out and her fingers hit something hard. Stone covered in leaves. Ivy. She could smell its bitterness over the roses. There was carving on the stone. Old writing. The ivy was growing right over the top.

A gravestone.

Instinct forced her body still, choked the scream rising up her throat. She froze, listening to the rustling in the trees, the far away traffic, the hammer, hammer, hammering of her heart. And something else. A sound like a blade on a whetstone. A slow rhythmic scrape.

She felt the echo of something long known and only just recognised. The shape of a familiar story. She was part of a narrative that had played out a hundred times before.

The sound like a blade on a whetstone stopped.

She fumbled at her pocket and her fingers touched the smooth screen of her phone. A while ago, when she had started internet dating, she had downloaded the ICE app – the 'In Case of Emergency' panic app. One press and a message was sent. She had never had to use it before.

She jabbed at the screen in the pitch dark. She could make out nothing, not even the glimmer from the home page. Had her phone run out of battery?

Someone was standing in front of her. She could feel them in the air.

'Who's there?' she said. 'Who are you?'

'I am Firestorm.' The voice sounded like her date.

Fear held her stiff.

She knew Firestorm. Everyone did.

Even though she had heard the words, she still couldn't make sense of them.

'Someone has taken out a contract on me?' she whispered. She couldn't believe it. Who cared enough to want her dead?

'No,' said the voice. 'You are an experiment. The first of twelve; now we are entering the final countdown.'

She could make nothing of this. What countdown? Her frightened brain skittered back to the question.

'Who are you?' she said again.

'I am the Guardsman.'

*

12 days to go…

In Paris, a Judge sat down heavily on the toilet in the end cubicle of the Judges' bathroom and wondered what a life spent in perpetual fear was doing to his insides. He had grown up with stories about Falcone and Borsellino, the selfless Italian magistrates who had stood up to the Sicilian mafia. As a young man he had been fired with the spirit of emulation and developed a burning ambition to follow in their footsteps.

Now he had got his wish and the reality was not glorious or heroic. It was terrifying.

He sometimes wondered what his old heroes would make of organised crime now. More powerful than any country and backed up by the might of the Firestorm website. An assassination market that had moved off the dark web and gone mainstream.

The Judge remembered seeing Firestorm for the first time and staring while his colleagues laughed.

Welcome to Firestorm
Cheating husband? Bitch wife? Hate your Boss?
Let Firestorm take care of your problem.
Safe. Anonymous. Cheap.

The Judge hadn't laughed – he had been too busy considering the implications.

By its first birthday, Firestorm had chalked up more than fifty thousand contracts and a whole new industry had been born. It passed a hundred thousand a few months later and by then its potential for intimidation had been realised. If you care, your enemies have all the leverage they need, and one by one the Judge's laughing colleagues had turned into shaking, twitching Firestorm shadows.

The Judge knew he should be glad that his parents were long dead and that he had no wife or children to be afraid for, but he felt alone and tired and fearful. He was afraid for himself and that made him ashamed, but no less afraid.

The Guardsman will find you soon, he had been told.

He looked at the grey, industrial toilet partition and the grey, hard-wearing floor and wondered what would happen if he never came out. The Guardsman could probably find him, even here, in the Judges' toilets, in the Palais de Justice.

The Judge thought about the Guardsman, Firestorm's most celebrated contractor, one of the Holy Trinity. Apparently, his page on Firestorm got more than a million hits a day. He was just a man, the Judge told himself, just an ordinary man. And that was part of the problem. No one knew what he looked like. The Guardsman could walk into a bar and order a drink right beside you and you would never know. The knife in the back you never saw coming.

The outside door to the corridor creaked.

The Judge sat very still, listening in the suddenly full silence.

Someone was standing right outside his cubicle. He could hear them breathing. It was strange there hadn't been any footsteps.

There was a *tap tap tap*. The kind of sound made by metal not knuckles. The kind of sound a blade might make if it was tapping lightly on a thin partition door.

'Hello?' he said.

The cubicle door crashed open, shattering the feeble lock. The door bounced off the partition wall and closed again.

No shoes, that explained the silence.

The door creaked slowly open again.

It wasn't going to be in the back.

*

8 days to go…

A man walked into a bar.

The barmaid checked him out as she worked the pump. Women were always checking him out. Up and down went her lashes, her mouth pursing as she finessed the head on a pint.

A flick of brown hair across the room caught his attention. A woman on her own. Desperate. He could read it in her body language. She was on the phone, laughing too loudly and sending flirty little glances around the bar.

Easy, the man thought.

She was Australian and it didn't take more than two martinis to have her spilling her life story, crossing and uncrossing her long legs on the bar stool. She had come to London as a student and never left. Her skirt rose mid thigh as she shifted again.

The man laughed. He could feel his knife, newly sharpened, pressing into his side.

'Because of our fabulous weather,' he said.

'Because of the fabulous men,' she replied.

And he knew it was a done deal.

She didn't mention her husband but that was fine because the man already knew all about him and in fact had had a long and detailed exchange with him in Firestorm's online contract room.

He glanced at the TV above the bar, it was showing a city in flames. It could be any one of a dozen cities in North America – New York, Chicago, LA. They were all burning. The man couldn't have cared less. He checked his watch. *No body* the husband had stipulated and that was fine too. The woman's face fell. She put her hand on his knee.

'D'you have somewhere you need to be?'

He could see her nipples through her thin blouse. He could taste her eagerness. She touched her hand to her ring finger, unconsciously rubbing the skin.

*

He opened the door to the rented house and breathed in deeply. The smell of old houses got him hard. He might start off outside, but, in the end, this was where he always brought them.

The woman hung on his arm, oblivious. She giggled as she stumbled on the hall carpet. She laughed as he closed the front door. He could smell apple martini on her breath.

His heart rate was accelerating. He looked at the metal door at the end of the hall.

Just a little bit further.

He could feel his blade under his jacket, against his ribs. It pricked through the thin shirt, pricked against his skin. He knew when he took his jacket off there would be tiny specks of blood on the white.

Now his hand was on the metal door. The room beyond was in darkness. She stumbled again and giggled again and then she was over the threshold and he slammed the door behind him.

Then he hit the lights.

Plastic sheeting draped the walls, taped high and covering the floor, filling the room with the chemical smell of cellophane. A couch and a chair stood in the middle at exactly the right height.

He would cut her first and take her from behind while he watched her bleed. He pulled the knife from its sheath and watched the light play on the serrated blade, little dancing beads of brilliant white. This was his favourite bit. It was all good, but this bit, when they realised, was the best.

He looked up.

The woman stood leaning up against the far wall. She put her hand to the top of her head and pulled at her hair. A wig. Her real hair was as blonde as his own.

'God, that thing is hot,' she said, and her Australian accent was gone.

The man stared.

The woman tossed the wig aside and put her hands in her pockets. When they came out they were wearing knuckledusters.

'Hi,' she said. 'My name is Winter. Welcome to the last night of your life.'

CHAPTER 1

I soak in the Guardsman's surprise. Fill myself up with the delicious, perfect shock of it. The most feared contract killer in history. Firestorm's top contractor. A cutter. A knife specialist. His body vibrates with halted momentum, the jolt of a gap where a step should be. Light reflects along the blade in his hand. His adrenaline is going full throttle. Only surprise is keeping him standing and that won't last long.

I'm not worried. I may be all alone but if I can't take an armed opponent one-on-one I have no business being Head of Field. Not that I am unarmed. I just want to use my fists. For all of GCHQ's technology, I have been punching air.

Until now.

Until I booked the Guardsman for a hit on myself.

I would like her to suffer, I had told the Guardsman, posing as my own husband in Firestorm's online contract room.

It will be my pleasure, he had replied.

I lever myself off the wall by my shoulder blades.

The Guardsman stares at me, confounded and confused.

A picture of a girl, bleeding out in a dusty graveyard fills my head.

Her name was Lucy.

I can see her now, hunched, half lying against a gravestone, the ICE app lit up on her phone. I can see myself running through the dark, tearing down the overgrown paths. I can feel her, sticky in my arms, feel the grass, dry as straw, feel the dust beneath me as I hauled her onto my body, trying to get her off the ground, trying to lessen the contact between dirt and missing skin.

She was alive. Alive long enough for me to find her. 'The Guardsman,' she said to me, and something else, and then she died.

It took three burly ambulance crew to prise me away from her. They put me in the back of an ambulance with a blanket. They pressed some hot sweet drink on me like I was a civilian and through the open door I could see her lying between the graves, abandoned in the dirt, and I broke away from the gentle hands and lurched out of the ambulance and gathered her in my arms again, while forensics screamed and scene of crime officers cursed my name.

I clench my fists and clench my jaw and the blackness rises. I breathe it in, draw it around me, wrap myself in it like a mantle.

His mouth opens. Here it comes. What will it be?

Who are you?

What's going on?

'Did the Guardsman send you?' he says. 'Is this some kind of test?'

'*What?*'

'Who are you?' he says. 'Are you a contractor? Do you work for the Guardsman?'

'No,' I say. 'I really don't.'

We stare at each other. I can see his brain ticking. His lips move as if he is working something out. His face twists in confusion. Something is wrong and indecision makes him rock like a metronome. Smart would open the door and run like hell. Stupid would carry on as if nothing has changed.

I can already tell which way he is going to go.

This is not Firestorm's top contractor. This is not the person I booked. Where is the Guardsman?

He tenses with coiled momentum, telegraphing his move.

Behind him, the door slams open, smacking him in the back.

What the hell?

The contractor staggers forward and a slim Chinese girl strides into the room. She is wearing dungarees, Doc Martens and a murderous expression. She sizes the contractor up through narrowed eyes then swings sideways and lands a stinging heel strike on the back of his neck. He keels over face first.

The newcomer kicks the fallen cutter. Plenty of welly.

I blink.

'Don't worry,' she says. 'I am here to save you. You are going to be fine.'

'Great.'

'I would've been here earlier,' she says. 'But I dropped my bus pass in his front garden.' She pats her huge pockets as if to check she still has it.

Priceless.

I kneel down beside the body. Two fingers on the jugular. Nothing. I pick up the wrist. Still nothing.

Shit.

'Blimey, will you look at this place?' she says, taking in the specialist décor. She pulls at a dungaree buckle, the strap is slipping off her shoulder.

I roll the body over. Blue eyes stare at the ceiling.

'What are you doing here? Were you following me?'

She nudges the body with her boot. 'I knew he was on a job.'

I am up and in her face before she can move. 'You hacked *Firestorm*?'

She shrugs. 'And?'

I get her by the scruff of the neck and haul her out the door, along the hall and into the front garden. '*And*, I want to talk to you,' I say.

CHAPTER 2

Simon glares at me. His gaze sweeps the Chinese girl then returns to me. His hair looks like he just got out of bed but then it always does. He folds his arms. As the orange street light catches his face, I see his lips tight over his anger. It is a familiar look. My quartermaster; my biggest supporter and toughest critic.

The night is quiet. Traffic from the nearby Lewisham High Road. Maybe the odd fox, otherwise nothing.

'He's dead?' he says to me.

My eyes slide across to my would-be rescuer. 'Self-defence.'

'Entrapment.' Simon glares some more. 'Are you honestly expecting the Met to believe you just bumped into this guy?'

Somewhere, a fox shrieks.

He scowls. 'Please, Winter. I understand, but we talked about this. You have to stop doing this alone.'

I pat my quartermaster's arm. 'It wasn't him anyway.' An image of Lucy bleeding out in a dusty graveyard fills my head. Disappointment soaks through me. I push it away. Close it down.

Simon's scowl deepens. 'Are you out of your mind?' he hisses. 'You tried entrapment on *the Guardsman*?'

It is my turn to scowl. Does he think I'm not up to the Guardsman? We glare off under the orange street light. A siren sounds in the distance, getting closer.

Both of us have forgotten my rescuer. She looks from Simon to me and back again, her eyes tracking to and fro like she is watching tennis. Her cute oval face is baffled. She puts her hands in her outsize pockets.

My head aches. Weeks of monitoring the police channels and the ICE app are catching up with me.

'So,' I say. 'Tell me about hacking Firestorm. The website we have teams and teams of analysts trying to take down.'

'I didn't exactly hack it,' she says.

'I never thought you did.'

'I knew he was on a job.' She fiddles with a dungaree strap.

I narrow my eyes. 'How exactly?'

She looks round at the street, up to the cameras, down to Simon. There are cameras everywhere, even in this anonymous corner of South London.

'I heard him on the phone,' she says. 'I was watching him outside the bar, before he met you. At first I thought he was nervous and then I decided it was excitement so then I thought he was probably waiting for a date. Then I heard him on the phone.'

'Go on.'

'So, I thought I'd better check it out.'

'Why didn't you just warn me?'

'What if I'd been wrong? *Awkward.*'

'You could have called the police.'

'You're joking? Under that kind of time pressure? Couldn't find their butts with both hands and a sniffer dog.'

'Right,' I say, dealing with that mental image. It's not like I disagree. I fold my arms. 'So, let's get this straight. You decided he was on a job and you thought you would just pop along and stop it?'

'Yeah,' she says.

'What could possibly have gone wrong?'

'It was only one guy. I could have taken him blindfolded.' She thinks about this. 'With my head in a bucket.'

I consider the youthful vigilante in silence.

'Who the hell are you people anyway?' she says.

'I'm glad you asked me that.' I look down at her. She reminds me of myself about a hundred years ago. She reminds me of myself when I didn't care.

Her name is Xiu and she is third generation. Her grandparents ran a takeaway, her parents are doctors. She holds a black belt in karate and trains at the Xen-Do kickboxing centre in Finsbury Park. She is in her second year at the London School of Economics studying financial accounting and she is as bored as fuck.

Her words.

'So, you want to be an accountant?'

'Hell no,' she says. 'My mum wants me to be an accountant.'

I meet Simon's eyes over the top of her head. She turned up to stop a hit with nothing but her fists and a bus pass.

'What?' she says.

'Have you ever considered an alternative career?'

THE GUARDSMAN

I

The Guardsman watched as the trainee contractor woke up on the cellar floor and put his hands to his face. The chains around the trainee's ankles clinked.

'Hello?' said the trainee. 'Is this another test?' His head circled like he was searching for something.

No, it was not another test. There would be no more tests for this trainee; he had failed to meet the required standard and the Guardsman did not tolerate mediocrity. Luckily he fulfilled all the criteria for something else.

The trainee's hands started to shake. 'What have you done to me?' he whispered.

The Guardsman glanced at the shipping buoys squatting against the cellar walls. In the dim light from the single bulb hanging from the ceiling, they almost looked alive.

'You are an experiment,' said the Guardsman, 'the second of twelve. Now we are entering the final countdown. It is an honour.'

The trainee looked like he didn't understand. Which was fine by the Guardsman. The open-air graveyard had been a success, giving new meaning to the phrase 'blind date' and the enclosed cellar had also been a complete success.

Which meant the trainee contractor was now surplus to requirements.

The Guardsman looked down at the knife and felt the anticipation rise.

Whetstone, then dry stone, then polish.

Was it sharp enough? Maybe it needed doing again. That was the problem with knife work. Sometimes you had to sharpen the blade three or four times during a job. Not that the Guardsman objected to that particularly.

The Guardsman stepped forward and smiled as the screaming started. There was purity in extreme pain. Who was it who said that? Was it Freud? Or was it Nietzsche?

There was a knock at the door.

'We have a problem,' said the voice behind the door at the top of the cellar stairs.

The Guardsman frowned.

There had been too many problems recently. Twenty-two failed contracts in eight weeks, and every day it felt like something was pushing, prodding, testing the Firestorm defences.

'What?' snapped the Guardsman sliding the bolt and opening the door to the man with the strange eyes.

'Tonight's job. The one you sent Contractor 159 to. You were right to be suspicious.'

The Guardsman followed the man with the strange eyes through to the room with the banks of screens and the moving red dots against a London backdrop. Eighty jobs within the M25 tonight. Eighty Contractors had punched in and, so far, forty had punched back out, uploading the required photographic proof of death.

'The system has thrown up a partial facial match on the target.'

The Guardsman leaned forward and pulled up the live surveillance feed. A bar, as expected. Pale wood, widescreen TV, Contractor 159, the Guardsman's go-to contractor, the lights shining off his golden hair.

The Guardsman hated being right.

The blonde contractor shifted slightly and the target came into view. The Guardsman stared at the woman with the brown hair. She didn't look familiar.

'Who does the system think it is?'

The man with the strange eyes, blue on the left and brown on the right, closed the door and pointed at the life-size photo nailed to the back of it. There were holes in the picture like someone had been using it for target practice.

The Guardsman stared at the photo of the familiar face. The bright green eyes, the blonde hair, the distant stare. Public enemy number one.

Winter.

The name hissed out before the Guardsman could stop it.

The Government agent responsible for unmasking the Boss, eight weeks ago. All of a sudden, the weeks of sly prodding and testing were making more sense.

Winter.

Reckless, arrogant and unbelievably effective.

Rage rose along with frustration.

Winter was one of the few people on the planet with special protected status on Firestorm.

Untouchable.

Untouchable because the Boss wanted to do it himself. And he had to do it himself. Everyone knew she had tracked him down. He had to assert his authority. The world of organised crime was in crisis. North America was in open revolt and, thanks to Winter, Alek Konstantin was being hunted to the ends of the earth, not able to stay in one place for more than a few hours, not able to impose his authority where it was needed.

The Guardsman thought about Alek, forced to scrabble around underground like a mole in the dark.

There was sobbing coming up through the floorboards. It was getting louder.

The Guardsman turned to look at the picture of Winter. How the Guardsman would love to have her, right now, chained to the floor in the cellar, instead of some trainee.

A vein throbbed under the Guardsman's eye. How could anyone think with all that sobbing going on? The Guardsman opened the door and went back down the cellar stairs.

The trainee contractor stopped sobbing at the sound of footsteps. His head jerked backwards and forwards like he was searching for something.

'Please,' said the trainee. 'Just shoot me.'

The Guardsman frowned at the suggestion. Did the man know nothing? The Guardsman never used firearms, had never even held a gun.

The Boss, on the other hand, was all about guns. Quick, efficient and low risk. The thought of Alek Konstantin and his efficiency focused the Guardsman and a moment later the trainee contractor crumpled to the floor.

The Guardsman went back up the stairs, and back to the surveillance feed.

'Get out,' said the Guardsman, without looking round, and the man with the strange eyes hurried out, closing the door behind him.

Firestorm was a sacred trust and the Guardsman, as its Guardian and Administrator, was there to protect it.

Winter had challenged the Boss; she could not be allowed to do the same to Firestorm. Particularly not now, not when they were so close. Eight days away. The Guardsman turned to look at the picture on the back of the door.

It was time to meet her. You couldn't really know someone until you looked into the whites of their eyes. Until you were close enough to feel their breath on your face.

The Guardsman stared at the live feed from the bar. Contractor 159 and his victim were heading for the door. Soon they would be arriving at the house with the metal door and the cellophane room. What to do?

Winter had to suffer, that was for sure.

One way or another.

CHAPTER 3

7 days to go...

It is light and the air is already warm by the time I get away from the police and the cellophane room and the house with its secrets laid out under the forensic tripods.

It is properly hot, like the sun has been up for hours. 7 a.m. and I am alone and knackered and late as I arrive outside a grey office block on the fringes of Canary Wharf.

Late and baffled.

I couldn't find his phone and I couldn't find anything in the cellophane house to explain the missing Guardsman. The computer stood up to about ten minutes of direct attack before its security collapsed and it held nothing. Nothing that connected him to Firestorm.

What tipped the Guardsman off? He can't have recognised me. He had already sent someone else by then. I put my hand to my jaw; my mouth is numb from yanking out the facial alteration kit. It is easy enough to change your appearance for a short time. For anything longer than a few hours you need surgery.

For about the hundredth time, I go over Lucy's last words.

I am an experiment, she said, gripping my arm. *In the final countdown.*

What did the Guardsman mean by experiment? A death without a contract? Without being paid? If so, it is a weird way to put it. And will there be more experiments? The thought of finding another corpse like Lucy has driven me sleepless through the last week to the cellophane room and my showdown with the Guardsman.

And countdown to what? The world has already changed. Eight weeks ago I tracked down the man at the top of organised crime and the world exploded into violence.

The trees lining the dusty street are heavy with the dark green of summer. I look at the café across the way. Red awning down, already busy with bacon rolls and yoghurt and berries to go, the smell of coffee beans rich in the warm air. My stomach lurches, saliva pools. I slow my stride. *Surely I have time?* I don't.

The office block is not shabby, it is not smart, it is just dull. Nondescript. The eye slides right over it, unable to find anything to focus on, not a single line of symmetry, no interesting shiny facade, no pleasing coherence. There is nothing to say what the building is or what it does. Not even a number on the outside, and the small rotating doors which take only one person at a time are not impressive. In Canary Wharf, where status is measured in marble and square footage, this small door could not say more clearly, *nothing important happens here.*

I enter the rotating capsule, wait the mandatory ten seconds while the weigh platform does its thing and lean forward for the iris scan. I walk through the body scanner, through biometrics until it is time for the pat down. Then I am up the stairs and in another reception with a whole new level of security. The European headquarters of the NSA takes its visitors seriously.

A poster of the world's most wanted man stares down at me from the lobby wall.

Alek Konstantin.

Al-ek Kon-stan-tin. The very syllables are hard. They trip off the tongue, smack against the teeth. The Prince of Darkness. The head of organised crime. The man behind Firestorm. The mastermind who harnessed the power of the net to control people and just kept on going until whole countries did as they were told.

Eight weeks on and he is still on the run.

We had no idea how far his authority stretched until it wasn't there anymore. Mexico and the Central American cartels were first, then Miami, Chicago and LA. Law and order collapsed overnight and the police fought running battles in the streets until the President called in the army. Curfews were announced in a dozen American cities, but as governments all over the world were discovering, it is difficult to fight your own population. Anyone can be turned by a well-placed Firestorm threat, and the full power of organised crime has been revealed like something ugly under a stone.

Not that there is anything ugly about the man himself. I stare up at the chiselled cheekbones, the dark eyes, the shaved head, the distant look, and my heart rate accelerates.

Eight weeks since I crashed a cage fight to meet him and nearly died of my injuries. Eight weeks since he nursed me back to health.

The lift doors at the end of the lobby open and Brad, the London head of mission, comes out, a wide white smile on his wide WASP face.

'Sorry it's so early,' he says.

'Sorry I'm so late.' I don't tell him I've been up all night. 'Control is dialling in.'

'I know,' he says, leading the way. 'It's the principle, right?'

Alek Konstantin's eyes watch us as we walk away down the echoing lobby.

The incident room is chill, like a space that is rarely used. A trolley stacked with coffee cups beside the door is seeing some serious trade. Analysts confer in twos and threes. What is the collective for a group of analysts? A hive mind? A contagion?

They whisper to each other, shuffle from foot to foot, look down at their cups and stir their coffee and look round at the room and everywhere except at me. They all know who I am and what I am carrying in my arm.

Operation Atlas, the search for Alek Konstantin, is nearly two months in and showing no results. There hasn't been a positive ID since the early days. Now everyone is jittery, jumping at shadows, worried for themselves, for their families. With the emergency G20 summit in London dedicated to the war on organised crime in seven days, everyone is nervous.

Something has happened.

But then I know something has happened or we wouldn't be having this emergency meeting, 7 a.m. London time, 2 a.m. in Washington. Inconvenient for everyone.

The big screen is split in two: Langley on one side and GCHQ on the other. Our building is only three miles away but like I said, it is the principle of it.

James McKellen, Director of the CIA and head of Operation Atlas, comes into the picture from the far left. We can see him by a tiny door 3,000 miles away in Langley, Virginia, talking to someone, then he is up close filling our screen. The best career politician of his generation, Kennedy good looks and Clinton charm. In the old days he would have been heading for the presidency. When that was the top job.

Now, nothing is more important than the war against organised crime. In the first week, he and his family were kidnapped by the central American cartels. A lesser man might have called it a day after that.

There is not a shred of tiredness in his bright eyes. He radiates energy. I can feel it from here. The GCHQ incident room is still empty, waiting for Control to make an entrance. I recognise the horsehair chair. It has a stain on the seat.

Finally Control appears, a wrinkled, awkward contrast to McKellen. Everything about him is worn. He has more than twenty years on the CIA Director and it shows. The last of his generation.

An old-school spook. He looks like he slept in his clothes. If he slept at all. He gives a nod to say we can go ahead.

'Thank you for coming,' McKellen says. He waits a beat and stares round like he has been on a management training course about keeping eye contact. Which he probably has.

The contagion of analysts has stopped breathing. If you were watching the meeting through cameras, I wonder whether you could read the tension. I glance in the corners but there are no surveillance cameras here, not in the NSA incident room.

'We received this earlier in the evening,' McKellen says and his image shrinks to a corner of the big screen as the footage loads.

The analysts look up, eyes huge in pale faces. Anticipation blankets the room.

It takes me a moment to make sense of what I am seeing on the big screen. Satellite imagery overlaid with drone shots. Isoceles, the global super satellite. Both bird's eye and street views. Men kneel in a line in the dirt, their hands on their heads. Looks like a desert – sandy, rocky terrain. The light is bright, the shadows short – the sun is high in the sky.

A broad figure with a shaved head comes into view. My heart hammers. I rub the raised weal on the inside of my left wrist. He walks slowly up the line and back again.

'Where is it?' someone asks.

'Looks like Mexico.'

I say nothing because I am watching Alek Konstantin put a black barrel to one forehead after another. The heads explode like watermelons. My eyes prick and I don't know if it is for the men in the dirt or something else. I turn away.

'Identification is going to be difficult,' says an analyst.

No one says anything.

A broad white snake circles the shooter's right wrist. A scar. For years we thought it was a tattoo.

Alek gets to the end of the line and looks down at the final kneeling figure. Corpses stretch out beside him. He passes his gun to someone behind him and reaches into his pockets. When his hands come into the light they are ringed with metal.

I trace the warm curves of the knuckledusters in my pocket. I know what is coming.

I figure the guy is dead by the second blow but it goes on and on. I can imagine the thump, thump of fists on raw meat playing out under the Mexican sun. The heat and the spray.

'How long does it go on for?' The analyst stares down into his coffee.

McKellen shrugs. 'Another few minutes.'

Someone moves the cursor along, skipping time.

The punching has stopped. Now the broad figure is directing the action. A sweep of his hand indicates the bodies. His arm points. Men with semi-automatics slung across their backs work their way up the line, dragging drums of black cable behind them.

The scene makes sense as the image pans round to a leafless tree standing stark in the middle of the desert. Bodies hang in a line. They swing slightly with the heft and pull of the effort of getting them up. The lack of head has caused a problem in some cases and those bodies are strung up by their ankles.

I look at the table to get away from the swinging bodies. A perfect drop of coffee sits on the polished surface. A perfect, smooth hemisphere.

'Why didn't we take him out?' someone asks. 'We could have taken out the whole region.'

The CIA are tracking Alek Konstantin with everything they have. If they had footage this good on Isoceles they could have shot him where he stood.

McKellen shakes his head. He leans forward. 'Isoceles was jammed. We only just got this footage.'

Government grade satellite interference.

'What about the drone?'

'It was theirs. They released the images at the same time as Isoceles.'

'Why would they do that?'

No one says anything.

The tiny drop of coffee is edging ever so slightly sideways. There must be a microscopic slope on the table, a fraction of one degree.

'What does it tell us?' says McKellen.

I look up. 'It tells us organised crime just removed Los Zetas from the board and are sending a message to the rest of the world.'

McKellen fixes me with a look from across the Atlantic.

'Winter,' he says. 'Good to see you. Are you off suspension?'

'We are just waiting on psych clearance,' says Control smoothly. 'She is here in a strictly advisory capacity.'

I stare down at the table.

'What about the other sightings?' asks Control, taking over in a way no management training course can teach.

There are two further unconfirmed sightings. Both at night, one at an empty office building in Petersburg, Virginia, and the other at a garden centre in Marseille, France.

'Both this week. Within twenty-four hours of each other.' McKellen looks down at his notes. 'Petersburg, seven armed men broke into a vacant office building, held the guard hostage for three hours and left. There is nothing to suggest it was Alek Konstantin except a positive ID by the guard. We are treating it as highly circumstantial.' There is something smooth about McKellen's delivery, like he has said the words many times.

'Virginia? Is that likely?' says Brad. 'What the hell would he be doing there?'

'As likely as a garden centre,' says an analyst. 'What was he doing *there*? Buying daffodils?'

Analysts laugh, tension release after the hanging bodies.

'Marseille, we have nothing but a back shot.' McKellen puts it up on the screen.

Everyone leans forward.

Even at maximum resolution the image is impossibly grainy. It looks like him. The figure is certainly tall enough.

'And nothing unusual from your end, Winter?'

I shake my head. 'No one has been near me.' I rub the tracker in my arm again.

'She is overseeing our training programme,' Control says. 'Staying close to base.'

I stare at the table.

'He knows she has found the tracker and is on her guard. We believe he is biding his time.'

Walking, talking, living bait, which is an acceptable risk as far as Control is concerned.

'Mexico marks a new development,' says one of the analysts. 'He is losing control of the cartels and publicly asserting his authority.'

Analyst heads nod. Synchronised bobbing. A consensus theory from the hive mind.

'Like the final days of the Roman Empire; the violence and bloodshed escalated incrementally as the Emperor tried to maintain control. We are seeing the same with Firestorm. Contracts are up more than fifty per cent since Alek Konstantin was unmasked. He is losing control.' The analyst sits back.

'Let's hope it is the final days for organised crime and not the final days for democracy,' says McKellen. 'In a week, the world's leadership will meet for the first time since the crisis and we are no nearer to catching him.'

'Winter is still our best bet at this point,' says Control. 'She tracked him down. She turned him into a fugitive. A public humiliation. He is never going to let this pass and he has a tracker in her arm from the time when he held her captive. He knows where she is every moment of every day. He can see her right now sitting in this meeting.'

The room turns to stare. Morbid and curious.

'Why hasn't he put her on Firestorm?' says an analyst.

'He won't send a foot soldier to deal with the woman who brought him down. He will come himself.'

Now the room is really staring.

I flatten the coffee drop with one finger.

THE GUARDSMAN

II

The Guardsman watched the footage of tattooed faces exploding under the Mexican sun and felt a primal, almost visceral, burst of gratification. Los Zetas had been a thorn in the Guardsman's side for years. Now they had stepped out of line and they had been dealt with. Retribution had been swift and without mercy. Possibly it could have been a little slower and more lingering, but no one could say the Boss was losing his grip. No one could doubt his power.

Alek Konstantin was not in favour of lingering. He didn't see pain as a craft. He didn't even seem to enjoy it. Efficiency was what he liked, and guns. He was all about guns. Quick, clean and low risk. The Guardsman was repelled by the very idea. Some things were not meant to be done quickly.

The Guardsman thought with quiet satisfaction about the experiments they were running and what was going to happen in London in seven days' time. A knockout blow. The world would never be the same again.

The Boss would be pleased.

He had to be.

CHAPTER 4

The Bank junction is crammed with commuters starting their day. Mine feels like it has been going for hours. Faces scowl, newly showered and shaved. The pavement is dusty underfoot; the driest July on record. It is like it has never rained. The streets suffocate under a blanket of exhaust fumes and bins. You can't breathe through your mouth for the taste of it.

It has been a summer of weird weather, the sky full of sand as a wind blows from the Sahara. The heat is getting under everyone's skin, stirring the blood. I saw in a police report last week that sex crimes are up tenfold in the capital and I can't say I'm surprised. We're not used to long, hot summer nights. We are a temperate climate, mild and green. Now they have stopped the fountains and the parks are full of half-naked bodies lying on the straw grass.

A tiny Starbucks is built onto the old walls of St Stephen Wallbrook, a glass box huddling up against the ancient sandstone. Singing is coming through the stained-glass windows high above. The morning service. I have to duck as I enter the Starbucks – cardboard iced lattes are hanging like glittery stalactites from the ceiling.

The girl behind the till smiles.

'Name?' she says.

'Winter.'

'What, really? Like the season?'

'Yes.'

'Cool.'

She writes it down on a cup with a thick black marker.

'Can I interest you in our special ice-cold honeycomb latte?'
'No.'

I move down the line. The person ahead of me is having a lot of
trouble deciding whether they want marshmallows in their coffee.
My eyes look overlarge in the chrome of the coffee machine, the pink
rims making the green fluorescent. My short hair is still crazy after the
Australian girl wig. I turn my back and lean up against the counter
and close my eyes. The chrome is warm behind my bare shoulders.

I try to remember when I last slept properly. Weeks of watching
the ICE app are taking their toll and the past week, since I found
Lucy, has been one long sleepless search for the Guardsman. Not that
the Guardsman wasn't around before but my focus was on finding
the man behind Firestorm. Unmask him and everything would
collapse. That was the theory. It hasn't exactly panned out like that.

My brain is fried and it's not just the all-nighter. I am wired
and restless and off key. I need to hit someone. Or get laid. Or
both. And there I have a problem. There is only one person I want
to sleep with and he is unavailable.

I rub the tracker in my left wrist. It doesn't just give location,
it monitors well-being – extreme pain and extreme pleasure. The
thought of Alek Konstantin watching me orgasm electronically
is keeping me celibate.

I pass the bronze face of the Bloomberg building, consider the
GCHQ underground entrance and think better of it. At this time
of day, Bank's circular tube station will be packed tight like some
world record attempt at the most people in an enclosed space.

The wind is warm. It whistles between the high buildings
covering everything in a fine layer of grit. I cross Queen Victoria
street heading for GCHQ's main entrance.

The cup is hot in my grip. Above me, the tower with its clock
face looks down on the junction. 9 a.m.

'Hottest summer on record,' say Security. They hand me a purple cord with a plastic pocket.

I look down at it. It is for my staff pass. To hang round my neck. The purple lanyard has white writing on it.

I put my coffee on the security counter to get a better look, feeding the silky purple through my fingers.

Energise. Empower. Enable.

'What the hell is this?'

They edge back. 'Everyone is getting one. We just have to hand them out.'

I stuff the purple cord with its plastic holder into my pocket and head for the lifts.

Control looks up from his desk.

'Tell me this is a joke,' he says. 'You set up a Firestorm hit on *yourself*? Did it seem like a good idea at the time?'

I shrug. 'It was nothing. Just a little field practice. I was getting rusty.'

The walls of his office curve in a perfect circle. I can see out through the clock-face window all the way across the junction. The great metal hands of the clock creak. It would drive me mad. Seen from in here, time is running backwards. There's probably something very profound about that.

'Tell me this is not about the Guardsman,' he says. 'How many times do I have to say this? It is not your job to take out contractors. You are Head of Field now. You must not let this man get under your skin.'

Under your skin.

'Solo, Aveline, the Guardsman are fantasies, myths, urban legends – the Holy Trinity. Aspirational figures created by Firestorm. They are not real.'

He is wrong about that.

I stare out of the huge circular window at the Bank junction. Taxis crawl and pedestrians bustle.

'Firestorm will be defeated online,' says Control. 'Not by attacking one foot soldier at a time in a futile personal crusade. For every Firestorm contractor, there are another ten jockeying for selection. You have responsibilities now. Priorities. And top of the priority list is Alek Konstantin. He was there in Petersburg. Did you see McKellen's face? He knows it was him, but he doesn't want us near it. I want to know why.' His eyes snap back to mine. 'Look around you. Look at what is happening in the world. The G20 is a week away and we have nothing. You were single-minded in your pursuit of the man at the top of organised crime. You were prepared to wade through a sea of blood to find him. You dealt him a mortal blow. Now, it's like you're not interested. I find your attitude hard to understand.'

He is not the only one.

'Firestorm is the priority.' I stare at the number twelve. 'It always was. Finding Alek Konstantin won't solve the problem. Without him there will still be Firestorm, just no one controlling it. An army of hitmen roaming the globe. The Guardsman was bad before but he is getting worse – hits without contracts, escalating violence. It is like the Firestorm Administrator has lost control of him.' The exact mechanics of Firestorm's back office are a mystery to us but we know there is an Administrator overseeing contracts, matching payments, keeping an eye on the contractors. 'The G20 will be a magnet for him. All those world leaders? It is like an all-you-can-eat buffet for Firestorm. Come on in and stuff your faces.'

Control grunts. He doesn't disagree. He has argued against holding an emergency G20 from the start. 'We know the G20 will be targeted,' he says. 'It is expected to take four and a half hours just to get into the ExCel Centre, then there's the bomb detectors, the nerve agent sirens, the panic rooms, the separate ventilation systems, the field hospital and don't even get me started on the quarantine zone nearly a mile out from the building. The place is a fortress. It is not a summit, it is an exercise in advanced military planning which has nothing to do with you. You must not get distracted. Alek Konstantin is the key. Take him down and we won't even have to have the bloody G20.'

'McKellen thinks it will be the turning point.'

Control snorts. 'The day the world gets its act together?'

The sun shines through the backwards numbers on the clock face.

'Do you ever wonder whether we might have gone beyond the point of no return?' I ask. 'That, if the man at the top is removed, everything really will collapse into chaos?' I turn to face him. 'In Mexico, at the first sign of Alek Konstantin's authority weakening, they used mustard gas to settle a turf war. Twelve thousand dead.'

'And Los Zetas haven't got away with it.'

'That's my point. He is still in control. Still doling out terminal justice. It wasn't us sorting it out, it was the Prince of Darkness. But he can't be everywhere, especially not now.' *Now I have betrayed him and left him running for his life.* 'His eye is off the ball. We need to deal with Firestorm ourselves. That analyst was right, it is getting worse.'

'And we will. As previously discussed.' We have had this argument before. 'But first we cut off the head. Cut off the head and the body dies.' He looks at his screen. 'What do you make of the Marseille sighting? We could be missing a trick in our own backyard.'

'Or it wasn't him and we are wasting time chasing shadows.'

'There is a new boss in Marseille. Armand. A professional. A different proposition to Ferret entirely. You might ask that Marseille kid you hired about him.'

'His name is Léon.'

'I don't care what his name is. Most people come back from a mission with some injuries and a minor venereal disease, not a teenage petty criminal.' He sits back. 'How is the hiring going by the way?'

'Fine,' I say. 'Fine.'

I think about my session with the candidates. A bunch of soldiers and marines keen as scholarship kids, not a hint of maverick amongst them. Exactly what you expect from years of military training. Exactly what I don't need. I get a picture of a vigilante with ready fists and a bad attitude.

'I met someone last night,' I say.

'Who?'

'An LSE student, financial accounting.'

'An accountant?'

'Kind of.' I try to picture her as an accountant and fail.

'Well, he can't be worse than Léon. And ask Léon about the garden centre while you're at it. If you can fit it into your busy schedule. If it's not too much trouble.' He looks at me. If he still had his half-moon spectacles he would be peering over them. 'I don't know what you are doing all day. I need you off suspension. I need you out there. Stop fixating on Firestorm and the Guardsman and focus. You have a lot of skills Erik didn't have.'

My old Boss. The old Head of Field. I wait for the compliments; it would be a first, but you never know.

'What you don't have is gravitas.'

'Grey hair, you mean.'

'Dignity.' He sighs. 'Believe it or not Winter, there is more to running a department than fighting people and playing hooky. Diplomacy, people skills, sensitivity—'

'I've got people skills.'

'I want you to check in with HR right now. No excuses, Winter. I want you to go straight to Beth's office. You are physically fit, now you need psych clearance to get off suspension and she is in a position to provide it. She says you are avoiding her.'

No shit. I have been avoiding her for weeks. I have no intention of wasting my time back on active. My focus is the Guardsman.

'And if you want to make a good first impression—' he continues.

I don't.

'—I suggest you wear your staff pass.'

'The purple garrotte?'

'You will cooperate, Winter, with her efforts to improve the department's HR standards.'

'Shall I slip her some tongue?'

Silence.

Tumbleweed.

Not a muscle moves on Control's face.

'Did it sound funnier in your head?' he says.

'I can't say I really thought about it.'

'And there,' says Control, 'is your problem in a nutshell.'

CHAPTER 5

She is waiting for me in the corridor outside her office. Black suit, silk blouse, shiny hair done up in some kind of a twist. Way better looking than I was expecting. The strip lighting flickers. The brand new GCHQ Head of Human Resources, fresh from the Treasury, a psychologist with a doctorate in well-being and a mission to modernise.

Well-being.

What a colossal waste of my time.

'Beth Garner,' she says formally, holding out her hand.

I ignore it. My attention is now all on the man with her. Young, dark-haired, floppy fringed. High cheekbones. Great smile. Not that I ever see it. Everard, GCHQ's chief medic and when I say medic, I use the word in its loosest possible sense.

Everard and HR – an unholy double act.

'Doctor,' I sneer the word.

'Winter.' His eyes are a blue Siberian wasteland.

He purses his mouth.

'Beth and I were just finishing.'

I nod.

'When are you sending me some recruits to test, Winter?'

My stomach churns. My own interrogation training flashes back to me. Chemically-induced pain that leaves no mark on the skin.

'I have been developing something new for them,' he says.

Of course you have.

His blue eyes stare into mine with the intimacy and indifference of someone who has broken your guard, broken your defences, broken your mind, until you are nothing but a grovelling, slobbering mass of pleading.

Beth's eyes flick from Everard to me and back again. Senior colleagues shooting the breeze about matters of national importance. This is more like it, she is thinking. In the thick of it. This is where the action is. Not like the Treasury. She smiles. Her teeth have the perfect brilliance of expensive orthodontics.

'Get lost, Everard,' I say. 'Crawl back under your stone.'

Beth flinches. A full-body reaction. She stares at me like she honestly can't believe it. Like it is inconceivable anyone could be that rude in the workplace.

Her office is cosy. Rugs on the floor, shelves of books behind her. It feels like the room of an Oxbridge don. I can smell perfume in the confined space. Something classy and expensive that I can't quite place.

'Shut the door behind you,' she says, sitting down at her desk, making a vain bid for the upper hand.

If you want to make a good first impression...

I plonk myself down in the small, hard chair facing her and put my feet up on her desk. My heels scrape as they hit the wood. I shift to check. I have left two long scratches in the polished surface.

'I was surprised to hear you speak to a senior colleague like that,' she says, carefully avoiding looking at my boots. 'Is there a history of conflict I should be aware of? As Heads of Departments, I imagine you have to see quite a lot of each other?'

'Not if I see him coming first.'

She stares.

I sigh. 'Do you know who Everard is?'

'He is GCHQ's chief medical officer,' she says.

'That too,' I agree.

She looks at me. Somewhere in the room, a clock ticks. I stare back at her. If she thinks I am going to break the silence, she has no idea.

'I have just been reading your last assessment,' she says, folding. 'Since it ended with you offering to suck the interviewer until he screamed, I thought it best if I conducted your review myself.' She gives a prim little smile like she has said something clever.

'You're not really my type,' I say. 'But I'm willing to give it a go.'

She gets a furrow between her brows as she works this out, then her face tightens.

She glares at me.

I steeple my fingers at her.

She gathers her notes together and taps them on the desk, breaking the glare off.

'OK, fine.' I sit up, pulling my boots off her desk. 'Ask me what you need to. Let's get this done.'

'Tell me about Alek Konstantin.'

'He runs the biggest crime network in the world. He controls Firestorm. He is the richest man on the planet.'

'Why do you think he let you go?'

'He didn't let me go. I escaped.'

She sits back, considering me. She flicks her pen lid on and off, on and off, her hazel eyes curious. 'And yet you are still alive. Somehow I can't help feeling if Alek Konstantin wanted you dead you wouldn't still be sitting here in my office.'

I shrug. I've got no answer to that because she is a hundred per cent right. Her gaze is appraising as if she is trying to work out the answer to some puzzle and I get a sudden, sharp, cold feeling that I shouldn't underestimate this woman.

'Tell me about the tracker,' she says.

'Standard procedure for a high-risk prisoner I imagine.'

'And why haven't you had it removed?'

'Control believes Alek Konstantin will come for me himself, up close and personal, and that it is our best chance of catching him.'

She looks down at her notes.

'Firestorm won't accept a contract on you. Did you know that?'

Yes, but I'm surprised you do.

'The man likes to pay his debts in person,' I say.

'And how does that make you feel?'

Conflicted.

'It doesn't make me feel anything.'

'What were your impressions of him?'

I shrug.

'What did you think of him personally?'

'What has that got to do with anything?'

'Just answer the questions, Winter.'

Alek Konstantin. Billionaire crime lord. Hot as hell.

'He was exactly what I expected.'

'That is no answer.'

The clock ticks.

'OK,' she says. 'Take a step back. What happened in Marseille with Marcel Furet?'

Marcel Furet, aka 'the Ferret'. The King Rat in the Marseille criminal underworld.

I tell her about the drug shipment and Detective Fresson, a straight copper in a bent world and about wrecking his drug bust so I could get in with Ferret. So Ferret would take me to Alek Konstantin.

She watches me. 'What do you think would have happened if Marcel Furet had realised who you really were?'

I shrug.

'And what happened to Furet?'

'He didn't make it.'

Hazel eyes bore into mine. 'And, in your opinion, did the results justify the loss of life?'

'Yes.'

'Tell me about Paris,' she says. And now she is getting to the point. 'Tell me everything you remember.'

I stare at the rows of criminology textbooks behind her. The 'well-being' is some kind of cover.

'Winter?'

Paris. What do I remember? A desperate, panicked hurtle to stop Slashstorm, the live torture site. Fighting the contractor behind it – the Marquise de Mazan – on a slick grey rooftop. The sound the Marquise's skull made as it hit stone. Seeing Alek on the roof across the street and realising I had been wrong about him. That he was never behind Slashstorm. That he was there to stop it, like me, even though he was on the run. The world's dark policeman.

'I have already been over it,' I say. 'I can't really remember. I was tired. Overwrought. Four days in captivity. I panicked.'

She makes a note on her pad. 'Panicked?' she says. 'The satellite imagery is very clear. You used unnecessary force to subdue the suspect and then you dropped her off a building.'

'It's all a bit of a blur.'

'Shall I tell you what I think?'

'No.'

'I think you wanted to do it. I think you knew exactly what you were doing and you did it anyway. I believe, and the French prosecutor agrees with me, that you think you are above the law. This is why you were suspended, pending psych assessment.' She sits back. 'Your behaviour was also ill-advised.'

'How do you figure that?'

'Because, Winter, there are people who will view your actions as a direct challenge. We are in the middle of a global power struggle. Have you seen what is happening in America? We are at war. And you announced yourself as a player. You stuck your head above the parapet. Sooner or later someone will accept your challenge.'

'This department kills people. It isn't the Ministry of Agri-culture.'

'And how does that make you feel?'

'Wasted. I always wanted to be a farmer.'

Her face closes down. 'We are done here,' she says. 'I have heard a lot about you, Winter, and I am disappointed to find it is all true. Under the terms of your suspension you may not engage in field work or carry arms.'

I get to my feet.

'I love these purple things by the way,' I say, tugging my staff pass. 'Very empowering, very enabling.'

She smiles.

'Great for tying wrists to bedposts.'

I slam the door on her reply. If there was one.

CHAPTER 6

Ten seconds after leaving Beth's office, I'm in the stairwell heading for the detainment floor. This level, like so much of GCHQ, has been extended and improved over time. State of the art interrogation suites with digital locks and 360-degree camera surveillance.

It wasn't always the case. The old cells lock with iron keys and there are sloping drains in the concrete floors for when interviews get hands-on.

I pull an old-fashioned, three-point key out of my pocket and look both ways up the corridor. Nothing. These old cells were abandoned years ago. The corridor cams all point the other way. I turn the key, duck inside and pull the wooden bar down quick. It slides into iron slots in the wall. Old-fashioned. Impregnable. If you had to break into this room, it would be easier to go through the wall.

The cell is little bigger than a store cupboard, with a table and a laptop wired up to a standalone router. The tools of a hacker. I am off-reservation within GCHQ. Flunking psych reports, hiding out, playing hooky, listening to the police channels. Just like being a teenager again.

The yellow Post-its stuck on the wall above the desk flutter slightly in the draft from the back of the laptop. Thirty-eight false alarms. Twenty-two Firestorm hits stopped. Twenty-two lives saved.

One hit, in a graveyard – not fast enough.

I write a location and yesterday's date on a new Post-it and add it to the rest. The contractor with the cellophane room wasn't who I booked, but he is part of the puzzle.

Another piece of the Firestorm jigsaw.

The disappointment swamps me.

I break that night down again, minute by minute, proving to myself I couldn't have got there any quicker. It took me twenty minutes to reach Lucy. Faster than ICE, but not fast enough. Twenty minutes is a long time to spend in the hands of a knife expert. I can see myself now, on my knees, trying to triage her injuries, knowing it was hopeless.

I wrap my arms around myself, gripping tight above the elbow. *Breathe in. Breathe out.*

Lucy used all the strength she had left to tell me something she thought was important. She used her last words.

I am an experiment in the final countdown.

It has an apocalyptic ring. A ticking clock. I shiver in my cold cell. Countdown to what? Chaos is breaking out all over the world. What else is there? All week I haven't been able to shake the sense of impending doom. It is in GCHQ, crushing me. I am twitching at shadows, seeing the Guardsman behind every eye.

My heart thuds as my phone breaks the silence, vibrating in my back pocket.

'Where *are* you?' Simon says. 'The recruits are waiting.'

'I'm on my way.'

'How did it go with Beth?'

'Fine,' I say. 'Good.' I stare at the Post-it wall, willing myself to understand where I went wrong.

'Great. So you are off suspension?'

'I don't know,' I lie. 'Probably.'

I flick off the switch and turn to raise the bar. In the darkness, I can feel the Post-its behind me almost as if they are alive. Yellow, fluttering butterflies pinned to a wall. Questions I have no answers to. The bar grinds in the silence. As I pull open the door I can almost hear rustling.

THE GUARDSMAN

III

The Guardsman considered the errant contractor. He was trembling from head to toe. Wide-eyed and slack-jawed and wanting. His sin was one of omission but that didn't make it any less of a sin in the Guardsman's book. He had reneged on a contract. Pity for the target: the cardinal sin. He had accepted a contract, failed to carry it out and then tried to run. The target had become aware. Embarrassing all round.

Embarrassing for Firestorm.

The Guardsman put down the chopsticks. The wonton soup was getting cold in any case.

Only seven days left, but the man was of no use to the Guardsman as an experiment.

Embarrassing for Firestorm.

A vein throbbed in the Guardsman's temple.

Across the room, the contractor's account was open on the screen. Nothing could be left undone. Both the failed contract and any outstanding ones. Firestorm always honoured unfulfilled contracts and the Guardsman, as its Administrator, handled it personally.

The Guardsman flicked a finger and the guards either side of the man forced him to his knees, locking his arms straight out behind him.

The Guardsman picked up one of the chopsticks and walked around the table. The soup had been delicious. Now it was cold. Things were floating in it. Bobbing to the surface.

The Guardsman leaned forward, took the man's chin in one hand and inserted the chopstick in the corner of the man's right eye.

'Our eyes,' said the Guardsman, 'are sometimes like our judgements. Blind.'

CHAPTER 7

I sigh as the doors open on GCHQ's triple-height training arena with its huge football stadium lights and stale smell. It is air-conditioned like the rest of the building, but somehow it hasn't quite worked in the giant space. The lights shake when a tube train passes overhead. On the right, the long internal window of the staff canteen peers down on the action.

The recruits are on the blue mats in the centre with Viv, Erik's old quartermaster, putting them through some kind of combat exercise. The glare hurts my eyes as I pick my way down the metal gantry stairs.

The recruits speed up when they clock my approach. Viv stands watching them, impassive in a black crop top and baggy tracksuit bottoms, her knuckles taped. I come up beside her and we watch the pairs for a while. They are practising shoulder throws. That or weird sexual positions. It's hard to tell.

I turn my back, dispirited.

'How's it going?'

She pushes a lock of dark hair out of her perfect pixie face.

'Fine,' she says, 'but they need you. You can't keep disappearing. They need something to aspire to.'

'They can aspire to you. You were Captain of the British Karate squad. You are an Olympian, for God's sake.'

'I'm not their boss,' Viv says patiently. 'They like me. It is you they want to impress.'

I glance over my shoulder at the recruits.

She gives me a sideways look. 'Rough night?'

I shrug.

Some guy in the middle distance is doing weights. His six pack is impressive.

I rub the tracker in my wrist. Can he see me now? Is he watching? Does he know what I am doing every night?

'Viv?'

'Mmm?' she says, her attention taken by a dangling piece of knuckle tape.

'D'you think there is a "Mr Right" out there for everyone? You know, the perfect match? The One?'

She goggles. 'What kind of a question is that? Are you serious?'

'Yes.'

'In that case,' she says, 'of course not. It is a ridiculous idea. There are hundreds of people out there who are "The One" and who could make you happy. And who is to say, in any case, that "The One" – if there was one, which there isn't, obviously – but just to say there was, for the sake of it,' the tape dangles from her knuckle, forgotten, 'then he would probably break your heart and leave you when you get fat and old anyway.'

'Right.'

She looks at me, her face curious. 'What's got into you lately? If I didn't know better, I'd say you were mooning over some guy. You, of all people. What have you done with Winter?'

'Don't be ridiculous.'

'When did you last get laid?'

I shrug, but my mind has leapt to the memory before I can stop it.

The slide of skin, the smell of the sea, the slow chug of diesel engines, the freezing breeze on my damp back and my aching, sensitised body pushed again and again to pleasure. Alek Konstantin. He has ruined me for anyone else.

'So how do you normally tell when a guy likes you?' she says.

'He gets hard.'

'Is that it?'

'Pretty much.'

'So, what about Erik?'

'Erik was different. He was like a brother. It would have been weird.'

'But did he like you as a person?'

I screw up my face in thought. My old Head of Field. Boss, father, brother, punchbag. I trusted him with my life. No question. I think about my teenage years, the training and his patience and the number of times he had my back on missions. I think about him disobeying a direct order and rescuing me from the hold of a pirate ship. I think about the disciplinary hearing afterwards that saw him stripped of his command.

I made him vulnerable.

If you care, your enemies have all the leverage they need.

I stare across the room blindly.

'I think he loved me,' I say.

'Right,' says Viv. 'When someone loves you, they care about your safety, about your well-being, they look after you when you are sick. They bail you out. Maybe they don't even fuck you.'

I feel like she is trying to tell me something. God knows what.

I turn back to the recruits and clap my hands together. They stop instantly, as if they have been just waiting for a move from me. Nine guys and three girls. They stare like I am some kind of rock star.

I sigh.

'This next exercise,' I say, 'is all about endurance, staying power and stamina. I want you to hop on one leg for as long as you can.'

As one they start hopping slow measured hops, pacing themselves.

'And to control your breathing, I need you to bark like a dog.'

'Which dog, ma'am?'

Ma'am.

'A poodle is my preference.'

I turn my back on the high-pitched yipping.

'Keep the first and the last to stop,' I say to Viv. 'Get rid of the rest. And give them a copy of that movie, *Coming to America*, on the way out.'

The canteen is half full, breakfast winding down, lunch starting out.

'Everything, Winter?' says the guy behind the counter, pointing with a ladle the size of his fist.

Eggs congeal in pools of grease. 11 a.m., they have probably been there for hours. The bacon fat has gone solid.

'Right you are,' I say. Calories in lieu of sleep. Works for me.

I take my tray and plonk it down by the window overlooking the arena. The recruits are still hard at it, bobbing up and down. The best the combined military has to offer. The glass is soundproofed but I can see their lips still moving. I turn my shoulder on the depressing sight.

A tray slams down opposite me with a banana and a coffee. Simon.

'Hi,' I say.

'I have spoken to HR,' Simon says.

'I don't think I am her type,' I say mournfully.

'How could you?' he hisses. 'How could you make a pass at the Head of HR? Did you honestly offer to suck her till she screamed?' His mouth opens on the next question, but his attention is caught by the recruits. 'Is that your doing?' he says, pointing an accusing finger down at the arena.

'Yes.' I don't bother to look.

'You can't keep sending them away. We need agents. You need a team. They have to start somewhere.' He opens his banana. 'I get the last to stop, but why the first? What's that about?'

'I would have been the first to stop.' I think about this. 'If I ever started.'

'So, you are basically looking for yourself?'

I shrug, thinking about a contractor clever enough to detect a sting and field a substitute. The Guardsman suspected, but he didn't know. That's why he sent someone else to meet me, so he could check. If he had been sure, no one would have come.

Simon fiddles with a spoon, stirring his coffee. He looks up scowling, ready to continue the lecture, but I am already on my feet.

As I walk away down the canteen, the recruits are still bobbing behind me.

CHAPTER 8

The bar looks just the same as it did last night. Smells the same. Booze and plug-in air freshener. That distinctive smell that makes you think of stained carpets even when there aren't any. Bland pale wood, fake leather seats, downlighters doing a poor job at creating ambience. There must be hundreds of bars in London like this one. Anonymous offshoots of some national chain. The air conditioning is working overtime. After the exhaust fumes and heat of the street it is like stepping into a fridge.

They are serving coffee and croissant – a seamless transition. The lighting is just a little bit brighter and that is about it; you can still get a pint if you want one. Soon the lunchtime crowd will be here and the drinking will begin all over again.

The widescreen TV above the bar is showing twenty-four-hour news. The red Bloomberg ticker tape scrolls across the bottom. 'Martial law has been imposed on a two-hundred-mile area in South East China,' the newsreader says. The picture cuts to a familiar street scene: burnt-out cars, smoke, people running up and down. It could be any one of hundreds of places. Organised crime are running riot.

The barmaid is unloading a bar-top dishwasher. She has changed her blouse.

'Are you *still* on?' I say, flicking the brown wig out of my face and massaging the new ache in my jaw. Her hours suck.

'Back on,' she says. 'Eight on and eight off.' She takes the steaming glasses and stacks them neatly on the shelf. 'You got lucky then.' She gives me an envious sideways look.

I think about the cellophane room.

'I'll have him if you don't want him,' she says. 'I could do with a nice steady guy in my life.' She stops mid glass. 'I could do with *any* guy in my life.'

I look at her. I know she has a kid and I know her hours are long and that she only recently came to London and I know it was the only job she could get and she got it because the manager is a breasts man and part of the job description includes letting him have the occasional grope, but it is not too bad apart from that. I know because I made a point of chatting to her, while I waited for the Guardsman. Shooting the breeze, building my cover. Second nature.

I pictured the manager last night, a small lean guy, pushing her up against the beer barrels, taking a breast in each hand and solemnly hefting them.

'I hate not being there for him when he wakes up,' she said last night, talking about her kid. 'But you do what you have to do,' and I nodded and smiled because I wasn't really listening.

Her foundation is garish in the brighter light, more suited to the night. The cheap black material of her blouse is sheer from wear and too much washing. As she leans forward, I can see right down her top. I imagine what the contractor would have done to her. I imagine her there on that chair in the middle of the cellophane room. The air feels cold. Tiredness must be catching up with me.

I stare into the mirror behind the bar and a strange woman in a brown wig stares back at me.

'Are you OK?' she says. 'You look like you've seen a ghost.'

I pull myself together. 'Long night.'

'Weird,' she says. 'I could have sworn you were Australian.'

'Only sometimes.'

The news has moved on. The Hollywood sign smoulders. It makes me wonder how they got a metal sign to burn. LA was one of the first cities to collapse into anarchy. Now Firestorm do what they like and bands of men in clown masks loot the smoking streets.

The barmaid stares up at the TV. 'Clown masks?' she says. 'What is that all about?'

'Intimidation and anonymity,' I say.

'What?' she says. She wipes the bar top with a cloth. 'They are all crazy over there. I can't see it happening here.'

I wish I could be so confident.

Organised crime – perfectly organised, perfectly cooperative, ruled by one man. A dictatorship. The very antithesis of our side. It has taken nearly eight weeks for world leaders to agree to the emergency G20.

I picture the planet and the centres of organised crime and, connecting them, the Firestorm web and right in the middle of it, watching and waiting like a fat spider, the anonymous Firestorm Administrator monitoring everything.

I shake my head to get rid of the image of the world suffocating under a massive web and look around the bar like a field agent. Who was here last night? Any one of them could have been the Guardsman. Was he in here all along checking up on his hunch? Or was he just double-booked and fielded a substitute at the last minute?

I sit down at a corner table and get out my laptop. It takes me about ninety seconds to access the bar's CCTV. There are cameras at the door, behind the bar, in the corridor to the toilets. The feed is low-grade, grainy and cheap like petrol station cameras.

The barmaid comes over with a coffee.

'Get that down your neck,' she says. 'You probably need it.' She puts a plate with a croissant in front of me. 'On the house.' There is something awkward about the way she says it.

I stare because I know that she gets one free pastry a shift but anything else she has to pay for, so normally she doesn't have anything more because she needs the cash. She has just given me her breakfast.

'Don't eat it if you don't want it,' she says hurriedly.

'Great, thanks,' I say. 'I appreciate it.' I take a swig of coffee. My fourth of the morning. 'D'you mind if I just look at the lights?'

I am standing on a stool and flicking the metal casing off the fish-eye light with a screwdriver before she can argue.

'Why?' She stares up at me open-mouthed.

The socket is empty. I get down off the stool and move it beneath the next one in line. Nine of them. Easy to check.

'Just a whim.'

She stands with her arms folded under her chest. 'Just don't damage them, will you? They were all changed yesterday.'

I look down at her, the screwdriver poised in mid-air. 'A scheduled change?'

'What?'

'Was it planned that they would be changed?'

'No,' she says. 'That's the funny thing.'

I get down off my stool.

'This guy from the lighting company came and said he had to change all the bulbs because there was a recall.'

'What did he look like?'

She shrugs. 'I dunno really. Tall. He had a baseball cap and a beard. I'm not into beards.'

'Fat, thin, young, old?'

'Medium. Couldn't really tell under the coat. I thought it was a bit odd he was wearing a coat in this weather. Strange eyes.'

'Age?'

She screws up her face. 'Thirty-five? You can never tell with beards.'

'Would you recognise him again?'

'I'd recognise the beard again.'

'What about his voice? Did he have an accent?'

'What is this about?' she says, putting her hands on her hips. 'You could have seen him yourself if you were that desperate.'

'When?'

'You just missed him. Apparently he brought the wrong ones yesterday. He had to change them again.'

CHAPTER 9

I am back on the laptop pulling up the morning's CCTV footage, my fingers moving faster than they have ever moved on a keyboard. He came in and planted surveillance cameras, probably short-range receivers, and was back this morning to remove them.

'Hey,' she says over my shoulder. 'Is that the bar?'

I grind to a halt. The system is only carrying the last hour, the rest is uploaded automatically to the cloud. I need to get back to the office to pull the data.

I hand her a twenty. 'I've got to go,' I say. 'Keep the change.'

She smiles. 'Thanks, that's really nice of you. We could go out sometime, if you like.'

She says something else, but I am already out on the bright street striding away.

It takes me longer than it should to get the bar's CCTV footage from the cloud. I am rushing and cutting corners. There has never been a positive ID on the Guardsman.

Facial recognition software is an amazing thing. Once you have a positive ID there is nowhere to hide. Unless you are the world's richest man and even for him it is proving a grim daily struggle. In London, there are more cameras per square foot than anywhere in the world.

I check out the street cam footage while I wait. The moment it loads I am scrolling and there he is, massive beard, baseball cap as described, and my heart thumps, and straight away he is heading for the tube and my shot of excitement is ebbing away.

The tube cameras, although plentiful, are old-school and London Bridge is a vast station, easy to hide in. Almost as if it can hear my thoughts the network drive tells me the stairwell camera is non-operational as of 2 p.m. yesterday. There is a blind spot inside London Bridge. I check the next-nearest cameras and nothing. He has vanished. The blind spot was there on purpose to allow someone to remove a beard and cap and coat and disappear into the anonymous hundreds in the station.

The trouble with beards is they are the first thing any witness mentions. It is as if someone only has to have a beard to make all their other features indistinct and with London sporting hipster facial hair everywhere you look, they blend right in.

Finally, the CCTV footage from the morning loads. I study his time in the bar, his interaction with the barmaid. There's never any chance of a face shot. I remember my face in the mirror behind the bar and go back to the door cam I had discounted. I scroll through it frame by frame and there it is. A tiny face reflected in the mirror behind the bar. No bigger than a postage stamp but all I need. The imaging software blows it up, scrubs the white noise from the shot.

A pair of eyes above a massive beard.

The circle goes round and round as it thinks about it.

Insufficient data.

There *is* something strange about the eyes. They are different colours. Blue on the left and brown on the right. Probably a single contact lens. If anyone gets past the beard, the only thing they will remember is the eyes.

I go back over the timeline. When was the bar first mentioned by me in my role as vengeful husband? I said it was where my brainless bitch wife went on the pull and I knew because I was tracking her iPhone. *Find my phone? Ha.* I said. *It should be called find my cheating wife.*

I look through the exchange. The bar was first mentioned around 11 a.m. and by 2 p.m. the tube stairwell had lost its camera and the bar ceiling was carrying a fistful of specialist surveillance equipment.

Just *who* is the Guardsman? The whole thing reeks of black op experience.

I picture the barmaid, smiley and helpful. Could she identify him again? The yellow stickies flutter in the draft from the back of the laptop. I drum my fingers on the desk. Something about her is making me uneasy. If I am making that judgement, so is he. A loose end. Definitely a loose end.

I dial the bar on my mobile and realise I don't know her name. She worked an eight-hour shift and gave me her breakfast and I didn't even ask her name.

A woman answers. A co-worker. Not the manager. My description of her is obviously spot on.

'I'm not sure where she is,' the woman says. 'Can I give her a message?'

'When did you last see her?'

'I dunno.'

'I need her to stay there,' I say. 'I am coming to her. She must not leave the bar, do you understand?'

I am on my feet, shutting down my laptop when Security call from Reception.

'Winter.' And there is something in the man's voice. 'You need to come up here.'

I slam out of the cell, down the corridor, pounding up the stairwell, dust bunnies flying. Dread has me by the throat. It wraps its steely fingers round me and squeezes till the blood thuds in my ears and black bubbles pop in front of my eyes. I burst out of the door at the top, hurtle through Reception, hurdling the turnstiles. Through the lobby doors I can see a crowd of bare legs on the pavement. Behind me, Security shout but all I can hear is my heartbeat drumming in my ears and *please no* coming out of my mouth.

I burst through the front doors and the quiet hits me. The quiet of muffled whispers and horrified staring. Shocked gasps. I shove my way through the backs, the shirt sleeves and the bare shoulders and stagger into the sudden, empty space. Something is lying on the dusty pavement. Something that might once have been a person.

I fall to my knees with an eerie sense of déjà vu. The barmaid stares with sightless eyes. There are words carved on her forehead.

An eye for an eye, Winter.

CHAPTER 10

6 days to go...

It is night. Refuse lorries circle the junction. Control looks up. There is no sympathy in his eyes, just understanding and calculation.

'I want you out of here,' he says. 'Away from this. Go to Virginia. Find out what Alek Konstantin was doing in Petersburg. If he is on the Eastern Seaboard, maybe it will flush him out. Leave this to the police. It is not up to you. I told you to leave it. You are too involved. One girl is an irrelevance. And now you have made yourself a target.' He scowls at the thought that someone else might get to me before Alek Konstantin.

'Two girls. Before her, there was Lucy.'

'Who was Lucy?'

'The girl from the graveyard.'

Control shrugs. *One girl, two girls? What difference does it make?* 'There is no room here for personal. I want you in Virginia.'

I stare out of the window. 3 a.m. and the Bank junction is deserted. As deserted as it ever gets. The refuse lorries crawl slowly along the kerbs. Early morning deliveries get unloaded onto pavements.

No room for personal.

I watched a mother identify her daughter this afternoon. Dry-eyed, adrenaline keeping her up, her grandson with his bare chubby thighs on her hip. She wouldn't put him down. I watched her tilt her head, trying to understand the writing on her daughter's forehead, I watched the police sergeant try to explain the words to her and I watched the toddler fall as she understood.

I caught the child in my arms and I had nothing to say, nothing that could make up for a life without a mother, nothing but a promise that I would find this man or I would die trying.

If that isn't personal, I don't know what is.

Orange rotating lights scroll round the room, the rumble thud and clank of a refuse lorry blocking the junction. It is like I can smell it.

I close the door softly behind me.

I sleep six hours and fifty minutes of the seven-hour Virgin Atlantic flight to Washington DC.

A girl reaches for me in a dusty graveyard, a barmaid stares with sightless eyes, Alek holds out his hand in the dawn, 'First and last time of asking, Winter – come with me.'

Touchdown wakes me. I watch out of the window as we taxi. It looks as hot as the UK. A government sedan is waiting on the tarmac.

'It is an honour,' says the suit shaking my hand. He is forty-five to fifty. Streaks of silver. Nice smile. I'm guessing, CIA Desk Head.

The sedan whisks me a hundred yards to a back door in the airport. The Desk Head whisks me through some anonymous back corridors. Immigration tip their imaginary hats. Washington is like that: hierarchical. We walk seamlessly out of the airport via a side door and straight into another government limo. Time from touchdown? About nine minutes.

'No luggage?' he asks.

I put a hand in my inside jacket pocket and pull out a folding toothbrush and an eyeliner.

He grins. 'The stories are true then,' he says. 'I never thought I would meet you in person. What about underwear?'

'What's that?' I say.

He clears his throat.

I look out of the window. We are already on the freeway. I can see smoke on the horizon.

'How many eyes-on?'

His profile is thoughtful against the pale blue Virginia sky. 'Eight, including me and the escort.' He jerks his head at the car behind us.

I say nothing.

The road slides by, drab. Time to Petersburg: forty minutes.

'Wake me up when we get there,' I say.

The change in tone wakes me. The limo moving from state freeway to local roads. I look about me. Petersburg is red brick and colonial. Maybe it was prosperous once, it doesn't feel it now. Population: 32,000. What does it have to interest the Prince of Darkness?

'Do you want to see the security guard first?' he asks.

The hostage.

'Sure.'

We pull up outside a long, low building. The local police. The duty sergeant behind the counter has been well primed. 'Your room is ready for you, sir,' he says before we even reach the desk. There is no sign of the martial law that is paralysing half of America. Another hovering officer takes us five steps down the corridor and shows us into an interview room.

He clears his throat. 'Can I get you anything?'

'Bottle of water would be great,' I say. 'Don't open it.'

He nods and backs out.

It is a typical interview room. Grey walls, grey floor, grey Formica table. Camera in the corner. Four plastic chairs. Two on one side of the table, one on the other and one in the corner. I walk around the room once and lean up against the wall. The officer comes back with a bottle of Evian.

'Thanks.' I break the seal and down half the bottle. 'Are you staying?' I ask my escort.

He nods.

'Do I have a choice?'

He shakes his head.

Footsteps in the corridor. The door opens again and a security guard comes in. He has a sad, droopy ginger moustache, watery eyes and an air of resignation.

'Are you another Fed?' he says. 'Because I have already told them everything I know.'

'No.'

His eyes narrow. 'Are you English?'

'Russian,' I say in my best Russian accent. 'FSB.'

The watery eyes pop.

I grin at him.

I lean forward and hold out my hand. 'Winter,' I say. 'You were right the first time. I have just flown the Atlantic to speak to you.'

His stance softens, widens, like a whole-body exhale. His palm is warm and slightly damp. I take my hand back and he sits down on the other side of the desk.

'Well, OK then,' he says. 'What can I tell you?'

I pin him with a smile.

'Go through it from the beginning for me.'

On the face of it, he doesn't have a whole lot. He was two hours into the evening shift. He made his rounds and saw nothing unusual. About ten o'clock someone knocked on the door with a delivery package. Medium height, thin build, wiry.

'He had me in an arm lock quicker than I could blink.' He looks at me imploringly. 'He had me before I even saw him move. There was nothing anyone could have done.'

I let that pass.

'Then what?'

'Five more men came in and behind them a tall man with a shaved head and I knew perfectly well who he was, because his picture is everywhere.'

'Did he know you had seen him?'

'I guess. He gave me this long look, like he could see right through me. Then he shook his head.'

'He shook his head?'

'Yeah, then they locked the cupboard door.'

'What do you think they were doing?'

'Beats me. The building isn't even occupied. There's nothing worth stealing. Some old office furniture I guess, but they didn't take any of it.'

I am tempted to tell him the world's richest man doesn't need to steal second-hand office furniture to make a living but I leave it.

'Then what?'

'Then nothing. I was still there when Steve turned up.'

'For the morning shift?'

He nods.

'And you didn't hear anything else?'

'I think I heard them leave. A long time later. Two hours, maybe more.'

'And you've got no idea what they could have been doing in the building for that time?'

He shakes his head.

'Anything else?'

'I think I heard someone say, "Eyes Only".'

For Your Eyes Only.

The Desk Head, beside me, moves a fraction of an inch, not even that.

'You lost your job?'

He nods. 'There were seven of them. What was I supposed to do?'

'Harsh,' I say to the Desk Head.

THE GUARDSMAN

IV

'*A great sign appeared in heaven,*' the Guardsman told the man in the corner, '*a woman clothed with the sun, with the moon under her feet and a crown of twelve stars on her head. Revelation 12:1.*'

The man didn't say anything.

The Guardsman liked the Book of Revelations, it made perfect sense. Today's world was living proof of it. Maybe the man in the corner would be more interested in the Book of Joshua.

'*So, Joshua called together the twelve men he had appointed from the Israelites, one from each tribe... And Joshua set up at Gilgal the twelve stones they had taken out of the Jordan.*' The Guardsman wondered where Gilgal was.

Still nothing.

How about something from the New Testament? Everyone liked the New Testament. It was accessible.

'*Jesus appointed twelve, that they might be with him and that he might send them out to preach. Mark 3:14.*'

Still the man in the corner didn't say anything.

Tough crowd, thought the Guardsman.

The Guardsman remembered being appointed. The lights and the noise and the fighting and the purity of the blade and then the Boss appearing before them. The crowd had parted and Alek Konstantin had stared deep into the Guardsman's eyes and said, *I see what you are and where you dwell*, and the Guardsman had known he wasn't talking about the small house with the broken windows. *Follow me and I will make you a fisher of men.*

He had chosen the Guardsman out of everyone.

'*And so God pulled out his rib and made Adam,*' said the Guardsman.

The Guardsman glared at the silent man in the corner. He didn't seem at all grateful to be hearing the word of the Lord. It was never too late to see the light. Even when you didn't have eyes to see.

Even when you were dead.

CHAPTER 11

The office building doesn't look any better in real life. It was drab in the pictures and it is even worse in reality. Ancient *For Let* signs crowd the tiny patch of earth outside. The grass is knee high. I look up at the frontage. Five floors. The windows are filthy. Some of the fascia is slipping.

The Desk Head opens the door. Plain lobby. Reception desk. Old-fashioned switchboard. Utility cupboard as billed. Two men in dark suits waiting. More eyes on.

'After you,' the Desk Head says.

I step inside.

Beside the lift doors, a list of previous occupants is still on the wall. The stainless-steel doors are bowed and pockmarked. Right in my eyeline are three tiny horseshoe-shaped dents, like someone has hammered on the doors with a metal spike.

They remind me of something.

I run a finger over the dents and take the stairs.

I start on the top floor of the office building and work my way down. I am not expecting to find anything and I don't. Deserted and dilapidated are just two of the words that spring to mind.

Piles of old furniture. Square, hairy floor tiles you can smell at ten paces. Who do they imagine is ever going to rent this place?

No one. That's the point.

I go back to the lobby and look for a way down. There is no sign of the eyes-on crew.

'How do I get into the cellar?' I ask the Desk Head.

'There isn't a cellar.'

'Right.'

I stare round at the shabby lobby. The visitors book with no entries, the peeling veneer that might have once been imitation marble, the ancient switchboard. I look straight into the eye of the state-of-the-art camera trained on me. I rip the top sheet off the visitors' book, turn it over for a blank page and scrawl two words across it. Then I turn back to the camera and hold the paper up in front of my face.

Call me.

I walk round Reception, sit down and put my feet up on the desk.

The Desk Head stares at me for a moment then he goes outside. A moment later he is talking into his phone. He turns his back when he sees me watching. I set a timer, make a bet with myself and close my eyes. The smell of mould is too bad to sleep but that isn't going to stop me trying.

I figure five minutes for a surveillance grunt to call it in, thirty minutes to go up the chain. Maybe quicker if the Desk Head is rattling some cages. How far up it goes will tell me everything. And the higher it goes, the longer it will take – these people can't be hurried, they are in meetings, seeing politicians in the White House. America is at war. It could be hours.

The Reception switchboard clicks. I open my eyes. A line is flashing red. A moment later it rings. High-pitched and tinkling like an old-fashioned phone.

I pull my boots off the desk and look at the timer. Twelve minutes. Fast work. I pick up the ancient handset.

'Winter?' says the woman on the end of the line.

'Right you are.' I lean back in the chair, tipping it on to two legs. 'Please hold.'

The clicks and screeches on the line sound like the Langley switchboard. Gears grinding as they bounce the call through an infinite number of destinations. How does the world's most secure location get a secure line?

Slowly.

'Hello, Winter,' says McKellen.

'Are you going to tell me or do I have to blast my way down to the cellar?'

'I hope you haven't brought an unauthorised firearm onto US soil,' he says.

'Please. You have enough of your own.'

He sighs.

'What do you have here that is so important that Alek Konstantin came himself? Weeks of nothing and he shows up here. Goes to the effort of locking up the guard. Doesn't kill him.'

'Oh, people died,' McKellen says. 'Don't go thinking he's gone soft.'

'Who?'

'What do you want, Winter?'

'Where are you?'

'Where do you think? It's not like I can leave Langley.'

'I'll tell you when I get there.'

I stride out through the door. Somewhere overhead the sun is trying to break through. The air has a heavy feel like it might rain. I slide into the government limo and the Desk Head walks round and gets in the other side.

'Langley,' I say to the driver.

The Desk Head says nothing. He has the look of someone who has run for a bus and seen it pull away just as he got there. The look of someone chewed over by a superior.

'Sorry,' I say.

He stares out of the window.

We are on the main street. An American flag hangs limp on the corner beside a clock that looks like a lamp post.

I think about someone on the run, turning up here on US soil and then turning up in France less than twenty-four hours later. No detours to stay under the radar, no picking a safe passage. It is suggestive of some kind of cause and effect, some kind of urgency.

I call Simon. 'The Marseille sighting of Alek Konstantin, that happened straight after he was in Petersburg…'

'What about it?'

'Where was it exactly?'

I can hear Simon typing.

'Outside a garden centre. A Mom and Pop operation. They made fertilisers and kitty litter, small scale. Sold bedding plants. You know the kind of place, there was probably a café.'

'Was?'

'It got blown up the night the Prince of Darkness was there.'

'McKellen didn't mention that.'

I can feel the shape of something.

'Control wants to speak to you, by the way,' Simon says. 'I'm putting you through.'

'Well?' says Control. 'Petersburg – what does it have?'

'The same thing it had during the civil war.'

'Don't get cryptic.'

'Location. An hour outside Langley. At the apex of four national highways and two rail tracks. Next door to Fort Lee. Connected. A place things can get to easily. Container loads of things. Close psychologically. Under someone's eye.'

'CIA?'

'Looks like.'

'So, what was he after?'

'I'm not sure.'

Control grunts. 'And is there a connection to Marseille?'

'The timing is suggestive. He went straight to Marseille from here. No detours. I think whatever he found in Petersburg made him go to Marseille in a hurry.'

'Any sign of him now?'

'Long gone. Sorry to disappoint. And if he wasn't, eight eyes-on would be nowhere near enough.'

Control grunts again. It was worth a try, he is thinking.

The checkpoints start a mile or more out. Langley, a 258-acre fortified oasis. I wonder if there is any more guarded place in the whole of the US. The tree-lined approach feels like English countryside until the mammoth modernist front of the old building comes into view. The home of the famous lobby with eagles on the floor and the flying concrete porch, a monument to the days when concrete was king.

We bypass the car parks and pull up a short walk from the front of the New Building. The glass has a turquoise tint to it. They stop me at the door. I don't even make it into the lobby. I have been in Langley plenty so I conclude I must have royally pissed them off, but then I realise: it is the tracker, the hot link to Alek Konstantin that is worrying them. The idea that I might bleep, bleep, bleep, my way into the very heart of the CIA and give away the exact location of the Director's office.

The sun is back out. I put my shades on and wander off to stand in front of Kryptos, the huge iron sculpture with the uncrackable code and wonder whether its creator is still laughing up his sleeve. After a while, I sit down on the bench. The eyes-on crew wait at a respectful distance.

Ten minutes later McKellen appears. His bodyguards fan out, leaving us in the centre of a ring of steel. He is smaller in the flesh and bursting with energy. He looks like he could take off his jacket and run a marathon. The charisma rolls off him.

'So, what do you know?' he says, shading his eyes.

Typical CIA.

'What about mutual cooperation, Operation Atlas and the shared exchange of information, the pooling of human intelligence protocol?'

He gives me a look.

'Fine,' I say. 'Alek Konstantin breaks into the CIA Petersburg deep storage facility. Spends a long time looking for something. Finds it. Goes away.'

'What makes you think he finds it?'

'Because he leaves.'

'So maybe he just discovers it wasn't there.'

'Maybe. But less likely. Deep storage. Decent size, so something bulky. A long-term permanent facility. No sign of any cooling. I'm guessing paperwork. Files and files of paperwork.'

'There is no paperwork these days.'

'Old paperwork.'

'Everything was destroyed years ago, you know that. Or uploaded.'

'Really? Everything?'

He says nothing.

'So, to recap. Alek Konstantin breaks into deep storage to steal some grubby little CIA secret from decades ago. Maybe even longer. Something toxic but valuable. A weapon of some kind maybe. And you want to keep it under wraps, *Your Eyes Only*. You don't want GCHQ and the rest of the world poking their noses in. Did I leave anything out?'

He looks away from me into the middle distance, his face a smooth mask, 'What do you want?'

I stare at Kryptos, still undeciphered after all this time.
'I want the Guardsman.'

The silence stretches out.

'I heard about what happened,' McKellen says. 'A message carved on a corpse.'

'I'll leave you to make the calls,' I say. 'I want to see everything you have.'

McKellen lets out a long, drawn-out sigh. 'I don't need to make any calls,' he says. 'He is front and centre. The file is on my desk.'

'Why?'

For a moment I think he's not going to answer. He stares at Kryptos.

'The profilers think I am a target. Like, a status thing. A status scalp. Aspirational. That he will choose to do it. The biggest status target in the developed world.'

I grin. 'The big cheese. What does the President have to say?'

He doesn't smile. 'She's got bigger things to worry about than her ego. Martial law in eleven states and only getting worse.' He turns to me. 'The profilers think the Guardsman has a God complex, that he probably stopped seeing himself as a gun for hire a while ago. They think you're a status target too, for what it's worth. Except you are *untouchable*, reserved for the Boss.'

I look around. The back of my neck prickles. McKellen has the most dangerous job on the planet. 'Should you even be out here?'

'They think I'm OK as long as I don't go more than fifty metres out.'

'Right,' I say.

'It's worse for my kid. She doesn't want to live here. She doesn't understand why she can't go to school anymore, see any of her friends. I've tried to tell her it's like a "Take your kids to work day".'

'What else do the profilers say?'

'They just don't know. He has hundreds of contracts to his name. The most feared and prolific contract killer in history. Ruthless efficiency cut with experimental sadism. They are having a field day with their fragmented personality theories.'

'Is there anything about an experiment or a series of experiments?'

Disgust flashes across McKellen's face. 'He's always experimenting. A hundred and one ways to inflict pain.' He stares across the manicured beds to the old building. 'I will get you everything we have,' he says. 'You'll have to look at it here obviously. I would offer you lunch but you won't keep it down.'

'Are you worried?'

'Not so much for myself.' He glances down at the phone in his hand. A girl with braces beams up at us.

'What about a safe house? Or you could all go off-grid.' Even as the words come out, I know they are pointless. He is a political appointment, not a black ops specialist. Off-grid, they wouldn't last two minutes. Langley is the safest place they could be.

He sighs. 'I've always thought I would retire one day. That's never going to happen. There's no checking out from this situation.'

'Just don't leave here.'

He looks around at the courtyard of neat planting and the miles of concrete.

'I've got to,' he says. 'For the G20. Who else can do it?'

They let me in through the glass doors and take me down the walkway to the old building.

A quote from John 8:32 is carved on the lobby wall. '*And ye shall know the truth and the truth shall make you free.*' A door on the right opens on a small room with four neat desks separated by waist-high particle board, not a PC in sight. Hot desks for visitors presumably. Spartan but adequate. They don't want you getting comfortable.

The Guardsman files are on the desk nearest the door, in hard copy. I don't know whether they don't trust their own systems or whether they just don't trust me in them. Either way, the pile of files is ten inches high.

It takes me four hours to read everything they have. A lot is familiar from the Guardsman's Firestorm page. Now I have the detail. Pages and pages of case notes and witness accounts and forensic reports.

Profiling, as a science, is based on data. Collecting the data, analysing it, filling in the gaps, looking for patterns, for coherence and consistency, then putting it all together and coming to scientific conclusions about future behaviour.

The Guardsman defies this. Renders the process null and void. One hit is weeks in the planning and the next is spontaneous, on a crowded train. There is no coherence and consistency. There are no data patterns.

Except when it comes to the weapon.

The Guardsman always uses the same blade, six to ten inches long and razor sharp. Razor sharp is easy enough to say but extremely difficult to achieve. The Guardsman spends a significant, obsessive amount of time sharpening. His home page on Firestorm is full of examples of his precision skills.

I stare at the cubicle wall. Fluff has lodged in the gap between the wall and the desk. A thin, precise line of inconsistency in the bland grey smoothness. Inconsistent for a reason. It is below the surface, any cleaning implement just glides right over.

Probably no one, since this file was compiled, has sat down and read it fresh, cover to cover. Instead of looking for patterns where there are none, I should be looking for inconsistencies in the one pattern there is.

There was an occasion when the Guardsman didn't use a knife – an Appeal Judge in Paris in the Palais de Justice. A high-security set up with enhanced, airport-style screening you would have trouble getting a metal paper clip through. I pick up the SOC shots – the Scene of Crime records – turning them round and round. A grey toilet cubicle, flimsy door, flimsy lock, probably didn't stand up to a good kick. Institutional toilets. They look the same everywhere. A scheduled ancient monument and the bathrooms still look like airport toilets shoehorned into nineteenth-century architecture.

So, inconsistent for a reason. The Guardsman didn't use his knife because he couldn't get it through security.

I picture the beautiful Parisian building next door to the Sainte-Chapelle. I think about the fabric of it and the opportunities an old building presents for a makeshift weapon. Metal window catches and so on. I look back at the dimensions of the smooth, perfect holes that shattered the Judge's eye sockets, one after the other.

The weapon was three centimetres wide at the base, narrowing to a centimetre at the point. A metal stake of some kind. Machine-ground. There is nothing makeshift about it. The Guardsman must have brought it with him, expressly for the purpose, which means, somehow, he got it through security.

And the autopsy results confirm it. Not only were traces of steel found in the entry hole, but also traces of mud. Which, in itself, is inconsistent. One minute, he is obsessively sharpening and the next he doesn't even run a cloth over it.

The Judge was taken unawares, that much is obvious. Did the Guardsman tiptoe in, stake in hand? I wonder what the Judge thought in that split second before the door crashed open. Did he know? A straight Judge, trying to do the right thing. He must have known.

I pinch the bridge of my nose and refocus.

There is a photograph of the toilet door. Seen from the outside. The Guardsman's eye view. I stare. Then I take a picture of it on my phone and blow it up. Then I blow it up some more.

Three tiny horseshoes, just like the ones on the lift doors in Petersburg.

Three faint marks at head height, like someone knocking with a metal spike.

CHAPTER 12

I close the Guardsman's file carefully, leave it on the table and walk back out into the sunshine. After a while the doors open and McKellen comes out, trailed by bodyguards.

'Coke?' he says, offering me one of the cans he is holding.

I shake my head and he puts the can down on the ledge bordering Kryptos.

'What do you make of the horseshoes?' I say.

'You found the horseshoes then.'

'There were tiny horseshoes on the toilet door in Paris, and there were tiny horseshoes on the lift doors of your storage facility in Petersburg. I'm presuming someone has done the work and checked they are a match?'

He nods.

'So, the Guardsman was in Petersburg?'

'Possibly.'

I think about the fraction of a second's pause after McKellen said the Guardsman's file was on his desk and the excuse he gave. He already knew, he just didn't want to admit it.

A kid is watching us through the lobby doors. Sticky hands are leaving smears on the glass. McKellen turns his back.

'What about Marseille?' I say. 'What is the connection? Was he there as well?'

McKellen stares at Kryptos. 'Maybe.'

'Maybe? Hypothesise for me. Based on your knowledge of the contents of that storage facility, is it likely the Guardsman was there and if he was, is there a reason he would then have gone on to Marseille?'

'Yes,' he says. 'I'm afraid there is.'

The Guardsman was with Alek Konstantin in Petersburg and probably again in Marseille. Petersburg was an archive. Marseille is the implementation. And whatever it is, the CIA really don't want it out there.

Now the kid is scowling. It puts its hands on its hips and waggles its eyebrows.

'Someone wants you,' I say.

McKellen looks at the kid, then he looks at me, then he looks at the kid again. Making up his mind. Awkward, a bit embarrassed.

'Will you do me a favour?' he says. 'Will you just say hi to my daughter?'

'Sure.'

'She is desperate to meet you. The woman who tracked down Alek Konstantin. The star player in the top trump deck. She'll never forgive me if I don't let her say hello.'

He beckons and the kid catapults out of the door like she's been fired out of a canon.

'Great reaction speed,' I say, and McKellen beams.

She skids to a halt in front of us and gawps up at me.

How do you greet a ten-year-old? Handshake? High five?

'Hi,' I say.

'Ariadne, this is Winter.'

That's a hell of a name to lay on a girl.

'Nice to meet you,' I say.

McKellen backs off with a fond smile, labouring under the belief I want to spend alone time with his pigtailed offspring.

'You look like Elsa,' she says, braces gleaming in the sunlight.

'I get that a lot.'

'Are you seeing anyone?'

'What?' I goggle down at her. 'You mean, is there a Prince Charming in my life?'

'Or Princess.'

'Right. And no.'

'Who needs a Prince anyway?' she says.

'Good point.'

I look across at McKellen for help, but he has his back turned.

'When I grow up, I am going to be you,' she says.

I smile. 'Who am I going to be?'

'You'll be dead by then, Daddy says.'

I yank the ring pull on the coke. It hisses out in the warm air, the can ice cold in my hand. I need a sugar hit to get through this.

'I thought your hair would be longer,' she says.

'Someone cut it all off.'

'Did you kick their butt?'

'Kind of.'

'Who was it?'

'A bad man.'

'Who?'

'Alek Konstantin.'

'Alek's not a bad man,' she says.

Coke sprays out, turning Kryptos glossy in the sunlight. Bubbles fizz in my nose.

'Don't let your Dad hear you say that.'

'He gave me a Mars bar,' she adds as a clincher.

'*What?* When?'

'And he kicks ass.'

'I kick ass,' I tell her. 'He shoots people.'

She shrugs a full-body shrug. 'Same thing.'

'It is not the same thing.'

McKellen is coming over. 'Well,' he says to her. 'Was she what you expected?' The question dives out of his mouth, falling to earth between us, proving even the best career politicians can blunder. Never give a kid an opening like that.

Her face screws up. Time stands still. I can feel him holding his breath.

'She's not as big as I expected,' she says.

I stand up taller, straightening my shoulders.

McKellen laughs. 'Did you ask her your question?'

Are you seeing anyone?

'Yes,' I say firmly. I am not discussing my love life with any more McKellens.

'That wasn't what I wanted to ask,' she says. 'That just came out when I saw how pretty you were.'

'OK.' I take my shades off and eye her warily. 'Go on then.'

'When they come again, what should I do?'

McKellen's indulgent smile vanishes, draining away as reality dawns.

I look down at her serious face, at her spindly ten-year-old frame. I look at the trails of Coke running down Kryptos.

'You run,' I say, 'and you hide.' I take another swig. 'Let's be realistic here. Nothing else you can do.'

She nods and for a moment her eyes are wise and wistful, and I can see she knows how bad it could be. Kids have no brakes on their imagination. And yet she would face it down, if she could. Courage streaks through her, burning bright. She has the heart for the fight but not the body.

I meet McKellen's eyes over her head and see he is in his own private hell as parental anxiety paints horrifying futures.

I get down to her level. 'Give me your arm,' I say.

She extends a stick-like forearm. I pull a pen out of my jacket and scrawl a number up her skin like a tattoo.

'That is the number for my quartermaster, Simon. If you need me, call him and he will put you through.'

She stares at her arm.

'Only if you need me,' I say.

She nods.

'I will come. It may take me some time. I could be on the other side of the world. But I will come.'

She stares.

'Now beat it.'

She walks off towards the door, cradling her arm like it is a precious gift, her footsteps meandering like she is in a daze.

McKellen's eyes are bright. 'Thank you,' he says.

'You've got a great kid there,' I tell him and am surprised to find I actually mean it.

He stares at Kryptos.

'Tell your close protection people. If you are taken again, I will come and they must give me access.'

He nods.

'Now, explain to me how the hell she met Alek Konstantin. When did that happen and why have you kept it quiet?'

'It was nothing,' he shrugs. 'He was there.'

'When you were taken?'

He nods. 'And then we escaped.'

'There was no mention of him being there.'

He shrugs again.

'There's no way you would have escaped if he'd been there.' I narrow my eyes at him. I know bullshit when I hear it.

'You escaped,' he points out.

'That is a very different matter. You don't have my in-built, natural advantages.'

His eyes widen. 'That wasn't in the reports,' he says.

I put my shades back on, leaving him staring at the mirrored sky.

'What wasn't?'

THE GUARDSMAN

V

The Guardsman looked at the security guard with the ginger moustache.

Winter. Again.

How could she be here of all places? And with only six days to go. How much did she know? The carefully crafted message on the barmaid's forehead in London should have been enough to keep her busy. The Guardsman felt the panic rise. Was she on the trail? Did she know what had been kept in Petersburg? Something that would change the world.

'And what did she do then?' the Guardsman demanded.

'I don't know,' the guard with the moustache said. 'I think she went to look round the office building, although what she hoped to find I don't know, it's been empty for years.' He wiped his nose on the back of his sleeve. 'Can I go? I've already told you everything I know.'

The Guardsman felt the disrespect. There was a cold wind blowing now that the Boss had been unmasked. Disrespect and disobedience. The Guardsman didn't like disrespect.

'Tell me about the man who came before.'

'Alek Konstantin? It was definitely him. I don't know why everyone keeps asking. His picture is everywhere. It was him. Two hundred per cent.'

Two hundred per cent. That was annoying. The Guardsman liked numbers and liked them to be accurate. But irritation faded in the face of hope. In eight weeks, there had been practically nothing from the Boss. He had disappeared off the face of the planet and that was inevitable, but first Mexico and now this. It was a sign. The end was nigh. The time of reckoning was coming.

The Guardsman thought about what had been kept in the vaults in Petersburg. The Boss was on the same mission as the Guardsman. He was going to be so pleased and surprised when he found out what was planned in London in six days' time.

The Guardsman didn't begrudge the short flight, it had been worth it.

The security guard was watching with narrowed eyes. 'Who did you say you were?' he said.

'How old are you?' said the Guardsman, ignoring this.

'What?' said the security guard. 'Forty-two.'

'Too young,' said the Guardsman. 'Pity.'

The security guard tried to smile. 'That's the first time anyone has ever said that.'

The Guardsman pulled the blade and stared down at it. It was razor sharp. Whetstone, then dry stone, then polish. It was a shame there wasn't more time to enjoy it.

CHAPTER 13

5 days to go...

At Heathrow, I brace for Simon's scowling face but there is no sign of him.

There is no sign of him on the way into London, no sign in our office. The absence is unnerving. I clatter down the gantry stairs of the training arena.

'Where the hell is Simon?' I demand.

Viv turns to look at me. The new group of recruits carry on with their sparring. Another day, another load of recruits. They have no idea who I am. My heart lifts at the thought of a youthful vigilante turning up to stop a hit with nothing but a bus pass.

'Well, hello to you too,' she says.

'Where is Simon?'

'He's got a date.'

'A what?'

'You know?' she says. 'When two people who like each other spend social time together without fucking?'

'Doesn't ring a bell.'

'I told him to stop waiting and hoping and take that nice bug-hunter up on her offer.'

'Why was he waiting and hoping?'

She rolls her eyes. 'I have no idea.'

*

I can hear the canteen all the way down the corridor. And smell it. Breakfast. Cheap date. It is a moot point which sense hits first. As I kick through the double swing doors, bacon nearly knocks me over.

The noise level is at max: the clink of china, the scrape of plates, the chatter of voices shouting to make themselves heard. The queue snakes nearly to the door, brown trays clutched to chests.

I scan the room. And then I see him at a cosy little table for two by the window. He has his back to the door. A girl with a pretty, pansy face and soft, brown eyes sits opposite. Her shiny, dark ponytail hangs past her shoulder. I remember her being recruited, how unusual she was, an English Lit major who loved numbers. Her self-taught coding skills were forensically good. A Renaissance woman. In the Bletchley Park days, she would have been a codebreaker. I remember coming to watch her take the programming challenge and staring at her through the mirrored glass.

I am staring again now. Simon's arm stretches out along the table towards her. A couple of inches closer and they would be touching.

I turn on my heel and head back out through the swing doors. I am halfway along the corridor before I change my mind. I turn and go back into the canteen and up to their table. Simon starts. She looks up at me and smiles.

'Winter, this is Emma,' Simon says.

Pansy Face holds out her hand.

I take it and give her my best smile. Not a flicker of interest, her eyes are already heading back to Simon.

'Emma's just back too,' Simon says. 'She was at Fort Meade.'

The NSA exchange programme.

'They wanted everyone home for the G20,' she says. 'I've actually got jet lag flying from Washington. It's embarrassing.'

Silence.

'I've been hearing all about you,' Pansy Face says to fill the gap. *Bless.*

'You don't want to believe anything from Simon.'

She laughs. 'Not Simon, he is far too discreet. Beth.'

HR. Great.

'Did you want something?' she asks.

This time the silence has knives in it.

Pansy Face sits back hurriedly. 'I'm sorry, I meant... do you need to speak to Simon alone?'

He is practically head down in his plate.

Breathe in, breathe out.

'Yes,' I say. 'I would like to speak to Simon alone. When he has a minute. If he can tear himself away from playing footsie.'

Pansy Face is up like a shot. 'See you later,' she says to Simon. We watch her scuttle away down the canteen, ponytail swinging.

'Was that necessary?' Simon says quietly.

'I need a facial search run,' I say, 'ASAP. Male, five foot six to five foot eleven, Petersburg and Marseille, cross referenced with the Palais de Justice Judge murder. Three data points.' The hammering action of the stake gives a pretty good guide to shoulder height.

Simon nods. 'It'll take a few hours,' he says. 'That girl is here by the way.'

'What girl?'

'Xiu. The vigilante from the other night, from the cellophane room? Her background check came through, so I called her in first thing. I've sent it to your phone.'

'How was it?'

'Mixed.' Disapproval flickers across his face.

'What did you do with her?'

'Nothing. I left her in Reception.'

'Great.' I give him a big smile. 'Laters.'

*

My newest recruit is waiting for me, clutching her temporary pass and watching biometric security with interest. I haven't seen her for two days and she is still wearing dungarees like they are some kind of fashion statement.

The background check makes great reading. Xiu is a straight-A student with flexible moral values. She has nine police cautions to her name and next to no chance of becoming an accountant.

Nine cautions and not a single arrest. That takes talent.

'Hi,' I say. 'Did you get any sleep in the end?'

'Nah,' she shakes her head. 'I had three cans of Red Bull and a kebab.'

Perfect.

'So,' I say. 'I've got to put you through a few tests. Just routine, you know. Can you hop on one leg?'

She looks around the marble lobby.

'Yes,' she says.

'Go on then.'

'Why?'

'I need to see how fit you are.'

'You're not going to be able to tell that by me hopping on one leg.'

'Can you bark?'

'You mean like a dog?'

'Yes.'

'Not really. I do quite a good dolphin.' She squeaks and clicks and screeches.

'That was a dolphin?'

'And I can do a puffin. And a seal.' She claps her forearms together.

I catch Security's eye.

'OK,' I say. 'You can stop now.'

'Also an owl,' she says, hooting. '*Twit-twooo*. This is for covert signalling, isn't it?'

'Something like that.'

'I imagine bird noises are more useful than dolphins in the field.'
She stares back at me, guileless, wide-eyed in her dungarees.
I fold my arms.
'You're winding me up, aren't you?' I say.
'Hop on one leg,' she says. 'What is this? The fucking circus?'

CHAPTER 14

I open the door to the training suite and look around at the rows of PCs one step removed from the GCHQ mainframe, the public side of the firewall. The wide screens are twice the size of a normal workstation.

The place is empty except for a boy, head down in the corner. No one in GCHQ needs to take a lesson in Python. I poke my head back out through the open door and look both ways just to be sure. The corridor is deserted. I yank the door closed behind me.

My teenage hire from Marseille organised crime looks up. His eyes have the scarlet rims and tiny pupils of someone who has spent hours and hours staring at a screen without a break. His car-jacking skills are unsurpassed. His computer skills – not so much.

'Is this where you work?' Xiu asks, looking around.

'Only when she doesn't want Simon to know what she is doing,' Léon says, leaning back and putting long brown arms behind his head.

'I don't know what you are talking about,' I say, sitting down at a terminal. 'Xiu, meet Léon.'

Xiu considers his dark curly hair and tanned complexion with blatant interest. 'Are you French?'

Léon scowls. *Nailed after one sentence.*

'Léon has just started too,' I say. 'He has to learn Java and Pearl this month.'

'Nightmare,' says Xiu.

'*Ouais.*' Léon nods gloomily.

'Can you hop on one leg?' I ask him.

'*Comment?*'

'You know? On one leg?'

I nearly start hopping myself.

Xiu grins.

'*Non,*' says Léon firmly. 'I do not think so.'

'Do you know the factory down on the waterfront in Marseille like a garden centre? Part farm and pet supplies, part café?'

'Sure.' Léon leans back. 'Marcel went out there a couple of times.' Marcel Furet, the Ferret. Marseille's answer to the Godfather and Léon's old boss.

'D'you know why?'

Léon shakes his head. He stares off into the middle distance, something I've noticed him do when he is considering a question. His thoughtfulness gives his face maturity. I would have hired him for this still, quiet consideration alone.

'I got the impression they were doing something for him,' he says finally. 'He never took many out there.'

By which he means thugs. So, it wasn't something that needed muscle.

'He was stressed,' he says. 'I remember that, even more so than usual, but he always was after that woman came.'

'What woman?'

'Just some woman. She used to come and speak to Ferret in the back office and then go away again. You could hear her walking up and down like she had six-inch stilettos on. Then he used to go out to the factory. After she had been, he used to deal it out with a big stick.'

I'm not sure the analogy works in English, but I let it pass.

'Was she connected to the factory visits do you think?'

'Definitely.'

'Would you recognise her again?'

'No,' he says. 'I never saw her.'

So, the factory had links to Marseille's organised crime. How it could be connected to a CIA deep storage facility in Virginia, I fail to see.

It takes me a couple of minutes to bypass the training programmes and pull up Firestorm.

The Guardsman's homepage is beautifully designed. Part art house, part perfume ad. Case studies as stylised as a fashion shoot until you look more closely.

We all consider the page in silence.

The barmaid's eyes are closed and her hair fans out against a dark textured background. Bark. The picture was taken against a tree. There is a case number under the picture. I scroll back and there is Lucy, the girl in the graveyard. I scroll back some more and there is the French Judge, murdered on the toilet in the Palais de Justice. I recognise the picture from the Langley file.

'So, what conclusions would you draw from these case studies, team?' I say, thinking of the pages and pages of CIA profiling.

'Psycho,' says Xiu.

'Anything else?'

'Young.'

Léon nods.

Interesting.

'You look at this page and your first conclusion is that he is *young*?'

'Second conclusion. It's the design ethic – he grew up with Instagram. It's like the difference between being a native speaker and learning it.'

Léon nods. His English is really coming on.

I stare at the picture of Lucy. 'Can you think of any reason why the Guardsman would kill a girl without getting paid?'

'Yes,' says Xiu flatly. 'For the fun of it.'

I consider this. Not inconceivable. It is 'experiment' that is troubling me. That doesn't quite fit.

'What would you understand from the phrase "the final countdown"?'

'Coming from the Guardsman?' Xiu says.

'Yes.'

'Armageddon,' she says. 'End of the world. Four horsemen, apocalypse and wotnot.'

Léon is nodding.

I shut down the Guardsman's homepage.

'So,' I say, turning to my latest recruit and pinning her with a look. 'Explain your police record to me. Why do you steal phones? And let me warn you, right from the start, that I am looking for full disclosure.'

'I don't always nick them,' she says. 'Depends how new they are. Sometimes I just read them. You can find out a lot about someone from their phone. Other times, I mess with them.'

'What?'

'You know?' Xiu says. '*Send to All?*'

Léon grins.

It's like some secret teen society.

She rolls her eyes. 'You message the entire contact list, put the phone back without them noticing and film the reaction. It's a thing.'

Sheesh. Don't kids hack the Federal Reserve anymore?

'So, let's get this completely straight. You take a phone, send a message and laugh?'

'That's it.'

I stare at their grinning faces in silence.

Looking on the bright side, she has already mastered nosing into other people's business and laughing at their misfortunes. Two GCHQ basics.

I have a bad feeling that I know where the contractor from the cellophane room's missing phone is.

'Is that what you were doing that night?' I say. 'The night we met? Nicking his phone?'

'Am I going to get into trouble for this?'

'As opposed to the trouble you might get into for, say, killing someone with a blow to the back of the neck?'

'Fair point.' She fiddles with a dungaree strap.

'So, you didn't hear him on the phone? You just made that up?' She nods.

I fold my arms. 'Of course you did. You nicked his phone and saw Firestorm. He had just clocked in for a job.'

'Yeah,' she says. 'I nearly dropped it.'

The phone with his Firestorm account. The history of the contract, when he got it, when the substitution was made, whether it was him or the Guardsman talking to me in the Firestorm contract room. The phone with all the answers. Maybe it even has the Guardsman's number.

'I need that phone right now. Where is it?'

'I put it back in his pocket,' she says. 'When they took him out.' 'What? Why?'

She shrugs. 'I dunno. Seemed a bit incriminating.'

I roll my eyes. 'God forbid.'

I turn to the screen, pull up the Met Police and open the case files. The body is being held at the Greenwich Mortuary awaiting autopsy, along with the personal effects. The biometrics aren't back yet. They are probably still taking the house apart and patting themselves on the back for catching a contractor.

I drum my fingers. 'What time did our contractor walk into the bar? Call it 10 p.m. Sixty hours ago. That's a hell of a long time to take on a hit. But given his specialty, it's not inconceivable.' I try not think too closely about the people who came before me in the cellophane room. I shut the screen down. 'If we are going to get into his Firestorm account, we need to hurry.'

They are on my heels, bright-eyed with enthusiasm, like spaniels about to be taken for a walk.

They chat all the way out the door, all the way down the stairwell, ten floors and twenty flights of stairs, all the way along the brightly lit corridors.

'This is the interview level and medical,' I say to break the flow.

'Waterboarding,' says Léon, proud of his English.

'Wait here,' I tell them, pulling out the iron key and letting myself into the cell. I can feel them craning their necks behind me as I disconnect the laptop and stuff it into a rucksack.

I collect an iris scanner from one of the store cupboards and a basic facial alteration kit and put them in the rucksack as well.

'What's that?' Xiu says.

'A scanner. Firestorm is an interactive phone app. With an iris passcode.'

'Epic,' she says.

'Will we be able to get into his account?' Léon says. 'Won't Firestorm know something has happened to him? Won't they have closed it down?'

'The Guardsman definitely knows.' A barmaid stares with sightless eyes. 'But that doesn't mean the Firestorm Administrator knows. That is the person who monitors all the contracts. The Administrator doesn't allow sub-contracting so the Guardsman may well have kept it quiet. Either way, it is going to be tight.'

'You booked the Guardsman? Sweet,' says Xiu. 'I tried to book Solo once.'

I have to ask.

She shakes her head sadly. 'It told me I had to be twenty-one to open an account.'

We head back to the stairwell and end up on the minus sixth floor. Through security and we are out on the stairwell by the underground train platform.

'Cool,' says Xiu as we slide out of an emergency exit and into the oven heat of the tube. 'You never need to pay.'

'I never pay anyway,' says Léon.

'Come on,' I say. 'Brains, beauty and brawn. What a team.'

'Which are we?' They look at me expectantly.

'You are the team part.'

CHAPTER 15

Twenty minutes after leaving the detainment suite, we are pulling into Greenwich Cutty Sark. I take the escalator two steps at a time and vault the ticket barriers, Xiu and Léon scrambling in my wake. A guard shouts but he is way too late, I am already in the pedestrian alley that spits you out right into central Greenwich. White stucco naval college ahead, the Cutty Sark and Waterstones on the left.

There is a Café Rouge on the corner, its windows wide open in the heat. Everyone has a flushed, red-faced, sweaty look. Menus fan back and forth. Bare legs stick to plastic seats.

I pound down the pavement, jumping into the road to avoid the crowds. Greenwich is running with tourists. The traffic is stationary, cyclists dice with death. I don't let up until I am on a quiet residential street in front of the long, low wall of the mortuary.

Xiu and Léon come to a stop behind me. Léon rests his hands on his knees, gasping for breath.

I clap him on the back. 'More cardio for you,' I tell him.

Xiu hasn't broken a sweat.

'D'you work out?' I ask her.

'Nah,' she says, fiddling with her dungaree strap.

Greenwich Mortuary is etched on a discreet plaque beside the gate. There is a small parking area in front of a gracious Georgian villa. It is the only detached house on the street. Once upon a time it was the grandest house in the area. Now it is a government building, shabby and down at heel with council notices plastered all over it.

Greenwich.

The closest mortuary to the ExCel Centre. The field hospital uses refrigerated trucks in a pandemic but this is the nearest permanent facility. If anything happens at the G20, the body bags will end up here. I wonder what their capacity is.

'Will they just let us see the body?' Xiu peers at the building.

'There are three types of people who man Reception in a place like this,' I say. 'Type A get off on frustrating you, Type B have been funnelled around the system until they have wound up where they can do the least harm and Type C are well-meaning but useless.'

I push the institutional fire door open. Reception is beige and like local government buildings everywhere. There is no sign of the listed Georgian heritage.

There is a flat wide counter at the end and a woman sitting behind it.

We stare.

Ample bosom, in her fifties, eye contact, cardigan.

'C?' says Xiu.

'B?' says Léon.

'I can't help you without an appointment,' says the woman in the cardigan.

A.

Her eyes flick from mine to Xiu and Léon.

I give her my serious face and lay my ID down on the counter.

'Do you have an appointment?' she says.

I hold my ID up. 'What does this mean to you?'

'It means you don't have an appointment,' she says.

I think about the time pressure and look at the door behind her. A button release. An easy enough matter to force the issue.

What you don't have is people skills. Gravitas.

'Who is your line manager?'

'Derek Haines,' she says. 'He's not here. He works out of a different building.' She smiles with satisfaction. Game, set and match.

A all the way.

'Great,' I say. 'Thanks.'

I turn away and Xiu and Léon look at me in surprise. I sit down on a plastic chair and pull the laptop out of my rucksack.

'You can't wait there,' Type A says.

'In the waiting area?'

'It is the waiting area for people *with appointments*,' she says.

I shut the laptop. 'I do have an appointment. Check your system, Brenda.'

She glares at me suspiciously and turns to her ancient PC, peering at the screen, one finger on the keyboard. I can type faster with my toes.

I can tell the moment she sees it. She rocks slightly in her chair.

'Thanks, Brenda,' I say as she releases the door.

I roll my eyes. Which part of *GCHQ* does she not get?

CHAPTER 16

'Fast work,' says Xiu as she follows me inside. 'Women like that get on my tits.' She thinks about this. 'And not in a good way.'

'That's nothing,' says Léon. 'She hacked the Marseille police department from a coffee shop a few weeks ago.'

I scowl at him. 'Will you not go around saying that? It's not even true.'

'It was *formidable*,' Léon says, like I haven't spoken.

'Epic,' says Xiu.

We head down a corridor and down a flight of stairs to what must have been the servants' quarters when it was a private house. It gets colder with every step lower and the TCP smell gets stronger. Just like the detainment level back home. There is something about the sense of enclosure that makes me twitchy. It feels like a trap. Or maybe it's just the proximity of all those dead bodies.

A woman in a lab coat comes to meet us. The duty pathologist. She is youngish with long brown hair and an earnest look. I wonder if she and Brenda get on. Do they even know each other? Maybe their worlds never overlap. Above ground and below.

I tell her the case number and she checks on a clipboard. A landscape computer printout on a portrait clipboard. She half tilts the clipboard and half tilts her head.

Times are good for pathologists. Just as a whole new industry of professional contractors has been created by Firestorm so the associated trades have had a boost. Pathologists, for example. Pre-Firestorm, a really elaborate murder was a rare event. Whole careers were built on one good paper, written on one good case. Now there are hundreds of good cases.

'Twelve,' she says looking up from the clipboard. She stops, suddenly still and staring, a shade too close. Half a step too close. Close enough for me to smell her sensible, Sure deodorant.

'Beautiful,' she says, right in my face.

'You're not my type,' I tell her.

She blinks.

'Your eyes,' she says. 'Eyes are my speciality.'

'Gotcha.' I give her the two-fingered gun salute to show I understand.

She stands there blinking some more. I resist the urge to step back. I can feel them grinning behind me, feel their cheeky, knowing faces.

'Sorry,' I say. 'We are on a bit of a tight schedule.'

'Maybe I could look at them another time through a lens?' she says.

'No.'

I step sideways and edge past her up the corridor. A door at the end opens onto a long, low space, some kind of basement storage when this was a private house. Xiu and Léon stare round, wide-eyed. I can't say I blame them.

Metal trolleys fill the room. The concrete floor slopes inwards to a central drain. The low ceiling is lowered further by hand washers looped to the ceiling. They look like garden hoses. Two for each workstation.

A gleaming aluminium table is plumbed directly into the floor. Examination lights hang from the ceiling, small versions of the ones in the GCHQ training arena.

'Overshoes,' says the Pathologist, waving her hand at a wall dispenser.

Xiu snorts with laughter at the sight of her DMs covered in blue plastic, adding pig noises to her repertoire. Her dungaree straps slip as she hops about. The concrete is wet. I am not sure if the overshoes are to prevent contamination or protect our civilian footwear.

The Pathologist opens a door at the far end. When we are all inside, she shuts the door behind us and the feeling of a trap is back. This is the cold storage room. It is arctic.

A wall of freezer drawers, four drawers high and ten drawers wide, gleams. More aluminium. There are no bright overheads in here.

She checks the paper docket on the outside of drawer twelve and yanks it open. Spindly metal legs unfold and clatter to the floor. For a moment, I imagine the room tipping and the forty metal drawers crashing open, bodies rolling everywhere like some zombie apocalypse.

We peer inside.

His skin is pale, his hair the colour of guinea gold. His eyes are closed.

'Straightforward,' the Pathologist says. 'Neck broken from behind.' Xiu avoids my eye. 'We don't get many visits from GCHQ,' she says. 'Was he someone important?'

'No,' I say.

A latex glove dispenser is screwed to the wall. I pull out a pair and slide my hands in. 'I need an iris scan. And his personal effects.'

'Then we need to get his eyes open,' she says.

His irises are blue. Tiny, red lines dart through the egg-white eyeball. There is something so distinctive about the animation of life and its absence.

The retinal scanner is as big as a laptop and five times as heavy. It sticks to the face like a diving mask. I set the timer and step back. It takes at least ten minutes to get a good image. Eyeballs are complicated. An iris has a unique pattern. Like your own personal bank note.

'I saw one of those used on a living person once,' the Pathologist says. 'It almost sucked the eyeball right out of his head.'

'Could you just take the eyeball out and use that?' Xiu wonders. 'Would that work?'

Léon makes a face.

I consider this.

'I suppose if you were really desperate. Messy in the field and it would be a one-time use. Eyeballs are very delicate.'

The Pathologist is nodding. 'I've got a jar in my office, if you would like to see?' she says.

'No thanks.'

'Awesome,' says Xiu.

CHAPTER 17

Her office, in the bowels of the building, is more like a big janitor's cupboard. There is barely room for the four of us and a massive desk weighed down with paperwork and textbooks and the jar of eyeballs, as promised.

Xiu holds the jar up to the light and the eyeballs bob around, the irises iridescent and sparkling.

'Did you know the iris is named after the Greek goddess of the rainbow?' the Pathologist says.

The walls are covered with Firestorm posters. Top contractors, the posters slick versions of their home pages. If you don't look too closely, the effect is homely, like a student's room. Front and centre, in glossy technicolor, larger than life-size, is the Prince of Darkness looking like he could be modelling for Armani. The sight brings me up short, like I have stepped on a cartoon rake. His dark eyes bore down at me. The Pathologist catches my look.

'Honestly,' she says. 'Who knew Alek Konstantin looked like *that*? It would almost be worth being a victim.'

'He's not a contractor,' I say.

She waves this off. 'He controls Firestorm. He is the most powerful man in the world. Don't you think there is something darkly fascinating about that?'

'No.'

Yes.

'Know thine enemy,' she says. 'That's the thing, isn't it? These days you can really know everything about someone. Really get under their skin.'

Under their skin.

I glance down at the tracker embedded under my own skin, monitoring my well-being.

'Solo, Aveline, the Guardsman – we've had them all here,' she says, like she is proud of it.

Xiu's lip curls.

I stare at the posters.

Solo is a cross between Thor and the Incredible Hulk. The Guardsman is front and centre, cloaked and hooded like something off *Assassin's Creed*. Aveline has a blade in each hand, hair swirling to her waist. The Firestorm Holy Trinity. *Celebrities.*

Beneath them is a postcard of Lord Byron looking dishevelled and romantic and out of place in such deadly company.

'Who did the Guardsman send you?'

'A girl,' she says. 'Last week. It made the national news. A Firestorm contract without a client. She was found not far from here, in an old graveyard.'

The room swims.

'Her name was Lucy,' I say.

'You heard about it then? It was a most interesting case,' she says.

The breeze is warm on my face, the ground dusty beneath me. I can smell stone. In the darkness, a wall of yellow Post-its flutters.

In my pocket, the timer rings shrill.

He is still on his back in the freezer room, with the retinal scanner clamped to his face. I peer into the viewfinder to check the image. Perfect. She is right: irises look amazing magnified, like miniature galaxies.

The Pathologist comes back with the clear plastic evidence bag of clothes and personal effects.

I feel in the pockets. I turn out the trousers. I upend the evidence bag onto the stainless-steel trestle.

'Where's his phone?'

The Pathologist consults the list. 'No phone,' she says.

'I *definitely* put it in his pocket,' says Xiu.

Where the hell is the phone?

I slam down the corridor. The whole thing has been a waste of time. A dead end. I could have had the Guardsman's phone number and I've got nothing. My hands are dry and cracked from the powder residue in the latex gloves. I wipe them down my jeans, palms, then backs, then palms again.

'Well, that was creepy,' says Xiu, making no effort to keep her voice down.

'You have a fan.' Léon grins at me. 'I reckon you were in there.'

'If the Guardsman turned up here, I think she would ask for his autograph. Honestly, like he is some kind of celebrity.' Xiu scowls in disgust.

The door through to Reception opens as if Brenda has seen us coming.

'We've got nothing without the phone. Where the hell is it?' Frustration is so sharp I can taste it.

'This phone you mean?' Simon is standing leaning against the wall in Reception holding up an iPhone.

I don't believe it.

'What are you doing here?'

Simon waves the phone.

'You took it out of his pocket? That is interfering with the scene of a crime.'

'Do you want it or not?' he says.

'Did you track me, or did you have an alert in the system in case I showed?'

'Both,' he says. 'I thought we agreed you weren't going to do this without me?'

'You were too busy playing footsie.' I snatch the phone. 'I need a flat surface.'

I sweep the room freshener and visitors' log from the reception desk and plonk down the scanner. Brenda opens her mouth and Simon smiles at her and she closes it again.

People skills.

I open the laptop, plug in the phone to give it some charge and pull up the camera footage from the bar. Unlike the bearded man, our contractor made no attempt to hide from the surveillance and the door cam outside the bar caught him square in the face. He entered his passcode into his phone twice.

The phone slides open and there is the Firestorm contractor app, front and centre, asking for an iris scan. I fiddle around, settling the phone in the scanner dock. It takes four long seconds to decide and then the login screen disappears and there it is, our contractor's open Firestorm account, with the word *pending* right across the screen and behind it, the last thing he did before he walked into the bar.

A man walked into a bar.

I peer at the screen. The last thing he did was bid on a job. A husband/wife hit.

I slide *pending* to *closed* and hold my breath. Even for the most slow, careful and methodical contractor this has been a long, long time to take on the job.

The phone misses a beat while it communicates with the mothership.

Congratulations Contractor 159, it says.
Please upload photo proof of completion for verification.

'A picture of you dead,' Léon says. 'Easy.'

Brenda is staring at us from behind the counter. She has crumbs on her cardigan. I turn my back on her.

'The problem is,' I say.

'The plastic room,' finishes Xiu.

'Yeah. This guy was a specialist. We are not talking a cosy street mugging.'

'We could use the freezer room downstairs,' says Xiu. 'With the bodies. Authentic.'

'Not like cellophane though.'

Xiu shrugs. 'Easy to wipe clean. Same idea. And keeps the body fresh. Bonus.'

We clatter back down the steps. The Pathologist is in the autopsy room laying out a tray of stainless-steel instruments. She looks up in surprise.

'Can we just get back in the chiller?' I say.

'Sure,' she says. 'Didn't it work?'

She opens the end door and icy air blasts out. When she shuts the door behind us it is all I can do not to yank it open.

'We need an empty drawer,' I say.

The Pathologist stares.

'Don't see why.' Xiu grins. 'You can always cosy up with someone.'

I tear open the face kit and start filling out my jawline using the stainless steel as a mirror. I am all thumbs. My reflection scowls back at me.

Simon has a bottom drawer open. The metal spindly legs unfold and the trolley comes halfway out. 'In you get,' he says. He leans up against the cabinet and folds his arms.

'I sometimes get in myself,' says the Pathologist. 'Just to see what it is like.'

I climb on the trolley. The idea of being shut in a freezer cabinet has my heart racing.

'I don't imagine you would be dressed, do you?' says Simon.

I take off my T-shirt and Kevlar and slide my bra straps down. It is freezing. 'You can just do a head and shoulders shot,' I say. 'And darken the hair up on Photoshop. Hurry up or the system will time out.'

The stainless steel is ice cold against my bare back. I feel my whole body going into shock as my core temperature plummets. How long could you survive being shut in one of these drawers?

'You don't look very dead,' Simon says, peering at the shot he has taken.

I try to sit up and bang my knees.

He is right. I look pink and healthy with muscle tension through my body. There is a frown line between my brows.

'Try again.'

I lie back and try to relax.

'Just think dead thoughts,' Xiu says.

CHAPTER 18

The Pathologist's office is even smaller and cosier with an extra person. Léon and Xiu sit on the edge of her desk. Simon stares round at the posters and then down at the jar of eyeballs and then back up to the posters.

'Lord Byron,' he says, looking at the postcard, 'that well-known hitman.' He picks up a book from the pile on the desk. *Byron and the Sea-Green Isle.*

'He was very into eyes,' says the Pathologist. 'It is always the first thing he mentions:

> *And the eyes of the sleepers waxed deadly and chill,*
> *And their hearts but once heaved and for ever grew still.*

He had one eye bigger than the other, you know.'

'Right,' says Simon.

'Come on, hurry up.' I say. 'We must be almost out of time.'

'Pretty good,' says Simon, looking down at his Photoshop handiwork.

Slowly, deliberately he uploads the picture of me dead to Firestorm and immediately a case number is generated.

51.4733 0.00000 Pending client verification.

I let out a massive breath I didn't know I had been holding.

'The photo will be matched to the one supplied by the client, i.e. the husband, i.e. me. I will need to verify myself as dead and the account will open and then we will be able to see what's going on.'

I have my laptop open, perched on a pile of textbooks and my fake Firestorm account up on the screen, ready and waiting. Simon leans over and looks at the exchange between me and the contractor in the Firestorm contract room.

I would like her to suffer.

It will be my pleasure.

'Jesus,' he says. 'And you put yourself in a room with that guy.'

He is scowling again.

'Better me than someone else.'

He shakes his head, his lips tight.

We all stare at the last thing Contractor 159 tried to bid on while we wait. A wife booking a hit on her husband. In the profile picture, the husband is wearing a tank top. Contractor 159 lost out. Someone else won the contract.

'That's what he must have been doing when I saw him outside the bar,' says Xiu. She picks up the jar of eyeballs, turns it over and watches them bob slowly back to the surface.

'Look at that poor guy,' says Simon. 'What has he done to make his wife book a hit on him?'

'Could be the tank top,' says Xiu.

'Who is he?' Léon wonders.

Simon opens his own laptop, pulls the image and starts data mining.

'Harold Crane. Five Gardenia Walk,' he says.

The imaging software is ninety-eight per cent sure.

'There really is *nowhere* to hide,' says the Pathologist. She cranes forward to get a better look at state-of-the-art government surveillance.

'You've got no idea,' I tell her. 'Show her what you can do with street cams.'

Simon pulls up a file and we crane over his shoulder. 8 a.m. and Harold, in shirt sleeves, is walking down the street. The resolution is good enough to see nose hair.

On the sidebar, Simon is trawling through Harold's financial history.

'Small mortgage, some savings, pension plan, life insurance but not huge. Our Harold is a prudent guy.'

'Sometimes you just never know what is going on behind net curtains,' says Xiu sagely.

On the street cams, the wife is putting out the bins. She is well-preserved. Nicely made-up.

'Maybe it's an affair.'

'We have to stop it,' Simon says firmly.

'Oh, so now you want to interfere with Firestorm? That's not what you were saying two nights ago.'

'It is bad enough to book a hit on yourself; this is something else entirely. If we don't do something to prevent it, we will be accessories to murder.'

I consider the guy in the tank top. 'Probably be a relief.'

'*Winter.*'

'All right, all right.'

'It may be done already anyway,' Xiu says. 'He bid on it three days ago.'

'Easy enough to find out,' I say.

I pick up the Pathologist's landline.

They stare at me aghast.

'You are not going to *call* him?' Léon whispers. 'What will you say?'

I punch in Harold Crane's home number and turn away as a woman answers. Clipped voice, well spoken, middle-aged.

'Can I speak to your husband, ma'am?'

Xiu pulls a scream face, Léon is holding his breath.

'Harold!' the woman's face is turned away from the receiver, maybe pointing up the hall, maybe up the stairs.

I picture Harold emerging from the kitchen in his tank top, tea towel in hand.

I put the phone down.

'Still alive,' I say.

The laptop pings on the pile of textbooks as a new message hits my Firestorm account. The vengeful husband account I used to book the hit.

Please upload image to verify photo proof.

'It is asking for another picture. Why do I have to provide another one? They already have a photo on the account. I had to upload one when I booked the hit. Why would I have to load it again?'

Simon shrugs. 'Extra layer of security. Get on with it, before it gets suspicious.'

I click on load and stand back while it communicates with the mothership.

Something about this is making me uneasy. I look at the case number again.

In the jar, the eyeballs start their slow bob back to the surface.

'Do you think that was a bit quick? Maybe I should have thought about it more.'

'Why?' says Simon.

'I guess he will know his wife is dead.'

'Who will?'

'Me. As him.'

'I thought you were the victim.'

'Try to keep up.'

The circling timer on the contractor's phone stops. We all crane forward.

Verification failed.

Account suspended. Please await further instruction.

CHAPTER 19

I press my thumbs into the corners of my eyes until I can feel socket. The room feels hot with the five of us crowded into it. A moment ago I was frozen, now I am burning up. We have nothing except the specs for a job our contractor didn't even win and a suspended account. A wild goose chase. A dead end.

'I'm going back to the office,' Simon says closing up his laptop. His face is worried.

'Fine,' I say.

'I don't think you are taking this seriously enough. It is our responsibility to stop that hit.'

'What hit?'

Simon glares. 'Harold Crane, Gardenia Walk.'

'Tank-top man,' says Xiu helpfully.

'I can let you know if he turns up here,' says the Pathologist. 'Would that help?'

'No,' says Simon, turning his back on her. 'It would not.'

'Get back to the office and check where they are with the Petersburg, Paris, Marseille facial ID search,' I tell him. 'We are done here anyway.'

I watch him walk away down the echoing basement corridor, his worried shoulders hunched under the weight of two laptops and a retinal scanner.

'I wonder if they could tell I wasn't dead from the picture.'

'It can't be that,' Xiu says. 'The photo went through OK.'

I look at the case number on the contractor's phone 51.4733 0.00000. Then I stare at the Greenwich Council Health and Safety notice tacked to the wall.

Greenwich Council.

I stare at the case number again.

Then I swear.

Hell. It is practically staring me in the face. I think about the picture of the barmaid on the Guardsman's home page and the case number below it, nearly but not quite the same.

'What is Greenwich famous for?' I say slowly.

Xiu looks blank.

'Time?' says Léon.

'We are on the Prime Meridian. 0.000 in decimal degrees. Longitude Zero. There is nothing random about this case number.' I jab the screen. 'It is the coordinates of where we are right now.'

'They don't look like coordinates,' says Xiu.

'That's because you are thinking of GPS, but positioning can be expressed as a decimal, plus or minus the zero line. Positioning is embedded in the photo upload. That's what we did wrong. We just uploaded photo proof of death from the contractor and photo ID from the client in the same place.'

I punch the case number for the barmaid into my phone and watch the satnav function think about it. Where was she killed? I am about to find out.

'Get back to the office,' I tell them.

'Where are *you* going?' they chorus, indignant.

'To check a theory.'

I head down the corridor, satnav circling, leaving them staring.

South East London, the street is Georgian but shabby. Long since divided into flats and then divided again into bedsits. Dirty nets cover the windows. My heart sinks as I get close. I have only been here once before and at night, but I know where I am going.

The memories come in flashes. The ICE app, the night drive, the realisation, the feeling like wading through water. The body on the grass, the arm moving in supplication, a face desperate to tell me something.

A ten-acre oasis of calm in the middle of South East London. The Brockley and Ladywell cemetery.

I was right. There is nothing random about the case numbers, they are coordinates harvested from the photos taken at the scene of death.

Firestorm is tracking its contractors.

Of course it is.

I walk up the pavement and down the other side. I watch the gates, peer through the railings. No one comes. The gravestones are falling over, ancient, the writing long since crumbling into illegibility. No one is coming to visit these graves. The people who used to come have been dead a hundred years.

The gates are wrought iron, gothic Victorian with huge stone posts. There may have been a crown of thorns round the top at one time. It has crumbled like everything else. I pause for a beat on the threshold, then I have crossed and I am inside.

It is hushed, silent after the street, even though nothing separates it from the outside world but iron railings. A world apart. I stand on the path listening to the rustle of the knee-high grass, reading the space.

Last time I was here, it was night and the trees were dark silhouettes against the sodium sky. Grass crackled round my ankles as I tore across the space, heart pumping.

I look around, shading my eyes against the brilliance. There could be tens, hundreds of crime scenes here hidden between the graves. Cold pricks the back of my neck. I shiver in the heat. Cemeteries are creepy. There is no avoiding it. A blackbird shrieks and my heart thuds. The bird's alarm call arrows straight into my monkey brain, bypassing my senses, pressing buttons way below my conscious mind. Straight in at the kernel.

Watch out. Beware.

Fear is in the bone, hard-wired, bred in through thousands of years of evolution. Modern service training does its best to drum it out. I don't know why. Fear keeps you alive.

Childlike, my pysch reports used to say, *limited emotional range. Instinctual in her reactions.*

Like it was a bad thing.

A wide emotional range makes you as vulnerable as a snail with a broken shell.

I was the child who lay frozen while the floorboards creaked, who feared monsters that came at night in the dark, who heard death in every clank of radiator and every creak of wardrobe. And now I have grown, I know that the monsters who come in the night to kill you are real and that if they only kill you, you have got off lightly. So, all things being equal, there is every reason to be afraid.

There is a church and another building on a hill in the centre of the cemetery. Victorian gothic like the gateposts. A path leads through the trees, circling the hill, too narrow for a road. Maybe it is for hearses, maybe the church is still in use. It is hard to believe.

I follow the path round to the top. I yank at the heavy church door. Locked down tight. The other building is a church hall. Single storey. Glass lantern on roof. It is locked as well. There is a heavy bar across it, as if they are keeping someone in. I peer through a keyhole big enough for a castle key. A corridor lined with noticeboards, limp posters about toddler groups.

I go back down the path and edge between the gravestones. In the brilliant sunlight, black shadows gather behind every tomb, every fallen angel, every ivy-covered column. A serial killer with a fetish for knives. Some stories don't really change. They just get updated. I am in a modern take on a story ages old.

'Nice,' says a voice behind me. 'Spooky.'

'I heard you coming a mile off,' I say.

'Yeah? It was that bloody blackbird.' Xiu looks round. 'Check this place out. One creepy graveyard. I am expecting vampires.'

'What have you done with Léon?'

Léon rises from behind a gravestone like a slow-motion jack-in-the-box.

'Gotcha,' he says.

I smile, despite everything. 'Nice job,' I say. 'Good skills.'

He beams.

It's you they want to impress.

They've imprinted on me like a couple of ducklings.

'What are we doing here anyway?'

'I don't know what you two are doing here. I am looking for a crime scene.' I show them the satnav locator pulsing blue on my phone.

'What's that?' Xiu points at the string of numbers in the search window.

'A case number from the Guardsman's home page.'

Xiu looks round. 'So not that crime scene then?' she says pointing at the black and yellow police tape where Lucy was found.

I turn away. 'No. Another one.'

'But it is probably a trap, no?' says Léon.

'I don't think so.'

'So, what are we looking for?'

'Blood. A lot of blood.'

Their voices fade as they move off down the cemetery.

It is Léon who finds it. Between the heavy, spreading limbs of a cedar, the air full of the resin smell of dry pine needles and something else, rotten and putrid.

A stone cross is covered in lichen and barely legible.

'*The just man walketh in his integrity,*' Léon reads. 'What does that mean?'

I look up into the face of an angel. Her blind eyes stare downwards. Her hands are clasped in prayer. An old wild rose twines around her neck like a noose. Its dry yellow petals are spotted with blood. Dark stains spread across the steps of her plinth.

This is where the barmaid was killed. This is where her photo was taken before she was delivered to GCHQ.

Grasses rustle in the black shadows behind the cedar and my heart thumps.

I walk round the huge trunk. There is no one there.

I run my fingers over the bark, track the flies in the grooves, up to the nail holes and close my eyes as the pictures wash over me.

CHAPTER 20

Contractor 159's phone moves in my hand and my heart thumps again. I peer down. He has a new message.

Please attend photo verification

'What does that mean?' Léon whispers as if the phone can hear us. 'I thought the account was disabled.'

'It means they don't know what's wrong. The system threw up an anomaly that's all. It means we may still have a chance.'

The phone moves again.

W1A 1ER

The circle goes round and round like it is loading something. We stare at it like contestants on a quiz show. Sun beats down on our bare necks.

'It's a postcode. W1A – very central.'

Léon squints at Google Maps, shielding his phone against the bright light.

'Fortnum & Mason, Piccadilly,' he looks up. 'What is that?'

'*What?* Give me that.' I snatch his phone and check the postcode. I punch it in again. Up come the trademark turquoise and gold colours.

'Unexpected,' I say slowly. 'It's a kind of department store.'

'For old ladies,' adds Xiu. 'Tea and teapots and things.'

'*Tea?*' says Léon. At the end of his first day at GCHQ, he told me everyone had talked about the weather and offered him tea. He said it like it was a joke.

'Very public,' I say. 'Multiple exits. If I remember rightly it has a domed atrium right in the centre. You can see every floor from every other floor.'

On my phone the loading wheel circles like it is waiting for us to get moving.

I am tracing my way through the pathways, out through the gothic stone arch and heading up the road in search of a cab before Xiu and Léon have moved. They jog in my wake to keep up. I spin the contractor's phone, hefting it from hand to hand. Can Firestorm see me now? On my way? Can the Administrator see the speed of my movement? The velocity? The trajectory? Is he watching from the centre of the Firestorm web, tracking our movements? I can feel eyes on the back of my neck. I check the settings for the third time. GPS is disabled.

'Lucky we came,' says Xiu behind me. 'You can't go on your own.'

'Why not?'

'Because you are the victim. Too weird.'

'Well *you* can't go,' says Léon. 'You're a girl.'

Xiu pats her dungarees. 'What gave it away? Was it these?' Xiu points at her non-existent chest.

Léon doesn't dignify this with a reply.

'You have no training, no skills. You are liabilities,' I tell them.

'I've got skills,' says Léon, indignant.

I stop still and they cannon into the back of me.

I put my hand on Léon's shoulder and my heel on his right Achilles tendon. He is flat on his back in a tenth of a second.

'You have no skills,' I tell him.

He sits up on the dusty pavement, rubbing his elbow. 'Why did you have to do that? I am dirty now.'

Xiu is laughing. I look at her and she backs off, waving her hands in front of her.

'Oh no,' she says. 'You're not getting me too.'

Léon staggers to his feet. He has streaks of dust on his white T-shirt. He squares his shoulders. Xiu's eyes flick over him. He is tanned against the white.

'I really need to know how to do that,' he says.

The loading wheel circles round and round on the phone. It makes me stressed just looking at it. A childish computer game, a virtual reality challenge. I put the phone back in my pocket.

A cab is coming down the road towards us, its golden light a shining beacon of loveliness. I haven't got time to deal with them now.

'Just keep out of my way,' I say.

The cab heads through New Cross, round Elephant and Castle and then we are in central London where every street name is famous and you can't move for iconic views. The Palace of Westminster is like a film set.

We pass the statue of Eros and the giant billboards and then we are on Piccadilly and pulling up outside an ornate, eighteenth-century shopfront. Turquoise and gold gleam in the sun.

Crowds cluster in front of the window display, phones raised high. Despite the times, there is never any shortage of tourists.

A church bell rings somewhere. *Oranges and lemons say the bells of St Clements.*

Xiu and Léon pull out their phones and start clicking away at the display of flying teapots.

I clamp a hand on each shoulder and propel them forwards.

Torches flame beside the entrance, the door handles shine like burnished gold. It is a bit of a disappointment when the Fortnum doors swing open automatically, powered by twenty-first century artifice.

We are in a tea hall, hushed after the clicking tourists. Somewhere, a live piano tinkles. Staff waft back and forth in black tie. The place even smells expensive.

Rows of glass teapots sit on a low table: Lingia First Flush – *a truly elegant first flush tea*, Formosa Panchoug – *a flavour between green tea and oolong*, Golden Monkey, China Jasmine, Phoenix Pearls. Xiu and Léon lean over, poking. The man behind the counter scowls.

The next display has glass jars of sweets like an old-fashioned pharmacy. Colourful stands of sea salt chocolate, Lucifer's chilli chocolate, caramel pearls. Everywhere there are boxes and boxes of the distinctive turquoise and gold.

I give Xiu and Léon the 'spread out and recon' and they look at me blankly. I roll my eyes thinking longingly of the marine recruits for the first time ever.

Fortnum's is hollow, like a tube of Polos. It has a circular atrium, with a shiny chrome balcony down its centre. Looking up through the hole I can see all the floors above.

Somewhere, there must be stairs.

We find them in the corner. Two painted, wooden, regency bucks stand at the bottom, lace at their throats, candelabras in their upstretched hands, their coats the ubiquitous turquoise. Xiu reaches for her phone.

I shake my head.

The first floor is wall-to-wall teapots. China as far as the eye can see. Teapots in a dazzling array of colours and shapes. Butterflies, *Alice in Wonderland*, teapots in the shape of the shop.

Xiu and Léon stare nonplussed. There is no one around.

There is a reverent hush on the top floor like we have entered hallowed ground. Hats and handbags and glittering phials of amber liquid. Not a soul in sight.

I glance down at the phone in my hand. The wheel is still circling. I have taken it to every corner of the store and there is no change. The frustration starts to rise. Xiu and Léon peer down at it.

'It's like we haven't done something.'

'Maybe someone is going to come and meet us?'

I hang over the balcony and stare down three floors, considering.

Léon. Right sex, right kind of age, give or take ten years, right kind of look – cute, but otherwise, way off. Wrong nationality, wrong hair, wrong colouring. If someone comes who knows our contractor, he is not going to fool them. On the other hand, if someone comes, he will have me.

I drum my fingers on the chrome. The wheel spins. Reason wars with instinct. The Firestorm Administrator. It is too good a chance to pass up.

'I'm going to give you my Kevlar,' I say, 'and put you on display with the phone.'

'Sure,' Léon nods.

'It is not ideal, but life in the field rarely is. Sometimes you have to weigh the odds, take a calculated risk.'

'Is that a good idea?' says Xiu.

'Says the girl who turned up with nothing but her fists and a bus pass to stop a hit.'

She shrugs. 'That was only one guy.'

'Did you?' Léon's eyes track up and down the dungarees. 'You're not exactly big.'

'It's not about size. I could take you with one hand behind my back.'

Léon snorts. 'I doubt that.'

I consider them both and try not to smile. 'It is probably true,' I say.

Léon's face reddens. '*J'y crois pas.*'

I pat his arm. 'You can sort it out later.'

In the Ladies, Xiu holds the door to the corridor closed while I strip down to my bra and Léon leans against the basins.

He is dubious. 'Will I get into it?'

I hold the vest up. 'It's going to be tight. Kevlar is supposed to be snug. It was made for me.'

He pulls his T-shirt off two-handed from the bottom. In the mirror, Xiu's eyes widen.

She catches me watching her and winks.

Léon yanks at the zip trying to get the mesh to meet under his arm. It doesn't meet.

'Better than nothing,' I tell him. 'Your torso is protected.' I clap him on the back. 'Just don't raise your arms.'

'It's not comfortable,' he complains.

'Nor is a bullet hole.'

He takes a seat at a table for two in the tea hall, with the phone on the white linen beside him. Xiu and I head for the floor above to watch over the balcony.

We check out the clientele. Mothers and daughters, ladies of a certain age meeting other ladies of a certain age. The occasional model mummy, offspring decked out in Burberry. Léon's dark good looks are getting a few sideways glances.

Three o'clock and high tea is well underway. We watch it arriving at the next table on a filigree three-tier cake stand. A tiny lemon meringue tart, perfect mini scones, strawberry jam, clotted cream in its own little dish, mini squares of brownie, Florentines with glossy chocolate bottoms.

'I'm starving,' says Xiu. 'Can we get something?'

A boiled egg arrives at the next table with a domed egg cosy. The waiter lifts the dome with a flourish, a curl of smoke rises and *pouf!* disappears. Smoked. Probably with tea. The customer beams in delight. It has a neat drama, a theatricality to it.

A waiter pours Léon tea – loose, naturally – through a silver strainer. I can't help wondering how many get lifted a year. The amber arc curves perfectly into the cup. The phone sits on the table in front of him like a homing beacon.

I scan the room, up and back and round.

The stage is set.

Time ticks by. The occupants of the restaurant change. Léon orders more tea. The waiter is too polite to move him on.

Simon calls. 'The results are in on your facial recognition search. No matches.'

'None at all?'

'Nothing, nada, zip, not even a partial. What next?'

I think about this. A store detective heads my way, I give him a look and he retreats. 'Marseille. It is the key. Alek Konstantin and the Guardsman were in Petersburg and then they went straight there. Straight to Marseille. Like some kind of cause and effect. And something was going on at that factory. Get me on a flight out this evening.'

I can hear the sound of Simon typing.

'Where are you now?' he asks. 'You're not in Fortnum & Mason?' He knows I am, my locator is pinpoint accurate. 'What are you doing there?'

'Training.'

'What, trying to blend in over a nice cup of tea? Are you sure you are up to it? I wouldn't want you to strain something lifting a scone.'

'It's kind of beautiful here,' I say. The teapots are getting to me. 'Nice for Léon to see.'

Simon snorts. 'He's meant to be back here learning Java. Is that girl still with you?'

'Yes.'

'You are on the 8.30 p.m. BA flight to Marseille by the way.'

'Right.'

More typing.

'There aren't any cameras,' he says after a bit. 'Strange. What kind of self-respecting department store doesn't watch its customers?' He is genuinely indignant at not being able to see what I am up to.

It is heading towards five o'clock and closing time. Léon is still hanging on to his table in the face of waiter outrage. Xiu is the other side of the atrium, draped over the chrome balcony like a rag doll.

I watch the patterns of movement from above. It is like a ballet. Artificial, brittle, beautiful. Something is wrong, I can feel it. My heart rate accelerates, my eyes scan the crowd. What has spooked me? I try to pin the feeling down. Isolate it.

The waiter is back, threading his way through the tables towards Léon with one of the boiled eggs under a smoky dome.

I imagine his movements ahead of time – the gracious, stately arrival, the placing of the plate, the whip away reveal as the dome is removed. I imagine Léon leaning forward to savour the smoke and then I am leaping, leaping out into nothing, vaulting one handed over the balcony and dropping like a dead weight to the floor below.

Not an impossible jump. About four metres, a good distance, not something you want to try without training. My biggest problem is the landing site. It is crowded with tables and chairs and prams and screaming women and with the best will in the world I am going to have to roll or break half the bones in my body.

A table crashes as I fall against it, brownies fly and then I am on my feet and striding forward and lifting the plate gently out of the waiter's hands. He stares at me open-mouthed. Léon is up and Xiu is arrowing through the tables towards me and I realise with a jolt that she must have jumped as well. An astonishing jump for a civilian. I press my thumbs to the top of the dome to hold it in place.

'Sellotape,' I order, jerking my head at the chocolate gift counter.

They are both on it, scurrying back to me with shiny pink tape. Xiu rips it with her teeth and Léon sticks it gently from the top of the dome round, down and under the plate. His giant puppy paws are surprisingly dextrous.

'You really think?' Xiu says, staring wide-eyed at the dome.

'Yeah. I really think. Where did you get this?' I ask the waiter. 'He didn't order it.'

'Off the pass,' he says bemused. 'He did order it – it's in the system.'

Léon shakes his head.

Customers scramble for the exit, fanning out, away from the epicentre – a boiled egg under a smoky dome. The cake stand on the next-door table has tipped over and the white linen is smeared with chocolate.

'Kitchen,' I say. 'Although I'm betting he is long gone.'

'That was some kind of ninja jump,' says Léon looking at Xiu, awe writ large across his face. 'Not in a racist kind of way,' he adds hurriedly. The tips of Léon's ears are reddening. I bet if I could see his neck there'd be a tide of crimson flooding it. 'I don't think it was the waiter,' he says. 'He's been here all afternoon.'

'I don't think it was him either,' I say, pushing through the swing doors.

The stainless-steel kitchen is long and full of people scrubbing down workstations. No one has told the kitchen there is some kind of crisis. The guy behind the counter looks up.

'Can I help you?' he says.

'Just passing through.' I cut down the aisles of stainless steel, past the freezer room and we are out in an alley at the back of the store. Wooden crates of vegetables are stacked against the wall.

A dead end.

Another dead end. Contractor 159's account is locked down permanently and whoever the Firestorm Administrator sent to deal with us is long gone.

I look at the gas swirling in the dome and think about all the many things it could be. I turn on my heel and go back into the kitchen.

'I need some containers,' I say. 'Preferably several.'

Léon whips away and a second later he is back with a cake tin and Xiu is holding up a Tupperware box of what looks like egg mayonnaise. She tips it out on the stainless-steel workstation and a chef shouts.

I put the dome and eggcup inside and seal it up, then place the Tupperware in the cake box. The lid is a tight fit.

'If this is what I think it is, this is in no way adequate, but in the field you make do.'

They nod, wide-eyed.

I pull out my phone. 'There are only two places in central London with the containment facilities to handle high toxicity analysis.'

Brad, the London head of the NSA, answers on the first ring.

'Winter,' he says, full of enthusiasm. 'How are you doing?'

'I need a favour.'

'Has it got anything to do with the G20?'

'No.'

'That's a relief.'

'It's a little below the radar. Meet you in the café outside your building in twenty minutes.'

'I'm intrigued,' he says.

I look back as we get in a cab. People are milling around outside Fortnum's, wondering what all the fuss is about.

CHAPTER 21

The cab goes straight through the heart of London, through Holborn, across the Bank junction, round the Tower of London and we are on The Highway, the dual carriageway to Canary Wharf. We go up the ramp through the ring of steel and pull up opposite the grey NSA building.

We troop into the café with the red awning, heads down against the hot Saharan wind funnelling between the buildings. Panattone hang from the ceiling. The smell of roast coffee beans is still strong. 6 p.m. Do they ever close?

I plonk the cake tin down on the wooden table.

'Can we eat?' says Xiu picking up the menu.

'Where are we?' asks Léon.

'Canary Wharf E14.'

He looks blank.

'NSA.'

'Friends in high places,' says Xiu.

'Something like that.'

'Why didn't we just go back to GCHQ?'

'Because she doesn't want anyone to know what she is up to,' says Léon.

'Are you OK after that jump?' I ask Xiu.

She shrugs.

'It was pretty awesome,' Léon says. 'You both jumped at the same time.'

'So I guess we know now,' Xiu says. '*Please present yourself for photo verification* means Firestorm are going to delete you.'

'We don't know that for sure,' I stare at the cake tin. 'It may be nothing.'

'Or it may be something.'

'There may have been some way to pass the test. Léon didn't pass because he is not a contractor. Maybe there was something he didn't do.'

'Like what?'

I stare out of the window thinking about the Firestorm Administrator and the wall of yellow stickies and the Guardsman and a final countdown, all pieces of the puzzle, all questions with no answers. 'There is something fundamental about the Administrator and the way Firestorm operates that I am missing.'

The door opens and Brad walks in. He is broad and brisk and such a stereotype that I find myself wondering if it is put on. He has always had a big smile for me, even back when we were foot soldiers.

He eyes Xiu and Léon. 'What's this?' he says. 'Work experience week?'

'These are GCHQ's top recruits,' I say.

Xiu and Léon preen.

'Deep cover,' says Brad.

He homes in on the cake tin on the table, gives it a long hard look then raises his eyes to mine.

'I just don't want to know,' he says. 'Is that what I think it is?'

'Do you want to know or not? I'm confused.'

'Go on then.'

'Probably.'

'*Great.*' He turns to the counter, jingling coins in his pocket and orders himself an iced decaf latte.

'Iced decaf kind of defeats the point don't you think?' I say when he is back with a tall glass.

'What, now you're criticising my beverage choices?'

'Sorry.'

Xiu snorts.

'So,' Brad stirs the ice round and round, 'I'm guessing you want whatever that is analysed under the radar?'

'That's it,' I say, glad to find him so quick on the uptake.

'And what's in it for me?'

'My undying gratitude.'

Brad looks sceptical.

'I'll owe you one?'

'Why do I never get the "suck you until you scream" offer?'

Xiu grins. Léon glares.

The phone in my pocket vibrates. I look down at it.

'If Simon calls you, this was just a friendly chat by the way,' I say.

Brad rolls his eyes.

'Hi,' I say into the phone. 'I know I'm cutting it tight. Hand luggage only. It'll be fine.'

'Harold Crane,' says Simon. 'Tank-top man. I think it's tonight. She just booked a taxi to take her to Paddington.' The unflappable Simon is practically hyperventilating. 'What shall I do? Shall I tell the police? Should I warn him?'

I stare out of the window. 'No. Cancel her cab and cancel my flight.'

'What? Why?'

'The last thing Contractor 159 did on Firestorm was bid on the Harold Crane job. He lost and someone else won. I'm going to go and have a little chat with whoever that was, ask them a few questions, get a few answers.'

I get baguettes to go and hustle Tweedledum and Tweedledee out of the door.

Brad stands with the cake tin in his hand looking bemused.

'Can I borrow your gun?' I say.

His face blanches. 'Absolutely not.'

It was worth a try.

'Call me,' I say, pointing at the cake tin. 'When you have something.'

'So, what have we got?' I ask Simon once we are in another black cab. This one is even older. Its seats are worn, the plastic sticky with heat. It has manual windows that slide down like those on an old train. I lean my weight against one, shoving it down. It doesn't make a lot of difference. It is still baking.

Capital is playing on the radio. Beside me, Xiu and Léon are munching like they haven't eaten for a week.

'I've just been though the bank accounts. Mrs Crane, the wife, booked train tickets two days ago.'

'Two days ago. It fits. Contractor 159 lost out and someone else won. Whoever that was gave her a day and she booked her alibi. How long is she going for?'

'Return is for Sunday afternoon.'

'So, she is going for the weekend.'

'Bottom line,' he says. 'Could be tonight. One other thing.'

'Hang on.' I check out of the window. The Mile End Road. Perfect. 'Can you pull up here?' I say to the cabbie.

I push Xiu and Léon out of the door. 'Out you go. Great first day. Go get some sleep.'

They look reproachfully up at me from the kerb, like abandoned kittens. I slam the door.

'Sorry,' I say to Simon. 'You were saying?'

'I've been talking to Beth.'

'Oh God, why?' HR are stalking me.

'She is a criminal psychologist, Winter. She is worried about the implications of provoking Firestorm. She thinks there could be repercussions.'

'Good.'

'Not you, Winter.' I can hear his frustration. 'What is the founding principle of Firestorm? If you care, your enemies have all the leverage they need.'

I stare out of the window at the urban sprawl.

On the radio, Blondie is telling everyone, one way or another, she is going to get you, get you, get you.

'Good job I don't care about anyone then,' I say.

CHAPTER 22

The street is broad and suburban and instantly recognisable from the street-cam footage. A cul-de-sac. Gardenia Walk.

Privet Drive.

I walk up the manicured path to the front door. Net curtains, stained glass, novelty bell. I lean on it. The Carpenters' 'Close to You' peels out, tinny and motorised.

The door opens.

The woman is cross. I can tell that before she has opened her mouth. Cross and going out. Her coat is on. She thought I was the taxi. She has probably been ready for hours. She probably woke up ready. Today is the big day.

'Hi, I'm from the Council,' I say. 'We're just canvassing opinion on the proposal to abolish wheelie bins.'

She was shutting the door, but this opens it.

'*What?*' she says. 'Abolish wheelie bins? And replace them with what?'

'The Council feels, in this recycling age of low emissions and zero carbon footprint, that there may be scope to do away with them entirely. The Council feels that any leftover household waste not covered by the recycling categories could be posted to them.'

'That's ridiculous,' she says.

'I'll make a note of your view,' I say. 'Do you have anything with proof of address on it?'

She stares at me. 'You rang my front doorbell.'

'I know. Data protection.'

'This is ridiculous.' She turns away and picks up a letter from the hall table and turns back to find a long, white blade in her face. I close the door quietly behind me. Her hand flies to her throat. Her eyes are pink like she has been crying a few hot, guilty tears.

'I thought you would be a man,' she whispers. 'You're early.'

Or right on time depending on your point of view.

I turn the knife in my hand, smack her on the side of the head with the hilt and catch her in my arms as she crumples.

Harold is in the kitchen, in a tank top.

'Hi, Harold,' I say. 'I'm Winter.'

'Are you from the Council?' he says. 'Because no one has collected the bins for two weeks in a row. One week is acceptable, but two?' He shakes his head. 'In this heat?'

'Listen,' I say. 'Here's the thing.'

I stop.

I've never had to deal with the victim end before. Not before the event anyway.

'Here's the thing,' I say.

Through the kitchen window I can see Xiu and Léon standing on the parched lawn in the back garden, about as subtle as the missing dustbin lorry. I roll my eyes. I might have known.

Harold looks at me expectantly. 'Yes? What's the thing?'

What is it about this mild-mannered guy that has his wife booking a hit?

'Yes?' he says again.

'Fuck it,' I say and smack him on the temple.

'Hurry up,' says Xiu as I pull the back door open. 'It's roasting out here.'

*

The carpet pile on the stairs is so thick it drags at my heels. My face stares from the landing mirror. I look gaunt, my green eyes large as a manga drawing. How long is it since I slept properly? In a bed?

There are three bedrooms. One at the front, two at the back. A bathroom squeezed in at the end. I turn into the front first. Twin beds with pink nylon counterpanes, melamine chest of drawers, a Christmas bag – probably the spare room.

I look inside the bag: rolls of twine. Gold, silver, blue, green. I pick up a roll, unwind a few turns and heft shiny gold between my hands. Too flimsy. I chuck the roll back in the bag and go out onto the landing.

The right hand back bedroom is much the same, only no Christmas bag. The second spare room. The air is stale. The last bedroom is the master. My hand rests on the china knob, eyes flicking around the room. Two single beds pushed together, alarm clocks, hand cream, earrings, books, glasses, pill packets. Shoes lined up against the wall.

I open a drawer and close it again, staring at nothing. What has made her hate him so much?

A lifetime of dodgy ties are stuffed into the wardrobe tie holder. There are so many, they have been forced in, higgledy-piggledy, some of them barely hanging on. Embossed and embroidered. Christmas ties with Santa on, stiff and cheap and viscose. I wrestle three silk ones free and shut the door.

There is a paisley dressing gown hanging on the back of the door. I slide the belt out on the way past.

The sitting room is chintz. Everything is flowered and pink and frilly. The lampshade has small pink pompoms hanging off it.

Léon and Xiu have dragged the husband and wife in and hauled them up onto the sofa. Now they are standing over them, radiating focus, trying to look indispensable.

I fling Léon the belt and ties.

'*Les deux?*' he asks.

'Yeah. God knows how he'll take it when he wakes up.'

I go back out into the hall, into the kitchen and look at the back door, at the keys in the lock, look at the single pane plate-glass window above the sink.

Next to the kitchen is a tiny utility. No window. There is a washing machine and a toilet and one of those old-fashioned drying racks that hang from the ceiling. Tan tights dangle. The door has a lock on it.

Good.

When the time comes, I am going to lock them all in here and wait in the master bedroom. I might even get into the bed. I grin at the thought.

What big eyes you have, Grandma.

What a big knife.

Back in the kitchen, I stare out of the window. The lawn is parched. Roses wilt in patio pots. This summer has been a tragedy for gardeners. Two buckets, one on the work counter, one on the floor bear witness to a careful approach to water. Every last drop is being saved for the roses.

The lines of sight from the sink are pretty good: ten-foot-high fences on all three sides and a squat prefab garage at the end. I wonder about access to the garage and go back up the stairs and peer down from the master bedroom. The window is wide. I stand in the warm air listening to the bird song.

A typical summer's evening in the suburbs. The murmur of voices. Open kitchen doors, cooking smells drifting through the gardens. There is an alley running along the back of the row and, beyond the alley, other gardens and the backs of other houses too far away to see into.

I picture the front of the cul-de-sac with shiny company cars outside every door. The garages are not in use, or not in use for their original purpose. They will be full to the brim with tools and all sorts of other things that homeowners put in garages. I have never had one myself, but homeowners love them.

No sign of the bins, full or otherwise.

So, all in all, we are looking at a relatively private back of the house, near perfect for covert entry, versus the front which has the windows of five other houses staring at it.

I drag a couple of pairs of tights off the rail in the utility room and go back into the sitting room. The chintz doesn't look any better, second time around.

Léon is just finishing up. He started with the husband which is an interesting tactical decision since the wife is clearly the more dangerous of the two, but maybe he felt his reaction would be unpredictable. Either way, he is finishing the wife's wrists which, like her husband's, are bound behind her. Uncomfortable and probably unnecessary but I can't fault his caution. In the absence of any other instruction he has taken the more prudent line.

Xiu is staying well back, standing guard and again that is exactly as it should be. One to tie and one to watch. I run my finger under the bindings, check the knots but there is no need. It is a decent job.

I hand him the tights and he binds them round one face and then the other, hard against their teeth. Uncomfortable, but way better than duct tape. He stands back.

'We need to bring them round,' I say.

I know what I'm doing when it comes to knocking someone unconscious, but I like to bring them round as soon as I can. There is always scope for the unexpected, the undiagnosed heart condition, the bad fall, the broken bones on the way down.

A tap runs in the kitchen and Léon is back with two glasses of water.

I flick water in the wife's face. Dabble my fingers and flick. Flick, flick, flick. She stirs, her head moves. Her eyes open and then she is bolt upright and feeling her wrist restraints and starting to panic.

I crouch down so I am right in front of her, in her field of view and take her face in my hands.

'I need to ask you some questions and I need to check that you are OK before I do. Nod if you understand.'

She nods once, sharp and emphatic.

I turn on my phone torch and check her pupils, one and then the other.

'You may be mildly concussed. Do you feel OK?'

She nods.

'I am going to take your gag off. If you scream, if you shout, if you do anything I don't like, I will knock you out again and I would prefer not to have to do that twice in one evening. Do you understand?'

Again, the emphatic nod.

I slide my fingers along the cheek and lift the tights out of her mouth slightly, a centimetre, giving her half a chance to scream.

Nothing.

I pull the gag down.

'Is it tonight?'

For a moment I think she is going to try and deny it. Her eyes flick around the room and then come back to me and her shoulders square.

'Yes,' she says.

'Staged to look like a break-in?'

'Yes.'

'How?'

'I don't know. He said it wouldn't be a problem.'

'What time?'

'Later; Harold was to be in bed asleep.' Her eyes find her husband, still unconscious on the sofa. 'Why did you tie him up? Was that really necessary?'

That's a bit rich coming from her.

I pull her gag up and move on to Harold. The same water flicking. His face is shiny with the heat, his breathing heavy. I don't like the look of him. Did I hit him harder than I thought? The water is already slightly warm, the chill gone. It still does its job.

He blinks up at me, disorientated, then he says something into the tights.

I pull his gag down.

'You hit me.'

'Yeah. Sorry about that.'

His eyes travel round and round, swivelling in his head, to Xiu and Léon, to his wife. Back to me. I can see him weighing it all up. Trying to fit events into the narrative of his cul-de-sac life. Trying to come up with some explanation to cover the facts.

'Is this a robbery?' he says finally.

'Good guess, but no.' I pull his gag back up, pick up the TV remote and plonk myself down in an armchair. 'Your wife took out a hit on you.'

I turn the TV on. The news. A talking head is sounding off about the global break down in law and order. He compares Firestorm to Brazilian army ants. The picture cuts to giant ants marching through the rainforest. There is a deer with a broken leg in the way. The feeling of impending doom is back. We watch the deer facing its final countdown. Harold stares at the swirly patterns on the floor to get away from the desperate three-legged flight. Now the talking head is telling us there is speculation about whether the G20 can go ahead in this climate of global violence.

'Site secured,' I tell Simon. 'Wife confirms timing.' I glance at her, she is staring at the television. 'Tweedledum and Tweedledee are here.'

'What? She hasn't even been through induction. It is not safe for them.'

'They turned up.' I look at them on their phones pretending they aren't listening to every word. 'It'll be educational. Easy hit like this. I was in Moscow at their age. We'll call it a training exercise.'

'About that. HR is causing trouble.'

'Oh God. What now?'

'Beth knows you were in Fortnum's and something happened. There is footage on YouTube of you base jumping into the Atrium. She says you have endangered civilians.'

'What did you say?'

'I said you were training.'

'So, what's the problem?'

'You don't understand. She is gunning for you.'

'I'm trembling. What can she do? I'm already on suspension.'

'She's looking to get you fired.'

It is the tail end of the TV news. None of it good. The developed world is collapsing into anarchy. Another talking head calls old Europe the last bastion of true democracy. Last bastion of total disorganisation more like. The weatherman tells us it is the hottest July on record. He points at a map of the UK. Smiling suns with numbers on their middles cover the screen. There is an almost perfect correlation between the abnormally hot temperatures and the breakdown of law and order.

Someone is walking up the path. We all freeze. The Carpenters sing. Electronic and shocking. I lie my face flat to the wall and look down the net curtain. The flock wallpaper is soft against my cheek.

A woman is standing on the doorstep clutching a bright pink thermos to her chest.

'There's a woman out there with a truly disastrous home perm and sensible shoes,' I say without taking my eye off her. 'If it is cover, it is the best I have ever seen.'

The wife jerks her head towards next door.

'A neighbour?'

She nods.

'Did she know you were away for the weekend?'

Nod.

'So she's come round with some soup,' I say. 'Nice. Kind. Maybe she's making a move on Harold with you away. If you had waited, maybe it would have all worked itself out. Maybe she would have taken him off your hands.'

People skills.

Honestly, I could be in marriage guidance.

The woman leans on the doorbell. She's not going to be deterred from her mission of mercy.

'D'you think there will be more than one contractor?' Léon whispers.

'No,' I say, watching the neighbour walk sadly down the path. She looks back up at the bedroom windows, a frown between her eyes. I am almost sure not. Almost. Something is making me twitchy. Something, somewhere in the back of my brain, the part that deals with fear. I can't put my finger on it, but something is not quite right.

By 9 p.m., the light is starting to fade. I draw the curtains. A bit early, but drawn curtains give freedom of movement. I go into the kitchen and let the roller blind down. The metal chain is warm under my fingers. The strip light flickers once, twice and comes on humming. There are dead flies trapped in the end.

I fill the kettle. An industrial-sized juicer sits beside it. I open cupboard doors looking for coffee. Box after box of herbal tea. There is a sad jar of hard Gold Blend in the back of a cupboard and that is it.

I turn the kettle off.

The shape of their lives is all here. A life for two: the buckets of water saved for the garden (him), the herbal teas (her), the biscuit tin (him), the juicer (her). If you could put coloured dots on their heads and trace their movements through a day, a week, a year, the pattern would look like an intricate interwoven tapestry, a dance of two entwined lives.

By ten o'clock, torpor has set in. It could still be hours. It depends how cheap she was, but *anyone*, even if it is their first time, will wait for darkness, wait for the target to go to bed, wait for the lights to go off.

There is some kind of naked blind date on the TV. A guy faces five girls behind partitions. The partitions lift from the bottom bit by bit, revealing naked feet, knees, thighs and so on. By the time the partitions have got as far as the waist, it is obvious who he will choose.

The wife shifts on the sofa. She is upright against the cushions. I wonder what she makes of naked blind date. Maybe it isn't her usual viewing.

'How did you two meet anyway?' I say. 'Did you kind of fall into it? Was it a whirlwind romance?' I look around at the florals. 'Maybe it was the unstoppable sexual chemistry?'

Two pairs of eyes stare at me from over the top of their gags.

Léon and Xiu sit side by side, heads together playing some game on their phones. Their knees are touching. The Cranes are lumped together, uncomfortable on the sofa. Their shoulders are touching.

Something is not right.

I think about body language and I think about a life for two and an intricate pattern of togetherness.

I mute the TV.

'How much was it?' I ask the wife. She speaks against the tights, her eyes wide. 'Give it to me in thousands,' I say. 'Five?'

She shakes her head.

'Ten?'

She shakes again.

'Not *twenty*?'

She nods.

No way.

The husband's eyes bulge. He is going to burst a blood vessel. He says something against his tights. I get up and pull down both their gags.

'*Twenty thousand?* You could have gone on a cruise,' he splutters.

'You have massively overpaid,' I tell her. 'That is ten times the going rate. Did you ask for something special?'

'You get what you pay for,' she says. 'I always buy the best.'

I bet she does. Pity there isn't a *Which?* survey on contractors.

It is not the wasted holiday opportunity that worries me, it is the amount. Twenty thousand on a single hit is a huge figure. We could be looking at the big league.

'Did he give a name, a contractor handle?'

She rolls her eyes and nods her head emphatically.

'Solo,' she says.

CHAPTER 23

We all stare at her. The cuckoo clock squawks in the hall.

'You two,' I point at Xiu and Léon. 'Out of here now. Out the front, walk away slowly, holding hands like you're a couple. Walk away and don't look back.'

'No way!' says Xiu. 'Solo. OMG. Firestorm royalty.'

And that is why you hire marines. That is why you hire people who will hop on one leg, because they do as they are bloody told.

I look at their faces. Xiu is vibrating with determination. Am I going to face Solo, unarmed, with civilians in the mix? Jesus. *Hope for the best, prepare for the worst*, Erik used to say. And I've come out with no preparation at all.

A bird shrieks outside the window. There is the fraction of a sound on the path and then the pop of a silencer at very close range. A popped cork, big clippers. Something crashes through the letterbox and I realise it is the sound of the front door lock being blown out and I am already moving.

All my predictions, all my expectations are wrong.

A competent contractor comes in the back. Waits for dark, waits for all the lights to go off, waits some more to make sure. Creeps in through the garden, breaks in through the kitchen, creeps their way upstairs.

The best don't bother with any of that. Normal rules don't apply. They walk up to the front door and blow the lock.

I look at the four frozen faces in the light from the TV and think about ammunition capable of blowing out a mortise lock and the gun that fired it. What would Solo carry? Maybe an M9, maybe a Glock 19, maybe the SIG Sauer P226. Whichever way you look at it, a gun chambered with cartridges capable of punching through plasterboard, capable of doing a lot of damage in a small room, crowded with people.

At the same time as I am thinking about his gun, the front part of my brain is anticipating his actions and my body is already moving. I know what he will do because it is what I would do.

He will have seen the TV flicker through the open doorway and will be coming down the hall, gun out. He will nudge the partly open door wide with the silencer and then he will be in the room shooting.

Not leaving me with many options.

I hit the deck, flatten myself on the carpet, jerk the door and throw. I have a split second to aim and only the white flickering light casting weird shadows on the hall wall to see by.

He is tall, much taller than I was expecting, my blade sinks into his right thigh, his arm jerks and the gun fires high and wide into the door jamb where I would have been if I was upright and not flat on my face.

I've got nothing, no advantage, maybe a little surprise and a whole load of disadvantages, chief of which are the roomful behind me and the loaded gun in front of me so I don't waste any time getting to my feet, but launch myself off the ground, straight at his body.

It is the trajectory of the second bullet that's worrying me. He's going to miss me coming in under his gun arm but where is the bullet going to end up? Hit him too slow and it is going to end up somewhere in the sitting room.

I push off, like a sprinter on the starting line, exploding forwards, charging him down. I need to put him on his back, down the hall. I hit him at speed, with the flat of my right shoulder, an explosive, mighty blow, velocity plus weight equals power and the second bullet hits plaster.

By rights he should go over but he doesn't, he jumps up and forwards using my momentum against me, a counter-intuitive move and for a moment it feels like a spear tackle, like I am going to drop him on his head but then he is twisting and falling forwards beside me. Head to toe.

The back of my heel smashes through the space where his head should be and hits nothing but air and I roll faster than the speed of fear. Someone reading a situation that quick has the presence of mind to hold on to his gun, which means it is even now coming off the floor. Not by much but it doesn't need to. A simple forty-five degrees will be enough.

He will brace his elbow, steady his arm and fire.

As I roll, I pull my knees up and they catch the barrel, knocking it upwards and the third bullet lands somewhere in the ceiling. I strike out with my elbow and get him on the ear but the angle is poor and there is no power behind the blow and then we are wrestling over and over in the tiny confined hall, crashing against the walls. A weird one-armed battle as I try to keep his gun arm clamped to his side and he tries to get the freedom to fire.

If I can't take an armed opponent one-on-one, I have no business being Head of Field.

In theory.

But the tiny hall closes me down, cramps my style, limits my options. The more confined the space, the less relevant the training and the more relevant factors such as weight and reach. Not that I think I am more trained than he is. Every muscle in his long sinewy body is screaming Special Forces. He gets the arm free and I hurl myself at it and then I am out of hands and he is rising above me and his left fist is coming full in my face, the size of a Thanksgiving turkey.

I twist at the last moment and take it on the side. Cheekbone and eye socket. Lights explode in my head and the panic hits as my brain clocks that I have just taken a disabling blow. Not a knockout but enough to change the odds. He grunts as his gun arm pulls free. Our faces are inches away from each other.

There is a moment when your training falls away and instinct kicks in, and in that desperate moment in no man's land, when everything is stripped away, you find out what your instincts are. Childhood shaped mine and they are rough and ready and dirty. No quarter and no surrender because children have no mercy. They have yet to learn. They don't know when to put the brakes on.

I have one weapon left and from a woman it is unexpected. I snap up at the waist and smack him on the bridge of the nose with my forehead. My brain jars in my skull, my teeth rattle. I can feel every molar in my head. He falls on me, the cartilage of his nose against my bare neck.

I look up over his shoulder, straight into Léon's face. His arm is raised. He is holding the pink table lamp. He brings it down hard on the back of Solo's head. The force punches through Solo, smacking me against the floor like a nail caught between the wall and a hammer. Fragments of china sting my face.

I shove, push and roll the dead weight off and lie flat on my back panting and staring at the ceiling, my ears ringing, shards of table lamp and slivers of glass in my hair.

CHAPTER 24

I should have expected Solo to be big. The pin-up Solo on the wall in the Pathologist's office looked like a cross between Thor and Tarzan. Massive. About three hundred pounds of honed muscle. The reality is similar but different. He is tall, really tall and strong. Not stacked like a body builder but hard and sinewy. His cheekbones are sharp, his face looks carved. I sit back on my haunches, staring.

There is something very familiar about the cheekbones. I hold my hands in front of his face, blocking the bottom half. I dig my phone out of my pocket and turn on the torch. His eyes are rolled back in his head, but the irises are just visible. Blue and brown.

Blue on the left, brown on the right.

'Duct tape,' I shout at Léon. 'Fast as you can.'

Léon is out of the hall and yanking drawers in the kitchen before I have sat back. Cutlery clinks, heavy items hit the floor. He is turning out. No sound of drawer slamming which is good. It means he understands the urgency.

Bolts screech, keys clink, the kitchen door opens and the air changes as outside invades. A far away siren, an owl hoots. Cool air travels across the kitchen down the hall, where I crouch, sweaty and wide-eyed. My senses strain along the path to the prefab garage following Léon, guessing where he has gone.

I listen to the breathing. The panicked shallow breaths of the husband and wife in the next room. The deep, slow breathing from Solo. Nothing from Xiu. Her watchful face is right beside me, alert and serious.

Running feet on the path.

Léon stands in the doorway, a roll of black masking tape in one hand and brown in the other. The huge body stirs, I snatch the duct tape and start yanking at the end, all fingers and thumbs.

More haste, less speed.

'Scissors,' I tell him.

Léon is gone and back again. The duct tape screeches as it unrolls and the body moves again. The breathing changes, speeds up, snatches through the broken nose.

He is waking up.

Xiu shifts to help, pulling his arms away from his body, shuffling the wrists clear for the duct tape. I wrap the shiny black tape round and round. Maybe ten times. Léon makes the cut and I turn to the ankles.

'Not enough,' he says, gesturing at the wrists.

And he is right. Not nearly enough for a decent hold but I am in a hurry to disable the feet. As Xiu shifts her weight, Solo's knee comes up. I move into the blow. Closer equals harder, but I get to choose where it lands. I take it on the ball of the shoulder and grunt with the pain. Ball joint to ball joint, nicely clear of the collar bone. Xiu throws herself on his head and Léon throws himself across his legs and for a moment it is a crazy, struggling mass of limbs.

He gets a wrist free. I throw myself across him and my head smacks the skirting board. There is a thump and all the tension leaves his body. I look up. Xiu's right arm is raised, elbow high and it dawns on me that my new recruit has hit him and knocked him out. A difficult, precise strike.

'Sorry,' she says. 'It was just getting too close there.'

I don't say anything. I carry on working, binding the knees some more and then moving back on to the wrists, until it is done and he is trussed up like an Egyptian mummy.

I sit back on my heels.

'Where did you learn a move like that?'

She shrugs.

The gun is on its side against the wall. I pick it up. A SIG Sauer P226 chambered for the .357 SIG, a high-velocity, high-penetration 9mm cartridge. More than capable of punching through plasterboard. I stick it, barrel first, down the back of my waistband. A really stupid place to carry a gun. There is no safety on a P226, just a decocker. Pull the trigger by accident and it goes off in your pants.

Xiu and Léon get to their feet and we look down at our prize, sleeping the dead sleep of the unconscious.

Solo. The contractor second only to the Guardsman. I'm not going to ask him just a few basic questions about how Firestorm works. He is going to know a lot more than that.

He is going to know where to find the Guardsman.

'Find a vehicle, preferably a van, and bring it round to the garden gate,' I tell Léon. 'There is an alley that runs all along the back.'

He nods, his eyes full of understanding and is gone, quiet as a cat burglar, out through the kitchen and down the path.

A ringtone booms out in the silence. My ears were straining, taking up the slack from my other senses and my heart jumps right out of my ribcage and I have to put a hand on the wall as Darth Vader's theme tune fills the hall.

Der der der der, der dee der, der dee der.

Xiu is patting her pockets.

Jesus.

'Did you not have the sense to put your phone on silent?'

'Sorry,' she says. 'It's my mum.' She rummages around in her dungarees and brings up a Nokia brick, not the smartphone she was gaming on a minute ago. 'I'll have to take it or she'll worry.'

'Fine,' I say, leaning against the wall and folding my arms. 'Don't let me stop you.'

She heads up the hallway to the front door and leans her forehead against the glass, keeping clear of the shards of wood from the splintered lock.

'It's not a great time, Mum,' she says. 'I'm a bit busy. I'm with the Boss.'

Pause.

'Yes, I'm staying safe.'

Pause.

'I'm working late.' She turns to me and pulls a massive eye roll, a 'what can you do?' face.

'Look I'll call you later, OK?' she says and cuts the call without waiting for a reply.

'Sorry,' she says. 'She worries.'

'Why the different phone?'

She rolls her eyes again. It is the most stupid question she has ever heard in the history of stupid adult questions. 'Find My Phone,' she says. 'Duh.'

I check Solo. He is still out cold, his breathing ragged.

'Just watch him,' I say.

I go into the dark kitchen. Tea towels hang from a rail on the front of the cooker. I lay one out on the table, open the freezer, empty ice onto it and hold it to my face. I am going to have one hell of a black eye. My forehead will be fine. There isn't a lot of soft tissue on a forehead. I roll my shoulder backwards and then forwards. The joint aches.

I stand in the open kitchen doorway. A night bird calls. Far off, I can hear traffic.

The air is soft on my face and full of the sweet, sweet smell of night. Jasmine and honeysuckle and lilac and old roses. It reminds me of a graveyard and dark shadows arcing in the bright sunlight and a smell like a butcher's shop of blood going off. I can see a stone angel with roses around her neck and a grave dripping with ivy.

A car lurches into the alley. It stops on the other side of the gate, the engine dies and there is silence. He is waiting to give the neighbours time to look out of their windows if they are going to. *Nothing to see here.*

He will wait a bit longer to give them time to go back to bed. Exactly as it should be. I count the seconds down in my head.

There are no tools kept in this van overnight.

Good to know.

Léon is in the driver's seat. He releases the van's back doors and I throw them wide. A black, empty interior, the floor ridged. A workman's van maybe or a salesman's. Nothing left as an incentive to break in. The air is stale. It smells of rubber and just a hint of iron filing.

Blood.

My imagination is working overtime.

I leave the doors open and head back up the path. Léon is silent behind me. In the kitchen, the fridge hums. The time flashes green on the cooker.

'How did you get the keys?' I say.

'Through the letterbox.'

Through the van owner's door. Textbook.

'Good skills.'

His smile is white.

In the hall, we stand looking down at our unconscious package. He seems to have grown, filling the space, skirting board to skirting board.

'We are going to have to carry him.'

'Can't we just drag him?' whispers Xiu.

'To the back door, after that we have to lift him. Too much noise. The neighbours are probably on a hair trigger.'

Léon and I grab a foot and we drag and haul him along the carpet and into the kitchen. The duct tape squeaks on the lino, sticky in the heat.

'OK,' I say. 'Let's try lifting him in here.'

Léon goes to his shoulders, I take the feet end and Xiu hovers with some idea of supporting his middle.

'Help Léon,' I say. 'The bulk of the weight is at his end.'

They take a shoulder each and we lift.

'*Mon Dieu*,' says Léon.

'Blimey,' says Xiu.

We put him down again.

I open the kitchen door and we take deep breaths and flex our knees and bend and lift and edge him out feet first, shuffling and swearing. It is not the weight, it is the awkwardness. We heft him down the path, stubbing toes and cursing.

Halfway along, we have to put him down again to get a better grip. I scan the bedroom curtains on either side of us.

I flip the van door wide with my shoulder and we swing and heave and grunt. Léon climbs in and hauls him up, his hands under Solo's arms.

'*Dieu*,' he says again.

Solo is still out cold, which is just as well. How do serial killers manage? The sheer weight of a dead body.

The van doors slam and we climb in. Léon in the driving seat, Xiu next to him and me on the outside.

'Are we just going to leave them?' Léon says. 'Tied up?'

Hell.

I go back up the garden path though the kitchen door and into the sitting room.

She is holding Harold, cradling his head against her as far as she is able with bound hands. Their faces are shiny and I can't tell whether it is sweat or tears. They are whimpering against the tights. Close quarters combat is a terrifying thing as a bystander, uncontrolled and violent.

I am out of the chintz sitting room and up the stairs in four strides. I burst into the master bedroom and stare at the thing that I saw on his bedside cabinet. I saw but I didn't understand.

I pull his drawer open. Industrial quantities of morphine. The paraphernalia of chemotherapy.

Twenty thousand? You could have gone on a cruise.

Not we. You.

I drag down the gags and start cutting through their wrist ties with the kitchen scissors.

I sit back on my heels and look up at them.

'I'm sorry,' I say. 'I didn't realise.'

Silence.

'How much time have you got left?'

'A couple of months,' he says. 'Four at most.' He picks up his wife's hand. 'I am ready now.'

'He wanted it to be quick,' she says, not looking at him.

I swallow at the weight of love in front of me. The life for two, the house, the garden, thirty years of Christmas decorations, that is about to be a life for one.

'Are you a contractor?' she asks.

'No.'

'But you kill people?'

I get to my feet. At the door, I look back. 'Yes,' I say.

CHAPTER 25

'Go,' I say, and we drive in silence.

I stare out of the window thinking about an interwoven life for two. The street lights dazzle, my night vision leaving contrails behind my eyes. Snatches of street sound fly by.

I turn to look into the dark interior behind me. For a split second I can see nothing, then my vision adapts and I get the slight shine off the duct tape and a mummified form comes into view.

The clock on the dash reads 12:10 a.m. The A2 is empty, the Blackwall Tunnel must be running smoothly.

I take my phone out and weigh it. I don't have to do it myself. There is someone who can do it for me. An expert. I think about calling him and the cold, sick dread rises. I put the phone back in my pocket.

'Come off here,' I tell Léon.

He yanks a hard left, down the slip road and turns east, parallel to the river.

We go past Woolwich dockyard, past the Royal Arsenal, take a left and then a right into a rundown light industrial estate. Chained gates and barbed wire on most of the units tell a story of optimistic over expansion and a ninety per cent plus vacancy rate.

Léon drops his speed to a crawl and looks at me.

'Keep going,' I say.

We run beside metal fencing. Beyond there are mountains of roughly cubed metal. A recycling plant. We turn in and drive down between the warehouses. Bays as high and wide as container lorries are full of sorted rubbish.

Plastics, metals, tyres.

Halfway along, one is almost empty.

I jerk my head and Léon drives in, nose first.

'Get out.'

They bolt out of the van. Léon first, Xiu scrambling after him.

I slam the door behind me.

The smell is indescribable. A wall of rotting rubbish, on top of ancient rotting rubbish, cut with burning rubber from the incinerator.

The night is quiet, the sounds of traffic far off. Forgotten corners of London.

I breathe in the smell. I breathe out.

I know the theory of course. I know the stages: pressure points, suffocation techniques, permanent damage, psychological injuries – eyeball removal, castration for a guy.

I know the theory, I just don't want to do it. I'm not good with pain. Other people's. I have to end it. Mine? I'm not too bad. I go somewhere in my head and it takes quite a lot to get me out of it.

I remember reading this study during training, into whether male interrogation subjects respond more favourably when threatened with castration or blindness. I read the ponderous, methodical notes and it made me want to heave. And the long and the short of it was that after many, no doubt messy experimentations, the testers were obliged to conclude there wasn't much in it either way.

Everard has no time for such methods – messy, impractical, inconclusive, almost as bad as waterboarding. I went to his lectures during training, he was a divisional head in those days. A rising star. Now he is the best. Or the worst, depending on your point of view.

I press my thumbs into the corners of my eyes.

Breathe in. Breathe out.

I throw open the rear doors.

He is awake. Eyes glitter. He felt the van stop and now he is braced, waiting his chance.

I climb in the back and pull the doors to behind me. It is about ninety degrees. I can smell him in the confined space. Fresh sweat and adrenaline.

He watches me clamber over. I put one knee on his chest and one knee on the metal. The ridges on the van floor bite. I wince and shift and in that split second, he bends at the waist using the same move on me, eighty pounds of forehead coming fast.

I take it on the solar plexus and slam his head to the floor. Hard but not too hard. I hold my knife above his face where he can see it. The white glimmers in the half light, like a ghost knife.

'Cut it out,' I tell him. 'This blade is sharp enough to slice off a finger. Do not move a hair, do not move a fraction of an inch. I want to talk to you, not slit your throat.'

I lean, heavy on his chest, holding his chin in place and working the tip of the blade into the space between his lips. When I have opened up a gap about two inches wide, he sucks in a huge great gasp of air and I know I have found the right place.

'Hello, Solo.'

'Hello, Winter,' he says.

I spin the blade on my palm, squatting on his chest, feet flat to the floor.

'There is no reason this has to go any further,' I say. 'We are both professionals. We have probably had similar training. We both know the order of escalation. All I want is a chat.'

He thinks about this. His breathing is laboured through his bloody nose.

'What do you want?'

'I want the Guardsman.'

'What makes you think I know the Guardsman?'

'You put up surveillance cameras for him the day I tried to take him out.'

He is silent.

'How did he contact you?'

'By phone.'

'Someone else came. Why was that?'

'What d'you know about the Guardsman?' he asks.

'Nothing,' I tell him.

'You are a dead woman.'

'I get that a lot,' I say, 'and yet somehow I'm still here.'

'The Guardsman will eat you alive for this,' he says. 'Take your skin off with a spoon and feed it to you.'

'He can try.'

He laughs, an awful sound, blood bubbles through his nose. 'If that's it, we can get right along to the next stage. You don't have the guts. I can see it in your eyes.'

I know the move of course. The psychological power play between captor and captive is like a game of chess and this is the equivalent of the Latvian gambit. Put up or shut up. An in-your-face challenge.

There's only one countermove.

I spin the blade and stab down behind me into his thigh. The tip hits bone.

His whole body tenses in a silent scream, cord veins rise on his neck. His fists are clenched, his breathing guttural through his broken nose.

I turn the knife and the scream hisses out, strangled on the way up his throat until it is nothing but a choked off groan. I adjust my position, straddling his knees and push the handle of the knife through a ninety-degree angle towards the horizontal, widening the wound.

He screams, loud and echoing in the tin can. I have got past his self-control.

There is a lot of blood in a leg. The blade is well clear of the femoral artery, but it is still gushing. Left unchecked, he will bleed out in a couple of hours. I grasp the knife; it is slippery under my hand.

'Is that it,' he says. 'Is that all you've got?'

'I can keep this up all night,' I say. I pull another knife, swap hands and hold it an inch above his right eyeball. 'You know how this goes.'

'Eyes, not testicles? The Guardsman is big into eyes,' he says. 'You'll have that to talk about.'

I brace my hand against his forehead. He stares up at the knife, unflinching, as it hangs like the sword of Damocles above his eyeball and all at once I know that I am not going to break him, all I am going to do is break myself.

There is more to running a department.

I pull off him and sit down with my back to the metal side, my elbows on my knees, my blade loose between my fingers.

'What did he mean by *the final countdown*? Is something planned for the G20? What experiments is he running?'

Solo stares at the ridged metal ceiling.

There is something about his words that doesn't fit. That strikes a discordant note.

The Guardsman will eat you alive for this, take your skin off with a spoon and feed it to you. Once you get past the imagery, it is a curious thing to say. Suggestive of extreme anger, suggestive of some kind of personal involvement. What my old boss Erik would have called 'skin in the game'.

I think about the Contractor the Guardsman sent as a substitute. The one with the cellophane room. *Do you work for the Guardsman?* he had asked. Another curious thing to say.

I think about Fortnum & Mason and anomaly algorithms and who would be in a position to see them and a lot of things fall into place. Now I understand why the Guardsman doesn't have to worry about the Administrator finding out he is sub-contracting. He *is* the Administrator. And that makes sense, in a way. You don't want some tech geek in charge, you want the biggest psycho in town.

Solo turns his head to look at me. 'I told you,' he says. 'You don't have the stomach for it.'

'The Guardsman is the Firestorm Administrator.'

Solo goes back to staring at the ceiling.

The final countdown. Not words spoken by some random contractor, but by the Firestorm Administrator. A man with access to a lot of firepower. A man with an army behind him.

I get out my phone and touch the number.

Everard answers on the first ring.

'Hello, Winter.'

'Are you up?'

'Yes,' he says.

'I'm bringing in a subject now.'

'Training?'

'No.'

Everard is silent.

'I'll see you in twenty minutes,' I say and cut the call.

Solo watches me, his eyes glinting in the darkness.

'Before, with the knife,' I say, '*that* was me not having the nerve.'

I close my eyes and lean my head against the metal sides and feel the prick in my sinuses at the thought of the decision I have just made.

CHAPTER 26

Night-time London is quiet but not deserted. Groups of lads shout on pavements. Girls shriek. Snatches of music fly out of open car windows and are gone. The bright lights of the Bank junction hurt my eyes. Xiu stares straight ahead. She and Léon had got back in the van without a word.

We pull up at the titanium bollards guarding the underground ramp into GCHQ. They could stop a Challenger tank. The same bureaucrats who commissioned a study of interrogation methods probably got involved in their design. They probably raised concerns about an open entrance into the heart of the building. They couldn't allow it. A psychological weakness, a breach in the fortified perimeter. So they decided to fortify the ramp itself.

The upshot is a titanium tube stretching deep into the core of the building like a metal condom. A tube split into containment pods and littered with grills. It has got to the point where the entrance ramp is the most fortified part of the building.

But even the humourless bureaucrats could concede there might be situations where fast, covert entry to the building might be needed. Sensitive material or sensitive personnel you don't want hanging about on Cheapside. So the initial stage is made to be fast. The titanium bollards that could stop a tank are for show, they slide right down into the concrete as you approach.

We swing down the ramp, turn round the corner out of sight and pull up in front of the blast doors. Behind us, the bollards rise silently out of the ground.

Security are there, ready and waiting, MP5s held loose. I raise my palm for the biometrics and catch their expression. My hands are sticky, my fingers glossy under the strobe lights. I wipe them on my jeans. Back and front and back again. Security stare.

Biometrics done, I get back in, the blast doors open and we drive into the containment chamber, a giant X-ray machine to analyse the contents of the van and everyone in it.

It is ten long, hot minutes before we drive down into the underground parking, rows of black cars on either side, lift shaft at the end.

A familiar figure is waiting, leaning against a pillar. Simon has seen my locator approach.

'Back it up,' I tell Léon. 'Left lift, door to door.'

Léon swings a wide arc and squints in his side mirror as he reverses.

Simon pulls himself off the wall as we come to a stop and I get out. The air is cool and stale, a steady ambient temperature this far below ground. Someone moves in the shadows. Pansy Face. Her shiny ponytail is dishevelled. How nice, how romantic. She was keeping him company while he waited up.

He stares at the van, out of the loop. 'Why the van?'

'I brought something back,' I say going round to the back doors. I can barely bring myself to say it.

'What?'

Behind us the lift doors open and two burly medics in white coats come out, rolling a metal hospital trolley between them. They have the thickset look of nurses in an institution. The trolley stops just short of the van. They already have their latex gloves on.

Simon looks at them and enlightenment dawns. He opens his mouth to speak but I am ahead of him.

'Get her out of here,' I say, pointing at Pansy Face. 'Now.'

He stands for a moment then walks away.

One of the medics opens the rear doors of the van and climbs in.

I crane to see what he is doing. A syringe flashes in the dark and all the tension leaves the mummified body.

'What was that?' I demand.

The medic in the van looks up in surprise.

The other medic shuffles over, the trolley comes hard alongside and together they shove and heave and heft until Solo is squarely on the metal. A lot less shoving and heaving and hefting than it was for us.

It is our first good look at our captive. We stare down at him under the bright underground lighting.

Fairish hair, 210 pounds, dark suit, white shirt with an open neck. Not dressed for combat, but why would he be? As far as he was concerned, the target was willing. His eyes are open, but the pupils are wide.

Simon is back.

'Simon, meet Solo,' I say, turning to face him.

He looks round at Xiu and Léon and back to my swollen face. 'Shit,' he says as he clocks my injuries and fills in the last few hours.

'Yeah,' I say, following the trolley into the lift. 'We can worry about the risk assessment later.'

The lift pings and the medics back the trolley out. The detainment floor corridor is bright. TCP disinfectant flavours the air. Somewhere, on the edge of hearing, a heart monitor beeps.

Everard is waiting, halfway down the corridor, his hands dangling from his sleeves, loose and awkward like they are not attached to him. The metal trolley clanks, the wheels clatter and we come to a halt.

Xiu and Léon hang back, teenage bravado and smart remarks gone. They don't shuffle, they don't sniff, they don't pick at their nails or look at their phones, they are still as stone. Here, standing in the corridor in a white lab coat, is a man who makes the hairs on the back of your neck lift. His eyes flick past me, checking them out and I get an urge to hide them from view, and then the blue eyes come back to me. He has analysed them, assessed them and dismissed them. They are not relevant.

He takes a pen from his top pocket and spins it slowly. I watch the long fingers. Any minute now they will be swabbing, preparing the soft, pale skin in the inside of the elbow for an IV. They don't look loose and awkward anymore; they look competent, skilled, merciless. My heart rate accelerates.

Breathe.

'He's all yours, Doctor,' I say.

For a moment, I think Everard is going to gloat, to say something that will change my mind and see me ramming my fist in his face. But he just nods through to the interview room.

The trolley wheels screech, rubber on lino, as they make the right-angle turn. The usually empty interview room is crowded with medical machinery. Three IV drips, a heart tracer, a blood pressure monitor and two other machines, function unknown.

Everard bends over the body, he and the medics murmur, he nods. He is checking what they've given. A pin light appears in his hand. He lifts eyelids.

He holds his hand out. He doesn't say anything, but the medics seem to know what he wants. Medical shears cut through the duct tape and trousers in seconds. Slice. Slice. Slice. Done. Quick and efficient. The socks go the same way. Soon Solo will be naked, laid out on a slab for Everard to play with.

His mouth purses at the sight of the hole in Solo's leg. It bleeds sluggishly.

'Was that you?' He gestures at the hole, his lip curling at the incompetence, the very idea of sticking a knife into someone and hoping that would work.

'I want him alive Everard, do you understand?'

His perfect sculpted lip curls again. 'Of course,' he looks at me. 'Are you staying?'

I shake my head.

'What do you need from him?'

'Everything. Call me when he's ready.'

He glances down at the man on the trolley, bare-legged, muscles like ropes. 'It will be quick,' he says. 'With his muscle tone.' Everard's eyes are a bleak Siberian wilderness.

Quick is a relative term. The longest anyone has ever held out against Everard is five hours and ten minutes and that was two hours longer than the next person. The top three slots on the endurance leader board are all held by women. I have always wondered why.

Everard attributes it to muscular-skeletal differences. Men's bodies naturally have a lower fat content and fat cells are wasted cells as far as Everard is concerned – they can't be made to feel agony. Sometimes I wonder if it goes back to the days when women were giving birth in caves and the ability to endure in silence was a key survival trait.

He raises a hand to my face and stops just short of touching.

'You should get that seen to,' he says, his breath whisper light on my cheek, his blue eyes staring into mine with all the intimacy of someone who has broken your mind.

I take a last look at Solo on the metal trolley. His eyes are wide. I want to tell him to cooperate, that he will break easily enough and that there is no point in holding out. I want it to be over for him, to help him get through the next few minutes. I want to tell him Everard practises 'topping up', the interrogation technique that takes the subject beyond breaking point and then keeps going that little bit longer, just to be sure.

'I want the absolute minimum,' I say.

'Of course.'

I turn on my heel. The exit of a coward, knowing full well that Everard will do exactly as he pleases and that my words do nothing but appease my conscience.

CHAPTER 27

They are waiting in medical, in the triage room just off reception. Léon sits at a table while a doctor uses something like superglue on the side of his head. Xiu is looking at her Nokia brick. Simon is pacing.

'That was Everard,' I say unnecessarily.

They nod solemnly.

'Winter…' Simon begins, his grey eyes troubled.

'Just leave it. I know what you are going to say. The ends justify the means.'

The disappointment on his face stings.

The doctor sticks butterfly plasters over the superglue. Part of me wonders when Léon got hurt. Did a piece of china catch him when the lamp smashed? Or a shard of glass?

Another white coat appears with an ice pack and a couple of sedatives. I take the ice pack but shake my head at the pills. The last thing I need is sleep. I wonder what my tracker is picking up. How much trauma does it detect? Is Alek watching now? Does he know I have been in a fight?

The backs of Léon's hands are covered in grazes. I can't imagine how he got them and then I remember him holding Solo down in the narrow hall while I bound his legs. He didn't let go.

Simon hands me a black coffee. I put the ice pack down and wrap my cold fingers around the cup. Steam swirls round my face like a coffee-flavoured facial. The surface shudders like ripples in a dark pool. Drums in the deep. Like in *Jurassic Park* when the T-Rex is coming. I stare down, my brain slow.

It is my hand shaking. I put the cup down on the table.

The interview suites are soundproofed.

In theory.

More or less.

Pretty much.

Léon flinches with every choked off cry from up the corridor. Simon's face is tense, his shoulders raised. Xiu's eyes are huge in her face. Her mouth has all but disappeared. I turn to go and then I turn back and then I turn to go again.

I stare blindly at their watching faces. Xiu and Léon round-eyed and silent. They are all looking at me. Waiting. Waiting for me to say something, to intervene. This was never a decision I wanted to make.

There is more to running a department.

I don't ever want to be the kind of boss who finds this easy.

The ends justify the means.

What an easy, pat saying.

'So, how's your first day been?' Simon asks Xiu in a pitiful attempt at humour that falls flat on its unfunny face. 'The hours suck, right?'

Footsteps walk down the corridor – slow, measured, heavy. They cross reception. We all stare. One of the burly medics appears in the doorway.

'Dr Everard is ready for you now,' he says.

I follow him up the long, white corridor past the empty interview suites.

Breathe in, breathe out.

The open doorway ahead is crowded with hot, complicated sounds. A heart rate monitor screams.

I walk in.

Everard, white coat just as before, a naked man on an operating table, metal restraints, IVs attached to the inside of elbows, electrodes on the chest linked up to the heart monitor, a metal gumshield to prevent him choking on his tongue.

And the wild, crazed eyes of a madman broken on the wheel of pain. Broken till he would kill his mother, kill his children, to make it stop.

Quick, just as Everard promised.

The same medic removes the tongue guard and the mouth opens and the screaming starts. I picture the last few minutes, the screaming and then the choked sound as the tongue guard went in. My stomach heaves, my hands shake but my face is hard. I made my decision in the back of the van.

Everard hands me a square plastic box the size of a big matchbox. I look down at it.

'Press to stop,' he says patiently. 'Press to go.'

I press.

The screaming stops. Just like that.

Wild eyes turn my way as I approach the bed.

'Let's start with your phone.' I hold his phone up in front of his face, fingers poised on the keypad. 'Code?' My hand is shaking.

Silence.

I press the button. The screaming starts. I count to ten, the heart monitor shrieks, I count another ten and press the stop.

He chokes it out.

I tap it in and the phone opens. I turn away while I search, leaning against the door frame where I can't see Everard with his loose hands or the blank faces of the medics or the broken man on the trolley. My heart is pounding like I have been doing circuits. My eyes blur.

Blink and focus.

I close the phone down, slide the power off, open it up again. It is the same. It is a completely empty handset. Even Safari has been disabled.

I check the call log, the text messages. The phone has never made a call, never received a message. It is nothing but the Firestorm app. And that makes sense. He doesn't carry a normal phone with him in case something goes wrong. His normal phone will have his life in it. Will have messages from his friends, will be easily traced. A real pro would always have two phones.

I hold the phone up above his face for the Firestorm iris scan. His knuckles are white on the edge of the trolley.

Firestorm opens.

Harold Crane.
Pending.

I flick through his account. The Harold Crane bidding history, a huge job in Moscow in a couple of days. A particular time frame is specified and I whistle at the size of the fee until I see the target. Sergei Stanislav, Head of the Bratva, Moscow's Mafia.

There is nothing from the Guardsman. I scroll to a week earlier to be sure but still nothing.

'Where is your other phone?'

Silence.

I press the button and the screaming and counting to ten starts all over again.

A minute later I am running down the corridor.

CHAPTER 28

The stairwell is echoing and silent. The black van sits where we left it, back door hanging wide, a roll of duct tape on its tailgate.

I fire up a Service Merc and barrel up the steep ramp to Security. They jump aside, the huge metal cylinders roll down and I am out into the night.

I wind down my window, sucking in the air, glad to be getting answers, glad to be out in the night and not stuck in a room listening to someone scream.

A group of guys stagger down the pavement, leaning on each other and shouting, so drunk they have no clue how loud they are. One of them is bare-chested. I punch in the address and put my foot down, overtaking the refuse lorries trundling along the curb.

Down Cheapside. Right at St Pauls, past St Barts Hospital and hard right onto the cobbles of Smithfield Market. London's biggest raw meat market is already open for business. I slalom between lorries hanging with carcasses, left, right, make a turn and I am on a narrow, residential street full of early Georgian houses.

I pull up half on the double yellow, half on the pavement, and sit for a second looking at my destination. Of all the places in all the world that Solo could live, this is the last place I would have expected – a quiet, expensive, residential street barely a mile from GCHQ.

The front door is black and dark and glossy with polished brass work and a period lantern. It is like arriving at 221B Baker Street. I look both ways, but the night street is deserted. There is something very perfect about it. A perfect example of early Georgian housing, white cyclamen and neat box balls in the window boxes.

Three Banham locks. No messing. I open the top and then the bottom then slide the key in the middle lock, hold my breath and turn. The alarm sounds the moment I break the circuit. Not the siren, just the beep that warns the homeowner to hurry up and put the code in.

I stare at the keypad wondering what I am going to do if Solo has given me the wrong code. It is an old-fashioned physical circuit. Break the circuit by opening the door and the bell sounds. Cut the power and it moves to battery and the bell sounds. No phone line out to disconnect, no wireless opportunities, nothing to hack. Simple but actually pretty effective, an analogue solution in a digital age.

I punch in the code and the beeping stops. I breathe out and stand listening in the silence. The hall is narrow with stairs rising up to the first floor. An ornate gilt mirror hangs on one wall, a long thin hall table in front of it.

The door on the right is the sitting room. Antique furniture and velvet upholstery. The street light shines orange through the open shutters.

I go from room to room. The place looks like it has been styled by Ralph Lauren. The home of a wealthy, cultured man. I picture him as I last saw him, naked on a metal trolley, and speed up. No landline, no computer, no router. What I took for a discreet TV cabinet turned out to hold a set of 1940s cocktail glasses on a silver salver with matching shaker and half a fresh lemon.

The desk has a street map of Moscow spread out on it. It looks out of place in the pristine order.

I flick through a neat pile of post. His name is Jim Grant.
Who are you, Jim Grant?

I wonder where he came from to live like this. What was his training? How did he get started? Was he going to carry on forever or retire at the top of his game? He will probably end up in a textbook in years to come with celebrity status and no one will remember his real name, only his famous alter ego.

I search from the bottom to the top and there is no sign of the phone, or of a laptop of any kind. Not even the trace of something removed – a line where a cable might have run, a charging dock, an empty but worn socket.

There is a stash somewhere. Paperwork, passports, a laptop, phones. I haven't found it.

I pull out my phone.

Simon answers first ring. 'Everything OK?' He is tense.

'I'm at Solo's place. Put Everard on.'

A few seconds and Everard is on the line. Simon must have run.

'Winter.' There is more warmth than usual in the Siberian wastes and the implications of that make me heave.

'I can't find it, Everard. I need to know specifically.'

The phone moves through the air, passing back to Simon and the screaming starts again before Simon cuts the call. Everard was so confident of getting an answer he left the line open.

I stand at the sitting room window looking out at the orange glow of the street. Light shines out from the window below me. A basement flat. Servant quarters back in the day. I go out of the door and head down the short flight to the front door below.

I lean on the bell, checking the time.

4 a.m.

There is a shuffling step, the clinking of chains, the drawing of bolts and the door opens. A woman in her fifties stands there in a dressing gown. She has a glass of water in her hand. She lives below one of the world's most famous hitmen and relies on a bolt to keep her safe.

'Yes?' she says.

'Sorry to disturb you,' I say, showing her my government ID. 'There was an incident on the corner of your street and Smithfield at 3.45 a.m. this morning. Did you see anything that could help us with our enquiries?'

Indignation vanishes in the face of drama. She will probably put it on Facebook.

'No,' she says. 'I was up getting a drink, but I didn't see anything. What happened?'

'I'm not at liberty to discuss the details but I can confirm that it is not, at this time, a homicide investigation.'

Her eyes are huge with interest. She clutches the dressing gown closed at the neck.

Not, at this time.

'What happened?'

'Who lives in the house above?'

'He's never in,' she says. 'I'd be surprised if he was there now. He won't have seen anything.'

'Does he work nights?'

'No, nothing like that.' She scowls at the idea that anyone on her street could be a shift worker. 'He travels a lot.'

I bet he does.

'His girlfriend might have seen something?' she says. 'You just missed her.'

'What, at 4 a.m.?'

'She works strange hours.'

That could have been awkward.

'Thank you,' I say. 'You've been very helpful.'

'You're young for a detective,' she says. 'Good for you.'

The phone rings, shocking in the silence. 'Excuse me,' I say, turning away to take it.

Everard has the answer.

'I want him alive,' I say. 'Do you understand me?'

Everard cuts the call.

I take the stairs three at a time.

A moment later I am holding Solo's phone in my hand. I dial Everard for the passcode. No answer.

I dial again.

Still no answer.

Something lurches in my gut and I am back out through Solo's front door, chucking my prize on the front seat beside me and craning over my shoulder as I back up the narrow street. I straighten up outside the market and put my foot down.

The leap forward from a standing start slams me back in my seat.

I slew round St Pauls and hit Cheapside at seventy miles per hour. The brakes screech on the GCHQ ramp. I pull up, leap out of the car, leaving the door wide and hurtle for the exit ramp.

Security shout behind me.

Down and round, down and round, leaping off the walls. I sprint into the underground car park. Black Service Mercs gleam. My handprint won't open the stairwell without the biometric sign-in. I pull Solo's gun, aim six inches from the lock and empty it. The lock clicks open and I am in the stairwell handing off the wall, leaping down the flights.

The detainment level is full of running feet and noise. I bolt down the end of the corridor.

Simon is standing, flushed with anger, up against the wall. White coats have their backs to me. The body on the trolley jackknifes with the shocks. Solo is lying on his back, his eyes staring.

Everard shakes his head.

The heart trace is flat.

Tortured to death.

I turn to Everard. I haven't got the words.

I backhand him with my right fist. A heavy, dirty, knuckle blow out of the lexicon of street fighting. Frustration boiling over into action. Words, even if I could find them, are not enough.

His head comes slowly back round, dark crimson seeping from one nostril and I drop him with a knuckle strike and he is over, quick and clean.

He pushes himself off the floor by an elbow and touches a hand to the blood. It smears red on his fingertip. His cheekbone thickens and swells under my gaze.

He gets slowly to his feet and starts to stack his metal instrument tray.

Tidying up.

I kick the stainless steel, smashing it upwards. It soars through the air, flashing bright as a mirror. Syringes, needles, tweezers go flying and Everard just stands there, hands dangling from his sleeves while the tools of his trade crash and clatter to the floor around him.

THE GUARDSMAN

VI

The Guardsman felt cold. Cold and sick and that was unusual.

Winter.

The name hissed out from between stiff lips.

When people found out Solo was dead, Firestorm would be a laughing stock.

The Guardsman thought about what had been done about Winter so far and knew with a cold Germanic clarity that nothing would be enough this time.

This time she had to die and only the Boss could do it. And that gave everyone a problem. How did you find the most wanted man in the world and how did you get Winter to him?

You set a trap. But would it work? There were a lot of variables.

The Guardsman drummed her nails on the table and picked up her phone.

CHAPTER 29

4 days to go...

I walk up the pavement. I watch the gates. No one comes. The gravestones through the wrought iron railings are sleeping in the morning sunshine.

The trees are still damp, the grass laced with a covering of dew that will burn off in an hour or two. The air is full of song. As if every bird in South East London is singing, piercing sweet about how good it is to be alive.

Early morning smells like mown grass.

They were waiting for me in Control's office, Beth shiny with groomed perfection, her glossy hair swept up in a French twist, not a hair out of place.

An unofficial disciplinary hearing.

Control nodded at Beth as if to say, 'take it away' and I understood. He was pissed, but my sin was one of omission. Not what I had done, but the fact that Control wanted me doing something else.

'Take a seat, Winter,' Beth said.

I walked over to the window. The Bank junction was heaving.

'You are on suspension,' she said. 'You may not engage in field work or carry arms.'

'Sure,' I said.

Anger flushed her face.

'You think you can take down Firestorm on your own?' she said. 'Your arrogance puts everyone you know at risk. What can you possibly hope to achieve by baiting an organisation the size of Firestorm? This will get the attention of the people at the top, people who have had other things on their minds, point out what a pain in the neck you still are.'

Control shifted in his chair and suddenly it was clear. He had been letting me get away with it all along, turning a blind eye, hoping I would stir something up.

I looked at Control.

You knew and you let me carry on.

I knew and I let it go, hoping for results.

Beth powered on, oblivious to our silent exchange. For a psychologist, she was slow on the uptake.

'The Guardsman is the Firestorm Administrator,' I said. 'Not some random contractor. Nine days ago, he was talking about a final countdown. Something that needed some kind of experiment. We cannot ignore this.'

'Granted, the Firestorm Administrator is more of a threat than an ordinary contractor,' said Control. 'But it is a known threat. If anything is planned for the G20 we are more than ready. The military capacity massing around the ExCel Centre could invade a small country.'

I was silent.

'If I could bring us back to the present,' Beth said. 'Your actions have put everyone you care about in immediate danger—'

'*What* people I care about?' I said. 'Selfish. That's what the profilers say.'

'But is that really true?' Beth asked. 'How will you feel if Firestorm takes your quartermaster, Simon?'

'Inconvenienced.'

Her face shut down at that, like it did in her office.

I stare out at the houses bordering the graveyard and wonder what effect it has on the inhabitants of this street, living their lives facing a graveyard. Does death fade into the mundane? Do funerals mean something different? The horse-drawn carriages with their flower biers, the old shires stamping their hooves, breath steamy in the cold, the plumes on their heads nodding. For this street, it means a car held up or a noise that wakes the baby.

But there are no funerals; the people who used this cemetery have been dead a hundred years. Now no one even remembers their names. No one comes to visit these graves.

No one except me and the Guardsman.

'The Guardsman will not let this go,' Beth said, back in Control's office. She sat and studied me with her hazel eyes, a few shades darker than her honey hair. 'What are the defining characteristics of psychopathy, Winter? He will see it as a challenge. What was it carved on that forehead? *An eye for an eye.* I would say you have about forty-eight hours, seventy-two tops, before someone you care about goes exactly the same way. Everyone knows you have a weakness for the vulnerable, that you don't like to see people in pain. We saw your reaction to the girl in the graveyard, to the barmaid with the message on her forehead.'

Faces cycled in front of my eyes, everyone I knew, everyone I'd ever met. I could feel the truth of what she was saying, the rightness of it. The fear clutched cold inside me. I could hear my breathing speeding up.

'You have crossed the line,' she said. 'This was a direct challenge to someone who doesn't get challenged and I'll bet my degree in criminal psychology it will not go unanswered.'

There was silence as Control and I locked gazes. Then he gave an infinitesimal shrug.

'Give me seventy-two hours to find the Guardsman,' I said.

'Forty-eight,' Control replied. 'And then I want you in Marseille looking for Alek Konstantin.'

As I closed his office door, his eyes followed me with a look that said *Make it count.*

I stand in the graveyard now, listening to the leaves, reading the space. The buildings on the hill look friendly in the early morning sun. The glass lantern on the church hall sparkles.

I walk between the graves, long grasses damp with dew bend as I pass. Below the knee, my jeans are covered with seeds. The sun is warm on the back of my neck.

The stone angel bends her head in prayer, her hands clasped together. She looks like she is crying. Her roses are dry as tinder in the heat. I sit down on the top of the pedestal. The stone cross is cold against my back.

I stare at the lichen-covered stone, the dusty scuffed weeds round the base, dry as tinder in the summer heat.

Samuel Palmer of Collingwood College.
Who passed away 26 February 1888. Aged 65.
The just man walketh in his integrity, Prov 20:7.

The just man.
What is just? I'm not sure I even know anymore.

*

I am in shade here, under the cedar, surrounded by the smell of dry needles.

I wonder about a tree this size in a graveyard. The way the root system must run as far below ground as the branches do above. Great, thick roots punching through the disintegrating coffin walls, through the bodies, through a ribcage, crushing a skull, feeding on the rich, decaying matter.

I look at the nails in the bark and think of the tracks of blood dripping down the splits in the bark, pooling around the roots. I think about the defining characteristics of psychopathy and about the man who came here with his victim for a bit of peace and quiet while he got to work sending me a message.

I think about a man dying on an aluminium trolley in GCHQ and I think about what separates those two things. About what makes me any better than the Guardsman.

I stare out at the bright sunlight from the dappled shade.

There is another way.

There is someone who can find the Guardsman. The ultimate higher power. The final court of appeal. A man with no compassion in his brutal body but a moral code of a sort.

Alek Konstantin. Billionaire crime lord. Head of Firestorm.
Lover.

CHAPTER 30

I'm not sure when I knew Alek Konstantin was going to be a problem. I remember when I knew I didn't want him dead.

I know I wasn't grateful he saved my life. I wasn't even grateful when he made me *untouchable*. I wasn't grateful but somewhere along the line, I began to understand.

I remember dark eyes watching me from the end of the bed, the Prince of Darkness leaning up against the bedpost, his long legs stretched out in front of him.

'The internet changed everything,' he said. 'And man doesn't have the emotional maturity to cope. Yesterday's rules and values are obsolete in this new dystopia. Like it or not, the world needs people who will do what must be done.'

I get up off the stone plinth, wiping my palms on the back of my jeans. My backside is numb. My T-shirt sticks to my skin. I pull out my phone, hunching over to shade the screen.

6 a.m. and Brad, the London head of the NSA, answers on the first ring. He has probably been at work for hours.

'I was about to call you,' he says.

'I need to see you.' The sun is already warm as I walk out of the shade. Crickets chirp in the grass. The road feels far away. 'I need your help.'

'And I need to know where that gas came from,' he says.

I picture the cake tin I handed him in the café outside his office. A gas sent by the Guardsman as the Firestorm Administrator. He knew Contractor 159 had not carried out the contract. He knew it was me on the other end of the phone in Fortnum & Mason.

'The chemists are going nuts,' he says. 'It has a molecular structure they have never seen before.'

'Government grade?'

'No question.'

I shade my eyes against the bright light. 'I need a favour.'

'Another favour? I'm not through doing the last one.'

'This is a really big favour.'

There is silence as he takes this on board, then he sighs. 'You'd better come and tell me all about it.'

I leave the phone and my locator on the stone pedestal and retrace my steps, moving between hanging branches, trying to keep something between me and Isosceles, the all-seeing satellite eye in the sky.

The building is still grey. Still doing a great camouflage job. It looks empty, not interestingly derelict, just unoccupied. The café is opening for business, unfurling the red awning, unstacking the chrome chairs.

I push at the rotating doors and they spring to life. Walk through the body scanner, through biometrics and up the stairs. It feels like a long climb.

Alek Konstantin stares down from the lobby wall.

The lift doors open. I muster a smile.

'Crikey,' Brad says. 'What happened to you?'

'It's nothing. Surface.'

'I should see the other guy?' Brad smiles.

Solo screams and screams on a hospital trolley.

'Probably not.'

His smile fades. 'Well he got a couple of good hits in, whoever he was.'

I stare up at the chiselled features of the Prince of Darkness. 'It was your fault for not lending me a gun.'

Brad's eyebrows shoot up. 'Did you have those kids with you?'

'They were quite useful, actually. Have you ever tried carrying a 210-pound deadweight?'

'No,' says Brad firmly. 'That is what clean-up teams are for.'

We get in the lift and Brad presses the button to take us up to the closed floor. They don't have the space we have in GCHQ and the incident rooms, interview suites and medical labs are all on different floors.

The doors open. The containment labs are over to the left. I remember them being developed back in the day when Anthrax was all we had to worry about. Brad leads us through to a tiny internal meeting room. Bare walls, table, no windows.

I lean against the wall.

A bearded white coat comes in. He looks up over his glasses as he shakes my hand. Breathless with some emotion.

'How much do you know about nerve agent degradation?' he asks.

I've missed the first half of this conversation.

'Can we go back to the beginning?' I say. 'What is the gas exactly? Is it a nerve agent?'

'Kind of,' he says. 'I have never seen anything like it.' He takes his glasses off and blinks rapidly as he wipes them on the corner of his lab coat. He looks like a tortoise with a twitch. 'Break it down to its molecular structure and it has a synthetic isobond.'

'Which does what?'

'We don't know. It is a chemically engineered isomer. Extremely sophisticated. Whatever it does, it does with pinpoint precision. We just don't know what. Yet. I could hypothesise for you, but that's not the exciting part.' He waves it away. 'Given the normal environmental factors for natural degradation, a classic nerve agent like VX oxidises at a rate of seventy-seven milligrams per

Watt hour of incident UV flux with quantum efficiency of 3.8 per cent, making it high risk to deploy, fatal for anyone in the vicinity and with a massive risk of cross-contamination. Worst of all, in cold wet conditions it can stay around in trace form for months.'

'Giving the game away.'

'Exactly. This one? After ten minutes uncontained, it has completely vanished. Complete 100 per cent degradation. It is perfect.'

Silence.

Overhead, the air conditioning roars. I shiver. The room is almost as cold as the mortuary. A muscle ticks beneath my eye.

'So, what does that mean?' I say finally.

He looks at me like I'm seriously missing the point.

'It is untraceable. Invisible. An invisible blow with no repercussions because no one knows you have used it.'

An invisible blow that the Guardsman tried to use against me in Fortnum & Mason. He knew all along it was me on the end of the dead contractor's phone. He knew the Australian wife was a fake. So what does the gas do? It's not going to kill – the Firestorm Administrator knows I am off limits. It is going to do something else. My skin pricks in the arctic room. I wrap my arms around my body.

'An invisible blow that does what?'

'We are still working on that. It has no effect on rats.'

'None at all?'

'Appetites, everything, completely normal. Possibly motor function is a little impaired, but within the margin of error.'

'So it could be completely harmless?'

The scientist shrugs. 'Pretty much anything that affects us, affects rats too. We'll know more when we have run further tests.'

Brad sighs as the lift doors open outside his office. He looks at me sideways. 'An undetectable nerve agent,' he says. 'Nice. You are spoiling me. So, any other little presents? Any little favours? Any other tiny thing I can do for you?'

'I'm so glad you asked,' I say.

Brad leans back in his office chair.

'Facial alteration surgery is a big deal,' he says. 'You know that. There is protocol, form-filling, a double signature.'

'Form-filling?' I raise an eyebrow.

'All right, maybe I can manage the paperwork. What about the expense? Three hours in theatre. How will I explain it on my cost code?'

'You are kidding? The agency with the biggest budget in the world, is whining about a few grand?'

He scans the biometrics. 'Who is this?'

'No one. One of my aliases.'

Snow White. The Russian hitwoman alter ego I used when I infiltrated organised crime. Nothing connects Snow White to Winter, the government agent. No one knows it is the same person except Simon, Léon and Alek Konstantin. Even Control never saw Snow White. Although Detective Fresson in Marseille could put two and two together if he saw Snow White again.

'I don't know how good a job we can do,' Brad says. 'It should be the people who created the face in the first place.'

'You mean you're not up to it?'

He smiles. 'Nice try. You know we're up to it or you wouldn't be here. Just explain to me why, with the unlimited, unquestioning resources of GCHQ at your disposal, you choose to come to us?'

I stare out of his corner window. The sprawl of Canary Wharf stretches out. The Thames, the flat white spaceship that is the O2, the curve of the Thames.

'This face can go places and ask questions I can't.'

'But can't he see you, whatever you look like? He can see you now in this building. He can see you everywhere you go. He knows how you are feeling. With a tracker in your arm, it is irrelevant what you look like, he will know you are coming anyway.'

'Not everything is about Alek Konstantin. Do you know where I got that gas?'

Brad raises an eyebrow.

'The Firestorm Administrator, aka the Guardsman.'

Brad stares.

I tell him about the yellow stickies, the pieces of the jigsaw, the planning, the contract on myself. I tell him about uploading the picture of me dead. I tell him about Fortnum & Mason.

His face closes down, just like Beth's. I have disappointed him. 'Jesus, Winter,' he says. 'What were you thinking? You're going rogue again.'

'Desperate times.'

'You don't get it. This is like chess. You are the Queen. The best player on the board doesn't get into a fight with a pawn.'

'The Guardsman is not a pawn.'

'Firestorm are like kids whose teacher has left the playground. First, they test the perimeter and then when they find the gates open, they run crazy and then after a while, the worst elements rise to the top. A load of things were being kept locked down and it only needed a weakening for them to start breaking out.'

'They're not running crazy yet,' I say. 'They are exploring the playground and finding the gates open. But I think they will be running crazy very soon.'

I walk to the glass corner and peer down. We are not that high up, not like the Canary Wharf towers, the status buildings, but still high enough to see all the way to the end of the Isle of Dogs. To see the curve of the Thames and in the distance the far bank and the white Palladian magnificence of Greenwich.

'You do well for yourself,' I say, looking round at the palatial corner office and thinking of my broom cupboard.

'Benefits of the boss being across the water,' he says. 'I get the best office.'

'What were you supposed to be doing today?'

'Before you hijacked my schedule? G20 surveillance. Four days to go.' He rolls his eyes. 'Everyone is terrified, but God forbid they are seen to be terrified. It doesn't look good with the voters. It doesn't sit well with their self-esteem. No one wants to be the first to blink. PR versus close protection and we are caught right in the middle.'

'I don't have to deal with that shit.'

'Thank goodness for MI5.'

'And there's a sentence you don't hear very often.' The glass is cool against my forehead. It must be tinted because it looks like an overcast day out there. 'Do you think the G20 will achieve anything?'

'I think we need to start working together. I think we need to get organised, like the other side.'

'The clue is in the name.'

'Right.'

'They have one man, however weakened, at the top,' he says. 'We, on the other hand, have to coordinate a hundred different governments and a myriad of different factions. All mainly concerned with their own self-interests.'

'We've got McKellen.'

His face goes sombre. 'And look at the job he has had getting everyone together. Cajoling, extorting, threatening. I don't think anyone else could have done it. He'll be flying in soon to try and hold it all together. When you think his family were kidnapped in the first week…' He shakes his head. 'I hear you went to see him.'

'I dropped in for a chat while I was there.'

'So, Virginia was a real sighting?' Brad tips back in his chair. The black leather squeaks.

'Yes.'

The chair hits the floor.

'What on earth was Alek Konstantin doing in Petersburg, Virginia?'

'You tell me.'

'Hmm.' His shrewd eyes narrow. 'Close to Langley. Was it a storage facility?'

I turn, lean my shoulders back against the window and smile.

'No wonder McKellen was cagey,' he says.

'Although, God knows what the CIA have left to keep under wraps these days.'

Brad shifts uneasily, caught between friendship with a foreign national and loyalty to his country.

'It's all right,' I say. 'I'm not here for answers.'

'What was he looking for?'

'Whatever it was, I think he probably found it.'

'But what could be worth that kind of risk? Breaking cover like that. Right in the heart of the US government. He knew there would be a positive ID.'

I think back to the security guard.

'*Five more men came in and behind them a tall man with a shaved head and I knew perfectly well who he was because his picture is everywhere.*'

'*Did he know you had seen him?*'

'*I guess. He gave me this long look like he could see right through me. Then he shook his head.*'

'*He shook his head?*'

'*Yeah, then they locked the cupboard door.*'

'He didn't just know there would be a positive ID, he made sure of it. He was sending a message. In the past, any time he has done that, he has had a good reason.'

'What kind of reason could he have? What could be that important?'

I shrug.

'And then he went to Marseille?'

'Yeah.'

'You know, I never got a chance to ask you…' He fiddles with something on his desk.

The whole surface is covered with executive stress toys. No paperwork. Not even a PC. That is a sign of the times. The London head of the NSA doesn't have a fixed workstation. Because he knows absolutely everything can be hacked. He drags a miniature rake across a miniature tray of sand and moves a miniature Japanese stone into the corner. He is very calm for someone with so many stress solutions.

'What is he like?'

'Who?'

'Alek Konstantin. The Prince of Darkness. The world's most wanted man.'

I turn back to the window. 'Exactly what you would expect.'

Brad scowls behind me, I can feel it against my back. 'Don't blow me off. I have known you a decade. I knew you when you were a kick-ass teenager with a bad attitude.'

'I'm glad you used the past tense.'

'Quit stalling.'

'Charismatic. He is controlling so many disparate things that you can't conceive how any one person could do it until you meet him and then it all becomes clear.'

'A charismatic, highly intelligent killing machine.' Brad looks disgruntled. 'No wonder half the building have a crush on him.'

'I'm surprised you don't have a picture up in here yourself.'

He shakes his head. 'I did but I took it down. It felt like he was watching all the time.'

I know the feeling.

I stare down at the toy train picking its way between the buildings then I turn to face him. 'I need to go properly off-grid.'

'Why?'

'I have my reasons.'

'So why not get your people to do the surgery?'

'Something is wrong,' I say.

'No way?' says Brad. 'Have you only just noticed? We are at war.'

I shake my head. 'At GCHQ. Something is wrong. I don't know what. I can't even tell you what I suspect. I can just feel it. Smell it.'

'Smell it? Not literally?'

'Kind of. You know that primitive back part of your brain, that tells you something is wrong long before your front brain spots it? The hairs on the back of your neck?'

Brad shakes his head. 'I guess that kind of thing only develops when you are in the field.'

'Or it is the reason you are in the field in the first place. On a packed train, I can tell you who is hungry, who is nervous, who is angry.'

'Four hundred years ago they would have called you a witch.'

'Lucky for me I was born in the age of technology.'

'The final age.'

'You think so?'

'Yes,' he says. 'Our generation are the midwives of the end of the world. We don't have the maturity to deal with our advances. We are developing faster than we can cope with. It's why authority is collapsing.'

As I lie in my hospital gown staring up at the operating lights and the three faces leaning over me in green surgical masks, I think about authority collapsing and about the man who holds the reins of power and how I am going to find him.

Three hours in the operating theatre and a further three hours recovering means it is afternoon before I am on my way, leaving the dusty, nondescript building as quietly as I came. Only this time I'm leaving as somebody else.

THE GUARDSMAN

VII

The Guardsman looked at the contractor, at the greasy hair hanging across his forehead. He was not worthy of Firestorm. He had allowed a target to escape in the middle of Central Park. It was embarrassing. Now he was trembling, a vibrating motion that made his outline blur.

'Please,' the contractor said. 'Please forgive me.'

The Guardsman picked up the knife, tilting it this way and that, considering the edge. Maybe it needed sharpening. It had only just been sharpened, but maybe it needed doing again.

Whetstone, then dry stone, then polish.

'*Parting is such sweet sorrow,*' said the Guardsman. '*That I shall say goodnight till it be morrow.*'

'Please,' the contractor said. 'Please forgive me. It won't happen again.'

Damn right, thought the Guardsman.

Only four days left but the man was of no use as an experiment.

He had no idea how much he dishonoured Firestorm with his incompetence. The Guardsman felt a sudden flash of rage so blinding it was almost painful.

'*Light seeking light doth light of light beguile;*
So ere you find where light in darkness lies,
Your light grows dark by losing of your eyes.' said the Guardsman.

CHAPTER 31

I stare at my face in the Eurostar toilet window and a Disney princess stares back. Long dark hair, big brown eyes, bruises gone. Snow White, my Russian hitwoman alter ego. There is only one person who can deliver the Guardsman and Snow White can find him.

It's good to see you, babe.

I swig ibuprofen for the swelling and Snow White winks.

Back in the game.

Snow White has never had to pass a psych test.

Which is just as well.

Paris is cooler than London, but still warm. Pollution hangs, a haze in the sky. Even the plane trees are limp in the heat.

Early evening and I stand on the cobbles, facing my past, looking down the narrow street at a high front door. The yellow and black police tape is tatty. The original tape has fallen down on one side. It is eight weeks since the owner died. French bureaucracy moves slowly.

This is where it all began. The home of the Marquise de Mazan, the contractor behind Slashstorm, the torture website. Eight weeks ago, I dropped her off this building while Alek watched. She died right where I am standing.

I slide my fingertips over the door. There is a thin layer of dirt. It is in the air. Give it long enough and everything gets coated with grit.

I lean my forehead against the dusty paintwork, picturing behind the door: the inner courtyard, the gracious sweeping red of the stairs, the slow climb to the first floor, the landing with its wrought iron balcony and then the room beyond with its blonde parquet flooring and its windows overlooking the Seine.

I picture the sun pouring through the windows and the balcony casting slanting filigree shadows across the floor.

There was a painting behind the door.

It was all there in that portrait. I never saw it. Never looked behind the mask until it was nearly too late.

Too arrogant, too hasty, too over-confident my psych reports used to say.

Not anymore.

In my mind's eye, I drift out of the sunlit room. My footsteps are silent on the thick pile, but my breathing quickens and my heart hammers, and then I am there, looking into a room lined with mirrors. I stare and a thousand Winters stare back at me.

My stomach clenches and my mouth fills with saliva. I am going to be sick. I take my forehead off the door and the cobbles swim back into view. The sun has gone over and the street is in shadow. Wind whistles off the Seine, funnelling its way between the buildings. I shiver even though it isn't really cold.

My eye falls on a patch of pavement. It is cleaner, like it has been scrubbed with industrial chemicals. Seen from the air it would be nearly circular. How many times did the Marquise's heart beat before she died? Once, maybe twice? There is a lot of blood in the human body, but it needs a pumping heart to bleed out.

The opposite side of the street is perfect Haussmann, but I know it is a facade, I have been here before. A perfect, beautiful exterior, derelict behind. I cross the street and slide a blade behind the lock. No police tape – it was never a crime scene. A push and a shove and I am standing in the hall breathing in the smell of old damp plaster and staring up at the sweeping staircase.

I ran up these stairs looking for Alek after I dropped the Marquise to her death. After I realised I had been wrong about him. I called and called but he had gone.

I hit the top floor and stand listening. Ahead is the door that leads out to the roof; beside me is the attic room where a tramp used to live. Did he watch, day after day, peering through the dusty windows to see what the police were up to? Did he find any kind of closure?

I push the door to the attic room. Empty. The air is still, it hasn't been disturbed in weeks. A heavy stillness, stifling in the lungs.

I push out through the fire escape, onto the roof. The air is cool and crisp and fresh after the closeness. The wind is stronger up here. The tall thin buildings act like a chimney, dragging the wind upwards. I stare up at the sky. Sirens sound in the distance. It is peaceful here amongst the sloping roofs and slick grey gullies.

I go back inside, back to the attic bedroom and hunker down in the corner, knees up, arms wrapped round my legs, the floorboards hard beneath me.

It feels right. I don't want to be comfortable. I want to wait with a degree of discomfort. And I know it will be a long wait. I touch my fingertips to my tracker. Even supposing he is still watching, it will take him a while to notice where I am and to realise. He will know I am waiting.

And then?

Does he come? Or does he send someone? Will he think it is a trap? What if he is in South America? Or Japan? Or Moscow?

I lay my cheek down on my knees and wait.

The hours pass and the evening grows greyer. Grey turns to dusk turns to twilight.

Sometimes I get up and stretch and get the blood pumping. Twice I go out through the fire escape and turn a slow 360, arms outstretched, looking up at Misty spinning in its satellite orbit far above me. I will him to hear me and to understand. Will him to come himself.

From the roof, I watch the lights come on all over Paris. I watch night fall. When I am cold to the bone, I go back inside to the attic room and the corner. I want the tracker to pick up my cold and hunger and tiredness. I want him to understand my need.

I count in my head, long complicated sums to while away the hours, my photographic memory painting the walls with numbers.

Midnight comes and brings exhaustion with it.

Something is knocking for attention in my brain, but I can't pin it down. Tiny horseshoes hammer behind my eyes, they ring against lift doors in Petersburg, they knock on a toilet cubicle in Paris. Lucy holds my hand in a dusty graveyard, a barmaid stares with sightless eyes, a gas swirls under a dome in Fortnum & Mason. Something connects them all. They are all pieces of a puzzle I don't understand.

My mind spreads out from the attic room, running across the Paris rooftops, looking in the windows at everyone sleeping, at the pigeons with their heads under their wings, at the stars, shining bright on this clear night.

After midnight, the sirens quietened. Now, in the small hours, it is all but silent.

I lift my head and listen.

Something.

Way off on the roof. Moving fast. Footsteps, several booted footsteps and the fear stabs through me. *Who is it? What if someone else has the tracker? What if someone else has come?*

The footsteps stop.

CHAPTER 32

There is murmuring outside on the fire escape. A voice raises and another voice cuts it off, closes it down. A voice you don't mess with, a voice that lifts all the hairs on the back of your neck. A voice that has my heart thumping and adrenaline firing through my body.

The fire escape door creaks open and footsteps sound on the landing outside. One set of footsteps; everyone else is waiting outside.

And then he is there, standing in the open doorway, larger than life, a black silhouette, his dark eyes glinting in the gloom. Dark trousers, dark T-shirt, Kevlar.

Pale moonlight falls across the chiselled planes of a face so perfect it pulls the eye. Why are humans so attracted to beauty? Why do we rate physical appearance so highly? What does it achieve? The longing arrows through me and the past weeks fall away and there is nothing but him, vivid and vital and as brilliant as a flame in this derelict room. A numbness I didn't even know I was feeling is melting away as if my mind and body are thawing out. Like I have been sleepwalking through the last few weeks.

He is tired. There is a new scar down one cheek and I wonder who got that close. I want to put my arms out, I want to touch my fingers to his face. The sight of him is like a body blow. For a long moment we stare at each other, me on the floor, him in the doorway.

'Hello, Alek,' I say.

'Winter.' His voice is heavy with some unspoken question.

I push to my feet slowly, my knees aching, the blood pouring into my calves.

'I wasn't sure you would come,' I say, pressing my palms to the cold wall behind me, trying to calm my rocketing heart rate. My voice is loud in the silence.

He makes no move to come into the room.

'Now I am running for my life?'

The distance between us is wide, a yawning aching chasm of floor.

'What do you want, Winter?' he says, switching to Russian.

'I want the Guardsman.' The words sound tiny and hollow and insignificant in the empty room.

He stares at me.

'I have travelled halfway around the world for you to ask me about the Guardsman?' His voice is light and curious.

I feel the words there, words I should be saying but they flit away, leaving me grasping at nothing, floundering and bewildered. His voice is light, but he feels angry.

He stares at me in silence and I think of the chaos and the burning townships and the gangland shootings of the last few weeks as the world erupted into violence. I see skulls exploding like watermelons under the hot Mexican sun and the pursuit of one hitman seems trivial, pointless in comparison.

I have travelled halfway around the world. Something sings inside me at the thought. I want to ask him how long it took him to notice, how long before he decided to come himself.

'I didn't know if you were still watching.' I look down at my wrist.

'So you thought you would test it out? Watch me come running?'

I get that feeling again that the right words are there if I could find them. He is angry. The gap across the floor is a wide, unbridgeable chasm. *What is it he wants to hear? What was I supposed to say?*

'I am sorry I interrupted you,' I say. 'Tell me who the Guardsman is and you can get back to it.'

'You have no idea what you are getting yourself into. Even I can't protect you from the Guardsman.'

'What are the experiments he is running? What final countdown? What was he doing in Petersburg? What is in Marseille?'

'Why don't you ask your Langley friends?'

'I have asked them. What do you want me to say, Alek? You know I can't leave this.'

'I thought...' He shakes his head. 'It doesn't matter what I thought, I am not leaving here on my own. Come with me.'

'I can't come with you, Alek, you know that. We are not on the same side.'

He swears, explosive and Russian and turns to go, and then turns back.

'There is no time left, Winter,' he says. 'We are out of time. I could die tomorrow. I could die tonight trying to get out of here.'

He stares at me for a moment like he is waiting for something. Then, with an oath, he is gone.

THE GUARDSMAN

VIII

The Guardsman shifted. Where was Winter? Had she taken the bait? It was impossible to tell – she had disappeared from under their noses. Gone to ground like the coward she was.

Not a coward, thought the Guardsman. *Arrogant.* With a vast, misplaced confidence in her own abilities. She thought she could challenge Firestorm. Sooner or later she would surface and then she would be made to pay. Once and for all.

Except they were having a hard time finding anyone she cared about. Everyone had someone they cared for, someone they didn't want hurt. It was the guiding principle of Firestorm. But not Winter. The Guardsman almost felt a grudging respect for her indifference. Almost.

Whetstone, then dry stone, then polish.

The Guardsman put down the blade, smoothed her long, sleek ponytail and glanced at her Patek Philippe. It had stopped. Again. That was expensive Swiss workmanship for you. Complicated and ineffectual.

The clock was ticking. Four days to go and before Winter died, she must be made to suffer.

CHAPTER 33

3 days to go…

The room is cold and dank now he has left it. I never noticed before. The small mean proportions, the low ceiling, the night through the grimy window. The whole room looks different. I slide down the wall onto the floor and curl up as waves of disappointment roll over me.

I thought he would help me. Did I think he cared? How ironic. How ridiculous. I lie for a long time watching the pale light of dawn until it is strong and clear and unmistakable.

The fear that I locked down in Control's office is back. How long have I wasted in this cold, dank room with the walls closing in? How long since Solo's death? Thirty hours or more. Thirty hours the Guardsman has been busy making plans, deciding on his revenge, choosing a victim.

I get unsteadily to my feet, my body exhausted from the lack of food more than the hours of watchfulness.

I push open the fire escape door and the morning hits me. Cold, crisp air, clean and fresh, whipping off the river. I suck the air into my lungs in great gulps.

Breathe in, breathe out.

The balustrade is cold after the night chill. I lean my elbows on the stone. A woman in a black suit is walking away from me up the street. An early commuter. In the UK she would be a solicitor or an accountant or a lawyer but here in the home of Parisian chic, she could be anything. She crosses the street, her stilettos slip-sliding, skittering on the cobbles. Two figures pass her, their silhouettes recognisable long before their voices are in range. I don't need any gait analysis software to identify the Doc Martin stride.

Surprise holds me as still as the stone on the roof.

'I'm telling you, this is where she will be,' Xiu says, her annoyed voice carrying all the way down the street, on the thin morning air. 'She will have gone back to where it all started. Slashstorm and the Marquise de Mazan.'

'What makes you such an expert all of a sudden? You hardly know her.' Léon, irritated.

'I just know, all right.'

'I don't see why. Last night you said she would definitely be at the graveyard.'

'You just have a massive crush on her.'

'I do not,' Léon says. I can practically see the blush.

Xiu's expressive shoulders shrug. She could give the French a run for their money on the shoulder shrugging. She is still wearing her dungarees. 'No one is *making* you come.'

They have reached the house opposite with the yellow and black police tape. They stand looking at it.

'See?' says Léon. 'No one has been here. I told you.' He kicks the door.

Xiu doesn't dignify this with an answer. She stands looking at the door with her hands on her hips then she turns a slow half circle.

'Come on,' she says crossing the street.

'Why would she be in there?' Léon's voice rises on a crescendo of disbelief.

Their bickering voices disappear under the lee of the building. I crane forward trying to hear.

'Are you going to do it or am I?' Xiu says.

I withdraw my head and go back through the fire door to the top landing.

There is the sound of a door being expertly picked, or rather the absence of sound, just a click, a loaded, breathless pause and then a shove and they are inside. Their voices hush to a stage whisper.

'Come on,' hisses Xiu. 'Don't be shy.'

I roll my eyes.

I can picture her shoving Léon in the small of the back. No doubt it was him picking the lock.

'Check this place out,' she says. 'Spooky. I bet there are ghosts and traps and a spooky caretaker. "I would have got away with it if it wasn't for you pesky kids".'

'What?' says Léon.

'Oh, come on, don't tell me you don't have *Scooby Doo* over here?'

I lean over the bannisters, looking down. 'If it isn't Tweedledum and Tweedledee.'

They jump like startled deer and gawp up at me like I am a ghost or a creepy caretaker. It's almost enough to make me crack a smile.

'Winter!' shouts Léon taking the stairs two at a time. Xiu is right behind him.

'You two need to make a lot less noise,' I say straightening up and heading down the flight to meet them.

They stop in front of me.

'That is A-MA-ZING,' Xiu says. She is staring with open-mouthed curiosity. 'That is un-bloody-believable. I wouldn't have known you.'

She reaches out.

I bat her away. 'No touching,' I say. 'Like Stringfellows.'

'Are you impressed we found you?'

'No,' I lie.

They look ridiculously crestfallen.

'So what are we doing here?' Xiu says.

I consider commenting on this but let it go.

'I was following a lead,' I say. 'A contact.'

'And?'

'He couldn't help.' I bite the words out. Slam Alek Konstantin back behind iron bars in my head.

'Couldn't or wouldn't?' says Léon.

'Wouldn't,' I say shortly.

'Where is he?' he says, craning round like he is expecting to see a body lying on the landing.

I consider, for a moment, the idea of beating the truth out of Alek. I toy with the attractive image of him bending to my will, cowering on the floor, while I stand over him with a flaming sword of righteousness.

The image dissolves, unsustainable even in fantasy land. I have never been able to take Alek Konstantin in a fight. I can't picture him bending to my will or anyone else's. And as for cowering…

I push past them and carry on down the stairs and they clatter after me.

The street is empty and fresh in the early morning. Another woman in a suit is making her way to work. Effortlessly elegant in six-inch heels.

There it is again, that feeling at the back of my brain, hammering for attention.

The woman walks away from us up the street, her stilettos ringing on the pavement.

'What?' says Xiu, cannoning into the back of me.

'Stilettos,' I say. 'I was thinking about stiletto heels.'

'Is now really the time?' she says.

I stare after the woman.

Shit.

What if there was no metal stake? What is the horseshoe-tipped weapon you can just walk in with?

A stiletto.

We are only a few streets away from the Palais de Justice where the judge was murdered on the toilet. I picture the Guardsman tiptoeing into the bathroom, shoes in hand.

I break into a run.

'Slow down,' says Xiu. 'Where are we going?'

We round the corner and onto the Boulevard de Paris. A minute later we stop in front of a nineteenth-century masterpiece of French architecture. A stone palace with turrets and iron work and French military police with their sub-machine guns.

'What are we doing here?' says Xiu, eying the magnificence with disfavour.

'This is the Palais de Justice, home of the Court of Cassation,' I say. 'France's highest Court of Appeal.'

'Whatever,' says Xiu.

There is only one entrance serving the law courts and the Sainte Chapelle. We step into the lobby and see exactly what I was hoping for. Super tight, airport-style security: a metal detector, a conveyor belt X-ray machine and a body scanner with a circular lino base. A small soft circle every person in the building has to stand on.

A policewoman steps forward. Her MP5 juts.

'We're closed,' she says. 'Guided tours start in two hours.'

I'm surprised they are still doing the guided tours, although maybe she means for the Sainte Chapelle.

I get down on my hands and knees beside the body scanner and glide my fingertips over the lino base, back and across, back and across in sweeping movements. This has to be the longest of long shots in a city where high heels are an everyday occurrence but there is nothing everyday about the heels I am looking for.

A modern stiletto is made of coated plastic, hollow and light-weight and tipped with a rubber horseshoe. The weapon that was used against the Judge was metal and heavy. It sheered straight through the soft eyeball, smashing the bone socket behind, destroying the temporal lobe. It had heft and weight and stopping power. The stopping power of a heavy stake with a sharp-edged metal tip.

The policewoman is not impressed. 'What are you *doing*?' she scowls. 'Have you dropped something? I am going to have to ask you to leave.'

Security are never as efficient as when a judge has just been murdered in the building.

I can see Xiu and Léon out of the corner of my eye, gaping. My fingertips slide across the floor. It is like trying to read braille. I close my eyes to see if that helps and then I feel something. A deep horseshoe cut into the lino, driven in by weight and a sharp cutting edge. I slide a hand to the side and there is the other one. The matching pair, as someone stood on the lino, rocking back on their heavy metal heels as the body scanner did its thing. Totally inconclusive and yet suggestive. Everything and nothing.

'What the hell was that about?' says Xiu, as we head back across the forecourt of the Palais de Justice, the policewoman glaring at our backs.

I shake my head. 'I'm not sure.'

It would explain why they found traces of mud in the wound.

'Tell me,' I say to Léon. 'Everything you know about that woman who used to come and see Ferret.'

'What woman?' asks Léon.

'The one you used to hear walking about in the back office.'

'Oh yeah,' he says. 'Like she was wearing six-inch heels. She only came a few times and then he used to go out to the factory by the harbour. They will know more at the café obviously.'

I stare out across the lines of traffic. Horns blare. It is already starting to get hot. Exhaust fumes hang in the air. I feel like I've got hold of a corner of the jigsaw.

'What now?' says Léon.

'Marseille. Give me your phone.'

Simon answers first ring.

'Lucy,' I say. 'Pull up her dating history.'

'Who's Lucy?' says Simon.

'The girl in the graveyard.' I can feel her, sticky in my arms, feel the grass as dry as straw. 'The first Guardsman victim without a contract. She was on a blind date when she was killed.'

Simon doesn't question, he just does as I ask. I can hear typing and then scrolling and then a grunt.

'Well, that's a surprise,' he says.

'She was into chicks.'

'How did you know?'

'I think the Guardsman could be a woman.'

CHAPTER 34

Marseille's central square is dusty. I run my fingers under the icy water from the fountain. Tourists sit on the edge tipping their heads back to catch the spray. Across the way, Léon is taking Xiu into his café. The café where he used to work when he was part of Marseille organised crime. A junior. But a junior with prospects. Ferret had spotted his potential. And then I came along and he jacked it all in to work for a foreign government on the side of law and order. Not that they know that here obviously. Snow White is a hitman as far as they are concerned.

Léon stands back to allow Xiu to enter first. *This is my turf.* His shoulders have got broader and his stride wider, the closer we come.

I remember the café the first time I saw it, checked tablecloths, wicker chairs, a round white-aproned proprietor and Ferret surrounded by muscle, in the middle of a poker game. Apparently, the new Boss, Armand, is a different proposition entirely.

I duck inside. The place is full of the lunchtime crowd. The same round, white-aproned proprietor is working the bar.

He exclaims at the sight of Léon and bustles and wipes his hands on his apron and takes him by the shoulders and kisses him once, twice, three times. He looks over Léon's shoulder at me and nods. Not enthusiastic. The nod of recognition. He remembers Snow White. The hitwoman who turned up and took over. The only one still standing when everyone else was dead.

Léon will get more out of him without me around.

I walk past them, through to the back, into the corridor with the crates and the smell and open the door of Ferret's office. More crates – San Pellegrino in orange and pomegranate. The room that used to be there is gone. I stand with my hand on the doorknob and half turn, wondering if I have come in the right door but there is no other door and I know this is the place. Even the picture of Ferret and the Marseille football team is gone. A sad, pale outline against the darker wall.

The floor is poured concrete, ideal for picking up the sound of heels walking up and down, useless for footprints. I get down and feel but I know there will be nothing. I go out and stare at the dirty lino in the corridor. The space is dark and narrow and made narrower still by the crates that are stacked up against the wall. They are always stacked up against the wall, which means everyone has to perform a sideways shuffle as they edge along. Perfect for slowing up a footstep. I get down on the floor and there it is again. A single, deep horseshoe. Almost as good as the ones on the lift door in Petersburg, made when someone hammered on the metal.

I can picture her now, tapping on a toilet cubicle in the Palais de Justice. Tap, tap, tap.

The Guardsman was here in Marseille and in Petersburg, Virginia, looking for something. But what? Some kind of weapon? Part of a CIA programme from way back when things were more relaxed?

Léon appears at the end of the corridor. 'He only ever saw her back. Apparently Ferret used to say he had a VIP coming and to keep everyone away. Then he used to go out to the factory on the docks.'

I feel the frustration rise. 'What was she like?'

'Well dressed. Heels. Suit. Long hair tied back. *Séduisante.*'

Sexy.

Whatever business the Guardsman had with Ferret and the factory in Marseille, Ferret's replacement is going to know about it.

'Where is Armand?'

'He has an office in the business district,' Léon says. 'But he is out on a job. He won't be back until 9 p.m. at the earliest.'

On a job.

Yet more delay. I clamp down on the panic. How many hours has it been now? If Beth and her criminal psychology degree are right, I am running out of time.

We go back into the restaurant. Xiu has sat herself down at a table with her legs up on the red, velour booth seat. Ferret's table. Instinctively she has gone for the table with the best vantage point.

We get steak frites and a green salad. A late lunch.

'We should tell Simon where we are,' Xiu says. 'He was pretty annoyed you snuck off. And that hot HR chick.'

'Beth?'

'Yeah, her. She was going on about an induction course.'

'You think Beth is hot?'

'Yeah,' she says. 'Don't you?'

I consider. 'Not really.'

'Simon thought we knew where you were.' Léon is aggrieved. 'As if we would have told him.'

'Simon knows where we are. He will have been tracking your phones since you left London.' I point out through the open door at the lamp post opposite the café. There is a street cam mounted on the ornate ironwork. 'He's watching us right now.'

I throw a few notes on the table.

'See you later,' I say. 'Try and stay out of trouble.'

'Where are you going?' demands Xiu.

'To take a shower.'

Hôtel de Police. The words are carved into the stone. A massive tricolore flag hangs limp from a flagpole.

The front desk is busy as always. Stray cats, lost phones, street muggings. The duty sergeant is like the triage nurse in A&E.

I wait my turn.

'Inspecteur Fresson,' I say when I get to the desk.

'*Capitaine* Fresson,' he says.

I feel a little spark of pleasure at the news.

'Name?'

'No name.'

The sergeant leers.

I go and lean up against the wall, fold my arms and wait. I can see the duty sergeant on the phone saying the words. It has been a few weeks since I sabotaged Fresson's drug bust to get to Alek Konstantin. I wonder if he has forgiven me.

About five minutes later, Fresson appears at the foot of the stairwell. He stares. Then his face cracks into a smile. 'Winter?' he whispers. No wonder he's not sure. He has only met Snow White once – in Ferret's office the night of the bust – and she wasn't wearing any clothes.

I smile back, pleased to see him.

He kisses me on one cheek and then the other and then back to the first again and stands back to get a better look. He could be Léon in twenty years' time. The tanned skin and dark curly hair of a Marseille native. There are new streaks of silver at his temples. Being the boss is taking its toll.

'I hear congratulations are in order, Capitaine.'

He grins, waving it off.

'It is so good to see you like this,' he says.

I feel a moment of irrational jealousy of my alter ego who gets so many smiles she doesn't deserve. Then I remember Fresson saw Snow White in her underwear and cut her some slack.

'I need to take a look round at the docks,' I say, linking my arm through his and steering him towards the sunshine. 'Will you come?'

*

We drive through old Marseille to the harbour. A huge, red-hulled container ship sits at anchor, boat cranes loading and unloading.

Fresson pulls up in the shadow of an old warehouse. He puts the Renault in park.

'That's as far as we can get,' he says. 'We have to go on foot from here.'

I get slowly out of the car, assessing the scene, the wind soft against my cheek, the traffic far away, the screech of a seagull, the smell of docks and diesel.

Fresson leads the way and we head inland, leaving the clanking of harbour cranes behind.

'I was wondering if someone would come,' he says. 'I never expected it to be you.'

We walk on, turn a corner and there it is. The site. Like a bomb site. If it was an insurance job, someone was pretty thorough. We duck under the police tape and pick our way over the piles of rubble. A row of faded flags flaps in the breeze.

'So, what happened?'

Fresson kicks at a piece of brick. 'They made fertilisers, cat litter, pesticides – just small scale. Maybe safety wasn't what it should have been. Piles of ammonium nitrate. Night guards on the minimum wage, maybe they got careless, a butt got flicked the wrong way, at the wrong time. Maybe the wind gusted.'

'And how do you explain the fuel oil?'

'How do you know about the fuel oil?' Fresson seems genuinely surprised.

I roll my eyes. 'Give me a break. Five parts ammonium nitrate, one part fuel oil accelerant, what have you got?'

Fresson smiles.

'What really happened?' I say.

He is thoughtful. 'We're not sure. You would think a clumsy insurance job, except…'

'Except what?'

'The owner died the same night. Thirty miles away.'

'Suicide? Money worries?'

'Not unless someone has worked out a way to commit suicide from six thousand feet away.'

Sniper.

'Definitely six thousand? Because that is a serious distance. What was it exactly?'

'6,079 feet.'

'So not just any old contractor. A pro sniper.' He nods. 'How many sharp shooters are there who can manage that range? Not many, even with all the practice they get nowadays. What was it chambered with?'

'Hornady A-Max .50'

'Definitely a pro then.'

I look at the bones of the building. The shape it used to be. It reminds me of an archaeology dig. I step over walls a couple of bricks high, trying to work out where the doorways were, what used to be where. I squat down in the rubble, I trace the line of storage bins, the small area of kilns, the thin, one-skin brick wall. What were they making here? Something for Alek and the Guardsman organised by Ferret? Some kind of special explosive to give Firestorm the edge?

I stand in the very centre.

The wall structure is different here. There was another building. A building within a building. Self-contained. Two rooms leading, one after the other, into a third. A dead end. It bore the brunt of the blast. I trace the distance to the storage bins and make some basic calculations.

I look up at the sky. Wind pricks the back of my arms, whipping across the bay, gathering speed across the water. I look at a piece of metal tubing with thick aluminium plating. I crouch down on my haunches and look at the site from ground level. Beside me Fresson reaches for the piece of piping and my hand closes on his wrist whip fast. I shake my head.

'What?' he says.

I look at the bare bones of what is left of a government-grade decontamination suite and shake my head. 'Whatever they were making, it wasn't for the domestic market.'

Fresson stares at the remains of the coffee shop.

'What do you think?'

'I think you need to get a chemical analysis team out here right now.'

He stares.

'I think they were making VX.'

CHAPTER 35

Fresson's eyes are wide in his tanned face. He looks around helpless. 'But they don't have the scale here. You need 500 degrees and an incinerator for the gas output. Think of the power requirements.'

'OK, maybe not VX, something else. Something next generation.' I think about this, about the CIA and their grubby little secrets. I can feel the shape of something. 'Or maybe something really old.'

'Why do you say that?' says Fresson.

There is something. A fishy smell. Maybe I am imagining it or maybe it is in the air – we are by the sea. I can feel the pieces starting to slot into place – some kind of nerve agent, invented by the CIA and long ago outlawed. The only record of it held in a deep storage facility in Petersburg, Virginia.

'Have you ever smelt QL?' The penultimate stage in VX production.

'Once,' he says. 'In Paris, when I was training.'

'And you can't smell it now?'

He shakes his head. 'It has to be psychosomatic. No smell could have survived the blast.'

I stare out across the rubble.

'Do you want to talk to anyone? Any of the employees? Six worked the factory end, three women in the coffee shop. Two security.'

'Let me make a few enquiries under the radar.' Snow White can get better answers than the Chief of Police. 'I'll come back if I need more. In the meantime, get some chemists up here. We need some answers.'

'What are they looking for?'

'Ammonium nitrate, phosphoric acid, limestone, dolomite, calcium sulphate, sulphur. Originally they would have looked like piles of aggregate, a bright yellow powder and a blood red liquid.'

'And fuel oil.'

'Not fuel oil. He brought the fuel oil with him.'

'When?'

'When he came to blow the place up. When he came to cover his tracks.'

'When who came?'

I stare out across the rubble towards the sea.

'Alek Konstantin.'

'*Merde*,' he says. 'So we definitely need a hazard team.'

'Typically, these are binary events – totally harmless chemicals that go to make one lethal combo. The final chemical is so lethal it can't be handled in anything but a government grade setting. But we shouldn't take the chance, something massive was going down here – this has Alek Konstantin all over it. He broke cover to come to Marseille.'

He nods, worry grooves on his forehead, two deep vertical lines between his brows. 'How is it?' he says. 'I know you can't tell me. It is way over my pay grade but are you close to finding him?'

I jam my fists into my pockets. 'I don't know. Sometimes I think it will be any minute and other times I think he will never be caught.'

He puts his hand on my arm. 'It must be very difficult for you.'

Yeah.

'If there is anything I can do, you will tell me? Any help I can give you.'

His hand is warm on my bare skin.

I turn into him, right into his personal space. His eyelashes are thick and dark, his body hot through his shirt.

His breathing hitches.

'Winter,' he says.

'The fact that you even want to help is enough,' I say. 'You are trying to do the right thing. In a world of people accepting, you are still fighting.'

We stand there quietly while the seagulls screech.

The apartment block is a modern grey piece of Marseille suburbia. The lift has an *Out of Order* sign. I breathe Fresson's embarrassment, read it in the shift of his shoulders and his sideways glance. Then his shoulders square as he makes the best of it.

'Welcome to the glamorous life,' he says.

'I slept rough last night,' I say. 'Frankly, it's a palace.'

He smiles down, two steps above me and I feel the shape of something in the air, in my accelerating heartbeat. I can taste anticipation against my teeth.

The long corridor is lit by energy efficient twilight bulbs. They do nothing to dispel the gloom. Front doors stretch away on either side. Somewhere a child cries. Kids' TV keeps pace with us as we walk up the grey corridor.

Then we are there. Fresson has his key in the lock, it turns, the door sticks, he shoves it with his hip and we are inside.

One glance tells me all I need to know. Outsize widescreen TV, foil takeaway container still on the coffee table, brown corduroy sofa lolling like an armless teddy bear.

Fresson stands awkward by the door, struggling again with his attempt to make the best of it. Seeing the place through my eyes.

I walk to the window, push the nets aside and look down. The view is out onto a supermarket car park.

'Do you think there is one right person out there for everyone?'
I say.

'I used to think so,' he says. 'Until she took my house and
kids.' He drops his keys in a plastic bowl on a ledge by the door.
It clatters overloud.

I look at him from under Snow White's hair. An honest copper
in a world all but destroyed by Firestorm. A man trying to do
the right thing. He couldn't be further from Alek Konstantin
if he tried. I think about how many hours there are until I can
question Armand.

I slip my jacket off my shoulders and throw it down on the
brown corduroy.

'I need to take a shower,' I say. 'Want to help?'

CHAPTER 36

Detective Fresson lies on his back and blows smoke at the ceiling. His silver lighter is folded into his palm and held against his bare chest like he hasn't got the energy to sit up and put it on the bedside cabinet. He is tanned against the sheets.

'Christ,' he says.

I touch my face to his stomach, breathing in the fresh sweat and exertion. His hand strokes the hair back from my forehead. I can smell Gauloises on his fingers. It is strangely comforting. He lifts his hand to take the cigarette out of his mouth.

'Tell me about the new guy,' I say.

'Armand?'

I nod.

'Better and worse. More efficient. He runs a tighter ship. Same old prostitution and extortion, less trafficking. If I have to have someone I would far rather have him than Ferret.'

And that's it in a nutshell. *If I have to have someone.*

'Uses Firestorm sparingly.'

'Is he a contractor?'

Fresson sighs. 'We don't know. There is a professionalism now that there never used to be. I'm not saying it's a bad thing but it makes me wonder what will happen when Alek Konstantin finally falls. It is already pretty bad in some places. What state has the world got into that it can't manage to police itself?'

'And how is Henri?' I picture the man behind Marseille's sex industry when I last saw him.

'He's a changed man. No one knows what happened to him.' He takes a deep drag and blows it at the ceiling. 'Apparently, he's lucky to be alive.'

'Yes,' I say. 'He is.'

I trace the raised bump of my tracker, then I trace the writing on the silver lighter with a fingertip.

With love from your wife

I think about the value of that love. The lukewarm currency of it. More powerful in the reverse. Maybe it was powerful. Maybe it burned bright and died like a falling comet in a blaze of light and fire.

I take the cigarette and stub it out. He tracks the movement, his face half amused, half fearful and full of anticipation. My hands slide under his shoulders and down into that warm place where buttock meets thigh and flip him, face first, onto the pillow.

He grunts as the air is knocked out of him. I stretch my full naked length along him, feeling every inch under my skin. I want the tracker to feel this. To know what I am doing. The damp dark curls around the nape of his neck are streaked with silver. I bury my teeth into his shoulder and he screams into the pillow. I flex my hips.

'You don't think you're done, do you?' I say.

His back is as hairy as his chest. Dark and wiry and full of sweat. I could get hot just from breathing in. I drag my nipples round, feeling the friction, feeling them harden. I straddle his hips and grind down against his tail bone. He grunts into the pillow. Snow White's hair hangs in my eyes. I straighten up as I come and lean back and stab two fingers into him. He bucks and flips and rises, trying to throw me off and I get a hand under him.

He is hard against his stomach.

He freezes and we hang motionless, him on his hands and knees, me on his back.

His breathing hitches. His body trembles.

I speed up and slow down and speed up and slow down until the sweat is dripping off him onto the pillow and his arms are shaking with effort. When he is nearly there, I slide round underneath him and take him in my mouth, while he bucks and thrusts and screams and empties himself down my throat.

An hour later, showered and dressed I swing back down the stairwell into the evening air, leaving a snoring Detective Fresson sleeping it off. He lies flat on his back, the silver lighter on the floor.

Snow White's hair sways with a clean tide of male body wash. As I move, I get the cinnamon hit of male deodorant.

I wish I could be there when Alek looks at the tracker readings and works it out.

If he is still looking.

The sudden thought is so shocking it pulls me up sharp. I teeter on the stairs, staring down at the concrete, seeing nothing but a black well in front of me.

CHAPTER 37

Marseille's newly funded business quarter is a sleek glass and chrome affair. Armand's office is on the top floor of the tallest building.

Nine o'clock at night and Armand is still open for business.

A coiffured boy and girl sit behind a high counter. I punch through the rotating doors into the vast reception space feeling underdressed. Olive trees, the size of small cars, stand in the corners. Armand is doing well for himself. Extortion and prostitution must be paying out. My boots ring on the marble.

The boy glances up and away.

The girl gives me a look from under smoky lashes that hits me in the pit of the stomach. My libido is back.

'Snow White to see Armand,' I say.

Armand's office is nearly as big as Reception. The desk is over by the window. He gets up and comes round it to meet me.

'The famous Snow White,' he says. 'I am honoured.' He looks me up and down, matching what he sees in front of him to what he has heard about the Russian hitwoman, Snow White.

Silence.

We don't shake hands. We stand, two professionals, weighing each other up. He is medium height and medium build with a pale, chiselled face and hair swept back. I get a curious feeling looking at him and it takes me a while to place it.

Respect.

I know I am looking at a fellow professional. I know under the impeccable business suit and white shirt and Hermès tie, his body will be as hard and lean as mine. He's a contractor. And now he is here running the show. An iron fist, a professional. He has been put here by Alek. The air shifts, thickening. If a pin dropped it would take light years to hit the ground.

'So,' I say, clearing my throat. 'Just a courtesy call. I have business in the neighbourhood.'

'Anything I should be aware of?'

I shake my head, dismissive. 'Routine.'

'Drink?' he says. His gaze drops as he turns away and I feel the tension release. He crosses to a mini fridge, pulls out a bottle of beer and holds it up with an arch of the eyebrow.

'Sure,' I say, taking the bottle from a perfectly manicured hand.

He slips his jacket off. His twin shoulder holsters balloon the sleeves of his shirt like he's a seventeenth-century nobleman. The tops of silver Walther PPKs are just visible. He gestures to the seating area with a panoramic view of Marseilles. I flop down and rest my ankle on my knee, my hand on my boot.

'Busy day?'

He shrugs. 'You know how it is.'

'You got the silver finish,' I say, nodding at the weaponry.

He shrugs. Rueful. It's the look of a man who drives a convertible XK8 because he loves it. Who knows it's not perfect but can't help himself.

'James Bond's gun,' I say.

'And Adolf Hitler's.'

'I heard there was an impressive distance job done here last week,' I say, taking a swig. 'Some factory owner. What was it? Six thousand feet?'

'6079,' he says.

'McMillan Tac-50?'

'Could be.'

'I don't have the patience,' I say. 'It's not the accuracy. It's the waiting – I get twitchy.'

'It is the hardest thing to master.'

'Do you know what the factory was making?'

He shrugs but his eyes narrow.

I pick at the label on my bottle and change tack. 'Do you see much of the Guardsman down here?'

His pale eyes bore into mine. 'No,' he says. 'I don't give the Guardsman any cause to pay me a visit. And there hasn't been any need for a clean-up. We haven't lost anyone on a job, touch wood.' He leans forward to the polished surface of the coffee table. 'We don't need a lot of administering.'

I take another swig of beer, willing myself not to say the wrong thing.

'Clean-up?' I lay on the Russian accent like I don't understand the expression.

'Carry out the outstanding contracts,' Armand says. 'So nothing is left in limbo.'

'Oh yeah. If someone dies on the job,' I stare down at my boot, weighing my options. Time to get some answers. I look up, meet his eyes and go for it. 'Have you ever met her?'

He shakes his head. 'And never want to,' he says.

'Amen to that.' I take another swig of beer. 'Have you heard about the experiments she is running? Victims without contracts.'

Disgust flickers across his face. 'We keep our heads down here. There is enough going on without getting involved with the Guardsman.'

I pick at the label some more. 'Solo is dead, did you know that?'

Armand shakes his head. 'I didn't but something is making sense now.'

I arch an eyebrow.

'I've heard rumours about the mother of all clean-up jobs in Moscow.'

Sergei Stanislav. Head of the Moscow Bratva.

I remember the details on Solo's phone. A particular day was contracted, in two days' time. Not leaving a lot of time for the Guardsman to plan a revenge hit for Solo's death. Not leaving a lot of time for her to be worrying about me.

The whirr of the air con and the buzz from the back of the fridge under the counter are the only sounds in the room.

'Is it always her that cleans up? I hear she plays a substitute.'

He gives me another look over the top of his bottle. 'Yes, it is always the Guardsman who fulfils the contract. It is fundamental. Part of the Firestorm guarantee. It is the principle of it. A binding contract between client and Firestorm. What would be the point of an Administrator if they outsourced to someone else?'

He looks at me with his pale eyes, having no clue he has just given me the one piece of the puzzle I needed.

CHAPTER 38

I step out into the warm air straight into Tweedledum and Tweedledee.

'What are you doing here?' I ask them.

'Waiting for you, *obviously.*'

'I'll see you in the morning at the airport,' I say, pushing past.

'Where are you going now?' They wail in unison.

'To get laid.'

The look on their faces is priceless.

'But what about us?' demands Léon.

'No one asked you to come.'

Fresson is still awake by the time I get back to the grey block. Some match is playing on the widescreen TV.

'I didn't know if you'd come back,' he says.

'I'm on a flight out of here in the morning, can I stay till then?'

He folds me in his arms and buries his face in my neck.

'Stay forever.'

'I'll settle for the night, a shower and a coffee.'

He smiles. 'How was Armand? Did you get what you came to Marseille for?'

'Yes,' I say. 'I did.'

*

The apartment phone is the most retro thing I have ever seen. The cream plastic holder is attached to the wall and the handset is attached to the cradle. You have to stand beside it.

Fancy that.

I lean up against the wall pulling the spiral through my fingers. Fresson watches me with a smile in his eyes.

The TV display is reading eleven o'clock. Ten at night in London. Simon answers first ring.

'I need some kit,' I say.

There is a fraction of a second of movement as Simon gets ready. 'Go,' he says.

I give him the list of equipment I am going to need. Nothing particularly difficult but problematic for someone not allowed to carry arms. I can feel him considering this, his busy brain finding solutions, not telling me problems.

'You're in a good mood,' he says. 'Have you got something?'

'Maybe.'

'Where do you want it?'

I tell him.

He grunts.

'By lunchtime.'

'No sleep for me then. What did you find?'

'He was here, no question.'

'Where are you?'

I picture him checking out the apartment block, peering down the wire at me. He's probably got the schematics up by now. Probably looking down the list of owners.

'With a friend.' I look across at Fresson and he winks.

'You don't have any friends,' says Simon.

I grin. 'I'll see you tomorrow. Don't be late.'

'Control wants to speak to you,' he says. 'McKellen is here by the way. I'll put you through.'

There is a pause on the line and then it reconnects.

'Well?' Control says. 'Have you got something?' Hope fills his voice. She tracked him out of Marseille last time, he is thinking, she is going to do it again.

'Maybe.'

'So it was him?'

'It was him.'

'What was he doing there?'

'Making VX or something like it.'

Control is silent. He remembers the Novichok days, before the global ban on chemical weapons, miles of countryside contaminated for ever.

'It was the next logical step,' he says. 'Anarchy breaks out and Firestorm defend their power base any way they can. I just hoped it wouldn't come to this.'

'We need to find the shipments. From something Léon said, I get the feeling the facility wasn't in production long.'

'Your priority is Alek Konstantin. You can worry about the shipments, if you survive.'

'Thanks.'

'No problem,' says the Boss.

'Is McKellen with you?'

Control grunts.

'Put him on,' I say. 'I want to speak to him.'

There is a sigh and the sound of a handset hitting a desk, then McKellen is on the line.

'That thing we were talking about,' I say.

'Go on.'

'It's a woman.'

'And I'm Daisy Duke.'

I tell him about the stiletto heels and the dents on the floor of the Palais de Justice and on the floor in Ferret's office in Marseille.

'Circumstantial,' he says. 'And in any case it makes no sense. He hung his last contract from the Brooklyn Bridge. That can't have been a woman. Have you any idea how heavy a dead body is?'

'Er.'

'Don't answer that,' he says. 'And since when were stilettos proof of gender? He could just be dressed as a woman.'

I tell him about Armand confirming it.

'A stiletto heel is not made of metal anyway,' he says.

'There is this brand in the UK,' I say. 'That have metal rods, like they used to in the 1930s and heavy, mirrored heels. You know they were called "stilettos" originally after stiletto knives?'

'So, she just pops to the UK for her shoes and then flies home?'

'I think she is based in London, like Solo. It makes sense. Everywhere is a short flight away. It's why London is hosting the G20.'

'You Brits, always thinking you are the centre of everything. No offence,' he says to Control. 'There is categorically no way the Guardsman is female.'

'Just be careful,' I say. 'I have my reasons for thinking she is about to go out of town but she could be in London.'

'Don't worry,' he says. 'He's got me locked up in an interrogation suite.'

'We call them interview rooms in the UK.'

'Whatever,' says McKellen.

THE GUARDSMAN

IX

The Guardsman frowned.

Three days to go. There was no question the Boss had found the Marseille production facility and destroyed it. Covering their tracks, protecting them. He was going to be so pleased when he found out the truth but she wished there had been some word from him. Anything. There had been nothing but a renewed command to leave Winter to him. The Guardsman knew everything the Boss did was for the greater good of Firestorm and it was not for her to question his commands but it would have been nice to know what he was planning.

She went back to the question of revenge.

Surely there had to be someone Winter was close to? The Guardsman didn't just want to see Winter die, she wanted to see her suffer. The Guardsman considered the earnest face of the man on her phone. Simon. He looked bewildered, his hair sticking out all over the place. What did GCHQ call them? Quartermasters. *Dogsbodies.*

It was the same job the world over. In Italian they were called *Furieri* after the word forage.

The Guardsman scrolled to the next suggested target. A woman. Her name was Viv. A former field agent retired to a desk job after a mission in Siberia. A friend. If someone like Winter could be said to have any friends. Suspended from duty after the death of her principal, Winter's old boss.

Now, he would have been a worthwhile target. The Guardsman felt a flash of regret that you couldn't kill someone who was already dead.

Neither target had Solo's status. Firestorm had been humiliated and the Guardsman wondered whether a pair of insignificant nobodies was going to cut it.

Cut it.

The Guardsman drummed her fingers on the hotel room table and tried not to get distracted.

The phone on the bedside cabinet rang.

The Guardsman put the phone down and smiled. The question of who Winter cared for had just been answered and it had a perfect, beautiful rightness to it. A delightful symmetry. As if Fate had personally taken a hand. The Guardsman was not superstitious but, in that moment, knew with a blinding certainty that fate had designed the perfect revenge. The right piece of information had appeared at the right time. It was destiny. The Guardsman stretched out her legs, her boots scraping the floor. Status *and* a connection to Winter – it didn't get better than that. Would there be time to carve a message on another forehead, she wondered. She certainly hoped so.

It was all coming together beautifully. The Boss was going to be so pleased when he found out.

The knife shone in the half light. Whetstone, then dry stone, then polish.

The Guardsman had heard about a blade once, whose edge was so sharp it couldn't be seen by the naked eye.

The naked eye.

The Guardsman liked that phrase.

CHAPTER 39

2 days to go...

It is morning. I stand in Fresson's bedroom wrapped in a towel, holding my jeans up to the early light. A long rip has left a gaping hole at buttock height.

'You haven't got anything else I could put on, have you?'

Fresson looks panicked. He pulls open drawers in his small cupboard and eyes the contents helplessly.

'You are never going to fit into my jeans,' he says. 'They will be massive on you.'

I hold up a pair of boxer shorts wondering if I could wear them underneath.

'What about your wife?' I say, deciding I can't. 'Did she leave anything behind?'

He shakes his head. 'She never lived here,' he says, looking round. 'There is something.' He is awkward. 'I'm not sure you'll want it.'

'At this point, I'm happy with anything that covers my butt.'

He pulls a box from the back of his wardrobe.

I stare. A cheerleader costume. 'Marseille' emblazoned across the chest. Short rara skirt.

You have got to be kidding.

'She was wearing it the day we met,' he says awkwardly. 'She doesn't know I still have it.' He holds it out. 'It's yours if you want it.'

What kind of longing makes a man keep an outfit for twenty years? His hands hang helpless.

'It is the silly things,' he says. 'The things you never think of. Like her feet. For fifteen years her bare feet were there beside me in the morning, in the bathroom, in bed. I could tell you every tiny detail of every toe, every freckle. Not that I have a particular thing for feet,' he says hastily.

'I understand,' I say. 'It is the intimacy.'

'Yes,' he says. 'And then it is gone. Now I will never see her bare feet again.'

The phone rings in the next room and he goes to answer it, leaving me staring into space. I pull the rara skirt on. He may forget her for a while, even for a night, but she is embedded in his heart like a piece of shrapnel.

Whatever else she may have been, Fresson's wife was short. The skirt is butt skimming. Fresson is standing in the doorway.

'It's for you,' he says.

'Hello?' I say, picking up the phone.

'Go to the window, Winter,' says the icy calm voice of the Prince of Darkness.

I almost drop the handset. Guilt seizes me. Grips me round the chest and squeezes.

I slide the nets aside and look down. The spiral curly cord on the phone stretches taut. A huge black sedan is waiting in the supermarket car park, its back door open, a suit standing beside it.

'Are you nuts?' I hiss.

'Get in the car, Winter,' he says. 'I am on my way.'

I slam the phone down.

I glare at it and it starts ringing again.

I yank the whole unit off the wall and hurl it across the room.

Fresson comes in from the bedroom. He looks at the phone on the floor.

'There goes my deposit,' he says.

'Sorry.'

'So that was Mr Right then, I take it?'

'Mr Wrong. Oh, so very wrong. In fact wrong doesn't even begin to cover it.'

He sighs. 'You always think that and then they smile and you forget everything you had planned to say.'

'He doesn't really smile.'

I clatter down the concrete stairwell, leaving the building on the opposite side to the car park, and stride off towards town. The wind blows fresh on my bare legs. Mortification mingles with anger. How dare he? *I am on my way.* What does that even mean? He has turned round and come back from South America or wherever he was going?

The pavements are packed with commuters scurrying to get to work. A girl with shiny auburn hair walks past me then turns back.

'Have you got the time?' she says. She has a coat over her arm and a Glock 17 in her hand. Commuters stream past us like water round an island. Soft, defenceless, vulnerable commuters. Collateral damage.

She jerks her head at the black sedan idling on the kerb.

CHAPTER 40

I look around the room. A small bedroom, grey walls, grey nets. A toilet cubicle in the corner. The flimsy partition not reaching the floor. Worn pink sheets.

Henri's.

The home of Marseille's sex industry. This is where I stayed when I worked for Ferret. It is even the same room. It makes me mad that Alek has had me brought here. I know what I will see out of the window. I am not getting up to have a look. I haven't moved from where they dumped me when they took the bag off my head.

I roll my shoulders, flex my neck. How dare he? I scowl. I would like to fold my arms to signify my displeasure but my hands are cuffed in front of me. I content myself with stretching my legs full length and seething.

I sit listening to the familiar sounds from the corridor. Doors bang, footsteps clatter, girls laugh. A long quick stride. Everything stiffens.

He's here.

The door flies open and the Prince of Darkness stands on the threshold looking as mad as hell. He looms in the doorway, broad as he was in a Mexican desert, his face scowling as much as mine. He closes the door carefully behind him.

'Just what exactly do you think you were doing?' he says quietly.

'Is that a trick question?' My voice sneers. 'Shall I draw you a picture?'

'Don't push me, Winter.' A vein throbs on the side of his neck.

'Are you *nuts*? You have kidnapped me because I shagged some guy? It is nothing to do with you who I sleep with. I will fuck the whole Marseille police department if I feel like it.'

Something in his face gives. He is across the room to me in two long strides and losing it. He hauls me to my feet, twists me round and pushes me face first against the wall, my handcuffed hands above my head. He holds me in place with his hip while he unzips his trousers and I know exactly where this is going and I am not having it. There is nothing about Alek Konstantin that doesn't get me hot but I am not having this.

I spin at the waist, cracking the side of his head with my elbow and he staggers back. Then he is throwing me on the bed, on my back, my cuffs over my head, forcing my thighs apart. My cuffs come down and my knee comes up and smacks him behind the ear. A proper blow. He keels over and falls heavily off the bed onto the floor and I am on him, straddling his chest and pressing the metal cuffs against his neck.

Then I am kissing him hard enough to bruise so there can be no doubt who is running the show. His arms come up and he rolls me over, pushes my pants aside and a second later he is inside me.

Waves of heat surge up my body, crashing over me, dragging me down, one after the other, engulfing me, swamping me. There is good sex, there is great sex and there is Alek Konstantin. In a league of his own.

He holds my head in his hands, thumbs on my cheeks, fingers in my hair.

'You are mine,' he says.

My head thrashes, the ache burning through my body.

'Say it,' he orders.

My eyes squeeze shut, to get away from the sight of him on top of me.

'Say it.' He jerks my head upright.

'Fuck you.'

I crest a wave and hang, hovering out over nothing, suspended, until he shoves me over with a brutal hard shove and I am tumbling, tumbling incoherent into the depths.

I come to, weighed down by his hard, heavy body. My ribs scream. His shoulder is pressed into my cheek. I push and heave and shove and he rolls off onto his back. He reaches a hand underneath him and pulls out a gun. He had a Glock stuck down the back of his waistband.

I hold my cuffed wrists up. 'Take these off.'

He pulls out a key. He didn't even get his trousers down. My wrists snap free and I sit straight upright. The room is cold. Voices sound in the corridor. Someone is saying goodbye. Changeover.

'Are you going to give me the Guardsman?'

'No.'

Of course he's not going to give me the Administrator and risk endangering Firestorm.

I am on my feet in a single movement and slamming the door behind me.

The corridor is brighter than the last time I saw it, like it has seen a coat of paint. The girl in the room opposite is leaning against her door jamb smoking. She is on a break. She still has the purple mules with the peeling velvet. A teddy looks down from her wardrobe.

'You're back,' she says.

'Just passing through.'

Somewhere nearby, girls laugh.

'Been some changes,' she says. She takes a deep drag. 'We keep fifty per cent now. You should come back.'

'I'll think about it.'

I swing down the corridor and down the wooden stairs, my boots ringing on every plank.

Henri is behind the reception counter, twitching and shuffling. He turns his head 180 degrees at the sound of footsteps, as if he has no peripheral vision.

I reach the bottom step.

He focuses on me and skitters back. The chair scrapes and squeals against the wooden boards.

'I'm still watching, Henri,' I say.

Out on the pavement, I stand for a moment until I realise I am hoping Alek will come out, that he will come after me, and the thought annoys me so much I stamp off down the street without a backward glance.

There is no sign of Xiu or Léon at check-in, or in Marseille airport's tiny departures hall, or in the café purveying lethally expensive baguettes to the desperate. I come out of the airport and stand looking up and down. If you were two teenagers with a limited attention span, where would you go?

The amusement arcade is down at heel with several bulbs out on its fascia and wall-to-wall slot machines where you put a coin in and hope it knocks all the pennies off the ledge.

They are crouched over 'House of the Living Dead' in the corner. I lean against the wall and watch them shooting up the zombies. Judging by the score, they have been at it for hours. I lever myself off the wall.

'Time to go, kids,' I tell them.

'Great outfit,' says Xiu, blowing the head off an eyeless corpse.

'So, what have you two been up to?'

'Nothing.' Léon's answer is whip fast.

Xiu gives a big, heavy wink like you get from an old porcelain doll. Clunk, clunk.

I am tempted to give her a high five. I rein it in.

I look from one to the other. Crimson is flooding up Léon's neck, up his face, disappearing up past his hairline. The longer I look the deeper it gets. He drops my gaze.

'Well,' I say. 'Well, I never.' I fold my arms and lean against a slot machine. 'That used to be a disciplinable offence in my day. Mind you, I'm not exactly operating from a position of strength here.'

Xiu fiddles with her dungaree strap, nonchalant. Léon shuffles his feet.

'Just don't get too attached,' I say heading for the door. 'You might end up having to kill each other.'

They trail after me back to the terminal. We are just in time. I get us the last three seats on the BA flight to London, hand luggage only, whistle through security, run down the long corridors and straight onto the plane.

It is full to the brim. Everyone is travelling with just hand luggage, the overheads are crammed. Air hostesses scowl. We work our way down the aisle looking for our seats.

Xiu and Léon shuffle and apologise and slide into their seats and I carry on up the plane and walk straight out through the back and down the stairs onto the tarmac.

An air hostess calls. I keep walking.

In the terminal building, I watch the 737 climb steeply, banking hard to the left as it gains altitude and smile as I think about them realising.

I go back to the front desk.

'Kiev,' I say.

CHAPTER 41

It is early evening by the time I exit customs and baggage reclaim at Boryspil International. One and a half hours to Paris, one and a half hours' layover and then three hours to Kiev. I slept as much as I could – I'm not going to have a lot of sleep for the next couple of nights. I get in a cab and pull up on Brovarskyi Avenue en route to Kiev central.

'I'll walk from here,' I say.

The cabbie looks at me like I am crazy.

We are on the edge of the Hydropark. It is the best time of year for Kiev's city beaches. They will be busy late into the evening – families replaced by office workers, stripping down and relaxing.

The artificial sand is covered with bodies stretched out on towels or stripy sunbeds with matching parasols. A laughing couple splash at the water's edge. I walk towards them, kicking up sand.

A figure detaches itself from the shadows.

'Simon.' I wait for the backlash, the recriminations.

'What *are* you wearing?'

I glance down at the rara skirt.

'It doesn't do it for you?'

He looks away.

'Apparently, they swim all year here,' he says, watching the glittering water.

'I doubt that. Kiev gets serious snow.'

'They hack a channel in the ice and plunge right in.' He turns to face me. 'So, what's going on? I'm assuming you have a reason for being off-grid.'

'I'm going to stop a hit. You should be pleased.'

'Who?'

'Sergei Stanislav. Solo's next job.'

He stares.

'When a contractor dies, the Administrator carries out the outstanding contracts. It's part of the Firestorm guarantee.'

Simon whistles. 'Did we know the Firestorm Administrator was a contractor? That blows my image of some tech wizard.'

'Not just any contractor.'

Simon goggles.

'It makes sense when you think about it. Who else would have the authority to do it? You don't put some geek in that job. You bring in the biggest psycho in town.'

'Doesn't mean it has to be the Guardsman. All the way over in Moscow? She might just get someone else to do it. Delegate.'

I look across the water. The giggling couple have taken the plunge and are swimming out strongly into the current. 'It's always the Guardsman. It is a matter of principle.'

Simon stares.

'Tomorrow night she is going to be in Moscow on a job. And I will be waiting for her.'

'That's quite a fan you've got there by the way,' Simon says.

'Who?'

'McKellen's kid.'

'Ariadne?'

'She is going around showing everyone my phone number on her arm.' Simon smiles. 'McKellen says she won't wash it off. She told me not to worry, she won't call it unless it is an emergency.'

'What is she doing in London?'

'The G20 of course. Two days to go. They're all here. I guess after the kidnapping, he wants them under his eye. He had to come to London so he brought the family with him.'

'Did she ask you if you were seeing someone?'

'No. Why? Do I look desperate?'

I stare across the water.

'They should have stayed in Langley.'

'They are in the detainment suite, in one of the interview rooms. Guards outside the door. Watchers in the observation room. Control dropping by every two minutes. It doesn't get any safer than that. It's like Fort Knox.'

'They should be in one of the old cells. Give me a manual door release any day. I like to be able to barricade myself in.'

Simon smiles. 'That's what Control said. He had bolts put on the inside of the door. Now they have to let people in.'

'Security must be going nuts.'

Simon cracks a small smile. 'You would think London was hosting the second coming the fuss they are making.'

'Poor Brad.'

'He was asking if you were back, by the way,' Simon gives me a look. 'I'm assuming he was behind that.' He points at Snow White's face.

I shrug, non-committal.

He turns to watch the water. 'It is a pretty damning indictment of the Service that you don't trust us with your face.'

Us.

'I trust you, Simon. You know that.' I can't believe I'm even having to say it.

Across the river I can make out the rusty roofs of the yacht club. The wide span of the bridge curves away on our right, the golden tipped domes of Kiev's monasteries gleam in the far distance. The traffic sounds far away, muffled, on the light breeze. A seagull cries.

'What about Alek Konstantin?' he says. 'What did you find in Marseille? I see they've ordered a containment team to the factory site. Was he there?'

'No question.' I stare out across the water. 'And they were definitely making something toxic. Some kind of nerve agent. At the centre of the building was a decontamination facility as good as anything we have.' Simon stares. 'I want you to check out the factory's recent history. See if you can track any shipments out of there. I don't see how they had time to make anything between Petersburg and Marseille but we should get to the bottom of it. The Guardsman was there several times, setting something up with Ferret.'

'I'll check it out.'

'So, if you were the Guardsman, how would you take out Sergei Stanislav?'

He stares out into the middle distance. 'Assuming time pressure?'

'A specific time frame was contracted, starting at midnight tomorrow night.'

'Working within that time frame then, I would say a distance shot. Given the variables, it is the safest option with the highest probability of success.'

'Yes, that's what I thought.'

'But?'

'There is a problem with that. The Guardsman is a cutter. She doesn't use firearms. Ever.'

'It's not the only problem. You can't go to Moscow. They still answer to Alek Konstantin. Make no mistake. It is one of the least safe places on the planet for you personally. If they get even so much as a hint that you are there, you are dead.' He thinks about this. 'If you are lucky.'

'Snow White can go.'

'Don't be ridiculous. He knows what Snow White looks like and even if he didn't, your tracker will give you away. If there is anywhere he can go safely, it is Moscow.'

'That's why I had you bring a blocker.'

'It's not a foolproof solution. Basically, the copper blocks the signal. If the guard moves or even slips it will stop working. You can't get into any kind of fight.' He looks at me like this is going to be a really big ask.

'You wanted to be included, remember?' I say. 'I will do it without you if I have to.'

He considers Snow White's face in silence. 'I think you change into this person when you are going to break the rules. As if it gives you permission to do what you like.' He opens his bag. 'I brought two blockers. One for each arm, so they look like matching bangles.'

I slide them on. Wide copper arm guards like an Amazon warrior's armour. I hold them up and they glitter in the sun. Somewhere in South America, a signal just winked out. Will the tracker ring an alarm? Or will it just circle and circle looking for the signal? I think about his face as it dies and feel a wrench of satisfaction.

'It can't slip at all, do you realise? It is literally shielding the signal. If it slips even for a moment, the locator will transmit.' He grips my wrist trying to get his point home.

I roll my eyes. 'I get it.'

He opens the bag.

'You've got your CZ P-09s, your rifle, your phone, a locator, cash, all as specified.'

I look in the bag. The L115A3 combat rifle comes with a Schmidt and Bender Military MK11 telescopic sight, a metal transit case, a mount, butt spacers, spare magazines, a sling and a tool kit. It is not light.

'How did you get it all out? Who did you say it was for?'

'You. Beth has signed you back on active.'

'I'm off suspension?'

'Yes.'

I don't know what to make of that.

'How's wots-her-name?' I say.

He looks at me from under his floppy hair. 'Who?'

'Your girlfriend. Pansy Face.'

'Emma. I can't keep up with her,' he says. 'One minute she is quoting Shakespeare and the next it is all zero knowledge proofs and spooky maths.'

'Is she the one?'

He stares across at the flickering glittering water of the Dnieper. 'I'm not discussing it with you.'

'Fair enough.' I zip the bag up and sling it on my back. It weighs a ton. 'Get back to base and keep an eye on Tweedledum and Tweedledee for me.'

He glances round like he is expecting them to pop up from behind a beach umbrella.

'I got rid of them.'

'Are you sure?'

'I think they have imprinted on me. Like ducklings.'

He smiles. 'They are amazingly persistent.'

'In a catastrophically amateur kind of way.'

He reaches for my arm, turning me back to him. 'Be careful, Winter. You are way out on a limb here. Sergei answers to Alek. There is a high likelihood the Kremlin answers to Alek. Nowhere within Russian borders is safe for you. Remember that.'

There is a Toyota parked in the lee of the bridge. It has one wheel up at an angle on the sand.

I glance behind me. At a distance, the beach looks like a colony of multicoloured penguins, all crowded and squawking and bobbing.

The Toyota was old about forty years ago. Now it is practically vintage. I glance in the back seat. Open the boot. Get on my hands and knees and check the underside. Satisfied, I get in, adjust the driver's mirror and prepare myself for a ten-hour night drive to Moscow and the Guardsman.

CHAPTER 42

Dusk comes and night falls hard. The hours stretch out before me.

As I drive, I listen to everything GCHQ has on file about Sergei Stanislav. I knew a lot already but I am out of date – it's been a while since I was on mission in Moscow. He still lives in a sixteen-bedroom mansion in an exclusive suburb with his Russian wife of thirty years and he still owns Moscow's trendiest nightclub, The Mayfair Rooms.

Some things are new.

His daughter has a new baby and he now also owns the Maison Honfleur – Moscow's most high-end brothel. The report doesn't say what happened to the previous owner.

I track the pathways of his life. He goes to the club every day except Monday and Sunday and ends up most nights at the Maison Honfleur. He has never been into guys but women are another matter.

He uses muscle like an old-fashioned mobster but is wily and canny and smart.

Midnight comes and the lorry I had been following for three hours drops away and now there is only the occasional tail light ahead. I stare out at the lonely road thinking about my way in. My blockers glint in the light from the dashboard.

A combat rifle is accurate up to half a mile in average hands. Double that for someone who knows what they are doing. If it was me, like Simon, I would hole up and wait for my chance. It may be hours, it may be days, but sooner or later there's an opening.

Maybe you take down a bodyguard. Cue panic and confusion and you get your opening.

If you can put a team on it, even better. Street hijack. Or a building raid – assault and acquire. Probably not in the mansion, panic rooms can slow you down. The Maison Honfleur most likely. Constantly changing, transient employees.

By the time the border comes, Sergei has died a dozen times in my mind.

Easy enough, with time and distance. But the contract specified a particular day. Tomorrow. And tomorrow starts at midnight. The Guardsman doesn't have time and she never keeps her distance. In all her many hits she has never used a single firearm. Not a long range, not an assault weapon, not even a handgun.

She must be planning and considering, working out the parameters just like I am. Maybe she is on her way already.

The barrier raises, the border guard doesn't get out of his Perspex home and I breathe out.

It is long and time-consuming coming in by road. Until you are actually driving it, you forget how vast Russia is. You could fit the UK in five times between Moscow and the nearest border.

But necessary. I am not going in unprepared this time. I have my guns, my blades and a blocker to hide me from Alek Konstantin.

One day to go...

The Toyota does an impressive 700 kilometres per tank. I have crossed time zones again and it is early morning before I am off the M2 and arriving on the outskirts of Moscow. Nothing has changed about the road layout since I was last here. The one-way system is still crazy. Trams still criss-cross the road, oblivious. Black leather jackets continue to be in vogue. Early commuters bustle along the streets, darting in front of the slow-moving trams.

Like Europe, Moscow is showing none of the tensions that are dividing North America. In Europe, it is because the authorities are still in charge; in Moscow, it is the other way around.

I hit the third ring road, go up Leninsky Avenue, cross New Arbat, go down Tverskaya and turn into a twenty-four-hour underground car park.

My hand raises like I am adjusting the sunshade as the car passes the entry cameras. The barrier goes up and I drive down the ramp.

Rows and rows of cars stretch either side of a wide aisle, nearly a mile long. Just one level, one straight line of parking, right under Moscow central. Concrete pillars every ten metres or so, stairs to the street every hundred.

A whole other world, just below street level. I cruise down the line looking for a good spot and turn in nose first when I find it. A concrete pillar on one side and a BMW that hasn't moved in a while on the other. The space is too tight to open the doors and that suits me fine.

I scramble into the back to change my clothes – jeans, T-shirt, Kevlar – bending and flexing in the cramped space. Buckle on my shoulder holsters and slot in my CZ P-09s.

The GCHQ armourer had a version of the Glock 17 Gen 4 designed especially for the service but another armourer I met a couple of months back told me the CZ P-09 was the gun for me. And he was right. I check the chamber but I don't need to. Eight hundred and fifty-five grams. The heft is different if they aren't loaded. Twenty-one plus one bullets, the biggest capacity on the market, slim and light in a woman's hand. Just the weight of it in my hand makes me feel invincible. My own guns chosen for me by Italian organised crime.

I clamber out via the boot and slam the lid behind me. I feel primed and ready. Not the full-on adrenaline of a fight but mission ready.

A task to do and a set amount of time to do it.

It is warm in the gloom. Not as hot as London and Marseille but pleasant. No hardship to be sleeping rough. Movement makes me look up fast. The ceiling is a mass of cables from the street, strung with pigeon netting. It doesn't seem to be working. Pigeons flutter and rustle in the dark gaps. The BMW's roof is splattered.

I spent a lot of time in this car park when I was in Moscow before. The parking bays are like hot desks for the city's transient criminal fraternity. You come for a couple of nights, do the job and melt away again.

I walk up the rows checking there's nothing new. More cameras than last time, the plastic shattered, fractured right through, crazy-paved by gunfire.

Fifty cars down, I come to the first stairwell. I glance back over my shoulder. The Toyota is lost in the sea of black cars. I push open the heavy metal door and stand listening to the low murmur of voices.

A moment later, the concrete space is crowded with sudden silence. A gaping black hole where there was noise before. Green algae streaks the concrete. The smell is a physical presence in the air. Damp and urine and something else.

Some things never go out of fashion. The particulars change, tastes come and go, the method might alter but ultimately there are always people getting high in a stairwell. Far off, the street echoes with the sound of engines pulling away from the lights. I am pretty sure I know where it comes out but I would like to be sure. This is my nearest exit and it is tradecraft rule number one:

scope out your escape route and then find another. I take a step forward. Eyes peer down at me from the turn in the stair.

'Relax,' I say to the eyes. My Russian is perfect.

I wait a beat to give them time to check me out then I walk up the steps slowly, one stair at a time, scanning the space.

Junkies crowd the half landing, clustering together, peering up at me from under greasy hair. They have been at it all night. Two guys and two girls, although it is hard to be sure. Black leather is a good disguise. They pause to watch me pass, eyes on my back all the way up the second flight.

I push through the door at the top, head up the final flight to street level and do a full 360 absorbing the sights and sounds, sucking in the feel of Moscow.

Horns blare.

I am exactly where I expected. The buildings have barely changed since I was last here. There is a new giant blue Nokia sign on the apartment block opposite but that is about it. Early morning and the street is busy. People heading out for the day, others on their way home from the nightshift. Everyone has a fag in their hand. The Moscow smoking culture is still going strong.

I turn and go back down the stairs.

The junkies look up. They have had time to get used to me now, time to get familiar with the idea of a woman, in their stairwell, on her own. Time for things to occur to them. As I reach the turn, the man with the eyes bars the way.

About five foot ten, a three-inch blade in his hand.

I pull my hands out of my pockets.

'Hey, beautiful,' he says. His teeth are brown and broken.

'Really? That's what you are going with? You don't want to give it some more thought?'

'What?' he says.

Sigh.

'Is there nothing about this situation ringing alarm bells for you?' I say. 'Woman on her own? Easy pickings? Too good to be true, maybe?'

His eyes crinkle as the idea filters through. He gives me a lingering once over. 'You got some moves on you?' Lank hair covers his eyes. He looks like a poster for heroin chic from decades ago. 'Maybe we could show you a few moves.'

'Hurry up then,' I say. 'I'm on a schedule.'

Confusion flickers in his eyes, with hesitation hard on its heels. He raises his knife hand and moves forward a fraction and stops. I watch the knife and then there is movement in the space behind me. Someone else, not up with events.

An arm circles my neck, a blade touches my throat, smooth leather strokes the underside of my chin. His body presses up against mine, his breath warm on my neck. I grab the elbow, pull it towards my neck, push the knife past, lean forward and he flies over my shoulder, landing against the legs of the other guy like a bowling ball in a skittle alley. Heroin chic goes over with a stagger and a whirling, windmilling of arms. Bottom, back, head.

Classic.

'You need a few more people,' I say, stepping over the bodies. 'If you want to try that again.' I consider the stairwell. 'Although a closed environment is always unpredictable.'

I open the door to the car park and it slams closed under its own weight. More than a fire door, it has the heavy, weighty clunk of a containment door.

I walk up the rows of cars past the concrete pillars, past the Toyota, anonymous and uninteresting. The vehicular equivalent of the NSA building. *Nothing to see here, move along.* Overhead, the pigeons flutter and bob, majorly contributing to the smell. I carry on up the rows until the entrance comes into view. A glass kiosk is tucked into the inside curve of the ramp.

I make my way over.

There is a man sitting behind the glass. He is bald and spectacled and large. He was large when I first knew him and the intervening years have not been kind. If I was following suit I would be using words like 'gargantuan' and 'colossal'.

The Collector. A finger in many pies. He sits behind his bulletproof glass and manipulates events. As far as I know, he never comes out.

I step up to the glass.

In the corner, an old-fashioned TV plays some American soap. The dubbing is bad. Mouths open and close and no sound comes out.

I push a 5,000 ruble note down into the metal hole. He ignores me for a split second just to make sure I understand who is boss, then a huge arm comes up and the metal closes and the note shoots through to his side. Six inches of flab hang from his arm. Huge, gold sovereign rings are welded to his fingers, the flesh ballooning out on either side, like belted sausages. Better than knuckledusters.

He grunts as he looks at the note and stares straight at me. His face is completely hairless, no eyelashes, no eyebrows, no beard, nothing. It is disconcerting. It is still disconcerting even though it is no surprise.

The note has told him a lot. It has told him I know the form. I have not wandered in, thinking it is a public car park. I know the form and I am prepared to pay upfront for it. I am not cheap. I am not going to haggle. I had to guess the going rate. Too little and he would be pissed, too much and he will get ambitious.

'How long?'

I shrug, hands in pockets. I look away. 'A few days?'

'Do I know you?' The hairless, lidded gaze stares at Snow White's face.

Winter shudders behind Snow White's eyes.

I shake my head. 'I think I would remember…' *someone like you.*

Just enough attitude to let him know I am not a patsy. Not enough to challenge him. Urban legend has it, he once put someone in a meat grinder.

Feet first.

And watched them beg.

'Keep out of stairwell twelve,' he says.

'OK.'

He leans down, tucking the note somewhere out of sight.

'Am I done?' I say.

He considers me. Then he nods fractionally. Jowls wobble.

I can feel the hairless, lidded gaze on my back as I walk all the way down the car park.

CHAPTER 43

Sergei's garden walls are high and white, with cameras on poles and everything else you would expect from the home of the man who rules Moscow's streets. The guardhouse beside the massive automatic gates is like an embassy checkpoint.

A guardhouse on the outside.

I wonder if they can open the gates themselves or whether it has to be done from inside the house.

I do a full circle of the walls and it takes me twenty minutes. It is a whole block by itself. More than a mile round. The garden is thickly wooded. No sign of the house.

I get back to the start. The nearest neighbours are hidden behind high walls. There is no one else around. No sign of anyone else doing what I am doing and that's not a surprise. Tight time frame and the clock ticking down. It was always the least likely option. How often is Sergei home after all? He is probably pretty busy. I'm sure that is the conclusion anyone would come to.

I turn on my heel and head back to the centre and my car park home to catch a few hours' sleep before tonight.

Early evening and Moscow's nightlife is already well under way. Lovers meander, hands in each others' back pockets. Street vendors hawk their wares, restaurants compete for tourists.

I stand beside one of the grand subway exits. The domed ticket hall is like the inside of a church, the arched white roof stretching cavernous overhead.

I am getting my bearings, thinking about the terrain. A central square. The river on one side. Park on the other and at either end, facing each other, the Hotel Imperial and the Mayfair Rooms. Baroque eighteenth-century architecture. All turrets and spires and ornate ironwork. Really perfect terrain for a sniper.

Moscow's best hotel and hottest nightclub on the same square, one hundred yards apart. An easy distance for a sniper. Not too difficult even for an amateur. I look at the rooflines and I look at the entrances and I look at the distance and then I look back at the entrances again.

The Hotel Imperial has one of those long, covered tunnels leading to the main entrance. A VIP car can pull up inside it. There is no protection from the hoarding itself, it is probably oiled canvas but that doesn't matter. It renders a sniper blind.

I turn to look at the Mayfair Rooms. Fin-de-siècle Paris, all buttresses and pediments and little domes. Huge shallow basins flame either side of the door. Five or six steps up.

Five or six steps out in the open.

A no brainer. If he was my contract he would be dead the moment he showed.

I buy a doughnut on a stick and a coffee from a street vendor and sit back on an iron bench and watch the world go by. 10 p.m. it is still early for clubbing. The square is thronged with tourists and couples, a sax is competing with a techno act. I have never seen anyone spin on their head. I can smell the river and hot chocolate peanuts.

I scan the Hotel Imperial's windows but nothing moves. I figure it would have to be higher than the first floor. Higher than the second floor probably. No point in guessing – I might as well just ask. I pull out my phone for a secure line.

'What do you need?' Simon says.

I picture him in the cold, wide GCHQ incident room, a physical Faraday cage. The only place to run a live op from. He is stuck there as long as I am operational. He's probably glad to be away from the G20 circus.

'I want to know about the rooms on the front. Who's in them. When they booked. I'll wait.'

I hear Simon starting to type. 'How was your flight, Simon?' he says. 'How are you doing, seventy-two hours with no sleep?'

'What?' I say.

'Nothing.'

'How are Xiu and Léon?'

'Driving me mad. They are convinced I know where you are. I think they're camped outside in the corridor right now.'

Probably keeping Pansy Face company.

There is a pause while he opens the hotel's systems. 'Well, here's a weird thing. They are long-term. Three of the suites have had the same occupants for over a year.'

'So, no convenient booking today then? Could be the roof.'

'Or in the Mayfair Rooms or in the Maison Honfleur,' Simon says.

'Right. Where is Sergei now?'

'Still at home. Maybe it's a quiet night in.'

'And maybe he's decided to take holy orders. Balance of probability says he sticks to his schedule.'

Simon grunts. He can't disagree.

'I'll go and check out the roof while he is still tucked up safe.'

'Are you armed?' he asks, picturing the next ten minutes and getting to the point where I walk slap into the Guardsman lying in wait.

'Loaded and ready,' I reassure him. 'I've got everything. And she doesn't know Snow White, remember.'

'Just be careful,' he says. 'It could be literally anyone. It could be the cleaning lady.'

'Always am.'

*

I cross the square, head away from the street cams and walk down the side of the Hotel Imperial. It takes up almost a whole block. I turn again and walk up the alley at the back. It is full of bins, broken air conditioner units and about half the hotel's staff.

I pull out a cigarette and lean forward for a light. A chef in whites cups his hands around the flame. I lean forward, take a deep drag and blow it at the dark sky.

'I needed that,' I say.

'Long day?' He grins sympathetically.

'Just starting. You?'

'Dinner is done.'

'Now it's just room service?'

He nods. 'And the breakfast trays.'

I lean back against the wall and work my assets a little.

'What is the night manager like?'

'Andrei? He's OK.'

'I was thinking I might go and see him.'

He looks at me with dawning comprehension. 'Are you working?'

'Yeah.'

He waves me through.

'Tell him Nikolai sent you,' he says.

I stub out my fag with one turn of my boot, throw him a sideways smile from under Snow White's hair and slide through the kitchen door.

Back stairs on the left, kitchen on the right, corridor to the atrium straight ahead.

I make for the stairs. Wooden crates are stacked against the wall, narrowing the treads. Service stairs not seen by the public. Rubbish on every turn. No doubt the public areas are all marble and polished wood and thick red pile carpets. Maids clatter past, doors bang below. I keep on going right up to the top.

A fire escape leads out to the rooftop. It is closed down tight, alarmed contact points. Not much of a problem. I poke my head out of the service door to the top landing.

Red plush carpet, as expected. Guest rooms, the numbers picked out in gold.

The ceiling is lower up here. These rooms must be under the eaves. Cosy.

I go back into the stairwell, pull out my phone and give Simon the form.

'On three,' he says.

He counts it down and I jerk open the door as he cuts the power, the lights flicker and I pull the door sharp closed behind me.

The air is balmy. I can see all the way to Moscow State University and in the other direction, all the way to the outskirts. It won't be properly dark till 11 p.m. Mist hangs heavy over the deep green, wooded far bank. Like something out of a fairy tale.

A beautiful night to be roaming the rooftops looking for a killer.

No one has been through my door recently but there are three other doors, all fire escapes leading to the roof. I pick my way between the gulleys and the pointed roofs and the turrets, to the low wall of colonnades overlooking the square.

I crouch down, open my backpack, take out an optical gunsight and line it up on the doorway opposite. I track the route from the pavement to the door and back again, do some basic calculations and come to the conclusion that anyone could do it.

A laughably simple shot.

In the hands of a competent shooter, the L115A3 has a range of 1,400 metres at sea level and 1,550 metres at altitude. In the hands of an expert? Much, much further.

I rest my elbow on my knee and my chin on my hand and consider.

Too easy.

The Guardsman is many things. But nothing she does is easy. I circle the other three fire escapes but only manage to confirm what I have already guessed. No one has been through them recently. Whatever she is doing, she is not taking the easy way.

I stare down into the square at the fire-eater still going for it.

It was always going to be a big ask to catch the Guardsman before the event. Sergei is about to break cover and I have no idea where she is.

It is time to mark the target.

I am going down the car park stairwell thinking about outfits suitable for Moscow's top nightclub, when the same jokers bar my way. They have an extra two junkies with them – one thin and emaciated, the other, wide-eyed and staring.

Heroin Chic grins. 'Surprise,' he says.

I roll my eyes.

'Two extra bodies aren't material here,' I say. 'It doesn't tilt the playing field sufficiently. It doesn't alter the odds. When I said you need more people, it was misleading.'

'What?'

'I apologise. I should have been clearer.'

He blinks.

I pat his arm as I swing past. 'You need *a lot* more people, not two. Significant numbers.' I sweep my arm round. 'Enough people to fill this stairwell.'

CHAPTER 44

The car park is cooler than the fetid stairwell. Pigeons coo. I can see stairwell twelve across the way.

Stay away from stairwell twelve.

The car park has always been home to drug deals and contract sex. Blow jobs under the stairs. No area was ever out of bounds before.

I check the time. 11.10 p.m. Time to change, get to the club and find Sergei before midnight and the clock starts ticking. Not really time to get into anything.

Maybe just time to have a quick look. Check it out. Satisfy my curiosity.

I turn left, not right, and cross the aisle.

Stairwell twelve is the closest to the state precinct of the city police. I never went near it before. The last thing you need as a representative of a foreign hostile nation is to tangle with the domestic law enforcement.

Maybe the Collector was just warning me to be careful about this stairway given its proximity to about a thousand cops.

Maybe.

I push the door open.

Lighter and cleaner. Stairs down as well as up. That surprises me. I didn't know there were any stairs down. The whole car park operates, literally, just below ground level, a thin skin of tarmac and concrete between it and the world above.

The stairs come to an end, two short flights down, in a small lobby and a metal door.

Leaning against the door is some kind of a guard. Six foot, muscled, leather jacket, Moscow native. Not a junkie. Definitely not a junkie. Muscle for sale.

He levers himself off the door. 'This is a dead end,' he says. 'Keep going up for the street.' His tone is friendly, but his eyes are hard. Eyes that have seen it all and done most of it and are never surprised. I have seen that look before, but it still makes me falter, a gap where a step should be.

I come down the last step, jamb my hands in my jeans pockets and gesture at the closed door with my elbows. 'Where does it go?'

He moves towards me an inch. In percentage terms, no more than one per cent, but indicative. *I am ready. Come one step closer and you will have to deal with me.*

An important inch psychologically.

'Nowhere.'

I hold his eyes and see them register surprise as he re-evaluates. I wonder what there is in my eyes that is causing him to re-evaluate and then it is decision time. Do I make something of it? My eyes flick round the lobby area. How much do I want to see behind the metal door?

I should let it go. I am on a schedule. I can't get distracted by local issues.

'Sorry,' I say, breaking the stare off. 'I must have gone the wrong way.'

'Yeah,' he says. 'This is the wrong way.'

I am halfway back up the stairs when someone screams behind the door. A girl or a teenage boy.

I pause, my foot on the stair above.

'Keep walking,' he says.

I look up at the stone slope of the ceiling above me and down at the stained concrete treads beneath my feet. I listen to the sounds of the car park muffled by the closed door. I check the time. Then I turn on my heel and walk slowly back down the stairs. I stop just in front of him and pull one hand out of my pocket.

There is nothing friendly about him now. 'Let it go,' he says. 'Don't start something you can't finish.'

I throw the loose change in my hand, hard and fast at the door. The acoustics are just right. The metal door rings like the great bell on Notre Dame. His eyes close instinctively as the silver flies, just for a split second but long enough.

My fist plus knuckledusters catches him on the side of the head and he goes down and I step over his body, my front foot already on its way with the forward momentum.

Metal coins against a metal door surrounded by stone sound like a shrapnel bomb going off. The door opens and a guy puts his head out. *What the hell was that?* he is thinking. He gets as far as 'What the——?' before he is brought up short by the barrel of my CZ P-09 in his face. He backs up, quick and efficient, hands raised and I am through the door and looking about me.

An arched, narrow passageway, brickwork, not car park concrete. The passageway widens out into a much bigger space, but I can't see what it is – my field of vision is limited to the brick arch and the man in front of me. He is dressed the same as the first guy. I lower my gun arm slowly until the CZ P-09 is pointing at the floor, his eyes follow the movement down and my left hand catches him just behind the ear.

He drops like a stone.

Two down.

I edge along the passageway, gun arm stretched out, left hand, still with its knuckledusters, supporting the wrist. The recoil on a CZ P-09 is nothing like as bad as a Glock but at full extension it is still a bitch. I swing round.

The passageway opens out into a corridor lined with cell doors. I pull up in surprise, trying to work out where I am. Can this already be under Police Headquarters? Why would there be underground access from the car park to the cells?

There is movement in the space, muffled sounds from the cells as if they are occupied. Iron grinds against stone; I register it is a cell door opening and duck back out of sight just in time to see a traffic cop coming out of one of the cells. He is in full biking leathers, his identifier on his right shoulder. He locks the door, takes a clipboard down from its hook on the wall, fills in entry details, slides the pen back under the metal clip at the top and hangs it back on the hook. He takes a last look at his prisoner and walks away from me up the corridor, footsteps echoing in the silence.

I curse myself for getting involved, for totally misreading the situation. I have just put two undercover officers on their backs and broken into the police detainment level for what? Someone who has been pulled in for drunk and disorderly probably.

Don't start something you can't finish.

It was good advice. I wish I had taken it.

I edge silently towards the cells and peer through the rusty bars. A woman is sitting in the corner sobbing. She looks up and stares at me. Then she puts her head in her arms again.

I creep down the line.

The cells are full. A single occupant in each. Old man, old woman, middle-aged man, middle-aged woman. One young man, maybe in his twenties. It is like some kind of Noah's ark. A specimen from all the ages of man. There are seven in total, all asleep or staring at the wall. There is something weird about them. Not one speaks to me. I take a clipboard off a hook and look at it. Arrest date and signature. No offence listed.

I glance up the way the traffic cop went. There must be stairs at the end but I sure as hell can't go out that way. I will have to go back the way I came. I retrace my steps, silent on the stone. The undercover cops are still out. I creep through the metal door, back up the stairs and out into the underground car park.

Shit.

What an idiot. There is no way the two cops I punched out won't follow it up.

Control's voice rings in my head.

You are too confident, too reckless, too hasty. When will you learn to think before you act?

The dark tunnel lined with bonnets stretches away. Light shafts down here and there, a street grating or an ill-fitting manhole cover. Up ahead is the exit light for the junkies' stairwell and somewhere past it, in the gloom, the Toyota.

It is 11.30. Half an hour before midnight. I was here with a whole day to spare and now I am going to be late.

Half an hour later, I stand across the square from the Mayfair Rooms watching the club. The temperature is coming down fast and the wind is cold against my bare back. I have come dressed for clubbing. My arm guards gleam. My guns are stowed away in the back of the Toyota, but I still have my knives in my boots.

Midnight.

Showtime, Cinderella.

The countdown on the Sergei Stanislav contract just started.

CHAPTER 45

It is like arriving at a five-star hotel. Limos, Rolls Royce, Bentleys line the cobbles. Their drivers tucked up inside, an evening of internet porn ahead of them. Flaming braziers flank the entrance. Up close they are huge. Punters queue, anxious, behind a red rope. Mayfair Rooms operates a strict door policy. If you are not good looking, you are not getting in.

I am not worried. Snow White can hold her own.

I walk up the wrong side of the red ropes, smile at the bouncers and then I am in.

Blue neon from the giant hallway chandelier casts a weird Halloween glow over security as they check bags. I am not carrying a bag so I walk through the metal detectors with my easy stride and my eight ceramic throwing knives and then I am in the club and the blue glow is replaced by glitter and mirror balls and beautiful women with swinging sheets of shiny hair and big lip-gloss smiles.

I stare round.

It is like the interior of an opera house. Ornate gold and gilt and cream. A DJ works the stage, Europop pumping out of the twenty-foot speakers. Sequinned bodies wriggle on their high heels, giggling and flicking their hair. There is nothing cool about Moscow's top nightclub. It is bling on steroids.

The dance floor is where the stalls would be if it really was an opera house. The boxes are all VIP booths. I scan for Sergei's and there it is, right in the centre. Raised above the crowds. The Royal Box with its bulletproof glass and great view.

I carve my way through the sweating throng to the art deco bar and order myself a cocktail. It comes with an umbrella and a slice of lemon. I dig a nail into the lemon rind and get a burst of brilliant citrus. I can just about make out the figures in the Royal Box. I climb up on the end of the bar for a better look.

This is better. I can see all the way into the box. Sergei and a couple of bodyguards.

The crowd whoop, their arms pointing in my direction.

A waitress in a jewelled bikini goes past, a bottle of champagne held aloft. Fizzing firework fountains flare white, strapped to the neck of the bottle. The crowd part to let her go, whooping and clapping and I watch her make her way up the narrow stairs, shooting white sparks as she goes. I trace the peacock colours of her bikini and the flaring fireworks as she makes her way along the first-floor level.

Girls in the same peacock bikinis work platforms high above the dance floor. Rope walkways link the platforms, their gold tassels swaying.

It is a while since I pole danced, but it is all coming back to me. The pounding vibrations through the floor, the tiny dressing room behind the stage, gym lockers holding the dancers' kit. Not that there was ever a whole lot of kit. Sequinned thongs covering the essentials.

I am down and behind the bar in one fluid move. Backstage is deserted. Gym lockers stand wide. Bits of discarded costume lie on the benches, as expected.

It is the work of a moment to find a peacock bikini bra and thong. I pull everything off except my boots. The bikini is strapless, tying between the breasts, maximising cleavage. The thong ties over each hip. One size fits all. Basically, three good tugs on the strings will see the entire outfit on the floor. I can just imagine Xiu and Léon's grinning faces if they could see me.

I stuff my clothes into an empty locker and then I am back out on the dance floor pushing my way to an empty platform.

This is more like it.

I am on the same level as the Royal Box, looking in at point-blank range. Sergei lounges back staring at his phone, the bodyguards stand, eyes on the crowd.

There may be some skills I lack – no doubt Control would say they are legion – podium dancing is not one of them. I pull a few flashy moves, curling back into a flip, sinking into the splits, scissoring the air in a one-armed handstand until the oohing and aahing has ratcheted up a notch and the girl on the next-door platform has stopped, hands on hips, to stare.

Sergei is still on his phone.

I cross to the next-door platform with three easy strides on the rope walkway and stand, checking her out.

Her skin shimmers silver. Some kind of iridescent cream. It glistens in the deep valley between her breasts, curves a path up to her throat. She is spectacular. Really. Russian babe premier league. Not much of a dancer, but I doubt anyone cares.

'Are you new?' she says. 'You are meant to stay on your own platform.'

'Relax,' I say. 'It's all good.'

Girlie shows are ten a penny in Western Europe, but Moscow has always been a little more straight-laced.

I pull her gently towards me with a hand on the small of her back and stroke my knuckles down her cheek. She watches me wide-eyed, bewildered by the turn of events. I rub my thumb across her mouth. Below us, someone on the dance floor wolf whistles. I can picture them all beginning to stare upwards.

I dip her back, so she curves over my arm, over the platform rail, and touch my lips to her throat. Hairspray and sweat. I pull her up and look into her face, forehead to forehead. Her eyes are huge. I kiss her.

She gasps as my tongue touches hers.

'Shhh,' I whisper against her mouth, stroking the cotton-soft skin round her waist, snaking my hand up her back. Her sequins are rough against my bare skin.

Her eyes close and her mouth opens and she sinks into it with a sigh that has my hips flexing involuntarily.

I glance over her shoulder at the Royal Box. Sergei is gaping, his drink halfway to his face, his phone nowhere in sight.

I close my eyes again and get into it.

My hand slides under her thong and keeps going. I hold her in place with a hand in her hair, swallowing her gasp of shock with my mouth. After a moment, her arms circle my neck, her chest presses against mine.

The floor rocks and it is not lust, it is the platform moving beneath us. We are descending back to earth, the golden pole sliding down into the dance floor, the rope walkways retracting.

The management have called time.

I don't let her up for air all the way to the ground.

A circle of burly bouncers hold back the dance floor. One of them grips my upper arm and propels me through the crowd. 'The Boss wants a word,' he says, breathing garlic in my ear.

We go up the stairs and meet a wall of muscle guarding the door to the Royal Box. They pat me down unnecessarily thoroughly, given I am only wearing a few sequins.

Thoroughly and ineffectually. They miss the knives in my boots.

They shove me forwards.

Sergei turns as the door opens. 'You are hired,' he says, throwing his arms wide.

And there it is, as simple as that. The bulletproof gold fishbowl from the inside.

Hot damp fingers close around my arm and pull me close. Sergei Stanislav, living, breathing proof of power as an aphrodisiac. It is a bit rich his club operates such a tight door policy.

'Phenomenal assets,' he says, getting a load of cleavage at eye level.

I have spent time over the years looking at Sergei's file. I know plenty about him. But I have never been this close. Close enough to see the pores on his nose, the hair dye clogging his hairline, staining the skin. The air stills as I look at his calculating face and realise he is appraising me just like I am appraising him.

There is a buzz against my skin, against the bones in the back of my neck and my heart jolts as I understand.

Too late.

Way too late.

I slide sideways into someone's arms and it all goes dark.

CHAPTER 46

Flecks of colour spark behind my lids. I can smell cooking in the cold air. I open my eyes. A basement with bright lighting. My neck aches. My head is woozy. I am padlocked to a chair. Not good. Nothing good ever starts with 'I am padlocked to a chair'. The bouncer from the Royal Box is in the corner, smiling. I can taste his anticipation. Something is getting him hard. I hope it's not me.

I rotate my wrists behind me. Metal handcuffs. Snow White's hair hangs in my eyes. My copper arm guards are gone.

Shit.

'Hey, bitch.' Sergei is standing in front of me, snapping his fingers. He slaps my face.

I flinch a split second before impact and take it on the jaw.

He shakes his hand.

'Who do you work for?'

'What?' I say, playing for time, considering my options.

I work for the British Government, don't forget about the Geneva Convention.

I am FSB. Don't mess with me, sweetheart.

I am one of your pole dancers; what makes you think I'm not?

My eyes take in the basement. Crates in the corner, wide metal cooling ducts, concrete floor covered in stains. Good to see some people still do it old-school. I get a flashback to Solo in our modern medical facility. Pumping rock is coming from overhead. Pumping down the walls, vibrating the metal ducts.

Nothing to suggest this is any kind of a long-term solution. No rings on the walls, no chains. The floor is a DNA minefield, testimony to the fact that Sergei is master in his own town. He couldn't care less about physical evidence.

He brandishes a handful of white blades in my face.

'Assassins' weapons,' he says. He pulls at my arm. 'And a tracker.' His fist comes back preparing for another strike. 'Who are you?'

'I am here to protect you.'

'Right.' Disbelief rings in the air. 'Who sent you?'

Adjust and adapt.

'Alek Konstantin.'

'*What?*' Sergei's hand stops in its downswing. He vibrates with the halted momentum. It's a gamble, but not much of one. I'll bet Sergei still answers to Alek. 'I don't believe you,' he says. 'He would never send someone without telling me.'

'He has a scar running down his hip bone.'

Sergei shrugs dismissively, waves his hands. 'So, you've fucked him. Alek Konstantin sleeps with a lot of women.'

That annoys me even more than being handcuffed to a chair. I have no idea why.

He leers down at me. 'Especially women who look like you.'

I jut my chin and look him in the eye. 'Call him,' I say. 'Ask him.'

Now it's like I have slapped him.

'You don't just *call*.'

'It's OK, keep this up and he'll call you.'

He looks at me. He turns away. He chews at a nail. Then he rubs his face with both hands like he is washing it, like an ugly chipmunk. 'Hell,' he says. 'Tell me something else about him.'

I think about it.

'He has a scar around his wrist that people think is a snake tattoo. It is actually an injury from manacles he got when he was a child.'

Sergei's face moves. 'You might have just heard that.'

What would no one know? He fucks like an unstoppable freight train. Like a force of nature. Maybe other people know that.

'He uses knuckledusters not guns when he wants to make a point. He drinks neat Scotch and speaks Japanese.'

Sergei stares.

'He has a manservant called Kristophe.'

He holds a hand up to halt me and takes a step backwards. A full minute goes by while he stares at me and I am reminded who it is I am dealing with.

This man has been at the head of the Bratva for a decade. He didn't get there by making stupid decisions and he didn't stay there by ignoring his gut. His monkey brain is as good as mine and right now it is telling him there is something wrong. Something doesn't add up. Is it bad news he is thinking, or really bad news?

A phone rings in the silence. Sergei reaches into his pocket. He stares at the screen.

'Shit,' he says.

He strides out of the room without a backward glance.

Two minutes later he is back, kneeling behind my chair and pulling at my cuffs. Sweat shines through his thin hairline. This close I can see where the dye has bled dark brown onto his skin.

'Told you,' I say.

He pulls and curses and trembles, his hands shaking as he tries to get the cuffs open. They spring free and he yanks at them and they stick again.

Finally, I am free of the chair and he drags me to my feet and cuffs my hands in front of me.

The door opens onto a service passage full of old crates, boxes of vegetables and pallets of soft drinks. We round a corner and I can hear the kitchen. We pass the open doorway. Stainless steel and ultraviolet fly traps. The smell of frying turns my stomach.

Two bouncers keep pace with us. A waiter flattens himself against the wall to let us pass. His hands are raised beside his ears. Obviously Sergei dragging bikini clad, handcuffed women through the corridors is nothing unusual.

Sergei pushes me ahead of him, up a flight of stairs and out through a red fire escape door. The warm night air and the sound of sirens hit us. One bouncer comes through and the other stays behind. Locking the door.

A limo is idling, almost as wide as the alley. The back entrance. Sergei's discreet way in and out. A new load of bouncers nod their heads respectfully. Sergei shoves me towards the limo's open back door and climbs in after me. The bouncer from the basement gets in with us and the doors slam.

I slide a look at Sergei. He is sweating heavily now, pulling at his collar, loosening his tie. He turns to a drinks cabinet built into the white leather wall and then thinks better of it.

I weigh up the bouncer. Two hundred and sixty pounds, plenty of bulk, most of it for show. Black T-shirt, black trousers, black jacket. Hot night for a jacket.

I sit bolt upright on the white leather, my cuffed hands in my lap, cleavage gaping. My hair hangs in my eyes from the hit to the face. Snow White does sultry really well. I catch the bouncer's eye and hold it. The bikini string dangles.

He shifts in his seat, his stance widening, loosening, as he pictures me giving the string a good yank and the knot springing free. Or maybe he is picturing himself doing the yanking. Either way, his jacket falls open and I see the butt of a holster under his arm as his mind paints possible futures. I could have the gun off him in a fraction of a second even with my hands cuffed.

And there is the Guardsman's way in, right there. You are only as good as your personal protection. If you have a load of weapons around, you risk them being turned on you. You are only as good as your weakest link.

The bouncer is still watching me with a smile on his face. His eyes roam over my body, down to my ankles, up to my breasts, to my mouth. I know just what is going through his head. He is hoping there will be some left over for him.

Moscow's night streets slide by in a wail of sirens. Wide three-lane avenues, night trams running along the side, overhead lines criss-crossing the road. I don't know whether it is the trams or the technology but there are wires everywhere, running ten-deep between lamp posts and stretching, web-like across the roads.

On Tverskaya, the lines have been strung with fairy lights. It looks magical. The tall wide shop fronts are still open for business, lights bright and music blaring. The streets are thronged with people enjoying the night. Couples, arms round each other, groups of men standing smoking.

We pass the huge blue Nokia sign on the right, pass the building-mounted video screen showing some Russian housewife making gravy and now I am puzzled because we are heading in, not out. We are not leaving the centre. Pretty much every scenario I had imagined led out of town, not to Red Square.

The limo lurches as it mounts the curb and we are on cobbles. We pass a round modernist fountain lit from below and pick our way, unevenly, across the pedestrianised Theatre Square.

The limo swings round and Sergei has the door open before it has come to a stop.

There, in front of us, blazing in all its eighteenth-century glory, is the huge Grecian temple that is the home of the Bolshoi.

'Stay here,' Sergei says to the bewildered bouncer who has his fantasies popping in front of his eyes.

Sergei drags me out and up the wide stone steps and through the wooden entrance on the right.

We can hear the stage. A night performance is in full swing.

A doorman hurries forward, his hands out in a hushing motion. He jumps back when he sees Sergei.

The swell of voices rises. A huge choral production. Hundreds of voices. *What the hell are we doing at the Opera?*

Sergei drags me, hand in armpit, up the wide red staircase. I wonder what the doorman makes of it. A handcuffed woman in a jewelled bikini and he didn't even challenge us. It says a lot about the scale of Sergei's reach.

There is a white piano and nothing else on the vast landing area that overlooks the square. Sergei crosses the red expanse without a second glance.

It really is the most beautiful building, like a colossal, carved wedding cake, the barrel-vaulted ceiling a mass of intricate plasterwork, the cream walls picked out in gilt.

Sergei drags me up a flight and then another until we are in a curving corridor lined with weirdly narrow doors. The Dress Circle. The corridor arcs away from us out of sight. The doors to the boxes are tall and thin and regimented.

The centre box opens before we get to it.

The man that comes out is a medium, wiry build with an efficient intensity that makes me shiver. I wouldn't want to go one-on-one with him.

Oh hell.

The Praetorian guard.

I know what this means.

The Prince of Darkness isn't in South America. He is here, at the Opera.

CHAPTER 47

Sergei comes to a stop, his feet shuffling, his fingers pulling at each other. Tension is pouring off him. He is almost vibrating. He didn't know the world's most wanted man was in Moscow either. The Praetorian guard gives a tiny jerk of the head and Sergei dips his head and dips his knees and eases past him. I move to follow but the guard blocks my way with one arm.

A SIG Sauer sits snug against his side.

He sees me looking at the holster and gives a slow smile.

'Go on,' he says. 'Please.'

I step back, trying to look like it never crossed my mind. Through the open doorway to the box, I can see the vast black interior of the opera house and in the distance, the brightly lit stage. A woman in a long dress is going for it against a castle backdrop, a dead knight at her feet. *Tristan and Isolde.* The full company hovers in the wings, ready for the finale.

The opera box is lined in red velvet. Everything is padded, even the low ceiling. A small table near the door is crowded with champagne glasses. I shift slightly and see the back of a tanned neck tilted slightly to listen to Sergei.

Why am I waiting outside? Why doesn't he want to see me? He hasn't forgiven me for Marseille.

Sergei is whispering fast. A long hand comes up to silence him. The white cuff of a dress shirt. A black dinner jacket. Two inches of tanned skin at the wrist. Long fingers. Who would have thought a wrist could be erotic? Maybe it is because I know what is attached to it. Maybe it is the memory of our last encounter. The anger and the frustration. I can feel myself getting hot under the sequins.

I stare at the two inches of tanned skin, my heart beating faster, stare at the long elegant fingers, the raised broken knuckles, map the wrist back up the arm, the corded veins, the throat, the high cheekbones, the dark eyes…

Sergei is backing out.

I lean up against the wall like I haven't a care in the world. Out in the corridor, Sergei straightens up and gives me a sideways glance. What has Alek told him to do with me?

'After you,' he says and there is something different about him. He is less nervous.

The limo is still where we left it, idling on the pedestrian front outside the opera house. Tourists stroll by, staring. The door opens and Sergei leans in and says something to the bouncer. A moment later the bouncer is getting out of the car. Sergei waves me inside.

What has Alek said?

The limo pulls off and Sergei opens the drinks cabinet. This time he pours himself a drink. Whiskey fills the air. He stares down into the golden liquid for a moment then he knocks it back.

'So,' he says. 'You work for Alek Konstantin?' His eyes travel up my legs to my breasts, up to my mouth, taking the exact same path as the bouncer's. There is no less appreciation but a whole lot more calculation. 'Surprising,' he says, staring down into his empty glass. 'I would go as far as to say, unprecedented.'

I shrug, remembering how everyone who actually works for Alek behaves. You can't get a word out of them. I think about someone I met once. *He doesn't fuck the staff,* she said. I shrug again and stare out of the window. It is immaterial. I am right where I want to be, right beside Sergei.

He takes something out of his pocket, leans forward and releases my cuffs. The metal springs free. I rub at my wrists.

'I apologise for the restraints,' he says. 'Mistaken identity. I was expecting trouble tonight.'

He already knows he is a target. That makes my job easier.

'No one will get past me,' I say.

He looks across, weighing me up.

'Do you get more trouble these days?' I ask, curious.

He shrugs. 'Sure. There is more trouble everywhere. Certain elements will find any excuse if they perceive a weakness. Nature abhors a vacuum.'

'What weakness?' I say, thinking of the man sitting in the Royal Box at the Opera.

'There is this woman…'

'Yes?'

Sergei shrugs. 'I'm sure I'm not telling you anything you don't know. She works for the British Government. While she is still alive there are always going to be those who think there is a weakness.'

'Winter,' I say flatly. 'He will deal with her when he is ready.'

Sergei shrugs again. 'It's not my issue. But people are asking questions. When will he deal with her? Why hasn't he dealt with her already? While she is throwing her weight around, challenging the system, there will always be trouble. There will always be those that think they can take advantage.'

People think Alek is weak because I am still alive.

I cast a sidelong look at Sergei. His face slides in and out of the shadows. Orange and then dark. 'Do you think there is one right person for everyone out there?'

'I guess,' he says.

'So, who is it for you?'

'She died.' He stares out of the window at the orange scene. 'A long time ago.'

'Oh.'

'I don't know why I told you that.'

We don't speak again as the limo cruises smoothly through the night streets.

THE GUARDSMAN

X

The Guardsman looked in the mirror and a clown stared back. The Guardsman smiled behind the mask. She looked good. She stroked a finger down the blade and hummed as she worked.

> *'Awake, Arise, pull out your eyes,*
> *And hear what time of day;*
> *And when you have done,*
> *Pull out your tongue,*
> *And see what you can say.'*

The Guardsman sang behind the mask and sharpened the blade and sang some more.

> *'Three blind mice,*
> *Three blind mice,*
> *See how they run,*
> *See how they run.'*

CHAPTER 48

We pull up and I peer out into the night. The Maison Honfleur. The bouncer gets out of the front and opens the rear door.

I put a hand on Sergei's arm. 'Do you think this is a good idea? What is the security like in there? This is the obvious place to choose.'

'Tight,' Sergei says. 'I've got the place locked down. If she comes we will be ready.'

'But what about the girls?'

'I know them all personally,' he says. 'A stranger will stand out a mile.'

'She will use a blade.'

'Obviously.'

'And she will sound foreign. Her Russian probably won't be great.'

'Really?' he says. 'I heard her Russian is perfect.'

A cop is standing guard outside the building, his motorbike up against the railings, blocking the pavement. His black visor reflects the street lights. Another traffic cop. Moscow is running with them. Sergei throws a fur at me and I shrug it over my shoulders. Mink, boots and a sequinned bikini. Now I really look the part.

He stops to exchange a few words with the cop. No doubt telling him to watch out. The cop asks a question and Sergei shakes his head. The cop never even glances my way.

I stand, tapping my foot against the top step and watching the street, the buildings opposite, the rooftops, the parked cars, the moving cars. Sergei picks up some of my tension because he glances round, gives a final instruction to the traffic cop and follows me up the stairs.

A heavy, black painted door opens onto a wide hallway with stairs sweeping away in a curve. Faces peer down from the top of the stairs. Glittering girls and boys. Achingly beautiful and practically naked. Elongated Slavic eyes and high cheekbones. They belong to another species. I breathe a sigh of relief at the sight of their bare feet.

The maître d' bustles forward. Sergei is recovering fast. He is still tense but now there is an excitement behind it. His eyes gleam and he rubs his hands together. The action is obviously all above us, but Sergei wants to stay in the hallway.

We stand about.

The maître d' brings a whiskey and Sergei downs it in one.

The bouncers hover. They are not quite sure where I stand but in the absence of any other instructions they are going to keep an eye on me.

After a while, I shed the mink and sit down on one of the peach velvet chairs that line the hallway, looking round at the opulence. The building is beautiful – could be the same architect as the Bolshoi. He missed his vocation designing wedding cakes. A huge crystal chandelier hangs down the centre. Black and white marble chequers the floor. You could twist an ankle in the carpet pile on the stairs.

Ultra, high-end brothel chic. I would own the peach velvet chairs just for the pleasure of running a finger over them.

There is noise from the street. Movement. Someone is arriving. The opera is done and now he is coming.

I stand up and flex my fingers, rocking from side to side on the balls of my feet.

Sergei moves forward and back again and stands undecided.

A car door slams. The tread of feet on stone stairs.

We are frozen like a tableau watching the door.

'He is here,' Sergei says. 'Quick, move, let him in.'

Six men, wiry and unsmiling, come through the door in pairs. The Praetorian guard. These are the men who must have been with Alek on the rooftop in Paris. The men who never leave his side. The men who wanted to go in ahead of him and scope out the scene. And he didn't let them. He came in alone.

I recognise the last bodyguard in – he was on the door of the opera box. A short stocky figure is next. Kristophe, his manservant.

And then he is there on the threshold, tall and dark. Alek Konstantin in black tie. My heart thumps. It is a good look. I have never seen him in anything but T-shirt and combat trousers. A couple of times in body armour. The tailoring does nothing to hide what's underneath.

I close my mouth.

He greets Sergei with a forearm grip and a hand on the shoulder. His eyes rake the room, pass over me, and it occurs to me I have been taking a lot for granted.

Sergei relaxes, his arms drop, the tension in his neck goes.

Alek smiles.

Sergei is offering something. A drink? *Stay for a drink.*

Alek has accepted.

Sergei is pleased, he turns to an underling with quick, eager, shooing movements. *Hurry, hurry get drinks.*

Alek smiles round. He pulls his bow tie undone. He turns his head trying to undo the top button of his dress shirt. The starched white points stick up above his jawline. He grimaces and the button pops open. Sergei laughs heartily at something, the laugh of relief. Now Alek is walking up the hall towards me, undoing another button.

He stops in front of me.

'Hi,' I say.

He turns away as if to say something to Sergei and snaps back, slapping me around the face. My head swings round, I stagger, catch my balance, my eyes prick.

He loosens the black tie until it is hanging down in two long silk strips. He extends a white cuff from his sleeve and fiddles with the cuff link.

I watch the long fingers wrestle with the stud. Suddenly the hand comes up and he slaps me again, a ringing slap and now my temper is rising. Three hits to the face too many this evening. My hair hangs in my eyes, my fists ball. Forty pounds of power on the end of each arm, like a hammer blow. Anger is rising behind my eyes. Anger and lust.

The next slap comes whip fast and takes me down, quick and clean before the block is even halfway up. I stagger and fall, the marble hard under me. Even though I know how to fall, my forearm jars, my elbow shooting pain. The jolt knocks the wind out of me.

Somewhere above, a girl giggles.

Alek stands for a moment, then he turns and walks away back down the hall. He says something to Sergei and they both laugh and then they are moving towards the stairs and the clink of glasses and the giggle of girls, leaving me and my escort staring after them.

My ears ring, my cheek stings, the implants in my jaw ache. I run my tongue over my teeth along the inside of my gum. Blood. Not a lot. Alek tapped me. If he really wanted to hit me I would be out for the count.

I push myself up on my hands and spit blood onto the marble. On the stairs, Alek's head turns and his eyes track over me once, so fleetingly I am not even sure he looked at all.

A perfect hemisphere of blood sits raised and round on the white marble.

*

The marble is cold. I shiver, my limbs shake. Tiredness is catching up with me. I get awkwardly to my feet. I can't let Sergei out of my sight. My guard follows me down the hall, hovering, uncertain. I seem to no longer be a prisoner, but no one has told them that officially.

Kristophe bars the way. He shoos my guards towards the stairs, waiting till they have reached the top before he speaks.

'Hello, Snow White,' he says. He grips my shoulders, tilting me this way and that as he looks at the slap mark on the side of my face.

I remember how he cared for me when I was a beaten wreck after a cage fight; his gentle competence. I remember how I never said thank you. I remember that I made him a fugitive too when I betrayed Alek.

'I'm sorry,' I say, staring into his kind eyes, 'for everything.'

He shrugs. 'You were always trouble.' His smile takes the sting out of the words.

'How has it been?'

He shrugs again. 'I think he is finding it harder than he expected. He misses the daylight.' His eyes go up the stairs to where Alek disappeared.

I swallow. *The daylight.* That makes me feel really bad. 'What did he say to Sergei?'

'He apologised for your behaviour. He said that you are in training, that you are unreliable but effective, hence the tracker.'

'Training for what?'

'To work for him. He said you have a way to go.'

My mouth gapes. 'What? Like a training programme? Sheesh. That's not very flattering.'

'Go to the bathroom now and deal with your face.'

I put my hand up to feel the swelling. 'It's fine.'

'Go.'

'I can't leave Sergei,' I say. I look up the stairs to where Sergei disappeared into a crowd of eager glitter girls.

'I will watch him,' Kristophe says. He stares down at the black and white, speaking so quietly I can hardly make out the words. 'You have no idea how much danger you are in. Alek has never put a tracker on a woman before.'

'So?'

He rolls his eyes. 'What is the founding principle of Firestorm?'

'If you don't do what I say, I will have you killed?'

'Try again.'

'If you care your enemies have all the leverage they need?'

'Right. And how many people would like leverage over Alek Konstantin?'

My brain feels slow. What is the point Kristophe is making? When I get it, I almost laugh.

'You think I would give someone power over him? That's a joke. Alek sleeps with hundreds of women.'

Kristophe gives a sad smile. 'But how many of them can pull his heart out through his ribcage?'

'What is that supposed to mean?'

'Literally as well as figuratively,' he says.

CHAPTER 49

The powder room is dark but luxurious like everything else in the place. Incense burns in shallow bowls between the sinks. Candlesticks either side of the gold mirror cast a romantic glow.

I take a towel from the little basket by the sink and put it under the gold tap. The water runs hot and then cold. I wring the towel out and hold it up against my cheek.

The door opens.

Alek closes it behind him, leans against it and folds his arms.

My eyes meet his in the mirror.

'What are you doing in Moscow?'

I shrug and it is like a flame to tinder.

'You expect me to bail you out without a word of explanation?'

'Yes.'

'Is that why you keep it? The tracker? So I can bail you out whenever you need it?'

I hadn't thought of it like that. I look down into the sink. What should I say? The gulf that was wide in Paris has become wider still. It feels like a wasteland.

He still came.

In Paris he came and tonight he has come again, even though Moscow is both harder and easier for him. He was quick to notice and quick to act.

I put the towel down carefully beside the basin. The room is closing in, the tension swirling, circling, buffeting. My face in the mirror is flushed, wild-eyed. My sequins glitter in the candlelight.

The room is too small for the two of us and the emotions that are churning.

I lean my arms on the counter, either side of the sink, and stare down into the basin.

'Thank you,' I say.

In the mirror, his shoulders shrug.

'It is good to see you,' I say, lost and at sea in this world of the unspoken.

'Is it?' he says. His voice light and his eyes cold.

'What?' I say. 'What do you want from me? What do you want me to say?'

He stands scowling.

'*Men are monsters but that doesn't mean they have to be monstrous.* That's what you said to me on the island. *Come work for me*, you said. *Clean the place up.*'

'Yes,' he says. 'If you won't come for any other reason.' His dark eyes stare into mine. 'Come for the good you could do.'

'So, explain the Guardsman to me. We fought Slashstorm and the Marquise together. You and I. And here is the Guardsman, worse than the Marquise.'

His face closes down and for a moment I think he is not going to answer. 'The internet forced a thousand years of development into ten years,' he says finally. 'And human nature can't cope.'

'The internet facilitates crime,' I say. 'I know this. It is why you are in business. What has that got to do with anything?'

'No,' he says, 'you don't get it. It develops, magnifies, enhances all the darkest parts of human nature. The worst man is capable of. The dark will take over the world. And what do you do about that? You organise it, administer it, control it. And there is only one way to control it. And it is not by sitting around at an emergency summit talking. It is with fear. Who do the biggest killers on the planet fear? They fear the Guardsman.'

'You cannot control the whole world, Alek.'

'No,' he says, 'and right now, I just want to control one small part of it.'

'She is a monster, Alek. I cannot understand you protecting her, never mind employing her.'

'It is about balance. You can't erase the dark, you can only keep it in check.'

'Are you going to give me the Guardsman or not?'

His face shuts down again. It reminds me of when we were on the island.

'I don't want you anywhere near it.'

'Then we are done here,' I say, turning back to the sink.

My back is turned but I can still feel him, feel the pull across the room.

Sexual thrall. It has a weird archaic ring to it. Like *droit du seigneur*. My heart rate motors, my breathing is shallow and fast. At its strongest, sexual attraction is powerfully disorientating. And that is just attraction. Once you actually know the touch of fingers, the slide of skin, the hollow of the throat, the hard push of hip, then you are lost.

I look up through my hair and our eyes meet in the mirror.

'Winter,' he says, and his voice is full of menace. 'I want an explanation and an apology.'

'An apology for what?'

'For Marseille.'

Temper rises in me, cut with guilt. An awful, awful guilt that I don't understand, that makes me even madder.

'I will fuck anyone I like,' I say. 'I never asked you to be faithful to me. I have no interest in who you sleep with. It is none of my business.'

For a moment, I think he is going to hit me again. Then he is slamming out of the door and striding away down the corridor and I am sagging against the sink, my heart motoring.

CHAPTER 50

The room is exactly what I was expecting. A wide, elegant salon luxuriously draped in dark velvet, couches and sofas everywhere. Round the edge are separate booths, raised areas with their own couches and curtains that can be drawn for privacy.

The room's inhabitants are like another species. Beautiful girls, their bare limbs gilded. A few boys. Incense hangs heavy in the air. The glitter on bronzed limbs shimmers in the half light.

My gaze finds Alek. He and Sergei are sitting in one of the booth areas, an open bottle of spirits already on the low glass table between them. Alek lounges back, his arm stretched along the sofa, his ankle resting on his knee.

Girls cluster round their table like a plague of glittered locusts and I can't say I blame them. Given their usual clientele, Alek has to be like winning the lottery. A redhead with pneumatic assets is stroking his sleeve. Easing him out of his dinner jacket. He laughs as he moves to help. I can feel myself staring. My jaw hardens. The room is warm, but I shiver, rubbing my arms. Goosebumps.

One of the glitter girls draws the gauzy curtains partly across to give the booth more privacy and now my imagination is working overtime. There is a roaring in my ears. The colours swim before my eyes. I listen to the roaring and wonder if my blood sugar is low, wonder what the hell is wrong with me. I shake my head to clear the angry buzzing.

The redhead straddles Alek, the thigh slits in her dress easily accommodating her spread legs. She leans forward to his neck like a vampire. I crane to see through the gauzy drapes. She whispers in his ear. He lies back and she works her way downwards, unbuttoning his dress shirt with nimble little flicks of her fingers. She yanks it upwards out of his waistband and folds the shirt wide, smoothing long talons across his chest. It is like I can hear her purr of satisfaction. She leans forward out of sight and I picture her licking her way across his chest, across the satin smooth six-pack of muscle, the trail of dark hair heading downwards.

I can smell the spicy warmth of his skin.

My hands ball into fists and I sit, unable to move as she lifts her head and holds his gaze, then slowly and deliberately pulls at the waistband, left, right and he lies his head back against the sofa and closes his eyes.

Her glittery leg swings over him, she has moved round to his side. His head lifts and he looks down his long body, his eyes smoky, as she lowers over where the waistband would be if she hadn't already opened it wide.

One lazy hand goes to her hair to lift it off her face for a better view.

Blood pounds in my head, clouding my vision, confusing my senses. There is nothing but Alek lying back watching, while the red hair bobs up and down, up and down, and I can't stand it.

I am on my feet and bolting for the door.

I slam through the double doors into the upper lobby and run down the wide, red carpeted steps; Cinderella fleeing the ball.

Security stare.

I stumble out of the front door into the night air. It is warm on my bare arms and legs. My brain burns with the image of the red bobbing hair. It stabs at me again and again and my head shakes, trying to dislodge the images.

I run down the stone stairs beside the house to the river path and stand in the lee of a great metal upright. The ironwork of the bridge arches above my head, sheltering. A night barge goes past, its pilot light twinkling.

My eyes prick. I stare at the black swirling water. What is the matter with me?

Footsteps are coming down the stone stairs behind me.

A measured stride and my heart leaps in my chest but pride keeps me still, hidden behind the giant iron uprights.

The footsteps stop. Their owner is looking about. Looking for me.

I rub my wrist, the bloody tracker. It has led him here but now he can't see me. I have a sudden crazy wish I had ripped the tracker out so that he would come round the iron upright to find it on the floor.

I wrap my arms around my bare waist and stare at the river.

He turns the corner and comes into view. His shirt is still open.

'Well, that was educational,' he says. 'You can get jealous. Just like a normal woman.'

'I am a normal woman and I am not jealous. Why did you stop? It looked like you were having a great time.'

He closes the distance between us. 'Winter,' he says, his dark eyes focused on me like I am the only thing in his world, and I reach for him, my hands behind his neck, pulling his mouth down to mine with an urgency that swamps us both. The burning heat obliterates every thought except teeth and tongue and aching need.

I get my hand underneath the dress shirt, feel the hot silk of his back, smell the warm scent of his skin. My hands close over the handgun in the small of his back, shoved into his waistband.

'That is a really stupid place to carry a gun.'

His mouth curves against mine in a smile but he doesn't stop. The dress shirt is rough against me. The skin on my face buzzes, tingling with sensory overload. He lifts me onto the stone ledge, and I know it is going to be right here, right now, out in the open and there is not a thing either of us can do to stop it.

Gunfire from the Maison Honfleur splits the air. Explosive and close. A single shot. Louder than thunder. The iron of the bridge rings with it.

The Guardsman.

My brain paints the word in scarlet flaming letters in the air. It tattoos it against my skull. My eyes open. My thoughts are slow. I shove hard and Alek staggers back. A strange dry wind blows. Thunder cracks, rolling across the sky. Sheet lightning flashes and I am running, running for the stairs.

CHAPTER 51

I pound up the steps, two at a time, my heart rate crazy. The Praetorian guard are there looking down at us. The Boss is getting laid so they have moved up across the bridge. I reach the railings.

The traffic cop is staring. His helmet is off and his pale face is staring like he can't believe his eyes. Like someone has punched him in the guts. I recognise him, without the helmet. It is the traffic cop from the cells beside the car park.

'Call yourself a cop?' I want to scream. 'Did you not hear the gunfire?'

He turns to watch me. Not interested in the gunfire. Interested in me.

I pound up the red stairs, handing off the maître d' and burst into the room with the glitter girls. Sergei is standing in the booth, his trousers around his ankles, his gun pointing downwards. He fires again and a body jerks on the floor. It is the pneumatic redhead.

I vault up into the booth and fall to my knees beside her.

Sergei stands breathing heavily. Everyone else is as still and staring as glitter statues. As Christmas angels.

Alek bends down beside me. I can feel the Praetorian guard fanning out across the room. Blood pumps from the redhead's shoulder. The first shot got her in the top of the arm. Blood wells behind her teeth.

'I can't believe Winter was that easy.' Sergei sinks onto a seat.

'This is not Winter,' Alek says, holding my eyes. His irises are flecked with gold. Tiger eyes.

'I can't believe the Guardsman was that easy,' I say.

'The Guardsman is not a woman,' says Sergei; typical Russian male.

Alek looks at me. His face is achingly close. 'What makes you think this is the Guardsman?'

'I had good intel she was hitting Sergei tonight.'

'It was the Guardsman who warned me Winter was coming,' Sergei says.

Alek gets slowly to his feet, a scowl between his black brows.

'Firestorm intel?' he says to me.

'Maybe.'

He shakes his head. 'Firestorm won't take a contract on Sergei. He is *untouchable*. Whatever you saw was a fake. Someone wanted you out of the way.'

'Or over in Moscow.'

'Or over in Moscow,' Alek agrees, his eyes thoughtful.

'Who is this then?' Sergei says pointing at the redhead.

'No one,' says Alek. 'A decoy to lure Winter out.'

'So, where is she?' says Sergei, bewildered.

I stare at Alek. The Sergei contract was a fake? My brain scrabbles. Only the Administrator could have done that. The contract was on Solo's phone. The Sergei plans were there, on the desk, in his house.

The room is still around me, not a sequin moves as the pennies drop thick and fast. I have been lured here under false pretences. The Guardsman laid a trap for me and I took the bait. She invented the Sergei contract to get me to Moscow and then told Sergei I was coming. When he said, *I heard her Russian was perfect*, he wasn't talking about the Guardsman, he was talking about me.

I am here for Alek to kill. She probably thought he would be pleased.

And if the Guardsman had time to set that up before I looked at Solo's phone, before I went to his house, she must have known I had Solo before he was dead.

She must have been there in real time – in GCHQ.

I take the stairs at a run and then realise there is no point in running. Simon answers straight away.

'What can I do?' he says.

He thinks it is me with a problem. He has seen me go into the Maison Honfleur with Sergei, seen me close to the target. If I am calling it is to report success or request evac.

'You need to get to McKellen and Ariadne now,' I say. 'I think the Guardsman is in the building.'

Simon is the best. He doesn't stop and ask questions, he doesn't need any kind of explanation. He just does exactly what I say immediately.

'I've got a missed call from Ariadne,' he says, his face white when he reconnects on his own phone. He pounds down the corridor shouting for Viv, there is no sign of Pansy Face or Xiu and Léon, then he is in the stairwell and I can see grey concrete streaming past – he is holding the phone down by his side. He shouts to a passing pair of legs, I can't tell who, but they reverse and follow him and then we are on the detainment floor and he is running full tilt for the end.

'Oh God,' he says.

'What,' I shout. 'What?'

'The door guards are down,' he says.

He slows right down as he approaches. The door is ajar. Behind him, Viv and the legs from the stairwell are catching up.

He pushes the door open.

'Oh no,' he says. 'Oh Christ.'

I can see the hinge of the door and nothing else.

'Jesus,' Viv says.

'Don't go in!' I scream at the screen. My tiny, tinny little voice stretching, stretching, trying to reach their ears.

Simon holds me up to his face. 'You don't understand,' he says. 'I have to see if anyone is still alive.' He turns the phone so I can see the room. Ariadne is by the door. There are words carved on her forehead.

'Oh no,' I whisper.

CHAPTER 52

'Get away from me!' Anger makes it black and white clear. 'It is your fault that psycho is out there carving up kids' faces. You gave her a platform. You could have stopped her and you didn't.'

Alek's face is still in the dim light. He leans against the stair rail and folds his arms and for a moment I think he's not going to answer.

'It is better to have some people where you can see them,' he says. 'Where you can check what they are doing.'

'Better pissing out? Jesus, will you listen to yourself? There is nothing, nothing that can justify this, Alek. This is the line in the sand and we are on opposite sides of it. Whatever this was.' I gesture to the space between us. 'It is over. Finished. I will take down the Guardsman and then I am coming for Firestorm and if I have to go through you, so be it.'

'McKellen was one of mine,' he says. 'No one knew. I thought his family would be safe with you.'

The stairs rock.

'I don't believe you.'

'He was a realist. A big-picture thinker.'

'I don't believe it.'

'What do you think happened in Mexico?'

I think about McKellen's evasion, about his claims to have escaped.

'We spent a long time talking about the world's problems and possible solutions. About balance. Ultimately, we agreed that order

is better than chaos. Only I can control the cartels. He was no
traitor, he just understood – taking me out would make things
worse. He was going to tell the G20 we needed to work together
to restore some kind of order.'

I stare.

'He had a problem with the Guardsman too. Especially after
Petersburg.'

The Head of the CIA.

Shit.

A terrible thought occurs to me.

If he controls the Head of the CIA, who else does he control?

'What about *my* boss?'

He shakes his head. 'I only have the Head of Field at GCHQ
so far.'

I turn on my heel.

My footsteps echo all the way across the black and white
chequered hall.

He doesn't follow.

THE GUARDSMAN

XI

The Guardsman stared and stared. A strange wind blew, whistling round the buildings, tumbling litter into the gutters.

The Guardsman began to shake. The Guardsman began to fall. First knees, then hands, then forehead. The Guardsman rolled into a foetal position on the stone pavement as the waves of betrayal hit. How could he? How could he do this to them? How could he do this to Firestorm? He had betrayed them all.

In that one split second, everything had changed and the Guardsman knew, from this moment on, nothing would ever be the same again.

No wonder Winter was untouchable. No wonder the Boss hadn't dealt with her. The truth had been there all along, staring them in the face.

'*The truth shall make ye free.*'

Make ye free.

One thing cut through the pain of betrayal.

The Guardsman was not alone.

CHAPTER 53

The Day

I am too far away. Out of range. Too far from home. Even if I get an airlift back I am still the better part of seven hours away from GCHQ. The aftermath, the lockdown, the initial interrogations will all be handled by someone else and there is not a thing I can do about it. The G20's opening ceremony is this afternoon and the courage of world leaders will be dissipating like rabbits running for cover. There was no need to attack the G20. Taking out McKellen has done the job just as well.

The four-person close protection team who were in the observation room next door are dead. Control, who was with them, is in a coma in intensive care. The two door guards are dead, the McKellens themselves are dead and another body has my name carved on it.

Ariadne's forehead was too small to take a long message, or maybe the Guardsman was running out of time, but the words are clear enough.

Too slow, Winter.

Am I really so painfully predictable, so easy to trick?

You should have sent someone else. You should have outsourced. That is what delegation is all about says the voice in my head.

But who better to face the Guardsman than me? How could I have asked anyone else to do it?

That is the whole point. That is why you have a regiment full of recruits. You just couldn't wait to do it yourself. To change into Snow White, slip the leash of your responsibilities and get back in the field.

I feel like a mother bird who sees the jays swooping down on her unprotected nest and knows she can't close the distance in time. There is nothing to do but watch. And it is worse than that. The Guardsman is there in the building. It has to be someone I know. Someone who works for me. Someone I trust.

I turn the list of candidates over in my head. Who knew I had Solo? Who knew what I was up to that night? I pick up the phone to make the call a dozen times but each time I stop.

It is not till we are airborne that I realise I am still in sequins. I stare numbly at the back of the seat in front. Regret pricks in the corners of my eyes. Another kind of woman would be resorting to vodka or something stronger. A morphine-based optimism. That warm, golden feel-good glow. I am not that woman. I stare dry-eyed out into the darkness as the plane chases the dawn.

Simon will have sent a car. The whole of the UK's security services will be on red alert. I pull the mink around me, scanning the crowds. Mink in thirty degrees, I am going to roast as soon as we are out of the air con. Flushed faces wait for night flights to arrive, arms hanging over the Starbucks barricades.

'Have you tried our honeycomb latte?' says the Starbucks poster.

Families shriek, grandparents with over-bright eyes crane to see over younger, taller heads. Professional drivers hold whiteboards. I scan the signs and then I see him standing there like a chauffeur. Messy hair, lanky. My heart lifts at the sight of him.

'Hi,' he says, not meeting my eyes.

I want to give him a hug, to reach out, but he turns away.

'How is it?'

He shakes his head. His throat works.

'I should have been here,' I say. Morning shafts of sun slant from the high windows. Dust motes whirl in the golden light. 'I know that.' As soon as I face my culpability the better.

Simon swallows. 'If you had seen them…' he says. His eyes are shiny. 'Emma is in pieces. She got there just after me.' *Pansy Face.* He shakes his head again. 'It's the worst thing I've ever seen,' he whispers. 'Beth is making everyone go through counselling.'

If that isn't just typical HR.

I am about to say something sour, but I think better of it. Maybe she is right. Maybe people need a framework to deal with this kind of thing.

We pull onto the motorway. The M25 is practically stationary, we crawl along in the commuter traffic.

'Who is running it?'

'The Americans have brought in their own team. The place is in lockdown, obviously. Everyone who was in the building last night. Total news blackout. It is not something anyone is looking to publicise – free advertising for Firestorm. It has really brought home how vulnerable everyone is.'

'What about the G20?'

He shrugs. 'It may go ahead this afternoon, it may not. Either way, it is not going to achieve anything without McKellen.'

The final countdown.

It was never an attack on the G20. Take out McKellen and everything else falls apart.

'How is Control?'

He shakes his head. 'They think he may have a bleed on the brain. You know what that means, don't you? You are the acting head.'

'What have we got so far?'

'Nothing.'

'I need to see the footage,' I say. 'As soon as possible.'

'I knew you would. So I brought it with me.' He jerks his head towards the laptop on the back seat.

'You're the best.'

'But not good enough,' he says, his hands shaky on the wheel. 'The reality is that in unmasking Alek Konstantin, I weakened his grip, disrupted the system, wrecked the balance and now things are worse. It would have been better if I had never found him. That is the honest, unvarnished truth.'

'You sound as if you regret it,' he says. 'Make no mistake, Alek Konstantin is the true enemy. The Guardsman is just an instrument of his will.'

The screen clears just in time to save me from having to answer. Because I don't have an answer. I know Simon is right. I just don't want to believe it.

The file opens and the footage from the detainment suite loads. Second after second, minute after minute. McKellen is on the phone, his free hand slamming the desk in frustration. A TV flickers in the corner. Ariadne is glued to an iPad. Her mother stares at the TV. McKellen looks tired and frustrated. Every now and then, he comes off the phone and puts his head in his hands. I play the footage until it cuts out and then I play it again.

Night-time, the cameras are on infrared. The McKellens are asleep on their pallet mattresses, all in the same room. Something wakes them. Ariadne is up first, she sits up in bed looking at the door. What has she heard? Someone knocking? Tap, tap, tapping three times with a stiletto heel? Is that how it happened? Did she get up and open the door?

She shakes her mother.

It is painful watching their last minutes, they blunder into things, feeling with their hands, dazed with sleep.

Ariadne has her phone. She puts it to her ear. Her face changes as voicemail answers. Like a drowning swimmer who saw help coming and then realised it was an illusion.

Despair.

She turns towards the door, then she is talking to someone on the other side. The angle is wrong to make out the words but there is no mistaking her expression of delight. She fumbles at the bolts and the door opens and a figure in a motorbike helmet walks in.

You are only ever as strong as your weakest link.

The blade glints reflecting the light and Ariadne just stands there.

When they come again what should I do?

You run and you hide.

I can't understand her reaction. She should be terrified. Instead, it is like she can't see death staring her in the face.

The Guardsman moves over to the camera, no hurry, and the image dies and that is the last that we see.

CHAPTER 54

As we approach Junction 10, the turn off on the M25 for central London and GCHQ, I shake my head.

'Greenwich,' I say. 'I need to go back to the mortuary.'

Simon nods. He doesn't question, he doesn't argue. His silence makes me uneasy.

We pull up. I shrug off the mink and pull a raincoat over the bikini. It is typical of Simon to have a raincoat with him when it hasn't rained for weeks. I belt it hard around my waist.

The Greenwich mortuary looks the same as ever – cracked paving, tatty notice, sad neglected frontage. It feels like a lifetime since I came here with Xiu and Léon. The door rocks on its hinges.

Brenda is there behind the counter, the cardigan gone. Her eyes narrow as she watches me. I haven't done anything and she is already hostile. Snow White hasn't even walked in and she is going to make her life difficult.

People skills.

Then I think about all the people who come in to identify a body and wait, grey and sad and bullied on the hard chairs.

She opens her mouth to speak but I am ahead of her.

'Hi, Brenda,' I say.

I round the counter, haul her off her chair and push her up against the wall. The chair skitters away on castors. Brenda chokes and her eyes pop but she can't speak because my left forearm is pressing her windpipe.

'The thing is, Brenda, you can go for years – maybe even your whole life – getting off on people's frustration and that's fine. But one day you will run into someone who doesn't handle frustration as well as they should and who doesn't really understand the rules. You need to think about that.'

Her legs kick.

I let her go and she slides down the wall and drops in a heap on the floor.

I press the door release button under the counter and head through to the inner sanctum.

The Pathologist is in her office, hunched over her keyboard, scowling at her screen. Alek stares down from the wall. She looks up as my shadow blocks the light.

'Can I help you?' she asks. Snow White is a stranger.

I blink a brown contact lens into my palm, crouch down and look into her eyes at point-blank range.

She stares, then she smiles. 'That's amazing,' she says. 'I would never have recognised you. Are you undercover?'

'Something like that.'

I straighten up, blinking the contact lens back in.

'You definitely need the lenses,' she says. 'Your eyes are so distinctive.'

'Do you remember when I was here before? We were talking about the girl the Guardsman sent you? Lucy, the girl on a blind date. You said it was an unusual case. I assumed at the time you meant the lack of contract, but you didn't, did you? Did you get to the bottom of it?'

She shakes her head. 'It was academic. There was no doubt as to cause of death or who was responsible.'

The jar of eyeballs stare at me from the corner of the desk.

'Did you keep anything? A sample?'

'There are about ten statutes preventing the retention of body parts post-autopsy and about three ethical ones,' she says.

'So, did you?'

She glances at the corner cabinet. She has her hair swept back in a ponytail and it almost makes her look like a different person.

'No.'

'Have you ever been to GCHQ?'

'Once,' she says, 'quite recently.'

'I may need you to come in, some time later today. Can you do that?'

'In person?' She looks stunned at the idea of leaving her basement level.

'Yes,' I say.

I get back in the car and stare out of the window at the hazy sky.

'Where now?' says Simon. 'Back to GCHQ?'

I shake my head. 'Powergate. I need to ask Brad a question.'

The street is the same as ever. The building is still doing a great camouflage job. I unbuckle my seat belt.

'Did you ever think it would come to this?' I say.

He stares out of the window and doesn't answer.

'Go back to base. Let them know I am on my way. And then get back here with a suit for me.'

'Why?'

'I need a suit before I go into GCHQ.'

'Since when?' His lip curls.

'Since I became acting head,' I say. 'A jewelled bikini is not appropriate. It is no good doing the job, you have to be seen to be doing the job.'

Simon stares out of the windscreen.

*

Brad is there in the lobby, waiting.

'I'm sorry,' I say.

He nods.

'I was with him, Winter,' he says. 'Just before. I was the last person to see them alive.'

'Apart from Control and the guards in the observation room you mean?'

'The last person who's not dead or unconscious.'

I wait until we are in his office with the door closed. There is a small dent in the wall that wasn't there before, like an executive stress toy has been thrown at it.

I get in his face and ask my question. 'Did you know McKellen was working for Alek Konstantin?'

'*What?*' says Brad, answering the question. Jerking away from me for the first time in his life. A tide of red sweeps up his neck. There is no faking that reaction.

'I guess not.'

The remote chance that it was an inside job, that the NSA had put two and two together and decided to clean up and pin it on the Guardsman, dies. Brad is not that good an actor.

'Tell me you are joking,' he says.

'It wasn't us,' I say. 'Except indirectly. I think the Guardsman works for GCHQ.'

He stares, out of words.

'I have to get back,' I say. 'I have a killer to catch, but first I need my own face.'

The process is nothing like the way in. A short forty minutes in theatre. Twenty-four hours to recover. In theory.

I down an ibuprofen for the swelling and swing my legs off the bed.

Simon is there waiting behind the curtain.

'You have to stay in bed,' says the medic.

I strip off the gown and pull on the suit. Shrug into the tailored jacket.

Buckle on the thigh holster.

I stride into GCHQ, pinstripe suit, killer heels, all flags flying.

She is back, she is back.

The word goes out. She just walked into the lobby. The eye of the storm. The Guardsman's nemesis. I can hear the muttering and recriminations.

Security jump to attention. I beckon them over. They cluster round, wide-eyed and leaderless.

'I want constant vigilance,' I tell them. 'I want to know everything that goes on. Entrances and exits, I want everything locked down. I want the logs brought to me hourly.'

They nod, bristling with professionalism. 'Yes, ma'am,' they say.

It's utterly pointless. The horse has bolted. They don't need to be told that.

'And I want every member of staff currently detained in the building by the enquiry in the training arena as soon as possible. They can work out while they wait.'

'Yes, ma'am.'

I take the lift down to the detainment level. Americans with semi-automatics bar the way.

'Stand down,' I say with not the slightest hint of doubt in my voice, like the idea that they might not do exactly as I tell them has never occurred to me.

They glance at each other and then back at me. I see the curl of the lip and feel the unspoken blame. Then they shuffle aside and I step over the tape and consider the chalk outlines. I turn into Interview Suite 5 and the guy in charge is on his knees on the floor, looking at something on the lino. His eyes are red-rimmed over the mask. He gets to his feet at the sight of me.

'I'm sorry,' I say. 'You have my full cooperation. I want to move the staff into one place.'

He shakes his head. 'No one is leaving the building.'

'I understand,' I say. 'But I want everyone contained in one place.'

'OK,' he says.

I walk on into medical.

'Dr Everard, please,' I say to the white coat.

He scurries away and I follow, my heels ringing on the concrete. I can see the open door, the light spilling out. I turn in. Everard is bent over a body on a trolley. He holds his hand up, his back still to me. Latex gloves. They are yellow with post-mortem chems.

'Just hear me out,' he says.

'Of course I will hear you out. I apologise if you think I do not respect your opinion.'

Everard turns and stares.

'I'm listening,' I say.

'There was something very strange about their reactions on that footage,' he says.

'I agree.'

He looks up at me from under his floppy hair. 'You do?'

'Show me the McKellens.'

They are lying under green, post-mortem sheets. Two large bodies, one small one. Tags round their toes.

'Who do you want to see?'

'It doesn't matter. Any one of them will do,' I say, pulling on the latex gloves.

Everard looks at me, a puzzled line between his brows, but he folds down the sheet on the nearest corpse.

Mrs McKellen.

I bend over her, peering at her face, tugging lightly on her eyelashes.

'Have you tried to get her eyes open?'

He shakes his head.

'Are they all the same?'

'Yes.'

I pull the gloves off my hands and open the surgical bin with the foot pedal.

'I want to bring in someone else.'

'Who?'

'No one. A local pathologist.'

Everard's face twists. 'We have the best in the country in the building already.'

I try to smile. 'You'll like her, Everard. She has a thing for eyeballs.'

CHAPTER 55

The sky is shot across with pink and salmon, like a violent sunset. Dark clouds scud from right to left. Apocalyptic. The weather is getting weirder and weirder.

'Red sky at night…' say Security, rubbing their hands.

'It's not night. More like early afternoon.' I look at the clock. '2 p.m.'

'Red sky in the morning.'

'Right,' I say.

The Pathologist is standing there, clutching a huge, black doctor's bag and wearing an uneasy expression and I can't tell if it is GCHQ or the daylight. Unearthed from her troglodyte existence in a basement in Greenwich.

She notices the GCHQ version of the Alek Konstantin most wanted poster.

'I haven't got that one,' she says.

'Thank you for coming,' I say. 'I really appreciate it.'

'That's OK,' she says. 'I thought maybe you had changed your mind.'

'About what?'

'About me examining you.'

'I don't know if we'll have time,' I say. 'We'll see.'

Her face lights up.

In the lift, I press minus 24 for the detainment level and her eyes get wide. The lift doors ping open and we walk down the corridor, past the interview suites and medical and through to pathology.

Solo is still on the slab. Everard is bent over him. He turns at the sound of us. He has been up for seventy-two hours straight but you wouldn't know.

'This is Everard,' I tell her. 'He is GCHQ's Chief Medic.'

She stares. 'I know who he is. I read your paper on digital pathology,' she says.

Everard nods.

'You have beautiful eyes,' she says.

Oh, for goodness' sake.

'Would you let me look at them through a lens?'

Everard smiles a shattering, heart-bursting smile of perfect teeth that fills the room with sunshine and has even my blood singing.

'Yes,' he says simply.

An hour later, she and Everard are explaining their findings. The overhead lights bounce off the polished aluminium surfaces. Their excited voices ring loud in the enclosed space. The air is thick with formaldehyde. The trolley between us is scattered with the tools of their trade. Tiny thin scalpels sit in kidney-shaped dishes, sticky rather than bloody. There is something dense and waxy about eyeballs, the trails on the blades are pale.

I close my eyes and lean against the wall. The thoughts float like confetti petals on the breeze. They scatter, blowing this way and that, never settling, buffeted and tossed by the wind. Now they are coming hard and fast as a blizzard. My eyes spring open, my pulse races, shiny bright thoughts rain like daggers until the storm dies and my heart calms and there, under the white lights of the detainment suite, pale, newly washed, newly minted, is the truth.

I pick it up and examine it in wonder.

CHAPTER 56

I have my answer. I know what made Ariadne stand there, staring at death.

She was blind.

Blinded by a CIA manufactured nerve agent that attacks the cornea and then vanishes without trace. I have been circling around it for days – Lucy, Petersburg, the attack in Fortnum & Mason, the factory in Marseille – *this* is what connects them.

I remember the gas from Fortnum & Mason and the NSA scientist saying, *After ten minutes uncontained, it has completely vanished. Complete 100 per cent degradation. An untraceable nerve agent with no repercussions because no one knows you have used it.*

A nerve agent invented as part of a programme shut down sixty years ago. Forgotten. The paperwork long since destroyed. The only single record of its existence held in a deep storage facility in Petersburg, Virginia. Held in storage until it was stolen by the Guardsman and manufactured in a Marseille factory by Ferret to give Firestorm the edge. An untraceable gas that renders victims defenceless but doesn't kill them. It makes Firestorm all but invincible.

Lucy was the first. An experiment to see if it worked. Were there others?

For Your Eyes Only.

Not the security level of the CIA file but a project code name. A little in-joke by the CIA experimenters. *For Your Eyes Only.* See what we did there? Haha.

My phone goes and I answer it without looking.

'I don't know if it is still important,' says Brad. 'But they have an answer on the nerve agent. It does work on rats – they just missed it. In a familiar environment like a laboratory cage, rats use their other senses to compensate.'

'It blinds.'

'How did you know that?'

'I have nearly all the pieces now,' I say.

I stare down at the schematics for the GCHQ building. If the top of the building looks like an ocean liner in full sail, then beneath it is a vast iceberg. There are twenty-four floors below street level and that is just the documented levels.

Below and beside are the old tube tracks and the ghost platforms long since abandoned. Like the Bloomberg building next door built on the remains of a Temple of Mithras, GCHQ is built on something older, carved out of a subterranean warren, a state-of-the-art structure emerging from Victoriana.

'Is this really important, right now?' says Simon, shuffling his feet. 'You should speak to the staff. They are all waiting.'

'Very important. Right now,' I say. 'We have a perimeter breach and everyone is being held here. The whole building could be in trouble.'

'There was no perimeter breach.' He scuffs his toe. He still can't meet my eyes. 'It was someone in the building. Everyone knows that.'

I leave GCHQ by the subterranean exit that leads up to the Bank southbound Central line platform but instead of heading up, I keep going down. I open the door on the still chill air and step through into another world.

I trace the crazy paved tiles, the cracked glaze on the distinctive oblong tube tiles. Dickens was around when these tiles were fired.

There was smog and pea-soupers and men in top hats. Then power came, gas lights and steam went, and modern tube trains forged new routes and these old tunnels were forgotten.

Forgotten until the internet age, when they needed space with a good power supply in the heart of the city and Europe's biggest server farm was born.

Not long after that, inevitably, GCHQ arrived and the practical requirements of ventilation and cooling were squeezed into places that were never expected to have to cool five thermal tons of equipment. Ducts and pipes squashed in, boot-strapped on.

I think about the titanium entry tube to the building. The giant armoured condom and the ventilation system hanging piecemeal and chaotic off the wall in an abandoned station. Two extremes. The sublime and the ridiculous.

My footsteps echo in the silence. It is weird the way some of these deserted platforms are still lit. Old sulphur bulbs. It's like the stations are waiting. Silent. Brightly lit, waiting for passengers that are never going to come.

The place is thick with black dust and debris except for a sweep down the centre of the platform. Someone has been here before me and they have wiped their trail. Someone who knew what they were doing and where they were going.

I don't even really need to look, I can just follow.

I round the curve in the platform and find it coming to an end with nothing but black echoey silence ahead of me. I peer into the dark. The black soot that coats everything soaks the light, absorbing it into its matt depths until it is beyond dark. It soaks in sound as well as light.

I scramble and slide down the end of the platform, switch on my phone's torch and keep walking.

The line is littered with debris: half bricks, piles of soot, the metal of the tracks barely visible. Somewhere water is running and that's another thing we have forgotten. The paths of all the ancient waterways. London's rivers, rerouted and diverted but still flowing.

I don't find the exact place, the exact how, but I find enough to satisfy me that this was how it was done.

Security stares, bemused, at the Victorian wasteland that is so close to their front door. Somehow all this will need to be dealt with, the ventilation system made secure, the perimeter properly reviewed. It is on the list of long-term problems. For now, a security detail will guard this breached perimeter twenty-four hours a day.

'The nerve agent entered the ventilation shaft here, and was piped directly to the detainment suite, possibly by a secondary transmission pipe, possibly by remote control,' I say.

'But toxicology came back clear.'

Their faces are full of hope. They want it to be true, they want it to be a nerve agent filtered into the airways. Not human error, not a contractor getting past them.

'A nerve agent with 100 per cent degradation.'

'Why were they not dead in the cell then?'

The deserted station is silent. The black walls sucking the sound.

'Because it doesn't kill. It blinds.'

CHAPTER 57

Simon is heading down the sooty platform looking about him with wide eyes.

'Who knew all this was here?' he says.

'What's up?'

'I'm not sure if it's relevant anymore,' he says. 'I mean, the worst has happened, right? But I just got some results back on the search for shipments out of the Marseille factory.'

'Go on.'

Security are black shadows behind me. The sulphur lighting flickers.

'One of the yachts that is occasionally moored at Victoria Dock was in Marseille for a night about a month ago. There are thousands of trips from the Med to London and back again – I wouldn't have noticed if there wasn't something strange about it.'

Victoria Dock. Right next door to the ExCel Centre. Right next door to the G20.

What did Lucy say? *I am an experiment in the final countdown.* What if the worst hasn't already happened? What if '*Eyes only*' was never about giving Firestorm the edge but about something else entirely?

'No reason why a pleasure boat shouldn't be cruising the Med,' Simon says. 'Every yacht in London has probably been in the Mediterranean this year and everything within a five-hundred-yard radius of the ExCel Centre will have been checked and rechecked a dozen times.'

'How big was it? Could it have had any cargo?'

'Tiny,' he says. 'The only thing that struck me as odd was how many buoys it had attached. Like it was about to sail the Atlantic.'

'Buoys?'

'You know? The big inflatable balls filled with air that run alongside.'

I stare at Simon. 'What is the volume of the ExCel building?' I say.

'It's massive,' he says. 'Two separate halls, four hundred and eighty thousand square feet each. Got to be at least eighty-five feet high. That's forty-two million cubic feet of air. A nerve agent wouldn't get anywhere. Like a puddle in a thunderstorm. They have detectors there anyway.'

I stare at the black sooty walls. A heavily fortified position, sensitive personnel and an undetectable nerve agent. How would I do it?

'What happens if the building comes under attack?' I say slowly.

Simon shakes his head. There are two thousand armed police in a ring of steel. Seven battalions on standby a mile out. No. 3 Squadron out of RAF Northolt. A no-fly zone in force for fifty miles.

'But what happens to the key players? All the politicians? All the world leaders?' I say. 'Where do they go?'

'Air evac,' he says. 'Unless it is deemed too dangerous and then it's the Bunker.'

'Which is where?'

'About two hundred metres below Customs House station. Bombproof, bulletproof, their own ventilation system, just like our detainment level. Impregnable.'

The final countdown.

'And exactly how impregnable was our detainment level?' I want to say, but I am already running.

THE GUARDSMAN

XII

The Guardsman stood on the dock opposite the ExCel Centre, warm wind in her hair. Across the way she could see the huge modern facades of the Novotel and the Ibis and the sleek white shape of the Sunborn Yacht Hotel and beside it a tall industrial dock crane, a relic from the days when Britain was an industrial power.

The wind whipped across the dock, churning the water, feathering the surface until the dark expanse looked like rippling fur. It reminded the Guardsman of Lake Michigan at home. The same deep grey-green tone, the same smell on the air. Although, there the similarities ended. Lake Michigan was a natural freshwater lake, and the Victoria Dock a manmade structure filled with sluggish backwash from the North Sea.

The sky was a dark bruise overhead. The Guardsman could feel the tension rising. It was in the very air. Across the dock in the ExCel Centre, the G20 was finally getting underway.

The Guardsman liked the idea of panic rooms. She had heard they had taken a thousand cubic tons of soil out when they built the facility below Customs House and reinforced the concrete walls against the pressure of water from the dock. The Guardsman pictured the water pressing in. She liked the idea of a watery grave too but that was for another day.

Today, the world's leaders were going to learn a valuable lesson in vulnerability. Nothing, after all, was more debilitating than fear.

Men, used to having eyes everywhere, would discover what it was like to have none. Men, used to watching from every street cam, would find out what it was like to be blind and disorientated. It would be the perfect poetic moment, so-called authority scrabbling around in the dark, vulnerable as crabs without their shells. A symbolic strike against a world that watched everything.

She glanced down at her phone. Ten minutes to go. As the Firestorm Administrator she could raise an army if need be. People were easy to control if you were prepared to apply the fear. In this case, only a few people would be necessary. A few hotheads to make a lot of noise and force security to respond to the clear and present danger.

The Guardsman thought about the weeks of meticulous planning and adjustments. She knew she should be happy as Firestorm stood on the edge of this triumph, but there was no joy in it. It was a hollow victory, empty and sour. It had all been for Alek Konstantin. A single, knockout blow that would render the world's leadership incapacitated and Alek victorious. She stared out across the water and the betrayal welled up again so painful, she could hardly breathe.

He had put Winter first; before Firestorm, before the Guardsman, even before himself. The last was almost the hardest to bear. He had allowed himself to be weakened for Winter's sake. It was incomprehensible. It suggested a strength of feeling the Guardsman would never have believed possible. How or when it could have happened she had no idea.

She looked down at the tiny Guardsman blade tattooed on the inside of her right wrist. The Guardsman's knife. A symbol of the Guardsman's authority. She remembered the day Alek gave it to her. She pressed her arm to her side to feel the prick of her real blade against her skin but there was no comfort to be had.

Against the backdrop of seagulls and the whirr of army helicopters, on the very edge of hearing, the Guardsman became aware of a distant police siren. It was far away, across the water and travelling fast. She frowned. The area was in lockdown more than a mile out. Even the Blackwall Tunnel, the aorta of the London road network, had been closed.

Across the water, a black GCHQ Service Merc was roaring into view. It had to be doing seventy miles per hour at least. It screeched up onto the raised pedestrianised area in front of the Customs House station and came to a halt at an angle. Somehow, one wheel was higher than the other. The Guardsman craned to see. The car door flew open and a woman in a pinstripe suit hurtled out.

A single word forced its way out between the Guardsman's clenched teeth.

Winter.

There was only one thing that could have brought Winter to Customs House station at this time, and that was the truth. The Guardsman had underestimated her.

This time she wasn't going to be too slow.

Even though a moment before, the Guardsman had been feeling little joy at the thought of victory, to have it snatched away by Winter at the ninth hour, brought back the pain of Alek's betrayal all over again. Hatred flamed white hot and burning cold, the blood drummed in the Guardsman's ears and her vision blurred. She fell to her hands and knees on the gritty stone beside the dock and rocked until her palms bled.

CHAPTER 58

Control is there in the bed in medical like a cadaver. I expected him to be small and diminished in a hospital gown, but he looks just the same, except with the fat sucked out. Not that there was any fat in the first place. His cheeks are so sunken in, the breathing mask doesn't clamp properly to his face and there is a small gap between cheekbones and jaw on each side. The air makes a rattling sound as it sucks in and out through the gap.

His hands lie outside the sheet where they have been placed by some careful medic. Fingers straight and together. Brown liver spots, familiar and yet strangely alien.

He is still unconscious.

'So,' I say to him. 'I have nearly all the pieces… The how: a CIA-developed nerve agent that blinds the subject, stolen from the Petersburg deep storage facility, manufactured in a factory in Marseille and transported to London by yacht.

'The where: the Customs House facility. A small sealed unit so nearly full of politicians. A manufactured disturbance always intended to fail, to pull the key players inside.

'The why: a knockout blow in the war. A clever, disorientating move that would leave the world's leadership vulnerable but alive.'

'I have the how, the why and the where. I just don't have the who.'

Six people died at the ExCel even though I was in time to stop the main event. They approached security with explosives vests and for a long horrifying moment it seemed like the whole line might be wearing a vest. Bodyguards threw themselves on their charges, civilians screamed and the bombers marched forwards. The authorities, forewarned, were braced for a sophisticated attack and were momentarily taken aback by the direct approach until they calmed down, took a breath and blew the bombers to pieces. No one was evacuated to the Customs House.

Now Brad and his in-house scientists are taking apart the air filtration units in the Customs House facility, and the world's politicians are displaying unexpected reserves of courage. After a few hours of enforced idleness, where probably the bulk of any actual political progress will be made, the G20 is expected to resume.

And what of the Guardsman? Was she there watching the panic? Did she get round the GCHQ lockdown, get out of the building? Or was she pulling strings from afar?

My mind skates over the events of the last few days, the fake contract on Solo's account, the fake plans in his house, a girlfriend round at his house, a barmaid lying in the dust. Misdirection and misinformation. The Guardsman never once out in the open where I can pin her down, get a positive ID.

Solo. I stare up at the opposite wall, still with thought. The heart monitor beeps.

No. There *was* a moment she was out in the open.

The neat Georgian street round the back of Smithfield is sleepy in the heat. It looks as manicured as ever. Box balls and white cyclamen on every window ledge. I take the stairs down to the basement flat below Solo's house two at a time and lean on the bell.

There *was* a time when the Guardsman was out in the open, reacting to events, setting me up.

The basement flat door opens and I push forwards, shoving the woman hard back into her hallway. I slam the door behind me. She's not wearing a dressing gown anymore; it is the middle of the afternoon. She runs away up the hall.

'I won't hurt you,' I say. 'I just need to ask you some questions. You remember you told me a woman comes by sometimes to the flat upstairs? You said she was his girlfriend.'

She nods, wide-eyed, still poised to fly, although she's got nowhere to go.

'I need to know if you would recognise her again?'

'I don't know,' she says.

'If I show you a picture would you recognise her?'

'I don't think so. I only saw her legs go past.'

The hope that has driven me here in under ten minutes, that has caused me to practically break down her door, dies.

'She always wears these shoes,' she says. 'You can hear her coming all the way down the street.'

'Stilettos with metal heels.'

'Yes,' she says. 'How did you know?'

I turn away.

'Why,' she says. 'What has she done?'

'You have no idea.'

The metal gantry of the training arena rings as my own heels hit the ironwork. It is like the bridge of a battleship. I stand there surveying the arena and a sea of faces turn my way. Pansy Face is there, her eyes huge in her white face and Xiu, still and silent, for once not fiddling with her dungarees, and Léon beside her.

Eight hundred people were in the GCHQ building when the McKellens were killed; they stare up at me, faces glistening. Some are still in the same suits they were wearing, others are in gym kit. If nothing else, the place is going to get a lot fitter.

I wish I could tell them it was a training exercise. A drill. Disaster survival practice. I wish I could tell them that the rumours they have heard aren't true.

I haven't said a word and they have all stopped what they are doing to look up, as if they were waiting for me. Which I guess they were. The acoustics will be excellent. My voice will bounce off the metal overheads, the cooling pipes, the ventilation that goes straight up to street level and comes out under the statue by the Royal Exchange. It is the only place in the building you could release a nerve agent and it would have next to no effect.

It is not so much what you say, as the way that you say it.

I grip the railings in front of me, ignore the muttering and tell them how it is going to be.

'That's why you moved everyone into the arena isn't it?' Simon says. 'You already knew.'

'I suspected.'

'I'm thinking about all the things you didn't say. Like how the Guardsman got into GCHQ and how she knew we had Solo.' He leans against the wall on the stairs. 'The Guardsman works at GCHQ.'

'Yes,' I say.

'So why the wait?'

'Because some things don't add up and I need to be sure. It is better to wait. She wants me now. Not anybody else. Rage will bring her to me. It is a hunt and I am the prize.'

I open the door to my cell. Post-its flutter like dry yellow petals. The air smells stale, no one has been here for a while.

It is not better to wait. But this is something I have to do on my own.

Welcome to Firestorm
Please enter your job description

I load a new job sheet. I set a new target, set a location, set a
time. Then I upload the photo from my GCHQ pass.

The Latvian gambit. An in-your-face challenge. Put up or
shut up.

I close the system down, disconnect the laptop and drop it in the
bucket of water I keep in the corner. Saltwater. Nothing destroys
a solid-state drive like it. Forget all the software you can get to
delete your data. I have known data retrieved from bullet-ridden
hardware, but nothing gets past seawater.

The location I have chosen is symbolic. A personal affront.

She will accept the challenge and the plan has to be perfect,
airtight. No one but the Guardsman can know.

And since I don't know who I can trust, I will be trusting no one.

8 p.m. and the graveyard is deserted, the stones grey. A hot wind
blows. The days of haze have given way to rumbling activity. Clouds
scud across the strange mauvish sky. The Moscow storm is here,
or maybe the weather is finally breaking. The weeks of heat giving
way at last. The pressure at breaking point.

I can almost taste electricity in the air. A white streak of lightning flares horizontal across the gravestones. The leaves rustle in
the warm wind. No rain but it is there, just waiting. I can feel it.
Any minute now it will fall, first one or two fat, heavy drops and
then, the dam broken, it will pour down in a torrent. It is flash
flood weather. The water will run straight off the hard, bare earth,
washing away topsoil, making rivers of the roads.

I can see the tape where I found Lucy in the dust and I can see
the trunk of the cedar tree with its tracks down the bark. I drop
a small plastic box down between the roots. We have come full

circle, the Guardsman and I. Tonight she will answer my challenge. And tonight we will finish it.

I check the time. Five hours to get into position and I am going to need every minute of it if I am to be sure no one has followed me.

I turn my back on the graves as the first fat drops fall.

CHAPTER 59

It is midnight. The rain has been falling for hours. The neat Georgian street round the back of Smithfield glitters in the street lamps, the pavements washed clean of the summer's dust. Rivulets run down the gutters.

Dark windows look down at me. The building has windows on the front and another house behind. No gardens. Nothing at the back – the house behind sits straight onto it. It is like a street of dolls' houses. The only way in is through the front door.

I let myself in and stand in the hall, listening to the space, reading the silence. No one has been here. I am first but then I am expecting to be. I check the house from top to bottom, then I sit down in the velvet armchair in the front room and face the door.

I think back over my route and the length of time it took me to travel a few miles. There is no possibility I could have been followed. The next person through that door will be the Firestorm Administrator.

The room is beautiful. A well-considered interior. Every square inch thought through and maximised like an elegant yacht. A huge orchid arches, architectural, on the coffee table. It looks unreal, the soil parchment-dry, the fat white roots showing, and I can't tell if it is fake or not. I close my eyes and breathe and get the peaty smell of soil.

I think about the fake in GCHQ hiding beneath the surface like a fat white worm of root. Camouflaged by all the other roots. I should have listened to Beth and her degree in criminal psychology.

Sooner or later someone will accept your challenge.

That was the key to it. The Guardsman has been challenging me, trying to get my attention.

Well, now she has it.

It is time to stop chasing and double down.

Rain pours down, muffling and distorting, turning the street into a ventriloquist, throwing the sound, bouncing it around. A drainpipe echoes and gurgles loud in the night. Is it this side or across the road? I can't tell. Cars swish a long way off. Maybe around Smithfield. Metal clatters on metal in the distance.

A door slams on the street, high heels walk down steps. A car beeps as it unlocks, two tones; one short, one long. A car door slams. An engine starts, the tone changes as it lurches, angling out of its tight spot, tyres squealing as it roars off down the road.

Silence.

An orange glow seeps round the edge of the curtain. My eyes have acclimatised – I can see as well as daylight.

A Glock 17 sits right where I can lay my hand on it. I don't check it, I don't fiddle with the trigger, I don't trace a finger along the metal. I am too old a hand. There will be time enough. And it will be a kill shot. A double tap. No attempt to take her alive, no questioning, no hand wringing about the rights of the individual. The Guardsman distils in one person everything that is wrong with the age of technology. The new dystopia.

My senses search in the silence, stretching out and away from me, reaching blindly down the street, up to the silent floors above, probing, feeling. I close my eyes to bring everything into sharper focus.

I discovered long ago, in the dark childhood years, that I can read spaces, read the movement in the air, the sound on the very edge of hearing, at that point where it disappears into vibration.

I breathe long and slow to calm my heart rate, remembering my sniper training from a decade ago.

Lower your heart rate, remain motionless, alert, watchful.

I am a fair distance shot but I would never have made a sniper. I have never been able to empty my head, to just hang, suspended in time, alert but empty.

I try now and my brain teams with images: a bleeding girl in the dirt, a judge sitting on a toilet with holes for eyes, yellow stickies fluttering on a wall.

A car goes past in a swish and slick of tyres, soft brakes at the end of the road. My heart kicks. This street is not on the way anywhere. There is no reason for any through traffic. Is it a drive by? Recon? Nothing moves but my eyes flicking this way and that. I can feel the pulse in my wrists beating against the fabric of the chair. I force my eyes closed.

Silence from the street except for the patter of rain.

My heart rate eases back, my breathing slows. The room comes back into focus as my hearing dials down.

Footsteps on the front steps, light and quick.

My heart kicks again. A massive jolt of adrenaline. The sort they give you in a syringe through the chest. A muffled subtle scrabbling at the door, the click of the lock giving way. Footsteps in the hall.

The door swings open.

'Hi,' says the Guardsman, standing in the doorway in her dungarees.

CHAPTER 60

The first bullet gets her in the leg. Because I want it to. She screams as she falls, both hands to her calf, her golden skin greying instantly.

'No, Winter!' Xiu screams. 'No!'

'It was like someone was feeding you lines, you were so bloody perfect.'

I think about the cellophane room and a contractor clever enough to field a substitute. The Guardsman was there all along.

'No,' she says.

'You were just too good.'

I stand over her. She is lying on her side rocking to ease the pain. The sight disgusts me. Even for the Guardsman I want it over. I put my boot on her hip to hold her still and stretch my gun arm straight.

'No one but the Guardsman could have found me here.'

Her eyes close. She is sweating tears of pain.

'Your tracker,' she whispers.

'I'm not wearing a tracker. I took it out.'

'Your other tracker.'

I stare.

'I did have someone feeding me lines. He told me how to play you.'

My heart clenches as the breath leaves me. A sucker punch in the gut. Alek told the Guardsman how to play me? I can't believe it.

'Alek sent me to protect you. He told me how to get close to you. He gave me enough Firestorm access to get your interest.'

I don't believe it.

'I am a bodyguard. He trained me himself. Normally I look after Roman.'

His brother.

I stare down at her. 'Tell me about Roman.'

'The Colony Club,' she says. 'You were wearing white and Roman was looking for you. He said you were the most beautiful mark he had ever seen. He pulled the Ace of Hearts out of your French pleat.'

I can see it now, the faces, the peacock colours, smell the Elnet and the Colony lavender, feel the tension in the crowd as the Bank hovered on the brink. An Asian woman in silver…

Shit.

No wonder she found me in Paris. Alek must have called her as he left.

'I was supposed to keep you busy but safe. And then first time out we hit Solo. Dumb luck.' Her face is grey.

My own safe area to play in, plenty of edged weapons, someone to look after me. Jesus.

'You were talking to him on that Nokia brick in the house. You said it was your mum.'

'He knew from the tracker you had been in a fight. I thought you would hear him shouting.'

'Did he tell you to come here tonight?'

'I told him what you said to the staff and he said it was a bluff, that there was no way you would wait. He said you would do it alone.'

'What have you done with Léon?'

'He's fine, drugged, out for the count. I knew it was all going down tonight.'

Something moves in the hallway and in the still, pregnant silence, it hits me. If this is not the Guardsman then he or she is still out there. Still coming. I hold my hand up to silence Xiu and step over her body.

My heart motors.

I grip the Glock and fling open the door.

CHAPTER 61

A man is standing in the corridor, his face dim with the light from the street behind him.

'I thought we agreed you weren't going to do this by yourself?' Simon says.

I stare.

In my head I see a man standing outside a house filled with cellophane and corpses, scowling under the street light, the same man running down a corridor in the detainment suite already knowing what he would find.

I missed a call from Ariadne.

Did you? Or did you tell her to open the door?

His eyes widen as I level the gun. He stares down the barrel of my Glock.

He puts his hands up slowly.

'Winter... surely you can't think...?' His face is white, struck, filled with horror.

'How did you find me?'

'I followed Xiu.'

For a moment we stand there looking at each other, the Glock a symbol of my lack of faith. I lower the gun, walk down the hall and put my arms around him.

'I'm sorry, Simon.'

His eyes are full of tears. 'How could you even think for one minute that I could do something like that?' He shudders against

me in the dark. 'All I want is to protect you. It is the only thing
I have ever wanted.'

Running footsteps tear down the steps away from us. The
Guardsman's footsteps, running full tilt, running to escape at all
costs, not caring about being quiet, only about getting away from
the trap. I push past Simon, down the hall to the front door. He
is behind me.

'Stay there with Xiu!' I shout. 'I shot her.'

'*What?*' says Simon, but I am out of the door and it is too
late to answer. As I leap down the steps, the running figure is at
the end of the street. A woman. She turns right onto Aldersgate.
My legs pump, my breath coming loud in the wet air. If she can
make it to Smithfield she will lose me in the miles of underground
storage and market stalls.

I pound down the pavement, my strides eating up the ground.
I turn the corner and catch a glimpse of her ducking into an alley.
Glasshouse Yard. She has trapped herself. Adrenaline courses
through me.

The alley turns a corner, running parallel to Aldersgate, part
of the old medieval city layout. Tall office buildings loom on
either side. After a hundred metres or so it turns again and joins
Aldersgate. She hasn't trapped herself in – she can escape. I hammer
down the deserted alley, my feet slapping in the wet. I am fifty
metres away doing maybe ten miles per hour. I have to be going
twice her speed to catch her before she reaches the end. My brain
can't hold any maths; there is nothing but the hard acceleration,
the screaming muscles, the blowing lungs. It shouldn't be possible
and yet I am gaining on her.

A dark building spans the corner with wide, steel-framed grid
windows and yellow doors. I bring her down with a flying tackle
right on its threshold and yank both her arms back in a wrestling
hold. Then I roll her over.

Surprise almost makes me release my grip.

Pansy Face. Simon's girlfriend.

'I hate you,' she says.

'What?'

'I *saw* you together. Holding each other. I heard what he said. All he wants in life is to protect you. I *knew* he was going to meet you this evening.'

I sit back on my heels, my plan in tatters. Xiu was able to find me. Simon followed her. Pansy Face followed him. Now I can't be certain of anything. I look up at the dark building with the grid windows and straight into a breakout area for creative types burning the midnight oil. A man and a woman are staring through the window at me like they can't believe their eyes. The woman has long shiny auburn hair. There is a poster of an orangutan wearing headphones on the wall above them.

'Jesus,' I say. 'Have you any idea how close I was to killing you?'

'I don't see what reason *you* have to be jealous,' she says. 'He doesn't care about anything but you.'

'I thought you were the Guardsman,' I say.

'What?' she says. 'Why?'

'Because you ran.'

She twists and squirms away from me, her giant pansy eyes full of misery.

I get a picture of Xiu lying on the rug, her face a grimace of pain and Simon, absorbed, bending over her, tying a tourniquet and the street door, wide, wide open. Open to the person I was expecting with their lethal gas and their blades.

I am up and back down the alley and out onto Aldersgate in a few strides.

The cold and wet hit me. Taxis swish past in the rain. Drunken voices far off. Something is wrong. I know it. Dread is gripping me. I break into a run, my feet throwing up spray as I hammer down Solo's street, charge up his front steps. The front door is wide open. I stop abruptly on the threshold, listening. Silence. Panic grips me hard.

I swing around the door. The place is empty. The architectural orchid is over on its side, stem broken. Earth spills out of its pot onto the rug.

I back out, out through the front door and search up and down the road, my lungs heaving.

Nothing.

Far off a car engine roars. The drainpipe stutters. The gutters run.

How could she have come and gone so quickly? How could she have got two people out so fast?

I can't believe it. I go back through the front door. The room is still empty. The smell of loam on the carpet fills the air.

'Simon?' I say to the empty space.

I lean against the door jamb, suddenly exhausted.

Oh no.

There is a clatter of footsteps behind me and Pansy Face is in the hall.

'Where is he?' she demands.

I shake my head. My eyes pricking.

She takes in the orchid, the signs of a brief struggle, the line of blood. Her hand goes to her mouth.

This is your fault, stupid girl.

I want to slap her.

Your fault because you ran.

No. It is my fault.

Behind her, something is scrawled on the wall. It wasn't there before.

The just man walketh in his integrity, Prov 20:7.

There is something familiar about it.

The just man.

Of course.

'I know where they are,' I say. I grip her by the top of her arms. 'Get back to GCHQ and get armed response out to the Brockley and Ladywell cemetery.'

She shrinks away from me. 'I can't go out there. What if they are waiting to take me too?'

Jesus.

I slap her around the face. Then I hand her my Glock. 'You know how to fire this?' She nods, looking down at it, limp in her hand. 'I did the day course during induction.'

The day course.

'It's easy,' I say. 'Point and shoot. Mostly it's enough to point. And watch for the recoil.'

'Where are you going?' she says, gulping on her tears.

'I am the advance party.'

CHAPTER 62

The cabbie pulls up. The graves are dimly pale in the dark. Black trees hang with rain.

'Rather you than me,' he says.

He drives off down the road and I stand on the pavement watching the street. No one is out in this weather. The rain pounds down, plastering my hair to my forehead, dripping off my nose. I shiver. If it wasn't for my Kevlar, I would be freezing.

I breathe in, breathe out and duck inside.

It is quieter than the street but still full of the creak and movement of water. The long grass is heavy with water, my legs are soaked before I have gone four paces. The smell of wet stone fills the air.

I reach the just man.

Samuel Palmer of Collingwood College. Who passed away 26 February 1888. Aged 65.

I find the little box I left earlier, open it up and put in Snow White's contact lenses. It was always coming to this. One way or another.

I stand by the stone angel, listening. The dead petals of her roses have washed away. I close my eyes over the lenses, letting my senses do the work.

Silence.

There is no one here.

Lights blaze from the lantern on the church hall on the hill.

I turn to face it.

*

The church itself is in darkness. I try the door. Padlocked. I imagine what it must be like inside. Silent, the smell of damp and decay strong, old hymn books abandoned on the pews, dark with only the borrowed light from the hall. Creepy.

I try the door to the hall beside the church and it isn't locked.

The corridor smells musty and damp. The old damp of church halls. Years and years and years of minimal maintenance. Double doors to what must be the hall lie ahead. Frosted fire glass in the windows. They look like they could be the doors through to a gymnasium.

I stand listening.

She is in the hall through the double doors. There is no movement and no sound but there is a presence where emptiness should be. That feeling you get when you know you are not alone. The monkey part of your brain tipping you off.

The corridor is lined with noticeboards. A dog-eared flyer for a toddler group hangs by one pin from ancient cork. I yank the pin out without breaking my stride and drop it in my pocket. My fingers slide down the inside of my calf as I walk, checking the blades. Eight knives and one pin and my fists. More than enough unless there is a gun involved, and there won't be. The big showdown – she will get close enough to cut.

I put my hand on the vertical handles and breathe in and breathe out. The brass is shiny with use. Adrenaline fires. My heart motors. I open the door.

CHAPTER 63

The room is cavernous, rafters stretch across a ceiling arched like a church with an old-fashioned glass lantern in the centre. There is a small connecting door to the church at the far end.

For a moment, my eyes can't make sense of the scene. Figures stand in a semi-circle, so still they could be stone.

Twelve of them.

They are dressed the same, in bodysuits of lightweight black Kevlar and black helmets. They are holding identical knives.

The Guardsman blade.

'Hello, Winter,' say the Guardsmen in unison. Their voices are far away. The sound displaced by the helmets.

Not Guardsman. Guards*men*.

Twelve of them.

I am out of the door, back down the corridor, hurtling for the exit. The doors to the outside slam before I am halfway down the corridor and the bar falls. I canon into the door; it is closed solid. Heavy with years. The varnish is cracked. I touch my forehead to the hard, shiny surface – it is cold beneath my skin. The space is silent behind – they haven't come out of the hall. No one has followed me.

I turn and walk back up the corridor, pulling a knife out of my boot. I grip the handle in the reverse hold, the blade hard to my arm. It is made for throwing. Lightweight and aerodynamic. One-time use.

My heart hammers. I put both hands on the vertical handles and throw the doors wide. The Guardsmen haven't moved.

'Sorry about that,' I say. 'Pressure of the moment.'

'You wanted to find us, Winter, and here we are.'

All twelve of you.

'We accept your contract, Winter.'

As one, they raise their right hands with the identical blade.

The Big Boss battle.

How good am I hand-to-hand? Pretty good, but not superhuman. Against twelve? Nowhere near good enough.

My eyes scan the room looking for an edge, looking for the angle, anything I can use to tilt the playing field just a little my way. There is nothing. The place is empty. It could have been designed for the purpose.

'So,' I say. 'Are you all the Guardsman? Like some kind of job share, like some kind of hive mind? Twelve is a very symbolic number. Twelve tribes of Israel, twelve months in a year, twelve pairs of ribs in the human body...'

'The Guardsmen guard Firestorm,' one of them says. 'One for each of the geographies. We maintain the system. We police it. We watch over it. We are its guardians.'

'Right,' I say. 'Hence "Guardsman".'

The profilers are having a field day with their fragmented personality theories.

No shit. McKellen got that right.

'Where are Simon and Xiu?' I say, and I can feel the Guardsmen smiling behind their helmets, a vindication of everything they believe. If you care, your enemies have all the leverage they need.

'About twenty feet away from where you left them, bleeding out. It wasn't necessary to take them, only to make you think we had taken them. We'll go back when we have more time. Make it last.'

Something must have shown on my face because the same voice says, 'You can still save them if you are fast enough.'

I picture Pansy Face racing full tilt for GCHQ, all our lives in her hands.

'And I wouldn't hold out much hope for that girl you left wandering the streets on her own. We couldn't allow a message to get through. Sadly, there was no time to make it last.'

I can hear the smile in the Russian voice.

'Let me guess,' I say. 'You are the Moscow Guardsman?'

He pulls off his helmet and pale green eyes stare into mine. It is the traffic cop from outside the Maison Honfleur in Moscow. The Guardsman that Sergei knows. The one who stood staring from the bridge, not interested in the gunfire, only interested in me. *The Guardsman is not a woman*, Sergei said. I should have listened.

I look round the semi-circle. 'So,' I say. 'Where else? New York?'

A man steps forward. This is the Guardsman who hung his last contract from the Brooklyn Bridge. '*Parting is such sweet sorrow,*' he says. '*That I shall say goodnight till it be morrow.*'

'Right. Chicago? Miami? LA?'

They step forward. Three correct guesses. I am on a roll. Chicago is a woman. She raises her hand in greeting. There is a knife tattooed on the inside of her wrist. Her palm is grazed and bloody like she has been crawling on gravel. 'I saw you at the ExCel Centre,' she says.

LA is wearing a clown mask under the helmet. The effect is weird. Like looking at a clown through a goldfish bowl. 'Did you enjoy the three blind mice?' she says. 'I heard they didn't run.'

My jaw clenches. I can feel the darkness rising. 'Mexico City? Rio?'

Another two Guardsmen step forward.

'*And the Lord said, in the final hour ye shall be judged,*' says Rio.

I think about the shape of organised crime. 'Tokyo?'

The Moscow Guardsman shakes his head. He has put his helmet back on. 'We have an agreement with Yakusa.'

'Of course you do. Beijing?'

A man steps forward. 'Shanghai,' he corrects, his accent thick.

That leaves Europe.

'Milan? Frankfurt? Geneva?'

Another three correct guesses.

Geneva raises her hand. She has a Patek Philippe round her wrist. A long glossy ponytail hangs over her shoulder.

There is one Guardsman left. Slim build. A woman.

The Guardsman that killed a judge in the bathroom, Lucy in the graveyard and the McKellen family in the GCHQ detainment suite.

'You must be London,' I say.

She puts both hands to her helmet and pushes. She shakes out her long hair.

I do not fucking believe it.

CHAPTER 64

'Too easy, Winter, too easy,' Beth says. 'You are a disappointment.'

I grip the blade. A one-time shot. Without her helmet, I could get her in the face.

'Bitch,' I say.

'Is that it? That's all you've got? No offers to suck me until I scream?' She laughs. 'Do you want to know what I said to Ariadne through the door?'

'No.'

'I said you were on the phone. That you wanted to speak to her. She died screaming for you.' She laughs a tinkling musical laugh. 'I am going to carve my name on your face, Winter, until you beg me to kill you.'

Sooner or later someone will accept your challenge.

I challenged the Guardsman and Ariadne paid the price.

What did Alek say? *You can't erase the dark, you can only keep it in check... it is about balance.*

I disrupted the balance.

I can hear Sergei in Moscow saying, *While Winter is still alive there will always be trouble*, and doubt slithers into my mind, crippling and confusing. Am I the concession Alek has had to make to the Guardsmen to keep order? My life, to keep the peace, restore the balance? Are they here with his knowledge? The thought is like a stab in the gut.

The figures closest to me are moving fractionally. Just enough. Muscles tensing. Preparation.

I grip the slim blade.

'Come on,' says Moscow. 'We are wasting time.'

Rule one: if you are facing multiple opponents and insuperable odds, get your back to the wall, better yet, get in the corner. I edge sideways and they move with me like a synchronised dance troupe. They were expecting it.

Rule two: don't be predictable. But honestly, at this point, what choice do I have?

Here it is then, the end of the road.

The Moscow Guardsman closes in. Ten feet, six feet. I can see his eyes through his visor. Then a blade flies through the air. I don't have time to do more than jerk sideways and it gets me in the top of my arm just below my shoulder.

Not good.

Then they are on me. Moscow on the left, LA on the right. She is wiry and flexible as a dancer. She ducks my jab so it barely connects and lands a blow in the stomach that knocks the wind out of me. I block down with my right arm and the shoulder muscle screams and Moscow jabs me in the face. A boxer's move – my head slams back against the wall.

He closes in and I know I've got to get the knife out of my arm. I wrench the blade free and slash down double-handed. It should have disembowelled him but the knives ricochet, harmless, off his Kevlar. He grins and I smack up hard and fast with my forehead. Power equals weight times speed squared. He is taller than me and I get the helmet just under the nose. He staggers back, hands to his visor.

Stars dance in front of my eyes, my brain thuds around in my skull – two blows to the head in quick succession. LA sees my guard is down. Blades are useless against Kevlar. I drop the left-hand blade and slam the heel of my hand up under the edge of the helmet. It snaps back, revealing two inches of throat under the clown mask. I take a punch in the face, getting my knife hand up, but it is worth it. Someone screams a warning but it is too late, she staggers backwards, my knife sticking in under her jaw. I pull it straight out, shoving her away and then they are all coming.

A blade hits my thigh, then another, then another. Two in the right, one in the left. Thrown with their right hands. Right-handed people outweigh left more than two to one. I grapple the guy in front of me close like a shield. He has thrown his blade. I use my forehead again, in the absence of any other weapons, but the angle is poor and the speed is slow. My legs stagger with blades. Three crap shots and then I realise. The Guardsmen are knife specialists – they are not crap shots. The blades have landed right where they were meant to. I am like a deer with arrows hanging out of her.

My right leg is shaking uncontrollably and I know in a split second of freeing clarity that if I don't stay on my feet it is all over. I feel down, blind and groping – I have got to get the knives out. I grip a handle, but it is slick with blood. I yank as a swinging blow comes at my head. I block with my left, but now I am out of hands. The follow-up connects fair and square with the side of my face. A proper blow. The world rocks, reality wobbles, bubbles pop, blood roars in my ears. Only adrenaline is keeping me upright. My legs are trembling. Blood is pouring down my arm, pouring into my eyes.

'Pull back,' Moscow says. 'Give her some space or it will all be over too quickly.'

My lungs heave, my hair sticks to my bloody forehead. I get a hand to another blade and pull. It was further in and the pain is searing. Crippling. My stomach heaves, my mouth fills with saliva, pain is going to make me throw up.

The black figures waver in and out of my limited vision. They watch me, impregnable in their Kevlar. My legs are like pin cushions. I can feel myself starting to heave again.

It goes on and on. They press me to my limit then pull back. My lungs burn, my legs shake. I wonder whether I will actually bleed out before it is over. They are prolonging it. Like a cat playing with a mouse. And the mouse knows exactly what is happening and its adrenaline pumps round and round, making its flesh tender and more appetising. Poor little beaten, battered mouse.

They pull back again and stand watching me, and the fear is cold, clammy down my neck. I am not going to get out of this and long before I am dead, I am going to wish that I was.

CHAPTER 65

Pain hits me in waves. Washing over me, ebbing and breaking, rising, surging and breaking. My eyelids flicker. Someone is bringing me round. Bringing me back to consciousness and they are using pain to do it. Screaming. My screaming. Memory fills in the blanks and panic hits me hard. I struggle, flailing against my restraints, my body going into a frenzy.

My eyes fly open. I am still in the hall. My bare wrists are bound to the wooden arms of a director's chair, my jacket sleeves pushed up to the elbow. Surrounding me, like a stone circle, are twelve fat shipping buoys.

There is a knife sticking out of my right thigh. My fingers are splayed against the wood. Beside me, a heart rate monitor beeps.

Faces surround me. Faces without their helmets, now the threat has been neutralised. They swim in and out of focus. The beating heart of Firestorm: six men and six women. Alek Konstantin, equal opportunities employer.

No, five women – the LA Guardsman is dead on the floor.

There are wires taped to my wrist above my tracker.

Why are they are monitoring the tracker?

The Moscow Guardsman looks at it with satisfaction.

I think about the most famous twelve of all – the Apostles – and their unquestioning obedience. How much does Alek really know about tonight?

'There is a Firestorm ban on me. The man at the top is going to be seriously pissed if you take me out. He has sworn to do it himself.'

'Alek Konstantin has betrayed the founding principles of Firestorm, betrayed us all. Discovery has weakened him. He has grown soft with sentiment.' Moscow sneers. His nose looks broken.

'Really? I'd like to see you say that to his face.'

The mouth twists. 'You will get your wish. Then you can watch me peel it off him bit by bit. He has suffered you to live. Put your interests before the good of Firestorm. He has betrayed us all.'

My heart thuds as my brain plays catch up. The Moscow Guardsman was there on that bridge, ready and waiting for Winter. They had it all arranged: get her to Moscow, to Sergei, and wait for the Prince of Darkness to come and deal with her.

No wonder Beth signed me back on active.

And it all worked perfectly. Everyone was right where they were supposed to be, everything went according to plan. Right up until the moment the Moscow Guardsman looked down from the bridge and saw what was really going on – a picture painting a thousand words. And at that point, for the Guardsmen, everything changed.

He has betrayed us all.

They know about me and Alek. They know about the tracker. They think he will come for me. Tonight was never about me. I am just the means to the end.

Who is the biggest status target in their world?

Not McKellen. Not me.

'If you care, your enemies have all the leverage they need,' says Beth, reading my mind. 'You have given us the power. How do you find the world's most wanted man? You make him come to you.'

CHAPTER 66

And there it is. The reality. Stripped bare. The Guardsmen are challenging for the top job. Firestorm's Administrators have gone rogue.

Even I can't protect you against the Guardsman.

There was one right beside me in GCHQ. He knew that. He must have been holding her back all these weeks. Deal with her and there were another eleven waiting to step in.

The pin from the noticeboard is in my jacket pocket. Six massive inches away from my splayed fingers. An aching, yawning, unbridgeable gap. I shuffle forward in the seat. Four inches, two inches. I stretch my thumb and forefinger down. Tears of pain stand in the corner of my lashes. The movement makes my head swim with nausea. I close my eyes and breathe in, breathe out and the dizziness eases off a bit.

A lurch and a reach and I touch the tip of the pin.

I hook my nail under it. It slides from my grip. The pale green eyes of the Moscow Guardsman look into mine and for a moment I think he knows what I am trying to do.

'I saw you in Moscow,' I say to distract him. 'Who were those people in the car park cells?'

He glances at the shipping buoys and for a minute I think he's not going to answer.

'Experiments,' he says. 'We had to get the dose perfect. Sometimes it was less effective. Once, it didn't seem to work. We are not sure why. We thought it might be age-related.'

So, Lucy wasn't the only one – they got in a wide sample to test, all the ages of man. A man and a woman from every decade. Twelve experiments in total. They probably thought that was symbolic.

No wonder the people in the cells looked straight through me, they couldn't see.

'Did the Boss not understand? Did he try to restrict your fun?'

He turns away, but not before I see the anger as the question hits home.

Alek didn't steal *For Your Eyes Only*, he was destroying it. He destroyed the production facility in Marseille. He was in Petersburg getting to the truth. The Guardsmen had already hammered on the door and stolen the formula and taken it to Ferret weeks before. Maybe they thought the Boss would be pleased.

Will he come? Into the heart of London? Walk straight into a trap? Why would he?

I can hear Sergei's voice saying, *Alek Konstantin sleeps with hundreds of women.* But then I remember Kristophe saying, *You have no idea how much danger you are in… How many people would like leverage over Alek Konstantin?*

And if he comes, he will die and a new age will dawn. Only this time the Guardsmen will be in charge.

There is one thing I can do.

I still have free access to the weapons I was born with. I look down at my arm. I brace myself. *Breathe in, breathe out.* Psych myself up and punch my head down.

As my teeth close round the tracker, the Guardsmen scream in disbelief. I shake my head like a shark trying to bite off flesh, and hands haul me backwards. The director's chair hits the floor, my head bounces, my jaw unlocks, the wires pull free.

The Guardsmen shout in panting disbelief, scrabbling at my tracker. They right the chair. They check the machinery. Someone holds my head in a lock, while they reconnect the wires.

There is a pause as they wait for the machine.

I picture the signal winking out, the GPS going blind.

'It is still fine,' the Moscow Guardsman says, breathing out. 'It is still transmitting.'

I can taste the fresh blood in my mouth.

He backhands me. Puts the full weight of his arm behind it. My brain hits my skull, my vision darkens. Maybe I black out for a bit, because when I come to, I have a hand across my mouth and nose. The heart rate monitor shrieks as the tracker picks up my panic.

The Guardsmen gather round, their faces bright with interest, turning from me to the monitor and back again.

'That's interesting,' Beth says. 'Fear of suffocation – almost always goes hand in hand with claustrophobia. That wasn't in any of her psych reports. We should have used waterboarding.'

Far off, in the distance, there is a rumble in the night sky. The Guardsmen turn their faces to the glass lantern. It is the sound of a helicopter travelling at speed towards us, the roar of rotor blades getting closer, fast. The glass in the roof flickers with light. It has stopped raining.

How can Alek be here? Was he already on his way? Why?

The Moscow Guardsman smiles as he points at the ceiling. 'And here is Prince Charming just in the nick of time. How romantic. How heroic. What a heart-warming thought. The most wanted man in the world in love with a government agent.' He looks at my face and his smile broadens. 'And she has no idea. It's an unbelievable situation. The man with no weaknesses, falling prey to the worst one of all. We should have questioned the Firestorm ban on you – we should have put two and two together. It just never occurred to us. It is funny how close love is to hate, isn't it?'

He twists the knife in my thigh and the scream bursts out until I strangle it. He twists it again. The pain is so bad I am going to black out. I clamp my jaws tight shut.

He smiles. 'And is it reciprocated, I wonder? Maybe we can play a little game when we have him. Get you to choose which part we cut next.'

The Guardsmen pull on their helmets, checking the fit around their necks. They hit the lights and stand in a tight, dark group around me with the shipping buoys surrounding us like a stone circle.

The room floods with the brilliant, white light of a helicopter search beam and the thud, thud, thud of rotor blades. A moment ago, there was nothing but the distant rumble of the engine, now the noise is so loud it cracks the eardrums. I look up through the Victorian panes of glass. It is right overhead. The shipping buoys cast fat, black shadows in the white light.

I can hear nothing over the deafening rotor blades and then the ceiling explodes with a boom of shrapnel and glass fragments. They rain down, a shining shower of knives, slicing at everything in their path, indiscriminate and lethal. The Guardsmen hunch, protected by their helmets and kevlar.

I brace.

Glass hits my hair, my bare arms, glass dust coats my face, my lips and through the glittering rain I can just make out a tall figure standing on the roof.

CHAPTER 67

The figure looks down through the dust, at the woman bleeding in a chair with the Guardsmen tight around her. He is backlit by the search light, his face in shadow.

The Moscow Guardsman has his blade at my throat. 'No guns!' he shouts up. 'Or I will gut her, right here, right now.'

'What does it matter?' New York says. 'He will be blind. He won't be able to see to use them anyway.'

The figure in black is still, then he shrugs and an M-16 assault rifle on a heavy webbed strap hits the roof. It was across his back. He reaches down into his thigh holsters and the grip on my throat tightens. Two heavy handguns go the same way as the assault rifle. He pauses, then slowly and deliberately he reaches into his boot and pulls a long familiar blade. A Guardsman blade. He holds it up high. I feel the reaction all around me. It ripples out from the hive mind. They approve. Blade against blades. A symbolic gesture. Did he give them their knives when he appointed them?

As one, they nod in approval.

'OK,' shouts Moscow, on behalf of them all. 'Come and get her.'

The figure in black turns away and a moment later a rope flies down through the opening. The coil hits the floor with a slap and then Alek is sliding down, and the Guardsmen are punching great holes in the shipping buoys beside them with their blades and all around me there is the hiss of gas escaping from twelve containers.

For Your Eyes Only.

They are using their entire stockpile on Alek Konstantin. A massive quantity. It is not enough just to kill him. They want to blind him and cut him first.

'Shut your eyes!' I scream, slamming mine closed but my words swallow-dive out into nothing and disappear, lost in the thud, thud, thud of rotor blades.

Someone smacks me across the mouth, the chair crashes over onto its side, my cheek slams into the ground and my eyes fly open.

I taste blood against my teeth. The arm that has hit the ground has come loose. I yank and pull and tear at the masking tape, loosening it, millimetre by millimetre, my breath coming in great heaving sobs. The arm breaks free.

Alek is surrounded.

The Guardsmen cluster round him like hyenas round a lion.

Knives stick out of his thighs. He turns and the next three hit body armour. His eyes are clamped shut and mine are not and I can still see.

I was right.

For Your Eyes Only was developed in the 1960s, before they had a lot of things we take for granted today. Like contact lenses. It didn't work on Control, a man who has worn glasses his whole life until a few months ago.

Snow White's coloured contacts have saved my sight.

The floor is rough under my cheek.

A Guardsman closes in and Alek's right arm shoots out and yanks him close. The Guardsman kicks and thrashes but he has no chance. Alek clamps down and slices at the gap between helmet and Kevlar.

The Guardsmen howl with rage.

Alek spins, using the body as a shield, edging closer to me but he is surrounded and the blades are coming from all sides.

My free hand closes over the pin in my pocket.

Blood pours down Alek's legs from the knives in his thighs.

The Guardsmen pull back, keeping their distance as they circle him, and I cannot believe that he is staying on his feet and that his eyes are still closed. The instinct to open your eyes to face danger is overwhelming.

I slash down again and again with my free hand and the pin at the masking tape round my wrist. The tape is thick and bound tight, but I am accurate. I break free and roll out of the chair, landing in the shards of glass.

Alek staggers and I know we are almost out of time.

I wave my hands in front of my face and hobble forwards on my knees, arms stretched out in front of me.

'My eyes,' I scream. 'I can't see.'

They pause in their onslaught, visors turning my way, jeering faces smiling behind the glass.

The nearest Guardsman boots me in the ribs, and it is all I can do to take no defensive action. I keel over, sobbing in the dust and crawl towards Alek, bleeding and battered like a snail with a broken shell, leaving a slime trail through the debris.

One foot closer, two feet, three feet…

'Look at her, Alek,' Beth says. 'Look at her now. Was it worth it? Was it worth betraying us for this?'

He puts his arms out in front of him trying to find me and for a moment I think he is going to crack and open his eyes.

'Alek,' I say. 'I can't get up. Come down to me.'

He crouches down and reaches out and his fingers touch my hair. My hands flutter over him, over his face, his shoulders. The Guardsmen laugh with delight at the sight of us, broken and bleeding on our knees.

Look what sentiment does to you.

This is what they were expecting. This is what they live for.

Now the fun can really begin.

CHAPTER 68

The Guardsmen don't use guns, it is a point of principle, but the Prince of Darkness does.

My shaking, fluttering hands move over his face, over his shoulders, they slide down his back, and then they are diving under the waistband and Alek hits the deck and I am rising and firing.

One, two, three, four, five. I mow them down in a circle. Five kill shots, straight through their visors with a strange gun and an arm so weak I can barely lift it.

Bang, bang, bang, they slam down, eyes wide with shock. Helmets explode, body armour crashes to the floor and five is all I am going to get because the rest are charging for the small arched door in the corner. Pushing and shoving to get away from the loaded gun and the pinpoint marksmanship.

I catch number six in the back of the neck as he throws the door open but the rest shove past, clambering over his fallen body and escaping out of the hall into the darkness of the church.

Alek is on his feet, pulling blades from his legs, still blind. I grab his hand and drag him towards the door.

The cold, clear air of the church hits our faces. Footsteps run in all directions but the main door to the church is padlocked. In trapping me and Alek in, they have trapped themselves.

I slam the small arched door behind us and look around. We have come in a side door in the south-east corner of the church, some kind of side chapel. The opening to the main part of the church is ahead of us. A little oasis of quiet. The solid old door between us and the hall is acting like a containment facility, keeping the gas out. Running footsteps echo somewhere on the stone.

Tiger eyes glitter down at me.

'Can you see?' I say.

He nods.

I shake my head. 'I don't know how you did that.'

He cups my face, looking at the bruising, tilting my jaw this way and that.

'It's still a stupid place to carry a gun.'

My legs buckle and I stagger and lean against the wall as it all catches up with me. I've been cashing cheques my body can't cover. He takes the gun before it falls.

'It was a trap,' I say. 'They never wanted me. They wanted you.'

His dark eyes stare down. 'I know,' he says. 'And here I am.'

'Where are your bodyguards?'

'Outside. I couldn't let them die just because I am a fool.'

He reaches into a pocket and pulls out a medical supply bag and tears it open with his teeth.

'I'm going to give you a shot,' he says.

The syringe to the heart feels exactly like you would expect. Like someone has jabbed you with a cattle prod. I straighten up, my legs are numb. He stands back watching me.

'I'm fine,' I tell him. 'Give me the gun and let's finish this.'

He smiles a wide white grin in the darkness.

For a moment we stand together, shoulder to shoulder, and then he counts and we burst through the opening onto the main aisle and he turns left and I turn right.

CHAPTER 69

We got two of them earlier and another six with Alek's gun. That leaves four.

Two for him, two for me.

I see words carved on a child's forehead.

Please God, let me get Beth.

The interior is gloomy. There is a light burning on the main altar off to my right, everything else is in shadow. Wooden pews stretch away in front of me.

I edge along the pews until I am on the main aisle. I swing right towards the altar. An oil lamp is burning on the white and gold altar cloth. I shut my eyes too late – fireflies of light dance against my black eyelids. I have wrecked my night vision.

My neck prickles and my subconscious screams a warning as a black figure rises out of the pew beside me. I spin and fire as arms close around me. Light reflects off the black visor as it sinks to the floor. Kevlar is bulletproof but not at point-blank range.

I yank off the helmet and the Moscow Guardsman's dead eyes stare up at me.

Not Beth.

Behind me, from the back of the church, there is a shout and the sound of a helmet hitting stone. I am not worried. No one I have ever met is a match for Alek hand to hand.

I move forwards to the side aisle opposite to where we came in, swinging left and right, arm at full extension. There is a small chapel on this side too, with an altar behind a low wooden screen.

It is empty; visibility is one hundred per cent. I turn left towards the back of the church, keeping the altar and the low wooden screen behind me.

At each pew, I stop, point, look.

A scream comes from the main aisle on my left and is followed up by a massive crash – it sounds like someone has just been thrown against a wooden pew. I don't check, I just carry on with my stop, point, look, stop, point, look routine. Eleven down and one to go.

I reach the back and swing left until I am on the main aisle again, looking up the church towards the altar at the far end. A wooden painted woman hangs above the altar in blue robes, with a white shawl on her head. Her hands are clasped together in prayer. Divine intervention. The last hope of the desperate.

Alek is walking slowly up the aisle, towards the altar, his back to me. I look past him at Beth standing in front of the white and gold, her helmet off, her beautiful hair gleaming in the light. Facing him down.

No way is he getting there first.

He has all but reached her when my blade catches her in the thigh. A mighty throw. Thirty foot or more in poor light by an arm weakened by loss of blood. She stares as if she can't believe it, then she goes over and I am running, charging up the aisle on numb legs driven by the need to get there before Alek.

She edges and fumbles up the stairs leading to the altar, bottom shuffling backwards like a toddler.

'Alek…' she says, and there is a world of longing in the one word.

I shove him aside, swap the gun to my left hand and pull a blade.

The Guardsmen don't use guns, it is a point of principle.

'You wouldn't,' she says. 'Not here.'

I grip the knife in the reverse hold, the blade at right angles to my forearm and slash down. The strike takes out her windpipe. Her mouth works round the blood. I slash again and the whole throat goes. Her head crashes back and I swipe again and again until Alek catches hold of the tops of my arms and hauls me hard back against his chest. The white and gold altar cloth is crimson.

I look up. The church is full of white light. There is the thud of new rotor blades overhead. The cavalry has arrived and I hadn't even noticed.

My cavalry.

Sirens scream above the roar of the rotor blades.

I can feel the sharp shooters massing, the armed response units. Shoot on sight: that is the order out to every police force in the West.

I turn to look at the Prince of Darkness.

'GO, Alek.'

He doesn't get it.

I push at him trying to make him understand, words deserting me.

'You have to go. This is my police force. *You* will be shot.'

He blinks as he understands. Coming back to the present. He had forgotten where he was. He grips my arms. His kiss is full of blood and longing slams me in the gut, swamping my senses. And then he is gone.

I get down on my knees and then on my stomach and lie flat beside the altar, beside Beth's body, my hair in her blood.

My cheek presses the cold stone as I watch the red lights of laser sights circle.

CHAPTER 70

I open my eyes and stare at the ceiling. White cork square tiles, strip lighting, the beep of medical machinery, TCP smell.

The detainment suite.

I am laid out for burial. My wrist is in a cast again. It is hard and heavy against my hip. My hands lie neatly outside the sheet. There are cannulas in the back of both of them.

I can smell teenager over the disinfectant.

I turn my head. Tanned bicep, white T-shirt, ripped jeans. Léon is sitting on the chair beside me. I turn my head some more. He is holding the hand of the person in the next bed. I recognise the hand.

'Get a room,' I say.

Léon jumps at the sound of my voice. *You're awake!*

Xiu levers herself up on her elbows. Her eyes meet mine, wide and serious. 'Are we good?' she asks.

I look into the face of my bodyguard. She is utterly perfect. Unbelievably, counter-intuitively perfect. She could have been created in a lab. Léon is still holding her hand. Her eyes are full of the question.

I go back to staring at the ceiling tiles. 'Where's Simon?'

'Over here.'

Simon is sitting in the doorway, in a hospital gown. Guarding. Another man in my life who thinks I need guarding.

'What happened?' I say.

'They walked us upstairs, knocked me out.'

'Saving you for later.'

'Next thing I know, I'm staring up into Léon's face.'

'A nasty shock for anybody,' I say. I turn to Léon. 'How did you find them?'

'Tracked her phone.' He looks ridiculously pleased he managed to pull off this surveillance basic. 'She tried to drug me, I wasn't having any of it.'

'Thank God,' I say.

If you care, your enemies have all the leverage they need. And yet, if Léon hadn't cared, Xiu would be dead.

'Then they woke up in hospital and were making no sense. No one knew where you were, but it was pretty obvious you were in trouble.'

I think of the twelve figures in Kevlar waiting to play.

'Yeah.'

'I went back to the house, saw the message and the graveyard was the first place I thought of. Got myself over there, got armed response out.'

'Nice job,' I say.

'You did it alone, after all,' says Simon.

'Not entirely alone,' I say, looking at Léon and Xiu but thinking about someone else. About standing shoulder to shoulder. About throwing myself off the trust high wire into the void. If Alek and I hadn't worked together, the Guardsmen would still be alive.

A doctor's white coat approaches. Dangling hands, floppy hair, eyes a bleak Siberian wilderness. I am upright in one juddering heartbeat.

'You let Everard stick a needle in me?' I shout at Simon. The heart rate monitor screams.

'How are you feeling?' Everard says, checking the bag above my head and looking at the monitor.

'A lot worse since you got here.'

The corner of Everard's mouth twitches. 'Good to have you back, Winter.'

I glare at his retreating back.

'Do you think Everard has ever had a girlfriend?' Xiu says. 'Maybe he reproduces via assimilation like the Borg.'

'Like the *what*?' says Léon.

Xiu rolls her eyes.

Control appears in the doorway in a wrinkled hospital gown, looking none the worse for his near-death experience.

'So,' he says. 'He got away.'

'Should you be up and about?' I say.

He comes to stand at the end of my bed. Frustration radiates off him. 'He was actually here, in London, and I was lying around in bed.' He glares. 'I knew he would stop at *nothing* to take you down.' His eyes fall on the white dressing hiding my tracker. He grasps at this tiny silver lining. 'At least your tracker is still in working order.'

'Turns out there were twelve Guardsmen,' I say.

Control waves this off. *Not interesting.* 'And now they are all dead and Firestorm is down which gives him even more of a reason to take you out.'

'Firestorm is down?'

'As of last night. Firestorm is currently without an Administrator. There is no one to match contracts, oversee the system, keep contractors in line.'

'What about the G20?'

'Ongoing.'

'Do we need to talk about the drive to improve the department's HR standards?'

He doesn't even have the grace to look embarrassed. His gaze falls on Léon and Xiu.

'Have you met the team?' I say. 'This is Léon.'

Control grunts.

'And this is Xiu.'

'Greetings,' she says.

He focuses in on her and on her bandaged leg lying outside the covers.

'Hell of a probation period,' he says.

'I'm not sure I'm cut out for it,' she says, looking at me.

'You're done when I say you're done,' I say. 'Or I'll put a bullet in your other leg.'

I think about this.

'And watch you hop.'

She grins.

A ring tone rises over the medical beeping. The Darth Vader march coming from an ancient Nokia phone.

'Hi, Mum,' says Xiu into her phone. She looks up at me. 'She wants to know if there is anything you need?'

Anything I need?

Like an answer to the question I've been asking all summer.

'I need to know if she thinks there is one right person out there for everyone.'

Control stares.

My bodyguard leans back against the pillows as she listens to the answer.

'Yes,' Xiu says. 'She does.'

A LETTER FROM ALEX

I hope you enjoyed *Winter Rising* – and that you'll look out for the next book in the series. If you'd like to keep up to date with all of my latest releases, you can sign up at the following link. Your email address will never be shared, and you can unsubscribe at any time.

www.bookouture.com/alex-callister

If you have time, I'd love it if you wrote a review of *Winter Rising*. Reader reviews on Amazon, Goodreads or anywhere else make all the difference to the author and can spread the word to new readers.

When I started *Winter Rising*, I was thinking about where I wanted to go with the Winter series – spy thriller, romance, crime, dystopian tech, alternative reality? All of the above? I was pondering the point one hot summer's day in my local graveyard when my eye fell on a statue of a weeping angel. I pushed the ivy away, crouched down and read the inscription: *The just man walketh in his integrity. Prov 20:7* and the Guardsman and the plot for *Winter Rising* jumped into my head, right there and then, in that sunny graveyard in South East London.

I went home and wrote all twelve of the Guardsman chapters and came to the conclusion that, for this book at least, I would be writing crime.

I am fascinated by the idea of the just man, the fantasy hero so beloved by Hollywood: John McClane, Jack Reacher, Dom

Toretto, Jack Bauer. Someone who does what is 'right' as opposed to what is 'legal'. Someone who defies and transcends the status quo. What is the right thing to do in Winter's dystopian world? Alek and Winter tread very different paths but this is their common ground; they are both searching for the answer.

There is no such moral ambiguity about the Guardsman, a classic character from the nineteenth-century gothic horror tradition – knives, churchyards, gravestones – reimagined for today. My version of Jack the Ripper, if you like. It is interesting to write this kind of killer in a technologically advanced age and see what opportunities that gives him.

If you have finished the book, and are not reading this letter first, you'll know there is more to the Guardsman than meets the eye (see what I did there?). I won't spoil the reveal but will put the key to the Guardsman chapters below so you can go back to those chapters, if you want, and see how it was done.

Winter Rising owes a debt to Lee Child's *The Visitor*. I am a big fan of Child's terse, sparse prose and would like to apologise for killing him off in print. Ahem. Sometimes the characters get totally beyond the author's control…

I would love to hear from you if you have time to drop me a line. You can get me direct on *alex@acallister.com* or via my website, *www.acallister.com*.

Best,
Alex

I. London
II. Mexico
III. Shanghai
IV. Rio

www.acallister.com

@CallisterAuthor

alex.callister.winter.dark

Lightning Source UK Ltd.
Milton Keynes UK
UKHW010115060520
362827UK00001B/99